For Rachel Margaret Eller Wolfe

Upper Kuskokwim River

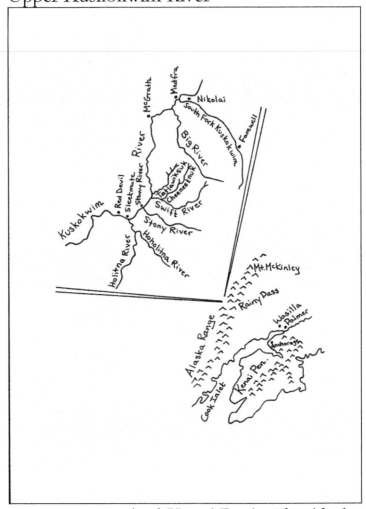

And Kenai Peninsula, Alaska

1

Something happened to the moose.

Something strange.

Isaac Bobby stared at the punctures in the crusted snow to read the silent message. He leaned from the seat of his ancient Polaris, its cowl torn from heavy use, its short windshield scoured nearly opaque by gale-driven ice. A wolverine ruff fluttered off his wind-burned face, deeply lined and marked by old frostbites. The frigid winter winds that had weathered the Eskimo's face now worked on the moose tracks he examined, slowly filling them with a fine dust from blowing snow.

Something happened here, an event frozen in time. Something odd.

Isaac Bobby stood on the Polaris and searched upriver, squinting into the low-angled glare of the sun off the Alaska Range, shielding his eyes with his marmot-skin mitts. The tracks proceeded straight up Big River at a high-stepping run. They dwindled into the far distance.

The moose reversed course and ran.

He had never seen this moose. Still, Isaac Bobby felt he knew it. He had followed its progress for several weeks. A young male, he first encountered its tracks near the headwaters of Jonetno' as they meandered down the Dhdlaghiyno', called Big River by the whites. He saw the tracks again while checking beaver sets a bit farther down.

He had watched the progress of this moose each day thereafter. His interest was purely academic. He and his brother didn't need another moose. They had sufficient provisions for the winter. With the success of beaver trapping they had more than enough fresh meat cached at the cabin. His brother dried extra beaver carcasses for the stew pot, their thin bodies dangling outside the cabin on high lines to discourage weasels. But Isaac watched for the moose tracks anyway, assessing, confirming, and learning from their progress. New seasons taught new lessons.

Like many moose in mid-winter, this young male was smart. It traveled circuitous, near-random routes as it browsed, tending towards the denser clumps of cover, constantly shifting locations against prevailing winds, frequently doubling back on its trail to confuse the wolves. Trying to track this animal by its trail would be a tiresome frustration. The moose left loops and blind endings like tangled string. Even so, its overall direction was constant. The moose moved downriver from the uplands toward the sheltered woodlands along the main Kuskokwim. Smart moose always drifted that way. So this morning, two days after the big storm, he expected to find the trail farther downriver and he was correct. He rediscovered the tracks along Big River a little closer to the Kuskokwim lowlands, not far from the Tatlawiksuk headwaters.

And then, the baffling change.

Isaac Bobby examined the marks leading to the event. The moose's path had proved especially difficult that morning, even for a strong, long-legged animal. The weak winter sun had melted the top of the new snow to form a hard thin crust. The snow beneath had consolidated, heavy and deep in the hollows. The moose had broken through the crust with each step, sinking into two to three feet of the old powder. It had walked slowly, carefully lifting and placing each leg, working toward firmer ground. Then abruptly, it stopped.

Isaac tied on snowshoes, long ovals of bent birch wood strung with taunt hide strips polished with wear. Stepping off the Polaris, he sank a few inches with the crust. Without the snowshoes, he'd founder to his knees in deep powder. He carefully walked around the moose's tracks, studying their sequence and placements, trying to read the event. The moose paused here. Suddenly it jumped, stumbled almost on its side, leaving a large mark. It whipped around and moved with difficulty, straight up the river valley, cutting its legs on the sharp ice, cleaving a bloodied path up Big River. It was a frightful, painful expenditure of energy. It ran for its life.

Why?

Isaac walked out from the moose tracks in a series of widening arcs, searching for reasons. He found nothing, just crusted snow swept by the frigid winds coming down the river valley. No prints of wolves. No snowmachine traces. No marks of anything that might have startled and terrorized a moose into a panicked run. He shielded his eyes and searched downstream. Big River disappeared around a long bend. Upstream, the brilliant white of the Alaska Range rimmed the horizon, bringing water to his eyes. To the east, the land rose gradually, offering small stands of aspen, birch, and spindly black spruce. To the west forested bluffs rose steeply to form the headwaters of several streams that flowed away toward the next drainage called Xelinhdi, Swift River. These were the streams that the Bobby brothers trapped for beaver, otter, and marten. At the moose tracks, views were unobstructed except for the west. Had something far off spooked the moose, something that left no sign?

Isaac Bobby returned to the Polaris and pulled the motor to life. He fixed the snowshoes behind him, straddled the worn black seat, and eased away from the tracks toward the cliffs to the west. He chose a saddle, gunned the engine, and quickly climbed to a rim that afforded an overlook. Leaving the engine idling, he removed his mitts and found binoculars. A keen wind knifed through his leather gloves as he scanned up and down the river, looking for signs of something that might spook a moose into a frantic run.

Isaac felt his heart beating. His ears, hotly pressed by the beaver hat, heard the dull thump that recalled his military service, that internal countdown of uncertainty and threat on missions stationed overseas. That was long ago. He was home now living in icy solitude, trapping with his brother months at a stretch, miles from other humans. His body's rhythms had readjusted with this quiet land, the vast subarctic that reached unbroken across the North American continent. Here on the upper Kuskokwim River he lived within the western-most edge of that wilderness. For generations these river drainages had sustained his people, the Deg Hit'an Athabaskans on his father's side and the Yup'ik Eskimos on his mother's. His body had adjusted to its cycles, its regular rhythms, reacting with discomfort to the discordant, the concealed.

He felt his tense shoulders as he scanned. He searched for something enigmatic, a force with sufficient power to threaten a moose and send it flying.

The day was clear and cold, thirty below zero in the still air by his cabin when he left to check his lines this morning. The breeze that whipped him on the bluff drove the temperature even lower. The beaver hat protected his neck and ears. The wolverine ruff saved his nose and cheeks from the wind. He scanned up, across, and down, examining each bend and hollow. During the second sweep he saw them, black specks mingling on the horizon far downriver.

Ravens.

Isaac repacked the glasses, pulled on his mitts, and maneuvered that direction, carefully following the steep rim of the bluffs that rose above Big River. He wove among the silence of the black spruce forest that blanketed the uplands, sliding down and gunning up narrow declivities formed by several steep, nameless streams. Finally he broke free of the forest. He pulled to a vantage perched above a slope that fell steeply, a bluff blanketed with thick snow undercut and sculptured by the winds into fantastic shapes.

Isaac spied the ravens. Just below the idling snowmachine was a querulous gathering within a glade of leafless poplars that gleamed like ship spars in a frozen harbor. The black tricksters hopped about a gray form.

A dead wolf.

Isaac surveyed the snowy patch with his binoculars. The gray carcass lay a fair distance from the edge of Big River. Ravens quarreled around it, pecking and cawing and jumping, some soaring up, circling the poplars, and descending to peck again. An ill feeling pervaded the scene, something aberrant and wrong. From a parka pocket Isaac removed the spotting scope he used for hunting caribou. Resting it upon a handlebar, he searched for the wolf. The image settled. His felt his heart within his ears. The scope resolved the scene in full detail.

He knew this wolf.

The wolf was a female from the pack that claimed the drainages from Stony River to McGrath. A vigorous adult, Isaac remembered, not the leader but one of her sisters. She lay dead in the clearing, legs splayed out on the snow, tongue slipped from a grimacing muzzle.

Isaac could clearly see the cause of death. The wolf's back was ripped apart, a corruption of mangled flesh and fur. Gaping wounds along her spine had released rivers of blood, now frozen. The ravens fought for bites from the bloody tears.

Isaac shuddered. What could have done this?

Isaac scanned the wolf's path from the river through the poplars. He found the trail easily, a splatter of gore and fur. There were no other obvious marks in the snow, no parallel tracks, no signs of attack or struggle. It looked as if the wolf's back had been shredded by giant talons from the sky. It was a frantic race of a wolf being torn asunder.

Isaac Bobby's stomach churned. The morning's coffee rose up his throat. He rubbed his eyes with his mitt and sucked breaths of fresh air.

He turned the scope again to the poplars and began another sweep of the grisly scene, moving up and down the trees, across the forest to the river, and upriver toward the Alaska Range. He saw nothing amiss. So he turned the scope away from the river to the steep slope on his left. He moved slowly along the forested rim. Finally he turned completely around to scope the dark forest wall directly behind him.

He screamed.

A monster swelled into his scope. Great flashing bug-eyes! It burst from the trees straight at him.

Isaac gunned the Polaris. Its engine roared. He launched in a shower of blinding snow and flew off the bluff. The Polaris soared. Isaac rose weightless from the seat.

He hit the slope hard, opened full bore. He fishtailed and raced down the slope's face, breaking cornices and ice walls. The face of the cliff released, a great slump of power. The ground melted beneath him, disintegrating in a cascade of powder and ice. Everything collapsed.

The Polaris rotated with the wave. It tumbled inside a roar of white. Isaac frantically climbed its side. He pushed free of the seat and swam like a fish up a waterfall, furiously fighting the powder for its surface as the chaos swirled about him.

Suddenly, everything stopped. The chaos froze, fixed like concrete, the world encased in solid cold. Isaac couldn't see. He was blind. Paralyzed. He could move nothing within the hard press of snow, nothing except the fingertips of one outstretched arm high above him, wiggling in the marmot skin mitt.

Black silence encased him.

Complete silence.

Isaac listened.

No... there was a sound. It plodded within the snow like distant steps.

Lump it went.

Chills went through his body.

Lump... lump...

Isaac Bobby knew it.
Lump… lump… lump…
That distant countdown.
Beside his ears pressed by the beaver hat it sounded.
Lump… lump… lump…
The beat of his buried heart.

2

She hunted birds in the silvery light. Or she played that she did. The irreverent rebel didn't care. That's how she was. Back home she was the playful one. She made games of everything. What did it really matter? She playfully hunted. Flush with excitement, she crept along the brook, her lithe body moving eagerly on the ice, her intense eyes reading signs in the fresh snow, exhilarated.

Today it felt especially naughty. Usually she trailed her brother. He encouraged her. She was the sister allowed to tag along on hunts. She watched, he killed.

Not today. She had sneaked off in the chill before dawn, pushed by a compulsion, a mischievous itch, a spontaneous usurping of familiar order. She'd given him the slip. Or if not entirely, her brother trailed her. She stalked the high drainage wonderfully far from home, exploring a winding brook bathed in a shimmering silver light, hiding her paths on hard ice. She'd learned that trick from him. Even he couldn't follow.

The canyon narrowed. She passed from the light into shadow. She paused to let her eyes adjust, examining the higher slopes ahead, the destination of the moment. Here the frozen creek zigzagged between a cleft in a broad hillside. The view brought up a memory. She'd hunted there before with her brother, a place of rock ptarmigans that browsed the hillside's berries, feeding in timid groups. Flushing a bird scared up a flock.

So much food!

Her brother showed how to cache the birds for later. They'd been praised. Even her sister had praised them.

Now her big sister was pregnant again. Confined close to home in mid-winter, she grew moody, demanding, and snappish, lording it over the household. How she came at them! Her vicious snits drove everybody out. She snarled and threatened to get her way like the place was hers. And they let her like before. Everybody retreated, leaving her alone with her foulness. Home was snug, too small for that.

They'd suffered much lately. There were accidents, sickness, departures, disputes. It felt ragged, almost fractious, a difficult struggle to endure the long winter in this out-of-way place. So they gladly left the churlish sister alone with her rotten mood. Like today, better to stalk ptarmigans on a blazing hillside, for real or play.

Cold air hung on the canyon floor. At the cleft, the breeze died. Some stench lingered in the stillness. She sniffed it cautiously and found the odor unsettling, ripe and annoying. What could it be? She warily tested the stale air, searching for the source.

Was it her? Did her own body stink?

How disgusting!

She fought an urge to rub down with snow. But then she heard it, a faint scrape above her beyond the turn of the cleft, a soft tamping on ice. The sound drove out her fret about scents. She crouched in the shadows and barely breathed. It came again, a scraping of snow beyond the bend. Something larger than ptarmigans!

Her pulse quickened.

No backup. Just her!

The prospect alarmed and excited.

She suddenly remembered the grizzly stuffing his face as the first snows fell. Was he awake, grouchy with hunger, walking the cleft? Or was it that wolf, the lone one, that shaggy dark pirate who slunk and thieved at the margins? She felt a thrill of doubt. Was she the hunter or the prey?

She ducked further into the shadow. Some part held her back. Caution tugged at her to turn aside from the narrow cleft and retrace the frozen trail toward home to find the brother she tricked. But something else pushed her on, a defiant readiness.

She moved ahead, creeping around the bend, stealthily placing each step, stalking at full alert. In the cleft she smelled it again, the ripe odor. It grew stronger, a wild stench that filled the space. She breathed in ragged pants.

It fell from the sky!

She threw herself aside, too late. It fell full upon her. Heavy. Strong. The dark wolf! The attack ripped out her feet. She slid helplessly on ice with the wolf on top. Great jaws gripped her neck with astonishing power. His legs wrapped fully around her torso, his weight squeezing her flat. She frantically rolled to knock him free but his jaws and legs locked firm. She instantly felt his loins tighten behind her. Terrified, she tucked her great tail to block entry. He entered anyway.

She yelped with pain.

With explosive fury, she surged to her feet and gave a stupendous shake. The violence threw him off. She viciously lunged at the rapist's throat with bared fangs. But he was done. Kicking aside, the dark wolf leaped up the hill, springing rock to boulder into the sun. With a snarl she sprang the other way, racing down the icy brook on a growing anger that gave surprising strength.

She sped through the silence of the white hills, dodging spruce and rock and log, moving up one draw and down another. A covey of ptarmigans flushed at her passage. She gave no chase. She just ran.

She finally broke from the forest. She slid to a halt on an overlook high above a great river. Shadows from the low sun shrouded the broad braided channel. The far side glittered with sun. In the dazzling white stretched a line of gray forms, a bobbing procession of high-crowned antlers. Caribou!

It captured her completely. Memories flooded her of chase and kills and gorging! She focused on the marching column. She felt a desperate need for her brother!

She circled the vantage, sniffed at the air, marked the sun, distant landforms, positions. She bounded away. This time she trotted. She fell into a steady cadence for distance. She loped with a purpose. The caribou drove her home to find hunting partners. They'd return to this place together.

She descended a swale where a stream had burst the ice. Steamy clouds billowed. She remembered her thirst. She cautiously approached the overflow, watching for danger in the skim of water, until her nose touched the pool. It felt cold and fresh on her long tongue. She lapped until her emptiness filled. Then she smelled the stench, a ripeness mixed with other disturbing scents. It recalled the attack.

She growled and displayed teeth.

She turned circle several times, looking for the dark outcast. He wasn't there. His smell came from her. It frightened and excited her. She whined in confusion and pushed her muzzle inside a leg and washed. Tasting the odors made her dizzy. She pushed her bottom to the wet ice and dragged through the overflow in an awkward squat. She scraped until the rubbing overpowered the smell. She washed some more.

When lengthening shadows stole her spot of light, she rose and trotted again, guided by landmarks, a hill, a dense copse, a long ridge. She came upon a prominent snag protruding from the ground and stopped. She carefully examined it. They all were there, brothers, sisters, and the scent of the strong one at the top. She backed to the stump to add herself when the foreign scent assailed again. Startled, she sprang into a clump of heather. It released its bitter pungency. She choked down bites.

The final path followed hard streambeds that left no prints. The smells of her brothers and sisters clung faintly. She placed her nose into familiar places, evoking memories of the trail's end. The last creek she followed narrowed and steepened. Brush clogged it. She ducked among debris and followed tunnels. Up she traveled until it opened to a draw. There it was, the dark entrance into the hillside, bright with afternoon sun. Home!

Happiness welled within her.

Vague feelings of dread.

She felt confused. She slowed and stopped short upon the frozen creek bed. She voiced a low whine.

A head appeared from brush on a ledge above the den's opening. The strong one! He voiced a happy yelp of recognition. Just as quickly, he swallowed it. His nose lifted. His stance stiffened. A menacing growl came from deep within his chest.

Another face emerged from the dark hole. Her big sister! She came out stiff, ready for a fight. She stood near the entrance, staring hard at her, nosing the air.

An anxious nausea gripped her stomach. She felt confused and ashamed. She retched, spilling bitter water and bracken. She flattened herself on the creek bed, pressing her belly to the ice in a submissive cower, her nose in the vomit, begging recognition. But she smelled her own stench, ripe with heat and sex. Her posture begged one thing. Her heady stench shouted another. The bold smells goaded. She fought a strange impulse to strut, the rebel, proud and flaunting. She tucked her tail over the reek, pressed her jaw to the ice, and plaintively whined.

Her sister's posture stayed unchanged.

She stretched further on the ice, displaying her narrow waist. She reached forward and behind in an exaggerated bend, defenselessly offering her white belly.

The strong one growled.

The young ones appeared from the brush at the sides, last year's pups, drawn by the commotion. She saw them at the edge milling nervously. The leaders ignored them.

Then she saw him. Her older brother!

He came from the brush by the creek. Another brother followed. Relief washed over her. She barked and bounded up to greet them.

Her sister attacked!

She swirled to meet it, fangs bared, a vicious snarl. Their jaws locked. She felt searing pain. The strong one bit deep into her shoulder. She rolled with them on top, crushed to the ground. Frenzied, they tore at her face and sides. Frantic, she lurched up, gathered her feet, and bolted, hot breath at her haunches. She dove into the creek bed, dodging through the twisted debris-clogged tunnels. She exploded from the creek and continued running, rasping for air, racing until the light and her body failed. In misery, she collapsed by a frozen pond, exhausted and suffering.

She lay a long time. The stars came out. They turned above her. A chill wind rose. Bitter cold crept through her coat pressed to the hard earth. Icy spears prodded like sticks through matted blood. With difficulty, she got up from the chilling ground. She looked about listlessly. An empty pond. No sheltered den. No sisters. No brothers. No young ones. Pain raked her shoulder. It brought back the shock of the attack. The fight. The run. She searched the pond again for signs of family. She found emptiness beneath a cold sky.

She lifted her thin face and howled.

There was silence.

She lifted her face again to the stars and howled, long and mournful.

Far off came a faint reply.

Her older brother.

Then silence.

She whined and curled in a ball on the cold ground. She heard nothing, smelled nothing, and felt nothing except emptiness and pain.

Falling snow woke her. Dry powder buried her. She stood stiffly and shook the snow from her fur, yelping at pains in her side. She shivered and looked disconsolately about her. Snow fell in huge flakes. A gray ceiling hid the tops of the spruce. New snow covered the pond.

Through the blur of flakes something rose from the flat surface. She limped that way. A vague mound of snow. She circled it. A faint scent lingered. It issued from cracks where water had subsided and ice contracted. She pushed her nose in a crack. A musky smell. It stirred memories, slick swimmers and food.

She dug, a painful effort. She pulled aside broken chunks of ice and earth. A dark fissure appeared among branches. Scent flowed from it.

She shook her face loose of dirt. She lifted her eyes to the surface of the pond. Falling snow completely veiled it. There was nothing there.

Everything had changed for her.

Some part of her knew.

She was alone.

She pushed her head into the hole. She dove into it. With a kick from strong haunches, her shoulders entered.

She burrowed into the earth.

3

Too many wolves.

Mel Savidge slouched with irritation beside the podium with the polished state seal where security guarded the third floor conference in Juneau's capitol building.

California had too much smog. New York City had too many people. And Alaska?

Too many wolves.

What crap!

Mel angrily waited for security clearance.

Like I'm some goddamn terrorist.

The bored, pot-bellied guard by the ground-floor metal detector had demanded to know her business and destination. He had singled her out from the crowd that passed unchallenged. That pissed her off.

"Anthropologist for the governor," she had snipped.

That prompted a phone call before she got past the elevators. Now a prim political Barbie doll had stopped her at the third-floor reception station to double-check her credentials. Her podium bore the official embossed state seal of Alaska. The receptionist normally intercepted tourists who had mistakenly climbed the three flights of stairs in search of Alaska's government. Her job was to redirect them one floor lower where the state legislature met, the floor where most public business got conducted. Lots of foot traffic down there. Here on the governor's floor the empty carpeted hallway evoked the hush of a cathedral.

Or a sepulcher, Mel smirked.

She expected the special treatment. She relished it. It affirmed her persona as the maverick anthropologist, the provocateur in Fish and Game, the specialist who couldn't quite be trusted. Mel rarely ascended this high in the state apparatus. Governors typically didn't consult cultural anthropologists. But the wolf crisis threatened to shatter the government, so the experts in Fish and Game got called to the sacred chambers. Underclass meets power… Mel was enjoying it immensely. If they ever opened the goddamn door!

Mel studied the round state seal affixed to the podium. It had embossed forests, mountain peaks, water, fish, even a tiny seal swimming along an outer edge. No wolves anywhere. Northern lights illuminated a mine pumping smoke over a bay. The artist got that one right. In the foreground a farmer ploughed wheat with a horse. What a fantasy! Wheat farming! She tapped the thick medallion lightly with a finger.

"Plastic."

"What?" asked a nervous voice.

Derby Peters, an assistant commissioner in Fish and Game, had just arrived for the same meeting. He rocked on his heels, breathless.

"What you'd expect on the third floor," said Mel. "Plastic."

"The state's seal," said Derby, squinting at the round medallion, stating the obvious, missing the point, as usual.

"It's fucking phony," declared Mel.

"Shhh!" Derby whispered, shocked at Mel's language. He glanced apprehensively at the conference room's heavy door. "The governor's in there!"

"Eavesdropping," scoffed Mel.

She resisted an urge to rap it too. But she knew the door would be solid wood. Alaska cut plenty of trees. Derby peered around him as if he didn't want to be seen

16

with this woman. Mel watched him fidget with perverse pleasure.

"Like the phony pillars."

"What?"

"Outside, the phony Greek pillars at the entrance."

"They're not phony, they're marble," countered Derby, defending the building's honor, remembering the tour he once took. The pillars were fashioned of genuine marble quarried from Prince of Wales Island.

"They're tacked to the building. They hold up nothing, false fronts on the saloon, bogus, like everything here!"

Derby gave her a sour look. Have some respect, he glowered. He checked his mobile.

"We should be in there," he muttered.

Mel shrugged, now feigning indifference. The biologists already had been admitted. Mel was forced to wait. She expected it. She was the wild card inside Fish and Game. 'Make her wait,' they probably told the Barbie girl, 'she works in the Division of Subsistence.' Subsistence researchers occupied the lowest rung of the department's ladder. Well, maybe not lowest. Subsistence ranked above the guys who studied bats and crows.

At the moment, Mel was the acting director of the subsistence unit. She oversaw a cadre of social scientists who researched hunting and fishing in villages. That bugged the big boys in the department, the biologists who worked in Commercial Fisheries, Wildlife, and Sport Fish, the divisions that generated revenue for the state. Tourists didn't come to Alaska to watch villagers smoke fish, they said. They came to see wildlife and to kill salmon and to take home the photos proving they did it. They left behind money. Villages just posed trouble for the package tours. No wonder she waited outside while the big boys caucused.

But why was Derby Peters waiting too? Maybe the administration didn't trust Derby either. This was intriguing. She considered Derby the iconic organization man, loyal to a fault. He'd go down with the ship of state launching the last lifeboat. Where did Derby fit in the wolf crisis?

"What's your take on this mess?" probed Mel.

"What?"

"The Board of Game… what do you think of the mess they've made for us?"

"The board's the board."

Chicken shit dodge.

The conference room door opened and the young receptionist stepped out, stylishly attired in a knee-length black skirt and low heels. Mel admired the tight calves. Her makeup was impeccable, her manners perfect.

"Dr. Savidge? Mr. Peters?" she inquired politely. "Sorry to keep you waiting. They're ready for you now."

Derby passed into the meeting room. Mel followed. A huge conference table immediately blocked them, long, heavy, and waxed to a blinding sheen. Plush chairs crammed around its edges.

Room's too small for the fucking table.

Tall windows filled an entire wall overlooking the flat snowy roofs of downtown Juneau. Mountains rose from the wind-swept water of Gastineau Channel. It was a stunningly beautiful winter day. The mid-morning light flooded in, glaring off the table.

"Where are the sunglasses?" joked Mel.

Derby grunted disapproval and went another direction.

Several men in suits stood by a lectern at the table's head. Mel recognized Marlin Fosburger, the governor's chief of staff, posed like a predatory insect. The others were aides or bodyguards or political hacks, she didn't know what. Where did they buy their identical suits?

Dan Crawford hulked among them, the commissioner of Fish and Game, her nominal boss, hugely overweight and sweating like he'd stepped off a treadmill. Dan the Man, the walking heart attack, bound someday to drop dead right before their eyes.

Mel squeezed behind game biologists arranged shoulder-to-shoulder at the table. They sipped coffees from diminutive china cups. On the end of this masculine

18

lineup sprawled the current superstar, Gary Gunterson, alpha male, the hotshot redneck game biologist currently ascendant in headquarter politics. Lean and mustached, he wrestled caribou from helicopters and drank whiskeys to brag about it. A real bully. She nodded squeezing past. Gunterson grunted.

God, he hates me. How can they stand him? He stinks like an ashtray.

Derby Peters found a spot beside Rod Boswell, a special assistant in Fish and Game, young, intelligent, one of the Santa Cruz preppies on missions to save Alaska from itself. To lock it up, the big boys complained. The wolf hunters hated this cadre of energized greenies.

So, Derby's choosing to sit with Boswell. Interesting. Maybe that's why he got stuck outside the door.

Two lawyers from the Department of Law sat at the table's foot. Bill Bolton, an old bulldog from the previous administration, hunched over his tiny coffee cup and stared out the bank of windows. Stewing about the new politics, guessed Mel. Beside him, Laurie Philips had her nose buried in papers. Laurie was a go-getter attorney in natural resources, single, smart, and exceptionally good-looking.

Everybody's trying to get into your sweet pants. I hear you're a screamer.

Mel decided to join them, choosing lawyers over biologists. Mel liked Laurie because she was one sharp cookie. She liked Bill because he was an unrepentant leftist from the old frontier, a descendent of Wobbly union reformers given the choice by Uncle Sam of exile in Alaska or jail terms in Wisconsin. His grandparents had chosen the far north.

"That's chief of staff, right?" asked Mel, plopping down without formality.

"Marlin Fosburger," said Laurie, clearing a space.

"Where's the governor?"

Bill Bolton, the old crust, laughed, a rumbling congestion in his chest.

"No show yet. You want coffee?" asked Laurie.

"I thought we came here to advise the governor. What's really happening?"

"Henny Penny," rumbled Bill.

"Sky is falling," said Laurie, interpreting. "We've been at it since yesterday. What's happening today? I don't know. More of the same probably. Worst case scenarios and defenses."

"Why are you guys here?"

"Politics," said Bill.

"No, not that. We get to listen in," said Laurie. "They ask for legal opinions occasionally. I read." She hefted a pound of legal briefs.

"But no governor yet?"

"Nope."

"Okay, let's get started again," intoned Marlin Fosburger as people settled into place. The chief of staff was top dog today. He strutted and gestured like a tent-revival preacher, already warmed up. He launched straight into hyperbole.

"So the Board's pulled the pin and tossed it to you," declared Fosburger, grandly pulling an imaginary pin and rudely pointing to the row of biologists. "But it's really a lob at the governor. What are you going to do about it? What are you going to do to keep the goddamn grenade from exploding in the governor's face?"

"Now Marlin, that's pretty strong," countered Dan Crawford.

"A fucking time bomb," Fosburger repeated, "and that pisser Richards is laughing through his ass."

Mel took out a pad and began scribbling notes. Is this how they speak on the third floor? She was in her element now, the anthropologist observing, noting, analyzing. 'Political grenade,' she jotted. 'Governor threatened. Richards gloating.' Richards was a political rival.

"This is great," whispered Mel.

Laurie rolled her eyes and found her papers.

"Henny Penny," muttered Bill.

"These are real biological issues," said Crawford. "Real emergencies. Not just politics."

"Okay, then let's hear it," said Fosburger, sitting on the table. "What's the emergency with wolves? The governor can legitimately respond to emergencies. Tell me how we convince the public that it's an emergency with wolves."

Hank Reisdahl cleared his throat, an area biologist in the row of biologists. Mel knew him as a scientific type, a by-the-numbers man, the antithesis of an ideologue.

"It's an emergency because the Board of Game defined it as an emergency based on wolf-moose ratios," stated Reisdahl.

"How's that?"

"Basically that's moose divided by wolves in an area. When there are too many wolves relative to moose, when the ratio dips below particular thresholds, it becomes a 'management concern' and then an 'emergency,' by definition. We applied the formula. Three areas fell below critical thresholds... the Upper Tanana, the Upper Kuskokwim, and the Copper Basin. The Board approved emergency plans for the Upper Tanana and the Upper Kuskokwim. It postponed the Copper Basin. The plans direct our department to take action in those places. The threshold becomes the measure of an emergency."

"But why that threshold?" challenged Fosburger, clearly following Reisdahl. "Why not set it higher or lower? Why put it there? Why is it an emergency at that point?"

"There's no purely scientific reason for setting thresholds at any particular ratio," said Reisdahl. "The Board made a policy call."

"They sure did," laughed Fosburger.

"But the ratios are poor," countered Crawford. "No one doubts that."

"But why are they emergencies?" pressed Fosburger. "What happens if we don't act? Do the moose disappear?"

"The moose won't disappear," said Reisdahl.

"But they stay low," said a gravelly voice.

Mel looked up from her notepad. It was Gary Gunterson, the darling of the lunatic fringe.

"They stay trapped in the predator pit and don't crawl out for a hell-of-a-long time."

"Predator pit," Fosburger savored the words. "Is that science? Can the governor say 'predator pit' with a straight face? Or will he get laughed off stage?"

"It's not a scientific term," said Reisdahl. "But there's scientific support for the concept. Population models show that predators can get the upper hand in an area. They drive a prey population to such low levels that most new recruits get killed. That keeps it low. The predators can be wolves, bears, whatever. The prey can't recover unless something drastically changes in the system. These are theoretical models. Removing wolves is a way to help the moose out of the pit. You reestablish another equilibrium at a higher absolute level. In the long run, you get more moose and more wolves."

"So the governor can say 'predator pit.'"

"No, he shouldn't," said Rod Boswell from across the table, joining the fray with a commanding tone.

'Boswell says no to predator pit,' Mel jotted. She quickly watched wonder boy in action.

"It's a politically-loaded term," said Boswell. "Whatever its scientific merit, the term infuriates environmentalists. They associate 'predator pit' with folk biology. The whole notion of a 'pit' is value laden, moose being stuck in a hole rather than simply being at a lower natural equilibrium. If the governor says 'predator pit' he'll be perceived as aligned with the wolf haters."

"Okay, then tell me this," challenged Fosburger. "Why not the Copper Basin? If it's an emergency in two places, then it's an emergency in all three. Can't the governor say the Board is being inconsistent?"

"Because of subsistence," said Crawford, pointing down the table.

All eyes landed on Mel.

"Mel Savidge, Subsistence Division," Mel began. "Subsistence economies are stressed in those places.

They're having a hard time putting food on the table. Few moose. Few jobs. Few options. Every moose eaten by wolves is one less for a family. That's how they see it. The Copper Basin has more economic options. So the Board found emergencies for the two areas under the greatest economic distress."

"Dammit! Using subsistence against us! Richards must be laughing out his ass!"

"Now, Marlin," smoothed Crawford, glancing nervously at his staff.

Fosburger turned on Mel angrily.

"Is this how they repay the governor? We've been throwing money out there. Community grants. Freight subsidies. Runways."

"It's not an either-or thing," said Mel coolly. "It's not 'money' instead of 'subsistence.' Villages need both. Sure, they need those subsidies. But that's no substitute for moose hunting. The governor is going to lose the rural vote if he talks like he's buying off subsistence."

Mel saw the glint in Fosburger's eye. He enjoys this shit, especially the part about votes. I'm speaking his language.

"Okay, Law, you've been listening. Is there any legal reason for Fish and Game to not implement the Board's directive?"

Laurie Philips looked up from her legal briefs without missing a beat.

"Legally, the state must manage big game for sustained yield. So managing wolves for the conservation of moose is the legal argument. There are budgetary constraints, of course. The department has discretion in prioritizing funds if it's consistent with statutory mandates."

"What about emergencies? Is the governor compelled to act because the Board has declared an emergency?"

"No, he's not compelled," said Laurie. "He's free to choose whether to act on the findings of emergency by a board, but not compelled to act."

Bolton silently sipped his coffee, adding nothing.

"Okay, it's legal but not compulsory. So what are some alternatives to carry out the board's directive?" Fosburger stared at Crawford. "What's the department going to recommend?"

The biologists sat like sphinxes, all except for Gunterson who seemed to scowl and smile simultaneously. Boswell jumped in from across the table.

"The department is recommending nothing at this moment... but we have identified a range of possible alternatives. You have them on that sheet. The options list monetary costs and a rating as to likelihood of success in achieving the wolf-moose ratio objective."

Mel had no list. The biologists never gave her anything before meetings. She looked to see if Laurie had it. She didn't either. Fosburger did. He perused it top to bottom.

"Shit! Who has this? Has this circulated?"

"Nobody, just us," said Crawford.

But it will leak, thought Mel. Somebody will leak it.

"Look at this!" said Fosburger. "If people thought we were even considering these things! Whose list is this?"

"We did them as a group," rasped Gunterson. "We were told that the governor wanted a full range of options, so we provided a full range."

"Bounties?" Fosburger read incredulously. "The department is considering hiring bounty hunters for wolves?"

"No, no, no," Crawford jumped in. "Of course not. We're not considering that. That's just an option, one used historically but unacceptable today. But we'd be remiss if we didn't list it."

"Aerial wolf hunting by the public?" read Fosburger, shaking the list. "The public is going to shoot wolves from private planes?"

Gunterson smiled evilly.

That asshole, he loves watching Fosburger squirm. That smile shows where Gunterson's political allegiances fall... not with this governor.

"We'd be remiss not to list it," said Crawford, "but like bounties, it's not likely to be acceptable right now."

"I don't want this list out," said Fosburger.

"Okay," agreed Crawford.

"I want all of them collected."

Boswell jumped in again, the soothing voice of reason.

"This is the most sensitive part, of course, identifying acceptable actions. I think it's reasonable to say that any actions taken by the department will be scientifically supported. Nothing the department does will be outside what science finds likely to be successful in sustaining wildlife populations."

"And who decides that?" challenged Fosburger. "Which scientists?"

"We have the expertise in our department. Our experts on wolves and moose are tops, the best in the world," said Reisdahl.

"But there's a public perception we have to contend with," said Boswell. "The public will be skeptical about any science coming from the wolf managers. They'll want an independent judgment from experts perceived to be neutral."

"And who's that?" pushed Fosburger.

"The universities could do it," said Boswell.

A head poked through the door, a silver-haired woman.

"It's getting about time," she advised Fosburger. "Pretty crowded out here."

Fosburger nodded.

"Okay," he said to the table. "Let's take ten. Crawford, you and I will meet with, uh, Boswell, Reisdahl, uh, Gunterson and, uh, Laurie Philips."

Mel rose and stretched. The group named by the chief of staff disappeared through a side door. Meanwhile, the floodgates opened. Bodies began pouring into the conference room, mostly paunchy commissioners and their youthful aides judging by heft and attire. They jostled for places around the massive table. Laurie Philips reappeared.

"So soon?" said Mel.

"I think some things were already decided."

"You know these guys?"

Mel waved at the new arrivals.

"Well, I should, but really, I can never remember some names," admitted Laurie. She started around the room, identifying a person's affiliated department. "He's with Tourism. He's Regional Affairs. That one's Rural Development. Over there is Seafood Marketing. There's Law, my boss. There's Public Safety."

"A convention," said Mel.

"A circus," grunted Bolton.

Boswell, Reisdahl, and Gunterson reentered.

"Gunterson looks pissed," said Mel. "Of course, he always looks pissed, but he looks really pissed right now. Did something happen?"

"I think he got rolled," said Laurie.

"Yeah?"

"I think."

"That's good," said Mel.

"It was the boycott," rumbled Bolton, hunched like a stone Buddha. "That decided things."

"Boycott?" said Mel.

The restart cut them short.

"Welcome, welcome everyone," intoned Fosburger. "Please take a seat. Anywhere. It's open seating today. Yeah, go ahead. That's fine."

The noise fell to a low murmur with heads turning toward the podium. The stenographer began recording on her strange machine.

"There's so many here today, I'm going to forgo introductions, but I'd like to especially recognize Senator Phil Watkins and Representative Cheryl Williams. Welcome! Thanks for your interest. I'm passing around a sign-up sheet so we get a sense of who's here. There's nobody here from the press, correct? Please identify yourself if you're press. Nobody? Good."

'Press excluded,' Mel scribbled on her pocket pad.

Commissioner Crawford reentered. He stood beside the podium. Fosburger continued the session, this time with decorum.

"I'm sure you've been briefed as to recent events. This meeting gives us an opportunity to connect, compare notes, and receive a heads-up on the direction the governor intends to take on scientifically-sound wolf management before the press announcements."

Mel wrote it down, 'scientifically-sound wolf management,' Boswell's term of art. Not 'wolf control.' Not 'predator control.' The approved sound bite was 'scientifically-sound wolf management.'

"Before I turn it over to Dan, let me summarize recent steps. Yesterday, the chair and co-chair of the Board of Game met with the governor. They briefed him on the wildlife management plans adopted by the Board. The governor thanked them for the briefing and the fine service they provide the public and wildlife management in Alaska."

"Yeah, thanks for the turds, guys," Mel whispered. Laurie giggled into her papers.

"This morning, the governor's staff met with the commissioner of the Alaska Department of Fish and Game and his game biologists, the state's wildlife professionals. Law was there too. We discussed a range of options. Yesterday, we kept in contact with the commissioners of the departments potentially affected by the management plan adopted by the Board of Game, especially those dealing with tourism and seafood marketing. This afternoon, the governor will be sending invitations to a number of universities and environmental organizations regarding a state-sponsored conference on scientifically-sound wolf management to be convened sometime next summer."

Mel wrote, 'state conference on wolf management.' Boswell won that point too. He's arranged the scientific cover for whatever Fish and Game does.

"The governor will join us momentarily, if we can steal him away from the Korean trade delegation. But before he does, Dan will brief us on the management options we covered. Dan?"

Mel saw her boss step to the lectern with tiny notes in his meaty hands. His baby face swelled with discomfort. He looked like a third-grader stung by bees ready to flub a class presentation. Dan Crawford was a political compromise, a good old boy, a malleable commissioner without political aspirations, a horrible public speaker. He stared at his notes like he'd never seen them before. Mel glanced at Gary Gunterson, the biologist who got 'rolled' according to Laurie. He sat unsmiling, arms folded across his chest, staring out the window.

"Yeah," mumbled Crawford. "Well, we explored lots of options. You know, the Board of Game passed a wolf management plan. It's a general plan for two regions, the Upper Tanana and the Upper Kuskokwim, places with problems. The plans call for unspecified management actions by the department to improve wolf-moose ratios. Uh, we explored optional actions today. Whatever gets implemented, the program will be based on sound science. The science, you know, it's complex. So to help with that, we will convene a conference of scientific experts on predator-prey relationships and management models."

He turned his notes over a couple of times.

"Thanks," he finished.

Several hands went up simultaneously.

"I thought the Board can't require you to do anything," was the first hand up.

"Regional Affairs," Laurie whispered to Mel.

"That's right," said Crawford. "But the Board found emergencies in these two places, so our department has decided to take action."

There was a general unhappy murmuring in the crowd.

"When will this happen?" asked a second hand.

"We start this winter."

There was more murmuring.

"What about the tourist boycott?" asked a third hand.

"Tourism," whispered Laurie. "They're nervous."

"I can respond to that," said Fosburger. "By now probably everybody has heard that certain animal rights groups outside the state have made statements to the press threatening a boycott of Alaska if the state begins what they call a 'wolf control program,' or a 'predator control program.' The governor knows only what the press has reported. He has not been in contact with any animal rights groups. Nor does he intend to be in contact with them. The governor does not respond to threats or blackmail. The governor does understand the legitimate concerns of Alaskans and other Americans about healthy wildlife populations and sound wildlife management. The programs implemented this winter respond to those legitimate concerns, not threats from extremists."

Mel wrote furiously, 'boycotts, blackmail, extremists.'

"This is great," she whispered.

"So Fish and Game is killing wolves this winter?" asked Regional Affairs, cutting to the quick.

Fosburger and Crawford exchanged glances. Who was going to answer? Crawford stepped forward.

"No, we're not killing wolves this winter."

There was a general murmuring again.

"We're not killing any wolves this winter," he repeated. "The Board adopted wolf-moose ratios as management objectives for the Upper Tanana and the Upper Kuskokwim. The Board directed the department to take actions toward achieving those objectives. After conferring with our biologists and managers, we have determined that we can achieve these objectives without killing wolves."

"How?" asked Regional Affairs.

Crawford took a large swig of water.

"With a relocation program," he burped, wiping sweat from his forehead.

Mel hardly knew what to write. A what? A 'relocation program?'

They were going to 'relocate' wolves?

She found the biologists. All sat stony-faced, respectfully listening to the boss. All except Gary Gunterson, who scowled over the flat roofs of Juneau.

You got rolled, eh? No killing of wolves. You must hate this town. Bet you need a smoke.

"And here come the handlers, right on cue," mumbled Bill Bolton from down the table.

The front doors swung open. A retinue of suited men entered. Inside the group walked the governor of Alaska, white-hair carefully coiffed, looking slightly befuddled, blinking at the glare off the giant table. A hush descended as he was ushered to the podium. He looked up and down the sea of faces as if searching for someone familiar. His chief of staff leaned close to the microphone.

"Governor. Thanks for taking a moment from your busy schedule with the Korean trade delegation. We appreciate it. Perhaps you can offer us some words of encouragement as we tackle this wolf issue that's been in the news the last few days."

A light came on in the governor's eyes. He smiled. Suddenly he beamed above the crowd of listeners.

"You know, I love to give encouragement. The people who know me best, they know I love to do that. Let me say this to you now, and I have said this many times before in the past, that we are so fortunate, you and I. We live in a great land. Alaska. And I know in my heart that there's nothing, absolutely nothing that we, the people of Alaska, can't accomplish if we join up, put our minds and our talents together, and work…"

Mel stopped taking notes. Clearly the meeting had ended. Laurie Philips read her briefs. Gary Gunterson slouched in his seat, staring out the wide windows at the whitecaps on the channel. Bureaucrats and aides fidgeted, hungry for lunch appointments. And beneath the governor's drone she heard a low chuckling, a well-worn rumbling, like an old film critic enjoying an old classic.

It came from the direction of Bill Bolton.

4

The wolf meeting ended. The capitol emptied.

Mel Savidge watched as hefty bureaucrats and politicians shouldered down the center stairwell with nubile aides in pursuit, rushing like salmon through a breach, bumping frenetically on common quests of noontime fulfillment, quick power lunches downtown, or just quickies before the afternoon grind. Red ties flashed like spawning colors. A few hook-noses even leered her way. Come with me, they beckoned, to promised lands, gourmet lunches, peak moments in the quiet backwaters to burst the mid-day doldrums.

Mel shuddered.

"Mel! Wait up!"

A rotund torpedo plowed through the crowded corridor trailed by a thin sprat.

Mel considered running.

Rex arrived, panting, adjusting his dangling black camera, an ancient single-lens reflex with a lens like a cannon refitted for digital. Rex Winkler, reporter, independent investigator of the Juneau political beat, disheveled and moist though the day was cold and dry from Taku winds off the ice fields.

"You at the wolf meeting?" he panted.

Mel reluctantly nodded.

"Let's get lunch," he belched.

He grabbed with meaty fingers and pushed her into the swell of bureaucrats. The thin sprat followed.

"This is Larry Feinberg. Larry, Mel."

"Pleased to meet you, Dr. Savidge! I've been hoping for a chance to talk to you."

"He's a lawyer," said Rex, plunging into the river of bodies. Mel entered the flow, resigned. Someone would pay for this.

"You're the anthropologist," said Feinberg, slipping beside her as they passed beneath the fake Greek columns.

"Yep. Where are we going?"

"Alaska Hotel," said Rex. "It's serving lunches."

"That place stinks."

"Then where?"

"Valentine's."

"Too crowded. Too many eyes."

"You planning to kill me?"

They slid down the steep street. Built on mine tailings dumped at the base of mountains, Juneau fell into Gastineau Channel. Anything loose went that direction. They veered left into Valentine's, haberdashery turned coffee house. Huge fans turned from lofty ceilings above round tables crammed with people. Everything was wood, so everything echoed in the old mercantile box. The lunchtime crowd roared.

Rex was right. No privacy here. That suited Mel. She didn't want to cozy up with Rex the boozer in a bar that stank of smoky velveteen and Lysol. She ordered a pesto frittata and found it covered by the lawyer. Rex chose a table in the back corner beside the water jugs and toilets, jammed in the path of the cheap drinkers and pissers. What an idiot. The window seats were more private.

"What happened in there?" asked Rex, his mouth full of pizza.

"Where?"

"The wolf meeting," said Rex peevishly. "What's the governor decided?"

"I don't think he's decided anything. Maybe his handlers…"

"Yeah, yeah, I know. What are the handlers going to do with the Game Board's proposal?"

"What proposal?" said Feinberg above the roar, spearing salad with a plastic fork.

"You want flatware for that?" said Mel, watching the fork bend backwards.

"Naw," said Feinberg, finding his mouth. "It makes me take smaller bites. Seems like more."

"Yeah," said Mel. She sometimes did the same. Feinberg was okay, kind of cute if you liked Dustin Hoffman types. No ring. But that didn't mean shit during the legislative session.

"Wolves. Haven't you been following the wolf story?" said Rex.

"Oh, yeah, too many wolves, right?"

"The Game Board has garroted the governor. They've got him, dangling and strangling."

"Now how's that?" said Mel, trying to decide if she wanted to leak to the press, especially to Rex the lout.

"Because it's a wedge issue," enthused Rex, hunching above his meatball pizza like a cheap gossip dishing dirt. "Splits the blocks in crazy ways."

Rex looked around the large room. Nobody listened, of course. He launched into his political analysis.

"The governor got elected as an independent, right? He got votes from the moderates in a three-way race. He stole the election. The parties hate him. But he's stuck with no base. It's a cobbled coalition. Wolves are going to shatter it."

"How? The wolf haters?" said Mel, incredulous.

"No, no, no. Nobody really hates wolves anymore, well, maybe the fanatics. But wolves eat moose. That's a fact. They threaten sport hunters, the big game guides, the outfitters. Those are big interests, big contributors. Plus, wolves compete with subsistence hunters. Natives aren't usually in that political camp. But if the governor doesn't do something with wolves, he's going to drive them over to the sportsmen."

"Strange bed fellows," said Mel.

Rex chuckled, guzzled Coke, and belched.

"But if he does kill wolves to appease the sportsmen and Natives, he's going to piss off the outside greenies. Wolves are their darlings, their pinups, their fundraisers. They'll go nuts. They're ready to boycott. A successful tourist boycott screws big business, and the governor lives to serve them.

"So he's fucked. No matter what he does, he's going to piss off somebody he needs. His coalition crumbles. They're squirming up there. Right?"

"I guess," muttered Mel.

His political analysis squared with hers.

"The governor can kill wolves?" said Feinberg.

"Nah, but his minions can," said Rex. "He appoints the commissioner of Fish and Game. The governor can steer him. But the Game Board regulates. The Board has stirred the pot. They've just told Fish and Game to take down wolves."

"How would they do that? Excuse me for my ignorance, but I'm out of Boston."

"Lots of nasty ways," grinned Rex.

Disgusting, thought Mel. He gets off on this. He's salivating just thinking about killing wolves.

"Bounty hunting."

"Bounty hunting?"

Feinberg mouthed it like an anachronism, like saying 'jousting' or 'spooning.'

"Bounties won't work," said Mel to throw water on the macho banter. "Wolves are too hard to catch. That's what trappers say at the board meetings. Even with a bounty, it's too expensive to trap wolves."

"Speak of the devil, look who's just walked in," whispered Rex, ducking instinctively. "Old Gatling Gun himself. Don't turn around!"

Mel looked up to see Gary Gunterson, God's gift to manhood, strutting into Valentine's. Beside him was a stranger, a bulked-up cowboy in rough denims and pointed boots, craggy face beneath a faded billed cap, skin peeled from sun and wind in the dead of winter.

"Who's that?" asked Feinberg, twisting like a tourist.

"Gary Gunterson, a biologist from Fish and Game," said Mel.

She flashed him a mean smile. Gunterson's eagle eyes caught it. He nodded back.

"He's seen us, Rex. Now he has to shoot you."

"Why is he called Gatling Gun?" asked Feinberg.

"Because he likes to kill wolves," grinned Rex, sitting back up. "He got caught ordering machine guns from a mail order catalog using a state budget code."

"Machine guns?"

"To solve the wolf problem."

"That never happened," said Mel, affecting boredom.

"Machine guns?" said Feinberg.

"Bolt them to a plane and shoot from the air," said Rex. "Aerial wolf hunts, more efficient than bounties. You buzz in at thirty feet and pull the trigger."

Rex swooped his hand.

What a cretin, thought Mel.

"Or take Haggarty," said Rex, nodding in Gunterson's direction.

Haggarty.

Mel instantly registered the name. She watched the stranger sit with Gunterson. They ate chili with heads together. She'd never seen him before.

"That's a real story," chuckled Rex.

"What's that?" said Mel.

"Joel Haggarty jawing with Gunterson. You know what they're talking about. Killing wolves. He's the Mosquito Man."

"Oh, yeah," said Mel quietly.

She now placed the name and the man. She stared at the table and memorized the face, recalling the story. She started to chuckle. Rex did too.

"Here's what happened," said Rex, leaning into Feinberg. "Joel Haggarty… he's the one-man wolf solution, the best wolf trapper in Alaska, if you can call what he does 'trapping.' He invented saturation snaring. That's a way to catch wolves so efficient the Board is under pressure to ban it. A real outdoorsman, he lives with wolves, studies them, learns to think like them. Then he kills them."

"What kind of snaring?"

"Saturation snaring. Wolves hunt and scavenge. They're attracted to dead things. Trappers set snares near carcasses, wire nooses beside dead moose and caribou. But Haggarty, he doesn't set one or two snares, he sets a dozen, two dozen, three dozen, hidden in every nook and cranny. Wolves are careful. They spot mistakes with a trap. But Haggarty's learned that when the first wolf gets snared, it freaks the rest. They scatter and don't look where they're jumping. Jump into a noose."

"And catch him?"

"Catch the whole damn pack."

"The whole pack?" whispered Feinberg, shocked.

"Yeah," laughed Rex. "So, Haggarty, he's bragging in a bar at North Pole or somewhere up there in Fairbanks, egged on by his fans who drool over lines of wolf pelts, explaining how to trap wolves, instructing his novices so they'll do it too, like anybody will trap at fifty below zero if he just explains it, how you check them and all that, how they'll chew to get out of a trap, chew off their whole damn foot, so you got to check or all you'll get is that bloody foot. He's bragging and they're buying and he's getting plastered. There's this guy in the crowd who, it turns out, nobody knows. He's buying rounds, egging him on. Anyway, it gets late and he's so wasted he leaves with this guy and passes out in his truck."

Rex laughed and choked down Coke.

Mel watched Feinberg. The Bostonian stopped smiling somewhere around the bloody stumps.

"He comes to," chortles Rex, wiping his dripping nose. "Haggarty wakes up. He's outdoors. Naked! Buck naked! It's summer, you know, and he's outdoors somewhere, waking up, hung over, buck naked. He thinks he was drugged. And he's covered in blood-sucking mosquitoes! Like a wooly blanket. Thousands of mosquitoes! They've got their beaks in him, pumping him dry. And his foot is stuck in a fucking leg-hold trap that's been bolted shut and chained to a six-foot stake pounded so far into the ground you'd need a truck to pull it. The only thing they left him is his pocketknife. It's wrapped in a note that says, it's scrawled in pen… 'if chewing's too slow.'"

Rex bellowed like a buffalo.

"Mosquito Man," Rex snorted between breaths. "They call him Mosquito Man."

Mel snickered slightly. She watched Feinberg's reaction to the punch line… if chewing's too slow. The East Coast lawyer looked slightly ill.

"Who did it?" whispered Feinberg.

"Who the fuck knows?" laughed Rex.

"Greenies?"

"Nah," said Mel. "Some random ET."

"Extra-terrestrial?"

"Eco-terrorist."

She was done with this stupid conversation. She checked her mobile. Rex read the body language. He jumped back on topic.

"So what's he going to do… the governor?"

He implored her, leaning on her arm, fixing her to the table like Haggarty to the tundra. His greasy hair stood at stiff attention. The windy fans couldn't budge it. Despite the free press, she found him despicable.

"Split the baby," said Mel.

"What?"

"A relocation program. Fish and Game's going to relocate wolves."

"Relocation," whispered Rex to himself. "Of course. The bastards!"

"What?" asked Feinberg.

"A relocation program," said Mel to Feinberg. The lawyer seemed much less depraved than Rex. "Capture wolves and relocate them from two areas, the Upper Kuskokwim and the Upper Tanana."

"So they don't have to kill any. So they're not blamed for killing them," said Rex, working through the political implications.

"Well, they'll die anyway," said Mel, trying to stand.

"Wait! Wait! Where will they put them?"

"The Kenai," said Mel.

She saw that meant nothing to Feinberg.

"The Kenai Peninsula," she explained to him. "It's a place west of Anchorage, a peninsula cut off by water and glaciers, Alcatraz, a gulag for wolves, no exit."

"Yeah," whispered Rex, impressed by the political brilliance. "Wait! Why will the Kenai take them? I mean, they've got their own moose troubles. Why will they take Kuskokwim wolves?"

"That sucks for them, eh?" said Mel. "But, you know, the imports will get picked off by the Kenai packs. And they'll be sterilized."

"Sterilized?" Feinberg's eyes got bigger.

"Cut, snip, a little present from the biologists while they're drugged. Can't have any unwanted baby wolves, can you?"

Mel stood to take off. She'd done her duty to the press. Feinberg stood with her, fumbling for his jacket.

"Can we talk as you walk?"

"Sure," said Mel, enjoying the attention.

She imagined the Valentine crowd watching her strut, trailed by the rich paramour. She pushed into a blast of frigid air. Feinberg ducked and followed. She gave a passing glance through the coffeehouse windows. Rex the reporter was sitting down with Gunterson and Haggarty.

What a weasel.

"Man, it's cold!" said Feinberg, striding up the street with Mel, cringing from the blasting wind.

"Yeah, the Takus, right off the ice fields," said Mel, pretending it didn't matter one way or another to her.

God, she was freezing! She hated the Takus! But she wasn't going to let an East Coast lawyer know that. She found her car tucked behind a friend's in a private drive.

"Get in, I'll give you a lift."

Feinberg slipped inside. She fired up the engine and heater. They sat in silence, watching ice crystals evaporate from the windshield, searching for feeling in frozen toes.

"Where to?"

"Uh, the Baranof?"

"Okay," said Mel, pulling out with a whine of tires on ice. The Baranof Hotel was just a couple blocks away.

"I wanted to talk to you about a case I'm working on," said Feinberg, shivering. "I was hoping you might be available to consult."

"What kind of case?" asked Mel, pointing the car straight down Main, sliding toward the channel like a toboggan, windshield wipers flapping wildly.

"Medical malpractice, a botched surgery," said Feinberg, frightfully watching them hurdle past bundled shapes struggling toward the capitol.

"Malpractice suit? What does that have to do with me?"

"Rex Winkler said I should talk to you. My client is an old woman, Eskimo. We need help defining her injuries."

"Yeah?" said Mel, pulling to a quick stop at the front of the Baranof Hotel, putting the car into a hot idle. "What kind of injuries?"

"Lost subsistence," said Feinberg.

"Yeah?" said Mel, suddenly more interested.

"The old woman doesn't work, that is, she doesn't work for money. But she cuts fish, puts up subsistence food, that sort of thing. Every year, she says. But because of malpractice, she lost two years of her subsistence, you know, her fish and game or whatever it is she does. We need to establish the monetary value of those losses."

Yeah, thought Mel, looking at the lawyer pulling his expensive overcoat tighter. And you don't know how to do that, do you? The lawyers are stumped. How does one attach a dollar value to Native traditions like hunting whales or smoking salmon? So the lawyers come running to the anthropologists.

"This is a Native woman?"

"An Eskimo, a Yup'ik," declared Feinberg.

"From where?"

"Sleetmute."

Sleetmute... a village on the Kuskokwim River in western Alaska. She'd never been there. But she had staff in Bethel who worked at times along the middle Kuskokwim, researching salmon fishing and moose hunting and other subsistence issues. Her division had funded mapping by linguists in the area to document Native place names. If she recalled correctly, her staff had nothing going on there at present.

"What kind of malpractice?"

"Knee replacement. Her left knee, arthritis. The doctors messed up. They replaced her good knee by mistake."

"Ah..." murmured Mel.

"After another year of suffering, they eventually did the left one, leaving her with two artificial joints. She lost at least two years, according to her family. We need someone to attach a monetary value on her losses."

"For the court claim."

"For compensation of injuries," said Feinberg. "The hospital's insurance argues there are no losses because there are no records and because there is no lost income."

"That's bullshit," said Mel.

"Of course," agreed Feinberg readily, looking hopeful. "Rex said you were the expert on subsistence in Alaska. You'd know how to do it."

Mel considered. It was an interesting question, one that had come up before in other cases involving wrongful deaths and incapacitating injuries. How do you valuate subsistence foods produced in traditional village economies when the foods never circulated in markets. She knew there was no single accepted method for placing a dollar value on Native foods. Because of that, Natives with subsistence losses got screwed in court.

The question of fair compensation had come up with the *Exxon Valdez* oil spill. Native villages stopped fishing and hunting from oiled areas. How much was a seal worth to a Native? She got sucked into that one. The lawyers were still arguing about it.

"Maybe," said Mel, "but it doesn't really matter, because I don't have time for it. You need someone to do field interviews with the woman and her family to document what was lost those two years. Then you need to apply some defensible method to convert that into dollars that fairly represents the values of the food and the customary pursuits to the injured. I've got no time for that. And I've got no staff available for researching something like that because it's a private suit."

"With public implications," pleaded Feinberg.

"Yeah, but I still couldn't justify staff time for it under state rules," said Mel, looking at her phone. "You need a consultant outside the state system. And I need to get back to work."

"Are you sure?" appealed Feinberg. "Please, could we talk some more about this later? Maybe we could talk over dinner? I could treat you to dinner. We could explore this more."

Mel looked into the sad puppy eyes of Dustin Hoffman, then through the thick leaded-glass doors of the Baranof Hotel. The dining room was one of Juneau's best and most expensive, a favorite haunt of the rich and powerful during the legislative session. She looked at the plaintive lawyer with the expense account, a green Bostonian, begging for the expert guidance of an experienced Alaskan.

"Well, okay... sure," agreed Mel, flashing him a playful smile. "I guess we can meet on this some more. How about... I'm working a little late today... how about we say eight o'clock reservations here? The restaurant, not the café. If we huddle together, maybe we can come up with something."

Feinberg smiled back. They shook hands. And the lawyer scooted out into the Taku blasts.

Mel zipped over the icy streets humming a little tune. She parked at Fish and Game. As she entered its threadbare hallway heading toward her office, tucked into a corner beneath fabulous views of the snowy mountains, Mel yelled for her administrative assistant.

"Hey, Cheri!"

"Yeah!" came the shouted answer.

"Get me Mac Cleary's file!"

Cheri appeared at her door, frowning.

"Camilla Mac Cleary," said Mel, though Cheri had heard correctly.

"In San Francisco?" said Cheri warily. "That whack job?"

"What whack job?"

"That's what I heard. Whacked in the head."

"No way."

"You going to try to hire her?"

"Just get me the file."

"She's not in state."

"I know," sniffed Mel.

"Why?"

Cheri waited, blocking the doorway to her office files.

"Why?" Cheri insisted.

Mel smiled slyly. She thought about what she'd wear tonight for her dinner date, something slinky.

"Because tonight, she's going to make somebody very happy."

5

Forty days and nights.

Still the rains fell.

For Camilla Mac Cleary, the clouds remained full. The rains never ceased. The night of pain came and Camilla stared at her image on the dark bay beyond the wet window. Bloody lights pulsed atop the bridge, ruddy smears on her cheek through the splattered glass.

Never ending.

Faceless workers scaled those towers, climbed against the freezing wind above the dark waters, inching toward the blood lights, and one slip would do it.

A single false step.

Her eyes fell to the stack of papers on the desk below the wet window, chapters in a moldering dissertation. Some had permanently curled. Others had acquired dust. She knew them all. Detested them. She no longer had strength to even clean.

The night of pain...

Nick came too.

They arrived together, partners within the neurological storm because the agony first began with him in that village on the Bering Sea. Not his face, though she knew that well, close her eyes and see it, a blend hard to place, Alaska Native, Asian, Russian, prominent cheeks, full lips, intelligent eyes. Nor his solid body that sometimes rocked when his mind was preoccupied, the unconscious sway of a hunter on dangerous ice, side-to-side, cautiously moving. She'd never told him, how he rocked with distraction.

It came with his hands.

She leaned from the chair upon the cluttered desk in the dark apartment, feeling the hands on her sweaty forehead, combing the hair that dripped with grit and blood, silently working. He didn't fear the silence, accepted her without a barrage of words, rough fingers working carefully, pulling the mess to ease the agony.

Nicholas John.

Camilla found herself crying with the agony, tears of hopeless desperation.

Biochemical, some part of her brain registered. It was a fucking chemical imbalance. But the pain and hopelessness remained. Unrelenting. Unbearable.

She slowly rose from the desk, rubbed her sockets with her palms, stood as she must, and stumbled for the bottles, modern medicine dealing with pain, one black pill from the wide bottle, one yellow pill from the thin bottle. No rustic fingers probing the gritty mess. She threw them down with water tasting of rust and stumbled back to the detestable desk clutching the wide one opened like a silent scream. The black capsules spilled to join the clutter. Her palms flattened upon them.

Rain pelted the windows.

The ocean refilled the clouds.

The smears of blood pulsed above the black waters as the unending pain precipitated off the brink where a single misstep, the singular errant choice... yet the pain that she began... it would still go on and on and on...

The mobile rang. A long time.

"Yeah?" she heard herself answer.

"Camilla?"

"Yeah, this is Camilla."

"It's Mel. Mel Savidge. Calling from Juneau."

"Oh yeah, Mel."

"You don't sound too good."

"Yeah, not so good right now."

She whispered into the phone.

"Gee, I'm sorry. Is it the migraine?"

"Yeah."

"God, I'm sorry. I'll call back."

"No, no, s' okay. I'm just sitting… waiting for the pills to kick in."

The fucking black ones, trapped beneath her palm.

"You sure?"

"It's okay… so… how are you doing?"

"Better than you, I'd guess."

"Yeah."

Five months. With effort Camilla worked it out. No… almost six since she had left them in Anchorage for San Francisco, almost half a year gone… somewhere during the count Mel's voice had resumed.

"I thought of you today. Something's come up, if you're ready for something. I've got a thing here. You said to call if anything came up."

"Yeah."

"So I thought about you. It's not much, but I think it could pay. I think they need somebody like you."

The red smear blinked.

"With somebody translating, it might be perfect, just right for somebody like you and maybe Nick, Nicholas John, if you wanted. But you'd have to call him. He doesn't know yet."

Camilla closed her eyes to it.

Pain pulsed within the blackness.

"Camilla? You still there?"

"Yeah. I'm here," whispered Camilla.

Her ear jammed hard to the phone in her neck, wet eyes shuttered, palms pressed hard upon the desk. Her fingers slowly groped the disarray, feeling, finding, pinning…

"Go on," Camilla whispered, working hard to follow.

It was exceptionally hard.

But slowly, she refilled the bottle, one by one.

6

Nicholas John, strangely detached.

It wasn't the booze, though he had consumed plenty. The warm buzz fortified against the unremitting cold just beyond the windows. Forty below. Winter in Fairbanks.

But Nick felt he'd just left the party. Or it had left him. Surrounded by revelers, he was suddenly adrift. Ejected. Strange as it felt, Nick wasn't surprised. It usually happened, university or otherwise, most parties eventually disengaged, floated off like bubbles on a flood, an amoebic mass separating in a cellular spasm, the odd piece left behind. Nick stood in a solitude.

A cultural thing. He decided that some time ago.

He swigged Chardonnay from the plastic cup as if that might return him to the main mass.

It was a cultural thing being raised Yup'ik in a village on the lower Yukon River, out of phase with the broad outside, out of sync with the at-hand flux.

He enjoyed the dislocations. Things appeared sharper, more exotic, a good drug trip without the brain injury. He could float, a mote between rooms, unnoticed, invisible, impressed by the foreignness of everything.

A tropical fish tank bubbled before him, bug-eyed carp gulping, fins sprouted like fungus. Glowing water divided nattering professors and students. None gave it a passing glance. Books walled him, a room with more printed words than in his entire village, sandwiched between covers that sandwiched him. Home had no floating carp or walls of books shaping social space. He had finished every book in the village by the age of fourteen, so they shipped him to boarding school. Get him out for his own good.

He got out. Now he was here.

Gulping fish and wine.

The party flowed off still further. The crowd moved through panes of glass into the biting night, a procession behind the piping grand marshal, the newly-tenured host, giddy and soused. A hand moved around Nick's shoulder.

"Coming?"

A friendly face and voice from earlier, some graduate assistant or something… Nick dug deep.

George.

"Where's everybody going?"

"The puppies," George laughed, pulling Nick into the brittle air.

The puppies came bounding out of a snug hutch near the back porch. They leaped about the knees of shivering guests, ecstatic fleas with uncontrollable tongues. Partiers ooed and aahed and petted. Pretty girls lifted fluffy pups for wet kisses. The drunken host beamed at his accomplishment, his happy progeny, his diminutive kids yipping beneath fuzzy skies curtained by northern lights that shifted from nauseous green to orange and back again. Detached, the presentation of puppies looked exceptionally strange to Nick.

"Don't you like them?" smiled George, flushed with booze and subzero air, catching him off sync.

"What are they?"

"Puppies," laughed George. "Lovable puppies. What else?"

"Yeah, but…"

There was something strange with the puppies he couldn't put his finger on… maybe it was the booze, the cultural thing.

"Huskies? A husky mix?"

"No… and yes," George flashed an enigmatic smile and lowered his voice confidentially. "The real question is, mixed with what?"

The party flowed back inside. The puppies yipped forlornly, puff paws on the chain-link fence, wanting to follow. Beyond the puppies, Nick heard a mournful howl. It turned into a chorus from the dark. Sled dogs howled somewhere on the property. Nick knew the professor kept horses stabled in a barn by the access road. He must also race dogs. Therefore, the puppies. Breeding dogs for a team. Inside the party crowd huffed and puffed from the painful cold and refilled cups.

"Sprint dogs," Nick guessed.

"So he hopes," said George, eyes twinkling. He shook his head and smiled knowingly.

"Why not?"

"Because they're not."

George poured Nick more wine.

"Not sprinters."

"Not dogs."

Nick snapped back to reality.

Not dogs?

"Then what?"

"Who knows?" laughed George, slurping his cup. "But I'll bet you this, next year this time they'll be the shits."

"Shits."

"Because they're freaks."

"Huh."

"Cute little abominations, cute little blends of ingenuity and pride, Siberian husky and…" he winked, "wolf."

"Wolf?"

"Shhhh!" said George, looking around. "Nobody is supposed to know. But of course, everybody does. Look at all of them laughing, congratulating dickhead like he's the sneaky father because he is. One-quarter wolf, but mostly husky and a touch of whippet… that's the claim, but you won't see any papers and he'll deny it."

"Why?" asked Nick, intrigued.

"It's not legal. Come on, get your stuff."

Bundled up, George lead Nick back outside. They took snowy paths that squeaked beneath their heavy boots, meandering among sheds and dog runs. Greasy colors shimmered in the sky, Halloween lights and jelly smears and scummy gauze as they arrived at a dog yard, a broad spread of tiny hutches surrounded by tamped yellow snow. Thin faces peered from kennel doors stuffed with straw, the howlers, chained to their shelters. It was too late for a feeding and too cold to bother with visitors, so they simply watched from the little doors, sniffing the crystal air sweet with wood smoke.

"They know me," said George. "I'm helping to train them."

"You race?" asked Nick.

"Yeah," he chuckled. "Come on."

They crunched through a stand of aspen so wide Nick thought George was lost when at a far edge they came to a high-fenced yard of indeterminate size. A forest of birch began beyond it, rising up the ridge above Fairbanks. A lone doghouse sat in the yard some distance from the fence. A face peered out from straw, resting on crossed paws.

"There he is," George nodded to the loner. "Dad."

Nick gazed uneasily into a large wolfish face.

"Dad?"

"Half wolf," said George, lighting two cigarettes, blowing smoke to the blurry heavens, and handing one to Nick, the real reason for the stroll. "But he'll deny it. That makes the pups quarters."

"Huh!" said Nick, considering the pedigree, nursing the cigarette. "How does it happen?"

George laughed, enjoying a substantial conversation.

"His mom was a local favorite," explained George, "a beautiful white husky, a real runner until she got stomped by a moose during the Quest. But his dad… they won't even tell me, his dad was a full-blooded wolf, not from around here. He bought the junk off the black market, shipped up."

"From where?"

"California, Minnesota, Texas? Plenty of wolves behind bars down there, or animals the dealers claim are wolves, raised and bred in captivity. That's the hard part, certifying you're getting the real stuff."

"Expensive?"

"Outrageous."

Nick watched the animal intently. George seemed to approve of Nick's reaction.

"And a total waste of money."

"What? Why's that?"

"Because they're fuck-ups," said George, lighting a second cigarette, blowing smoke for emphasis. "Fuck-ups. Racers buy into it, you know, especially the new racers. They think they'll breed some super-dog, a dog with wolf traits, strong, fast, tough, endurance. And they are. Like that one there, he's got that husky mom and wolf dad. One-on-one he'd destroy any dog in a distance race, absolutely destroy him. Durable, strong like a wolf. Trouble is, that's not all they come with."

George gave a sardonic laugh.

"They think they'll get some new kind of dog with wolf traits, or at the worst, some wolf with dog traits that they can breed again. But that's not what they get. What they get is this." He patted the chain-link. "They get an animal they have to pen up, separate from the kennel, cordoned off. Why? Because that animal in there isn't a dog or a wolf. It's neither. It's a freak. It fails as a dog. And it fails as a wolf."

Nick thought hard on this, watching the loner.

Intense eyes stared back from the hutch.

"Same with those quarter puppies," said George. "He'll find out. They're not dogs either. You can't breed animals as far apart as dogs and wolves and get a sled dog, not in two generations or two dozen. There's fifty thousand years between them."

"You think?"

"That's what I think. I know geneticists who'll argue."

Fifty thousand years.

Fifty thousand generations separating wolves from dogs. A long time for change. For difference.

Nick considered himself, his origins in western Alaska, his own community, the Yup'iks, the 'real people.' They had hunted the Bering Sea for several thousand years. So the archeology said. His ancestors had been separate from others like Europeans much longer than that, enough time for Yup'iks to develop distinctive languages, technologies, religions, world views. He was proud of his Yup'ik roots. Now he worked as a student of cultural anthropology among non-Yup'iks who mostly had Euroamerican roots. He studied and learned, aggregated systems of knowledge, bridged disparate worlds. He spoke two languages fluently. He survived in remote villages and in cities. He could successfully hunt a seal and debug a computer.

At the end of it, what was he?

Not a Euroamerican, whatever that might be. He was still Yup'ik. But an odd Yup'ik. He'd been wondering recently, did he fit anywhere?

"So what are they like?"

"What?" said George, absorbed by his thoughts.

"The offspring, the mixes, what are they like?"

"Who can say? It's hardly been done enough, though the breeders are trying. But I'll tell you what I've seen. There's a key difference.

"Dogs are programmed to like humans. It's in their genes. Don't ask me why they are, humans are such rats. But a dog is wired to like humans. You know the joke… to a dog you're 'the master,' to a cat you're 'the staff.'"

George laughed at his own joke.

"But to a wolf… I bet you know this better than me, to a wolf you're 'trouble,' plain and simple. A wolf will run from a human, nine times out of ten. He's wired to do it. Deep in his wolf genes he knows with a certainty that humans are trouble."

Nick nodded.

"So what do you get from breeding into that?" said George. "Fuck-ups. The mixes are useless as workers.

They won't pull a damn sled for a human. They're totally wrong for it. They're skittish around people. Unpredictable. Dangerous. They won't be trained, and not because they're stupid. They're a hell of a lot smarter than most dogs, way smarter. But they won't be trained to pull a damn sled. It won't happen."

This seemed right to Nick, but George presumed wrongly. Nick didn't know wolves. Wolves had left his homeland along the lower Yukon River during his great grandfather's generation after the failure of the reindeer herds introduced by the missions. That's the story told on the lower Yukon. The wolves left. So he didn't know wolves. But he did know dogs. He knew dogs worked for people, like George said. The Yup'ik word for dog was 'puller.'

Nick eyed the wire enclosure. He felt sympathy for this animal, genetically engineered, trapped in a cage.

"He'll find that out soon enough with those puppies," said George, flicking the butt. "He'll piss and moan but he'll get his money back. There are lots of crazy people who'll pay top dollar for quarter-wolf puppies. But I'll tell you something. I'd never have one. In a million years, I'd never keep a wolf-dog, never around kids. Dangerous. Absolutely unpredictable."

"Yeah," said Nick, putting his hand on the prison, thinking he'd like a better look at the beast in the cage.

"Speak of the devil, here he comes now," said George.

The wolf-dog emerged from the hutch like a shadow. The creature was large and gray, a thin waist with powerful hind legs, a broad expressive face and great tail. It seesawed across the yard, first one shoulder, then the other, watching Nick with ghost-like eyes. At a dozen feet it stopped, tail straight, silently eyeing him. To Nick it looked curious.

"I've never seen him do this," smiled George. "He never comes out to greet strangers. He's never come out for me and I'm here a lot. I think he's studying you."

Nick felt embarrassed.

He didn't know what to think or to say. He felt like he shouldn't gawk. But the animal stared, so Nick stared back. He wished he had something to offer, dried salmon or seal. But he had nothing.

"Hey Shadow!" said George. "How're we doing?"

The wolf-dog stood, eyes on Nick.

It did not acknowledge George.

Because that's not your name, Nick thought.

You have no name.

The animal bowed, set its haunches, and launched.

Paws smashed the fence where Nick's head had been. Nick sprawled on the snow. It ricocheted off the fence, shoved off, and landed in the yard. Its haunches raked the icy ground, a raw scouring like boulders in a landslide, flinging gritty snow through the chain-links behind him. With a great leap, it vanished.

"Son-of-a-bitch!" said George.

"Yeah…" said Nick, brushing off, watching the empty dark. "Well… I guess that's half right."

That called for another cigarette.

7

She burst from the den enraged. The yearlings scattered into the brushy hillside. She stood bristling at the mouth, set to charge anybody within reach.

The feeding... intolerable!

Crowded, suffocating!

The puppies fought. They quarreled and scratched and nipped. They bit her! Enough! She had thrown them off, snarled them to silence, and bolted, breasts swinging with milk. They whined, but enough! She left the foul hole and stood like a fury. The strong one, her partner, appeared at his perch. He nervously watched. She growled deep in her chest. Stay away.

She made a leap and slid down the icy slope. Entering the clogged creek, she escaped to the tunnels.

Down the frozen path she raced, breathing heavily, badly out of shape from her confinement. She sucked great gulps of the icy air. It tasted delicious. She emerged into full sun, panting and alert, turning in circles at the main channel. She felt elated.

Downriver smelled best. She broke that way and fell into an easy trot upon the thick mid-winter ice. She heard a faint bark and a howl behind her. The strong one called for her. She ignored it. She moved on familiar trails freed from detention.

The stone appeared at the great bend.

She stuck her nose upon it, read its messages, top to bottom. The strong one claimed the highest spot, her partner, the leader. That was right. Just below she found brothers, hunters, those who brought the food regurgitated at the den. She located a sister, the one who always greeted her and licked her nose and clung by her side. It took a moment, she found herself, a faint mark near the top. Too faint. She fixed that immediately. She sprayed the roster. Then she rooted further along the rock, searching out smells of yearlings, that one and then that other one. Oh, a fox! And a marten! They had plastered themselves among the community. Outrageous!

Further down, beneath these offenses she detected fainter spoors. There a yearling, a son. She remembered his face. There a daughter so faint it barely spoke. There a beloved brother, barely perceptible. The scents brought each back to memory, children from before, former den mates. The fading spoke of long absences, uneasy mysteries. She voiced a low whine.

What was that? Something jolted.

She shifted effort, crossed a few steps to a nearby snag that poked from the frozen ground.

Oh! That rogue! There he was, the dark one! His scent covered the snag and snow around it. So strong she lifted her head and searched. Wait, someone else was there too. Her nose touched the spot. Her sister! The playful one! She hid beneath the pirate.

She lifted her face quizzically. The land rose beyond the marker. Up there somewhere? Had she staked claim with the dark one somewhere up there? An intense curiosity filled her, a nervousness to confirm it.

She checked the river path behind and saw no pursuers. Her unemptied breasts ached, remonstrations about hungry puppies. Her nipples hurt from their teeth. She nosed the sky. The pale sun peeked above the ridge. The pissing stone marked a place for leaving the river.

Impulsively, she turned up the hill, nose to the snow. Back and forth she searched. She smelled the rogue. A well-worn trail lifted up along the rise. The rogue used it boldly. 'My path,' it proclaimed. She found the playful one nowhere. But she detected another, a brother, and too many foxes. Somehow this winter, the community had left this path to the rogue and foxes, deferring to their bold claims. She knew this route well. She didn't like thieving foxes.

Following her brother's scent, she climbed the path, moving upwards toward the crests of long ridges. She passed among stands of leafless birch and aspen. The smell of the rogue remained strong. The walk felt good. She paused often, catching her breath and sniffing the bases of naked wood. She felt a growing need to turn back to her pups. Ahead she saw the top of a higher ridge. She would go there.

As she reached the crest a strange buzz filled the air. Some blot darkened the light. She momentarily froze. The light returned. The buzz faded. She hesitated, uneasy. A vague fear tugged her. Retreat down the hill. But movement on the next ridge caught her eye. The dark one! He stood erect, watching her from across a narrow vale. And she smelled the playful one on the path that dipped into it. The smell of her sister drew her on. The dark one moved with her along the ridge at the edge of sight. This was how he was, the loner at the margins.

She descended the vale, crossed a frozen brook, and came up the other side. She ascended slowly, moving among fields of rocks obscured by deep snow. She momentarily lost the trail working among drifts. It was hard going. But ahead, she saw the ridge's end. She struggled up the rise, pushing a path, coming almost to the top. Suddenly, something was wrong!

She stopped, alert, tense.

A foreign smell struck her, brazen, sharp-edged with burning. She had never smelled it before. It screamed warning. She swung her nose to fix its direction. The wind was wrong. It gusted, broken by the ridgetop. Her stomach clenched. Her flanks shivered. She frantically scanned the ridge.

The dark one was gone!

She leaped backward and flipped about, setting her legs for a push downhill.

Something popped.

A sharp pain pricked her shoulder.

She yelped and leaped, springing down the slope. Numbness filled her shoulder. A freezing river ran down her flank. Her front legs collapsed beneath her, driving her face into snow. Everything went wrong. Her rear legs twisted. She couldn't feel them.

Her face plowed atop stinging ice.

She stopped sliding.

A fixed pale sun glowed at the corner of her vision. She could not move her eyes! The light turned fuzzy. Faded. Terror gripped her, a frantic desperation to find her puppies!

A crunching sound approached.

A shadow fell over her.

It took away the sun.

* * *

Keith Nichols was a by-the-books biologist. He had developed the solid reputation of an honest straight-shooter at McGrath, working there twelve years. He loved the outdoors. He loved the upper Kuskokwim region and its residents, who he now considered his people. And he hated ideologues. He hated fanatical anything. In the bush where he worked they just made for problems.

Today it was that.

He didn't much like the new wolf program. The ideologue who came with it he resolutely hated. But wolf relocation on the upper Kuskokwim had suddenly become department policy. And when Gary Gunterson came out to McGrath to lay down the law and oversee its first week of implementation, Nichols bit the bullet.

He went by the book.

But he didn't like it.

Keith Nichols muscled his hefty thighs through drifts at the ridge top, swinging his rifle for balance. An exuberant Gunterson leaped down the hill before him, sliding with his bulky pack.

"You got her!" shouted Gunterson.

Nichols already knew this. He was more concerned with the other wolf, the black male.

"You see the dark one?" shouted Nichols.

"He hightailed it!"

Nichols shouldered the rifle, grabbed his binoculars, and scanned the forested ridge. The dark wolf, a large mature male, had disappeared. He must have seen them land on the frozen lake in the swale between ridges and bolted for the riverbed. The female hadn't. The wind was behind her. They had cut the engines, scrambled to the ridge top, and set up just in time to make the shot.

What were these two wolves? Partners?

He doubted it. They traveled too far apart. Partners usually traveled the same trail in a line. The behavior and relationship of the two wolves were puzzles. He checked his wristwatch. Twelve ten. The time would be recorded. He sat in the snow, removed the paper log, and made entries. Beneath him, Gunterson worked efficiently to fix the stretcher. Nichols didn't bother to watch. Gunterson was expert in field procedures. But he was still an asshole.

"She's ready! Let's get her up!" shouted Gunterson.

Nichols stowed the log and slid down to the wolf some yards below the ridgeline. Gunterson had trussed her in a sling with side handles. Each gripped a side. Together, they hauled the animal to the top, huffing and puffing and sweating in the frigid wind. Nichols spied Hal Martin on the lake below, repositioning the plane's skis for takeoff. The lake was just long enough. Hal Martin was a friend and seasoned bush pilot. Nichols trusted him completely.

Gunterson broke out equipment for measurements. He set up the tripod to get a weight. He wheezed as he worked. Smoker's lungs, thought Nichols. The man can't breathe. Nichols removed the dart from the wolf's shoulder. The drug would work for several hours. Still, they must hurry to avoid another injection during the flight to the Kenai. The more injections, the greater the risks to the animal. He retrieved the logbook.

"You ready?" Gunterson squinted into wind that whipped the ridge. His mustache dripped above a broad smile. He loved this work.

"Go," said Nichols.

Gunterson positioned the tape, checking the wolf's length and chest girth. He had started the second measurement when Nichols saw them, peeking from the flap of the stretcher.

"Shit!"

"What?" said Gunterson.

"That!" said Nichols.

He pulled the tarp flap, exposing the underside. They stared at the teats of a nursing wolf.

"Yeah, I saw it. Haven't got there yet," said Gunterson, shaking the clipboard of instructions for recording data on wolves.

"She's nursing!" said Nichols hotly.

"I said I saw it."

"That changes everything."

"No it doesn't."

"Sure as hell does. That's an alpha with pups."

"Well, maybe… and maybe not," said Gunterson. "I see wet tits, but it doesn't mean that."

A gust hit the ridge. Hunkered against it, Nichols examined the full breasts.

"She's nursing. That's the goddamn alpha female."

"We don't know that."

"What?" said Nichols, incredulous.

"We don't even know what pack she's from, let alone where she fits in it."

"She's Big River."

"Well, maybe."

"No, definitely."

"Well, maybe, because you say it. But come on, Keith, we don't know squat about that pack. You don't even know where Big River dens. To say she's maybe Big River is one thing. But to say she's the alpha female of the Big

River pack is too much. I'd need a hell of a lot more than some wet tits to say that."

Nichols scowled. He turned back to the wolf in the stretcher. He gently stroked the fur, probed for injuries, lifted her face, scrapped by the slide on ice. She looked three or four years old, the prime of life, a beautiful animal. The teats were puffed and bitten.

"She's nursed recently," said Nichols.

"Looks like it," said Gunterson.

"She's got pups, she's the alpha," said Nichols firmly.

"Not so," said Gunterson. "She's more than likely a loner."

"What?"

"Why else isn't she sitting home, nursing? Because nobody's feeding her. She's out hunting with that dark one. That's likely her partner."

"Not likely," growled Nichols.

"I've seen it before. You've seen it too. Expanding packs. Excess kicked out. This one's excess. That dark one too, partnered up, hunting together. You can't just go calling wet tits an alpha of a pack. We know shit about Big River wolves. Pack structure. Dens. You said so yourself at the office."

Hal Martin, the pilot, arrived at the ridge. He instantly spotted a foul-up.

"What's happening?" he asked cautiously.

"The wolf," Nichols waved with frustration.

"Is she an alpha or not?" said Gunterson simply.

Martin eyed the men, both obviously agitated, engaged in an all-to-familiar pissing match. Nichols was the region's top biologist, the local expert. But Gunterson was Nichols' current boss out of Juneau. He wasn't going to purposely step in the middle of this one. But if he had to, he'd support his buddy, Nichols.

"It make a difference?" said Martin.

"The difference is what protocol we follow," said Nichols. He lifted the writing pad, red papers flapping in the breeze. "An ordinary wolf is red, an alpha is blue. Different procedures."

"Yeah?" asked Martin, who knew nothing about this part of the project. He just flew the plane. "Does that mean we're not going to the Kenai?"

"If she's blue, we don't," said Nichols.

"That's right," said Gunterson, sitting in snow. "The red form has the protocol for a wolf for relocation. We capture for a trip to the Kenai. We expect reds. The red form is on the clipboard. But if we happen to capture an alpha, the blue protocol is followed. That means sterilization and release at the capture site. We sterilize an alpha and release it back to the pack. That's the procedure."

"So what's the problem?" asked Martin carefully.

"Is she an alpha or not?" repeated Gunterson.

"She's lactating," declared Nichols flatly. "She's got pups. So she's an alpha. That means we measure and we sterilize and we return her to the pack."

Martin looked to Gunterson.

He slowly shook his head in disagreement.

"I don't see it that way," said Gunterson. "On its surface, that squares with the protocols, but it doesn't. I believe it's contrary to the purposes of the program, so it can't be right."

"How's that?" said Martin.

"This whole thing's been rushed," said Gunterson. "That's a piss-poor way to run a program but that's how it was, so the field plan doesn't spell out every field contingency. But one thing I'm sure of is the program's purpose. Improve wolf-moose ratios. That's the bottom line. Now, is this wolf a red or blue? If uncertain, I say look at the bottom line.

"If we follow the blue protocol, we sterilize and release back to the pack. This is why there's a blue protocol... it maintains the dominance hierarchy. Alphas are the top wolves in a pack. They keep others from breeding. If we sterilize and release, the sterile alpha still tries to breed but fails. So the pack misses one or several cycles of pup production before it's figured out. The sterile alpha gets replaced, fights for succession and all that. So with the blue protocol, the program uses the dominance hierarchy as a management tool to reduce pack fertility. It's a smart idea. It preserves pack structure and reduces pack size. In theory. Right?"

Martin followed the argument and nodded.

Nichols sat unmoving.

"Now this female's nursing," said Gunterson. "Here's something the protocol hadn't anticipated, darting a female already with pups. So I say, what's the bottom line in this case? Following the blue protocol does nothing to skip a pupping cycle. We release her. She goes back and nurses the pups the protocol was designed to prevent. It does nothing to reduce wolf-moose ratios. It's contrary to program goals. At least it seems that way to me.

"In a perfect world, we'd have thought of this in the office ahead of time, made a category of wolf like this one, and tweak the protocol to say what to do. But it doesn't, so we've got to figure it out ourselves, and we've got to do it fast. That drug won't last forever. I say we treat her as a red, a regular female, like we originally anticipated. We measure and relocate to the Kenai unsterilized. That squares with program goals."

Nichols exploded.

"By killing the pups!"

"Well, that may be," agreed Gunterson.

"How's that square with program goals? That kills wolves. That violates the non-lethal provisions."

"Yeah... it might," said Gunterson grudgingly. "But I always thought it pretty peculiar myself. You're going to reduce wolves but never kill any? That's what the public wants to hear. The public doesn't want state biologists to shoot or trap or snare wolves to kill them. So, we don't. And we aren't. We're capturing and relocating."

"That will kill her pups!"

"We don't know that," frowned Gunterson. "I mean, what pups? Yeah, she's lactating. There are small ones somewhere. Unweaned pups die without milk. But we don't know anything. They may be old enough already, almost weaned. She's out hunting for them. That black one's hunting for them. They're out hunting to bring them food. If we killed those pups directly, yes, that's a violation. You know, pulling them out of their den. I'd never do that. We're not doing that."

"It's the same."

"Well it isn't," said Gunterson. "But I sure as hell know one thing. We're not spending taxpayer money flying around and capturing wolves to worsen wolf-moose ratios. That's just stupid. That doesn't pass the red-face test. If we let her go, that's what we're doing.

"That's why this wolf is got to be red. If she's blue and we release her here, it increases the pack against the program goals. We're consistent with goals only by treating this as red. That's how I read it, by the books."

"That's by the books?" asked Martin.

"I believe it is," said Gunterson.

Nichols stared at the swollen nipples.

He grabbed his pack.

"I'm not killing pups," he growled.

"We're not," said Gunterson.

"Fuck off!"

Nichols stomped away.

Martin watched his friend slide down the slope toward the plane on the lake, taking huge steps. Gunterson watched too, smiling beneath the dripping mustache.

"Hey, Hal?"

"Yeah?"

"Can you fill out a log?"

8

Camilla Mac Cleary shuffled across the wet plaza beneath the glass towers, weary and demoralized. She detested herself for being there. The skyline of the financial district beat her down, reflected her failure as a human.

The towers moved with storm clouds.

Never go to law.

In her heart Camilla knew this.

Reject power and privilege. Address mistakes personally, honestly, face-to-face.

She knew she had fallen. She had sold flesh-and-blood like a commodity, abrogated a solemn contract, and fought against a needy family. Now she appealed to the rich and powerful to rectify her sins.

Law heals nothing. Makes nothing whole.

It feeds from the wound.

Before her an outlandish crowd choked the path. The plaza swarmed with people waving signs. In the spit of a noontime squall, lean shirtless men leaped about howling, stomachs bleeding red paint. Women in feathered headdresses circled in a dizzy dance to wildly banging drums. A cameraman filmed the spectacle. A reporter interviewed demonstrators.

Banners shouted in block letters.

STOP THE KILLING!

SAVE THE WOLVES!
BOYCOTT ALASKA!

"Mac!"

A tall bearded blond leaped from the throng, hands filled with flyers. Camilla recognized him from the university, Geoff Sturgis, an outdoor enthusiast and political activist on green issues. He was unassailably self-righteous, a global dilettante exuding the naïve confidence of the privileged class. Camilla liked him.

"Mac!" he smiled.

"Hi Geoff."

"Thanks for coming!"

Without dropping a flyer, he wrapped his great arms and swallowed her in a hug.

"You bet," said Camilla. "What is it?"

"What is it?"

"I'm here on business," she nodded reluctantly at a tower.

A bald female in huge spectacles and tea shirt proclaiming 'Save Them Now' plucked the flyers from Geoff's hands. She began to work the lunchtime crowd. A contingent of half-naked males converged. They lifted their faces to the sky and howled. A companion with black and yellow dreadlocks beat against a giant wheeled drum.

"It's a Howl-In!" said Geoff enthusiastically. "The first one ever! Join us!"

"Howl-In?"

"For the wolves!"

"Oh, yeah," Camilla remembered.

She had heard it advertised on campus, 'boycott Alaska' to protest the mistreatment of wolves. This was it, a demonstration against Alaska's latest predator control program.

"You've been up there! You can say something. You can speak for the wolves."

"Well, yeah," said Camilla, seeing a stage under construction, "but maybe not, sorry. I'm late for an appointment where they charge by the hour. And I'm broke. Maybe when I come back."

The giddy crowd swirled around them, dancing, chanting, and waving banners.

"Boycott! Boycott! Boycott!"

"Larry! Becka! Karly! Meet Camilla Mac Cleary. Camilla, Larry and Becka and everyone. Camilla's been up there! She's with the wolves, one hundred percent!"

"Right on, Camilla!"

"Save the wolves!"

"Boycott! Boycott!"

Camilla smiled and gave Geoff a friendly pat.

"See you later."

She moved through the crowd feeling affection for the oddball wolf protectors, but mostly discouraged. Did they think beating drums and howling could save wolves? It fed the media here. It got a message out. But howling? It looked nutty. Didn't they know that? The shouts for a boycott seemed better, launched from the heart of the financial district. Boycotts threatened business in its pocketbook, forced businessmen to think about wolves because of money.

Money was the real fuel.

Camilla rode a windowed elevator skywards, suppressing a sudden nausea.

She had passed way beyond money as fuel. Broke, she wallowed in debt, barely paying on school loans, foundering with her dissertation. No lender would touch her. She had crawled back to beg help from Scott Findley, an old Berkeley classmate and friend, now a corporate lawyer. He agreed to help from some combination of pity and duty and self-abuse.

She and Scott were briefly lovers. After passing the bar, he was ready for something more permanent. She wasn't. They had parted amicably enough, she for anthropological fieldwork in Mexican rural health and he for the corporate climb. Now she was fucked and had come slinking back. How did he feel now, helping her fight for a baby that wasn't even his? After drinks he must really detest her. He referred Camilla to an associate, Hugh Glassner, a new family-practice lawyer offering pro bono for the poor in Berkeley to expunge college loan obligations. Camilla accepted with self-loathing.

"Come in," greeted a pert receptionist. "Mr. Findley and Mr. Glassner are ready for you."

Scott's office today.

A meeting squeezed into a lunch hour.

The receptionist's lips curled with fascination, the voyeuristic appraisal of a mother who sold her child.

I'm projecting, thought Camilla. She knows nothing about me. I'm less than nothing to her.

They entered a spacious conference room. Hugh Glassner thumbed file folders from a leather chair. Scott Findley stared out the high window above the plaza.

"Mac, come in," gushed Scott. "How are you? Let me get you something. Green tea, right?"

Scott sent the request with the receptionist. He knew her drinks. He knew a lot about her. Camilla read his solicitous manner as discomfort, thinly mastered by professionalism. He didn't have to do this, but here he was, consulting and assisting Glassner. Maybe the new family-practice lawyer felt over his head, defending baby sellers.

"Good to see you, Camilla," said Glassner, taking her hand, smiling sincerely, overlapping eyeteeth uncorrected by orthodontia, working class making good.

"Nice to see you too," said Camilla.

"Is it raining yet?"

"Spitting."

"What's happening down there?" asked Scott.

"A demonstration... to protect wolves," said Camilla.

"Hey, free Willy!" Scott laughed, taking another look.

Glassner said nothing. Maybe whales and wolves were worth saving. Camilla sat opposite him. Scott perched on a chair to one side. Glassner had the lead today. The green tea arrived. Camilla took a deep breath.

She could do this.

Time for work.

She was good at social performances, an essential skill for cultural anthropology. In stressful surroundings she could wall up personal discomfort, lock down emotions, and convincingly perform as if they didn't exist. She could effectively present a public side despite the inner chaos and pain, for short snatches, play it out, perform. She'd do it now.

"We have a court date, three weeks from tomorrow," said Glassner, handing her an official document. "That's good news. I'll be there with their lawyers. So should you, to hear it argued and to respond to questions. It's not a trial. It's more like a preliminary hearing. The judge usually asks questions. It's before Judge Zimmerman. That could be good or bad, I'm told, depending on how he approaches it."

"What do you mean?" asked Camilla.

"Whether he approaches it as a contested adoption, or as a broken contract."

"Zimmerman's a traditionalist," said Scott from the sideline. "We're hoping he sees it the traditional way, as a contested adoption."

Scott took a long sip from a tall glass of ice water. He allowed his eyes to linger for the first time.

He's mourning me, thought Camilla. His eyes are full of hurt. I wounded his pride by rejecting him and he's still suffering, two years later. God, he shouldn't be here. I shouldn't be hurting him more. But he can't stay away. Camilla saw Glassner watching him too. Why did Glassner allow Scott to participate? His inexperience? Doesn't he know their history? What must he personally think of her, the cultural anthropologist who rented out her womb?

"You may remember from our last session," Glassner continued, "there are no laws specific to surrogacy in California. The state legislature hasn't passed any laws about surrogate mothers, on purpose. What they mean by that is who gets pregnant and how it happens is not the state's concern. The state doesn't peep into the bedrooms of consenting adults."

"I remember," said Camilla.

"That means fertility clinics are essentially unregulated. They enjoy broad latitude in assisting pregnancies. There's little binding between parties except the terms of specific contracts. That's how you and the Schofields did it. You drew up a contract through a clinic. So that's one approach for Zimmerman. He can treat the case as a contract dispute. Terms. Obligations."

Glassner extracted a set of papers from the file and handed them to Camilla. She took them reluctantly. Holding the contract made her physically ill. Her signature sat beneath those of the Schofields.

How idealistic she had been, how stupid, signing these papers, the legal basis for disposing a baby not even conceived or personally experienced. Memories flooded back with the papers. Brenda Schofield had found her, desperate for a child. Someone at the clinic knew her because Camilla was connected, part of the health networks. Would she be interested? Brenda Schofield cried, begged her as a last resort to make her marriage whole. She was Catholic, so was Camilla, at least on her father's side. She caught Camilla during a turbulent transition, emotionally, financially, and professionally, just entering the field in Mexico. Camilla found she empathized with Brenda's desperate hope. Yeah, carrying a baby for her to save her marriage... I'm young, I'm healthy, I can do that. Camilla had believed this.

She dropped the papers on the table.

"Okay, as a contract dispute," said Camilla.

"Or Zimmerman could view this primarily as a child custody case, a contested adoption. There's firm California law and case history on child custody. Unlike conception, it is in the state's interest to see that every child has a parent and a home. The contract still pertains, but the courts can go beyond its specific terms and apply criteria relevant to child welfare in general."

"That's how we've challenged it, as a contested adoption," said Scott. "That's why this case is before the court."

"Through the birth certificate," said Camilla.

"That's right," said Glassner. "We challenged the change of birth records at week three. You refused to sign. That's how it's before Zimmerman, as a contested adoption. We hope Zimmerman sees it as a question of who gets legal status as a parent."

Camilla remembered the horrible period after the birth. For her it was a disaster, like a flood or an earthquake, a catastrophic blur of pain and confusion. Camilla found her mind had changed. She couldn't give up the baby. But they took her anyway as she wept at the hospital.

She ran to Scott, inconsolable, barely coherent. Scott was shocked, hurt, and angry at finding that Camilla had given birth for somebody named Everett Schofield. But as a friend, he helped her. The surrogacy contract was clear, he assessed. The baby went to the Schofields except for certain medical exceptions, which there weren't.

Scott found Glassner, who identified the critical legal step at week three. The initial certificate of birth listed Camilla Mac Cleary as the mother and Everett Schofield as the father. At week three, the certificate was to be legally changed pursuant to adoption laws, making Brenda Schofield the legal mother. Her name would be entered as the adoptive mother on a revised birth certificate, the original sealed by the court with the signed concurrence of the biological mother.

'Don't sign,' advised Glassner.

It had given her hope. It pulled her back to sanity.

"What other criteria can he use?" asked Camilla.

"Biological facts," said Glassner. "We'll strongly argue these before Judge Zimmerman. You are the mother in two ways. You gave birth. This is one basis for establishing motherhood in California. Also, it's your egg. You're a genetic parent. That's a second basis. The biological facts conflict with your contractual statement to voluntarily relinquish legal status as mother in the surrogacy agreement. I'll argue that biologically you are still the legal mother. The second step of adoption was never completed. You changed your mind before that step. You are the legal mother and want to remain the legal mother."

"And you've received no payments," said Scott. "That's still correct, right?"

"Yes, I haven't touched it," said Camilla.

"We'll have to get verification and clarification about the status of that account in Mexico City before the hearing with Zimmerman. I must admit, I still don't have a complete understanding of that account."

The money.

What had she been thinking? Camilla couldn't believe she had actually agreed to this, selling her baby. But she did it because there was no baby yet, just an idealized concept. She didn't become real for Camilla until the long months of pregnancy and the hard delivery and the horrible infusion of hormones that had fucked her up completely. She knew this happened with some women. She never thought it would happen to her, a slave to biochemistry. She hardly believed it still.

"He wired money to an account in Mexico City," explained Camilla, "five thousand dollars for any medical expenses to use while I was pregnant in Mexico. I never touched it."

"It was in his name, not yours, right?" asked Scott. "It wasn't a retainer?"

"I never saw it. He told me it was in his name, but he listed me as somebody who could withdraw from it. It was never a retainer."

"His lawyer will contend that it was your account and taking it constituted an initial acceptance of payment under the contract's terms."

"That's not true. It was a contingency for doctors."

"There's over twenty-five thousand dollars in it now, which they say is your payment," said Glassner.

"That happened later. I wasn't even down there."

"We'll have to straighten this out before the hearing," said Scott, "but definitely, don't touch it. Don't even call that bank."

"Okay," agreed Camilla.

Money… in America, money could buy almost anything. But not children. Since Lincoln's emancipation proclamation there were no more markets for children in America. Buying and selling humans was now illegal and socially repugnant. Unless, of course, it was carefully fenced through the unregulated fertility clinics. You could buy them that way. And you could buy lawyers to dispute the terms. In America that was socially acceptable, as well as repugnant. Lawyers came expensive. The twenty-five thousand dollars in a Mexican bank sat like unclaimed collateral. How might a court award that money, should one side or the other lose? Attorney fees?

Glassner brought Camilla back.

"We hope Judge Zimmerman will choose to treat this primarily as a contested adoption, focusing on the dispute between a biological mother and biological father who aren't married. Mothers traditionally have an edge in that kind of dispute unless there's some other compelling reason such as child safety. That's something their lawyer may play up. They'll claim the Schofields' home is better economically and socially for a child."

"I'll bet," said Camilla.

"So we need to get a statement from you regarding your educational status and employment prospects to counter whatever they might contend."

"Uh huh," said Camilla.

"And your newest job, something on that too," said Scott.

"Okay, but I've only received a verbal commitment."

"Who's that lawyer again?" asked Glassner, flipping through the file.

"Feinberg. Larry Feinberg."

"Of Soames, Oakes, and Henry in Boston, right?" asked Scott.

"Yeah."

"Tell them Hugh or I will be calling for a copy of the agreement. I can do that tomorrow."

"I don't think there is one yet," said Camilla.

"You're flying to Alaska to work with only a verbal contract?" said Scott, surprised. "Law firms stiff consultants all the time! They're the worst offenders. I'll make sure there's a written contract by tomorrow, one we can send to Zimmerman to show you're employable."

"Okay," agreed Camilla.

There was a silence in the room.

The lunch clock ticked down.

"So how does it look?" asked Camilla, searching their faces. Glassner looked uncomfortable. Scott stared out the window.

"It's hard to say," said Glassner. "There aren't many definitive surrogacy cases. Rulings have been all over the map. One lower court has treated a couple's arrangement for a pregnancy through a fertility clinic, regardless of genetic donors, as legally equivalent to a natural, biological conception. If Zimmerman takes that position and rules on the basis of the contract, it may override our biological facts."

Scott turned away from the window. He looked sad.

"It may come down to who wanted a child most," said Scott. "The court might find that Everett and Brenda Schofield worked hard to conceive, really wanted to have it, while you didn't, based on the contract."

His sadness said, 'and you didn't want mine.'

"That was before," countered Camilla. "Before I carried her, before I gave birth to her, before I knew her. It all changed after that!"

"Did it?" asked Scott.

"Yes! I'm not the same person as the one who signed that contract!"

"I'm not sure the courts will concur."

"It's true!"

"Look, a pregnancy doesn't make a woman a different person."

"Wait, wait," said Glassner, looking worried. "How is it different? How are you different? Zimmerman might be persuaded by this argument, that a woman changes with motherhood."

"Yeah, I know," said Camilla, reining it in. "I know I'm the person who signed that contract. But look, I'm now also a biological mother. The old Camilla Mac Cleary wasn't. Now as a biological mother, I find I can't just give her up!"

"Lots of mothers do give up babies," said Scott.

"I know! I know! They do! But somehow, I don't know how, somehow it's like my body is no longer me! I can't explain it, how it happened, except biologically, some surge of hormones. I'm not the same person. Scott, do I even look like the Camilla you knew? I'm morose, depressed, incapacitated. I get fucking migraines almost every day! I never had that before the delivery. Never."

"I'm not sure we want those things on the record," said Glassner nervously.

"But it's not like a head injury, something where the doctors point to this or that and they say 'that's damaged so she's neurologically screwed.' It's totally invisible. But I can tell you, this isn't my old head!"

Camilla's eyes filled with tears.

Pain flitted across Scott's brow.

"I understand," said Scott. "I understand and I'm sorry. But you have to know, Mac, it's a hard argument to make. Will it persuade a judge? It's like, you can break a legal contract because of raging female hormones?"

"Not female hormones!" shouted Camilla. "My fucking hormones! My fucking head!"

Camilla buried her eyes in her hands and openly wept. Scott Findley stared uncomfortably out the window, a bay disappearing in a curtain of gray.

"So I can understand," said Glassner, "the hormones after birth. I know some mothers say they bond with their babies and that this may be hormonal, fiercely protecting them and so forth. You still have that?"

"No," whispered Camilla.

"No?" asked Glassner, surprised.

"No, that's faded. That's going. That's gone."

"But you have head pain since the delivery, because of the pregnancy?"

"Yes," said Camilla.

"A doctor can confirm this. You take pills?"

Camilla fished into a jacket pocket, found plastic bottles, one wide, one skinny, and passed them.

Glassner jotted prescriptions from the labels.

"I guess I should take one of those now," said Camilla, her wet lashes squinting into the light. "One from the big bottle."

She pulled out a capsule and downed it with her last gulp of tea. Camilla saw that Scott watched with morbid fascination.

"That's for migraines?" said Glassner.

"Yeah, it sometimes works."

"And the other one?"

"Depression."

"Oh," said Glassner.

Camilla tucked them in her jacket.

"I'll put together the strongest case I can," he said.

Camilla nodded and forced a grateful smile.

"I know you will. Thanks."

"Hugh?" said Scott from the window. "We'll need more information from the clinic about the specific medical procedures in case they argue that it's the legal equivalent of a natural conception."

"He jerked off in a cup," whispered Camilla dully.

She shielded her eyes from the overpowering light, couldn't see Scott's expression.

"But there'll be a longer history than that," said Glassner, "procedures involving Brenda Schofield that may be entered into the case as evidence they wanted the child more than you did. We'll argue it's irrelevant to this specific conception. They'll argue otherwise."

"Yeah," said Camilla.

They watched her silently, the thin face, the short black hair, the wet lashes, the eyes shut to the over-bright light, the pallor of death. In the distance, a bell tolled the hour, a single lonely strike.

"Where is she?" Camilla finally whispered, breaking the spell.

Glassner shifted uncomfortably in his chair. Scott stood unmoving at the window.

"We don't know," whispered Glassner.

"They're hiding her," said Camilla.

"Maybe."

Camilla looked to Glassner desperately, then to Scott.

"I haven't even seen a picture. Can't I even see a picture? One picture?"

"They've refused."

Camilla hid her face. Soundlessly the tears welled, spilling over, cascading down. Scott stared beyond the high window of his glass tower to a bay that had now vanished in gray sheets.

The afternoon storm, it had begun.

9

She had been dreaming. Something frightening.

Her dry tongue, open to the air, tasted foul. Her face stung. She tried to wet her teeth, found no saliva, swallowed and gagged. She struggled against the terror, trying to wake. Her body shivered. And suddenly the she wolf discovered that she no longer slept.

She cracked her eyes to twilight.

Fear materialized. Her foggy mind sensed it, a threat at a murky edge not far away. Memories woke too. Acrid smells. A snap and pain. A paralyzing fall. And the pups. The imperative fear. The pups!

She gathered her legs, heaved up sluggishly, tried to stand, and toppled. Kicking awkwardly she tried again. She came up wobbling, her head a great weight pulling sideways. She toppled again. Things were wrong! Get to the pups! Again she surged up. This time the legs held. Her heavy head moved one way and another in a search for safety. Salt struck her, a raw alien smell that covered an entire side like a barrier, the edge with the threat.

She tried to move, staggered, and skidded in snow. She regained her feet. Lights flashed behind her. She bolted. Her legs barely worked. Gulping air, she scrambled away from the frightening salt smell, away from its danger, plunging into murky wood. In and under, over and around, she struggled through tangled gloom.

The sense of danger faded. But the salt smell beat upon her. She fled from it. It took her upward. At an edge she stumbled, slid downward, and felt squeezing on her neck, a discomfort that weighed and constricted. She violently shook to throw the choking loose. She flew sideways against a bare trunk, shouldering the blow. Again and again, hard against wood. She twisted, rolled, and collapsed gasping, feeling her pounding ribs. The weight clung on her neck. She whined.

Water.

She smelled it. The scent recalled her thirst. She stumbled toward it, a flowing stream partially rimmed in ice. Flowing! Unfrozen! She sniffed the bank and water suspiciously. Thirst overcame fear. She lapped the flow, filling her empty stomach.

The thirst disappeared. An ache began. Her breasts hurt, distended, tender. She licked them.

Get the pups.

She nosed the air. Circled.

Everything was wrong... the salt smell, the murky wood, the flowing water. Warm air. Thick trees. No views. Nothing to guide her.

The stream came down steep rock. She turned from that and worked along its bank, followed it cautiously downwards. Smells came to her, odd and familiar. She examined them... hares... martens... foxes... the leavings of a moose... dogs! She put her nose to it. A trail. Dogs and humans! Their odors claimed it.

The trail crossed a shallow ford. Wide and icy, it disappeared into woods beyond. The stream fell steeply downwards toward the salt smell.

She waffled, torn by impulses.

Her breasts ached. She needed to nurse. That wasn't the salt smell. She knew that. She had never smelled it before. The pups weren't there.

She forded the stream and worked the trail. Her back stiffened.

A wolf! A strange wolf!

She stopped alarmed.

Why was it here? A strange wolf. Its trail?

No, dogs claimed the trail. Dogs and humans. She knew those smells, where they were found, far from the den. She voiced a confused yelp.

Nothing was right.

She circled, worrying. The salt had no pups. The odd-smelling stream had no pups. She surveyed the icy trail. The wolf went this way.

She took the trail.

The she wolf trotted. Her legs worked. The trail took a level course, twisted and turned within woods, dipped into vales with creeks, rose to resume the level way. Other trails appeared from the great salt smell. They joined the one she traveled, trails of moose, fox, and hare. Fresh wolf sign entered. She stopped and smelled it. A stranger. It left going upwards. She kept to the dog track. Her milk hurt. Get the pups. She loped.

Abruptly, the trail broke free. The she wolf stopped, an open vantage atop a ridge. She stared amazed. A starry sky flickered above a strange vista. Flat black water stretched in the middle distance, more water than she had ever seen. It rimmed a falling landscape. The salt smell blew from it. Beyond the land rose into great mountains. White glistened beneath the stars.

The she wolf whined. She and her pups lived beneath mountains, white above her home. Of everything, the mountains seemed most familiar.

Between ridge and water, lights twinkled in the dark. She sensed what they were... dog places, human places. They sprinkled the lowlands like another sky. She felt the thrill of fear.

She sniffed the air. She circled the open ridge, marking the lay of the flat water, the far mountains, the lowland lights, the salt smells, the starry sky, the flowing streams. The confusion of the wood disappeared. The world took shape and bearings.

White mountains.

The trail dipped toward them.

She took the trail down.

It entered woods at the bottom of the ridge. Thinner, brushier woods.

She trotted.

Mountains.

She sensed the coming of dawn.

Faint barks sounded.

She immediately entered the brush, moving cautiously. A path left the dog trail. It fell to a clearing. Light gleamed. The air smelled of smoke. Fish! The smells triggered memories, places of food, up the great river with dogs and humans. Places of danger.

She crept closer.

A cache! She recognized it. Her stomach clenched. Her body quivered. She was famished. She nervously assessed... a cache... dogs... humans. The acrid smells were everywhere. A pale light shined from a pole. It was nearly dawn.

Hunger pushed her. She crept down the slope hidden in trees. The smell grew. A wood path rose up the cache. She scrambled upon it, pausing, nervous. No sounds. She slunk up icy steps.

Oily fish smells flowed from cracks. She salivated, licked, and gnawed. Blocked. She explored with her nose, searched for entry, stood on hind legs, pushed. It creaked and moved slightly.

She began to scratch.

A bark!

She ducked into shadows.

A dog. It moved from behind the place with light. Shoulder hairs stood stiffly.

She gauged distances. The fishy cracks... so close! The woods... a quick leap and dash. Her stomach clenched with hunger. Her flanks trembled.

The dog barked at a tree. He stood on his legs, looked up into it. Barked again.

She crept off the steps and halted at the edge of dark.

A stout male dog.

She measured him, his heft, height, manners. The trembling tapered off and stopped. Her breathing slowed. Concentration sharpened.

She stepped free of the shadows.

The dog scrabbled at the base of the tree.

She checked the cache that smelled of food. Judged the woods behind, its distance, slope. Looked back to the stout male scrabbling at the tree.

She yipped.

Once, soft and high pitched.

The dog froze. Turned.

She turned a full circle, tail lifted high, ears pointed. Her head dropped, chin to front paws. She held his eyes, bobbed up and down, pushing with her front legs. She bounced forward, showed her tongue. Her breasts swung with the bounce.

The dog lunged and loosed a volley of barks, slid to a stop, legs wide and stiff.

The she wolf retreated and stopped.

She yipped again, soft, high pitched, and turned a full circle, tail lifted high, ears pointed, excited. She looked back and forth between dog and slope, bounced toward the slope, stopped, looked back, ears lifted high. She did it again, yipped, bounced, and jumped.

The big male launched. He came straight at her, great huffs of air, barking wildly.

She took off up the slope.

The dog chased, gathering speed, barking defiance.

She ran, not looking back. The barks closed the gap, timed it precisely... up... up... the dog trail.

She spun, set her feet, head down, ears back.

He drove his paws into ice to stop.

He skidded the final distance, mouth wide with teeth.

The wolf lunged.

* * *

Ben Langstrap wove his truck through the junk, eased around a derelict flatbed, and parked beside a mossy shed dusted with snow. The rear of the cabin looked much like the front, run-down and cluttered. He cut the engine, pulled on his official hat, adjusted the earflaps up, and carefully stepped from the cab. Dog scat littered the drive. The piles thawed in the unseasonable warm.

The dispute came from the backdoor.

This was the place.

He grabbed his aluminum case.

Two men in stained Carharts, one in a bulky wool cap, the other a Green Bay Packers cap, yelled at Jack Shiveley, the area biologist, trim in his lightweight jacket and official Fish and Game patch, the front man. Any local trouble, Jack took the first heat. He was earning his pay today.

Seeing Ben approach, the men backed off. The teams had evened up. Wool cap frowned sullenly. Anger smoldered in his eye. His partner in the Packers cap affected a cautious smile.

"Morning Jack," greeted Ben amicably. He nodded to the others. "Ben Langstrap, Fish and Game."

"This here's Ken Stratton and Fred Buhle," said Jack. He gestured toward his silent countrymen.

No one shook hands.

"Your place?" Ben asked the sullen Stratton.

"Yeah?" replied Stratton, neither confirming nor denying, a response full of suspicion.

"Ben is a research biologist out of Anchorage," explained Jack. "Working from Soldotna right now. Does our wolf studies."

That pushed the button. Stratton straightened and launched back into the tirade, shoving a finger angrily.

"Your wolf studies! Your wolf did it!"

"Now Ken, how do we know that?" said Jack.

"The goddamn collar," said Stratton. He viciously gripped his own neck.

"The wolf had a radio collar?" asked Ben.

"One of your wolves!"

"You saw it too?" Jack asked Fred Buhle.

"Pretty good light back here," Buhle said apologetically. The yard had a spotlight. "We watched from that window. She had the collar, all right. I was thinking, maybe that's why it happened. We never have wolf trouble."

Jack Shiveley considered this.

"That wouldn't do it."

"Do what?" asked Ben, pulling a notepad from a front pocket. He jotted down the date, place, and names of the two men. Stratton's look showed he didn't like the notepad. But he was too far in it to retreat now.

"Killed my dog!" snarled Stratton.

He pointed accusatorily up the path toward the woods. This confirmed what Ben already knew. Jack had called him in Soldotna to tell him about the kill.

Barks and scratches sounded behind them. They came from the rear door. The faces of several dogs appeared and disappeared at the door's window. The dogs were jumping and banging on the door.

"Shut up!"

Stratton yelled at the house. He turned on Ben.

"We got them all inside. They're going to tear the place up!"

"Where are they usually?"

"Round the side."

"Can I see?"

Stratton snorted and led the group around the cabin. An unfenced yard held several small kennels. The yellow snow and accumulated scat showed this was where Stratton chained his dogs.

"Five?" counted Ben

"Yeah."

"What kind?"

"Husky mutts."

"For racing?"

"Yeah," grumbled Stratton, moving back to the sun. The rear door still banged with dogs.

"The one that got killed, it was a husky too?"

"No, just a mutt," said Stratton. His downcast expression showed he liked this mutt.

"German shepherd, retriever mix," Buhle answered for his friend.

"He wasn't chained?"

"Watchdog," muttered Stratton.

"A good watchdog," said Buhle, pointing across the yard. "Never had bears in the fish. Scuppers kept them away."

A log cache stood on short pilings at the edge of the clearing, not far from the cabin.

"Scuppers?"

"Kept the bears away. He did it good. We never before had wolf trouble."

"You live here too?"

"Yeah," said Buhle.

"Suckered him," said Stratton angrily. "He could handle the bears. But he couldn't handle that."

"Couldn't handle what now?" said Jack.

"She suckered him! Flirted right there under that spot. Come on, big boy, come on and get it! Then tore up the path. Goddamn bitch!"

"How do you know?" said Jack.

"What?"

"The wolf was female."

"Her tits were flopping," snapped Stratton. "Come and get it, big boy! Then tore up the path!'"

"You saw it too?" said Ben.

"Well, yeah," muttered Buhle.

"Goddamn wolves killing dogs! They should be shot!" yelled Stratton.

"Now, Ken," said Jack.

"You saw it too?" Ben pressed Buhle again.

"Old Scuppers, he was a good old guard dog," said Buhle. "He was the best. You know he was, Kenny."

Ken Stratton looked away.

"Yeah, he was," Buhle answered himself. "He caught that wolf snooping around the cache. She smelled the fish. Scuppers caught her doing it. He was doing what he was good at. Guarding the cache. She ran. He chased her off."

Buhle paused, looked at his friend.

"He died doing what he was good at," said Buhle.

Stratton hid tears.

"He wasn't suckered," said Buhle.

Stratton said nothing.

"No, he wasn't," Buhle repeated gently, turning back to the biologist. "He was just being a watch dog. She was just being a wolf, I guess."

"Goddamn wolf," mumbled Stratton.

A long silence ensued.

The dogs listened quietly from the house.

"Can I see it?" asked Ben.

"I can show you," said Buhle. "We already showed Jack."

Ben followed Buhle up the path into the woods. Jack stayed behind with Stratton. The path came up from the dog yard. The snow was packed and smoothed by the regular passage of sleds. The surface glistened from the unseasonably warm morning. The incline had turned slippery. In less than a hundred yards, the path connected with a wide trail for snowmachines and dog sleds that ran along the hillside. Ben huffed the final steps to the level path.

"Where's this one go?" asked Ben, looking up and down the trail. He was still new to the Kenai trail systems.

"Anchorage."

"Anchorage?" said Ben with surprise.

"You could if you wanted to," said Buhle. "The trails connect all over the place, you know. This one heads toward Hope. You go from there over to Portage and Girdwood, then through Chugach Park into Eagle River if the pass is open. Then Anchorage. Or Palmer. I did that once."

"You run the dogs?"

"Yeah. Kenny doesn't do it much."

Ben dropped to a knee to inspect the trail. The snow at the intersection glistened a rosy red in the dappled light.

Tuffs of black hair scattered the path. There weren't many. The battle had ended quickly.

Ben opened his aluminum case and began the collecting. With tweezers, he retrieved samples of hair, tucking them into zip-lock pouches. He pulled out a digital camera and recorded images from the kill site. Blood splatters showed where the carcass had been dragged off the trail and up the slope into the higher forest. The slick surface offered little resistance.

"I followed it up a ways," said Buhle. "It just kept going until I lost it."

"This was a big dog?"

"Big."

"How heavy?"

"Oh, I don't know. Ninety, hundred pounds, I don't know. Scuppers was big."

Ben jotted notes.

"That's one strong wolf, dragging that weight up that hill," said Buhle.

"They can do it," agreed Ben.

"Nursing and all."

"You're sure about that?"

"I know what I saw."

"Large tits."

"Yeah."

Ben tucked the notebook away, repacked the case while Buhle watched.

"She'll eat him, right?" said Buhle finally.

"I expect she will."

"She couldn't get in the cache. If we had had that cache unlocked, she'd have took a bit of fish and left. No bears right now. But the foxes, you know. Foxes want to get in it. So we keep it padlocked."

"Yeah."

"Old Scuppers would still be alive except for that lock."

"Well, maybe so."

Ben stretched kinks from his back and took one last look at the kill site.

"Do you think they enjoy it?" said Buhle.

"What's that?"

"That wolf. Flirting. Tricking a dog so as to eat him."

"I thought you said she didn't."

"Oh, I said that for Kenny. He hides it, you know, but he loved that old dog. Yeah, she did it, but I don't think Scuppers fell for it much. He was a good watchdog. He was guarding the fish. But she flirted all right."

"Hmmm."

"So do they, do you think?"

"What?"

"Enjoy it? Tricking dogs to eat them."

Ben finished the stretch and shook his head.

"They're wolves, animals. You can't give them feelings like people, saying they enjoyed this and hated that, motives like they're human. You said it yourself. She was hungry. She smelled the cache. She was just being a wolf."

"Well, I said that for Kenny. But she did it all right, flirted to trick him. Then she ate him."

"Yeah, well, she's just a wolf."

Buhle gave a wan smile.

"You're a wolf man. Guess you can't say otherwise."

They walked together back toward the cabin.

"I'd like to see your huskies," said Ben.

"What for?"

"Scuppers, he'd hang with your dogs?"

"Yeah."

"Then I'd like to look at them."

"Okay, if you want."

Coming down the path, Ben saw Jack talking softly with Ken Stratton off to a side, like the parish priest. A stooped Stratton listened. Cracking it carefully, Buhle and Ben slipped through the rear door. Five frisky huskies jumped and licked, overjoyed for company. Ben petted and praised them. He was good with dogs. He examined them, looking at eyes and ears and skin beneath their lush winter coats. Ben opened his case again, extracted plastic pouches and a fine-toothed comb.

"Can you hold this one?" he asked Buhle.

Buhle held the husky's head by its ears and watched Ben comb from several places over glossy creased paper. He carefully poured contents into plastic bags, sealed them, and wrote on labels.

"Finding something?"

"Yeah."

"Something more than dog lint?"

"Something more."

Ben dangled a bag at eye level for Buhle. It held hair and skin flakes and tiny translucent globs.

"What am I looking at?" asked Buhle.

"Lice."

"Oh, yeah. Lice."

"Well, let's get these guys outside and to the truck."

"What for?"

"A nice dusty bath."

Ben bent down to a friendly face, taking it between his hands, and said it again.

"You'd like that, wouldn't you big boy? A nice dusty bath?"

The husky licked Ben's face.

10

Nicholas John bounced in the turbulence. Icy peaks jumped and shook outside the cockpit windows. Beside him, the pilot fought with unruly controls, forcing the Piper through the violence of Rainy Pass. Strong winds had pummeled them at takeoff from Merrill Field in Anchorage. Shears swept across Knik Arm. Now roaring hurricane gales spilled over the crest of the Alaska Range down their throats. They pitched and bumped like an amusement park.

"Pretty good ride, eh?" the pilot shouted.

Nick silently prayed. He hated this.

Snowy plumes whipped off the tops of nearby peaks, trailing like smoke into the distance. The sky shined a rich blue above them, cleared by a high-pressure cell that squeezed the hurricane winds through the passes.

"Equalizing pressure!" shouted the pilot as the plane dropped precipitously. They hit an updraft and bounced with a shudder.

Nick nodded. He understood the weather system and still hated it. Air rushed from high to low-pressure cells. The arctic air from the interior was screaming through the mountain passes toward the coast. His small bush charter flew straight into it. The plane bounced like a fishing bob reeled against a torrent. They sat inside the bob. Nick remembered someone telling him, under similar rattling

89

circumstances, planes were over-engineered for just this kind of punishment. The rivets wouldn't pop. The wings wouldn't snap. The windows wouldn't blow in.

Nick prayed anyway.

The views were stunning. Jagged peaks of the Alaska Range stretched to either side filling horizons, a massive upheaval erupting from the lowlands by the crush of tectonic plates. Nick craned around a wing strut. He found Denali on a far horizon with its twin, Foraker, the tallest points in North America. He had names for none of the others. Everything glistened starkly. Winter covered all, rocky cliffs, ice fields, glacial streams, white surfaces burnished by the winds into mirrors that hurt the eyes.

The pilot followed the Skwentna drainage through the wall of mountains. The river's cleft would lead them through to Rainy Pass, a landmark for the state. The Iditarod Trail traveled over the tiny pass. Nick leaned and looked straight down. He saw the Skwentna River disappear beneath him but spotted no trail. It was, after all, simply a track for dog teams. It followed an ancient travel route between the coast and the interior laid down by Alaska Natives. The annual Iditarod sled dog race gave it recent fame. Mushers climbed through Rainy Pass on the thousand-mile race from Anchorage to Nome on the Bering Sea. Dogs and drivers rested at the Rohn Roadhouse on its far side, an historic trail stop for miners. Nick squinted ahead. He saw a cleft through the mountain range.

"Is that the Kuskokwim?" shouted Nick.

"Yep! Upper south fork!"

Just ahead, the cleft sliced through the north shoulder of the mountains, the Kuskokwim River, one of its upper branches, hemmed within steep canyons. The plane quickly came above it. They were through Rainy Pass. The pilot tracked the river out of the mountainous jumble. The buffeting diminished. They left the mountain wall and sailed into a great interior basin on the east side of the Denali massif. The Kuskokwim's south fork bent across a broad tilted land scoured by myriad tributaries coming off the Alaska Range, a vast forested wilderness without any roads, a region nearly empty of people.

"Farewell!" shouted the pilot.

Nick easily spotted the narrow lake and tiny runway called Farewell. The dirt strip was the only straight line in sight. A quick stop, the pilot told Nick. Really, it was a request. This was Nick's charter paid by Feinberg's law firm to carry him to the village of Sleetmute. But the bush carrier wanted to combine Nick's flight with a freight drop at Farewell, substantial savings by combining runs. Made perfect sense to Nick, raised in a poor village. He didn't mind if the pilot stopped to make additional money. He got to see something new.

He wasn't disappointed. A network of trails fanned out from the dirt strip on the broad uplands. He spotted a few buildings, a miniscule affair by a frozen lake, the center of the network. The trail system was huge. Most villages didn't have this many trails.

"What is this place?" asked Nick, surprised by the evidence of such substantial traffic in the empty region.

"Hunting lodge," said the pilot.

"Hunting? The fall moose hunt?"

"All summer. This place is crawling."

That explained the trails. They were tracks of four-wheelers and other off-road vehicles. Nick guessed the reason. The flight from Anchorage to Farewell was short by Alaska standards, a quick jump over the Alaska Range. Bush carriers probably made a killing ferrying hunters back and forth between Farewell and town.

"All summer? For what?"

"Salmon, trout, grayling, moose, caribou, bear, sheep, you name it," said the pilot.

"You fly them in?"

"Yep. To Farewell, Holitna, Hoholitna. Drop and retrieve. Floaters."

"Floaters?"

"They float the rivers. We pick them up."

Nick was impressed. Clearly the area supported a substantial economic enterprise in summer. Somebody made big money here.

"Why are we stopping?"

"Freight," said the pilot. "Some outfitters want to stock up early, hedge against the weather. There they are."

Two snowmachines with sleds crawled toward the runway. The plane landed on the icy strip. They rolled to the snowmachines and cut the engine. Wind whistled around the wings. Not a pleasant day at Farewell. The pilot popped the door and jumped into a stiff breeze. Nick came out too. He wasn't going to sit shivering in the cockpit. With the pilot, two men began unloading boxes from the plane's rear storage. Nick moved in line to help. They lugged supplies to the waiting sleds.

In short order, the freight got moved. The pilot secured doors and prepared for takeoff. A bulky man sauntered over to Nick.

"Thanks, little buddy."

He shoved out a gloved hand.

"Yeah," said Nick.

Little buddy.

Delivered with undisguised arrogance.

Nick wasn't 'little.' Nor was he ever this guy's 'buddy.' The sneering asshole had positioned himself as biggest and best.

Nick took the hand reluctantly.

"Joel Haggarty," the man declared.

"Nicholas John," muttered Nick.

Nick turned to leave.

"Hey! Where are you headed, Nicholas John?"

Haggarty's tone was hard. He wasn't finished.

Nick stopped in mid-stride. He stared at Haggarty, didn't reply for several seconds. Haggarty's eyes grew even harder. This bully wasn't used to not getting answered.

"Sleetmute," said Nick finally.

"Sleetmute?" Haggarty smirked. "Visiting family?"

Nick found himself growing angry. He knew this type of kass'aq, self-inflated and condescending. He hated them. Nick treated strangers with respect. He'd never call an adult he didn't know 'little buddy.' Nor would he ensnare unwilling strangers with personal questions. He measured Haggarty, legs planted wide, big shouldered, skin peeled from exposure. Here was a rugged outfitter paid by sportsmen for wilderness adventures. He probably considered this his turf. It meant money to him. Haggarty was demanding to know what Nick was doing in his territory. Visiting relatives? This was Haggarty's best guess. Natives visited relatives.

"Research," said Nick.

"Research?" said Haggarty, his eyes narrowed suspiciously. "What do you mean, research?"

Obviously Haggarty did consider this to be his personal business.

"Medical malpractice, translating…"

"Ah… yeah, translating," Haggarty interrupted with a smile.

Nick found himself steaming. Haggarty had tucked him into another box. Natives translated. Haggarty's world fell back into order.

"I'm an anthropologist," said Nick darkly.

Haggarty's eyes narrowed again.

"We're assessing monetary compensation for lost subsistence in a medical malpractice suit."

Haggarty just stood, unable to find a response.

The pilot shouted.

Nick left Haggarty without a goodbye.

Chew on that for a while, 'buddy.'

Nick hopped inside and slammed the door shut. They taxied and took off. The plane shivered in crosswinds and rose fitfully. Nick checked below. The snowmachines rumbled off on a track away from the lake and lodge. He was still angry.

"Who's Joel Haggarty?" shouted Nick over the roar of the plane, the snowmachines disappearing behind them.

"You don't know Haggarty?" laughed the pilot.

"No."

"He's a character."

"An outfitter?"

"Yeah."

Nick waited. The pilot would want to say more.

"He guides. He traps. He's a real trapper."

"At Farewell?"

"Koyukuk, Tanana, anyplace. He does wolves."

"Wolves?"

"He likes to kill wolves."

The pilot turned the aircraft west. The Alaska Range passed on their left. They began crossing tributaries that drained north toward the main Kuskokwim.

"Nobody does it better. Nobody knows wolves better than Haggarty."

With that, the pilot began navigating. It was too noisy for extended conversation.

Nick returned to the forested lands passing below him. He put his mind away from Haggarty the outfitter, the braggart and bully who killed wolves. He hoped never to see Haggarty again.

Nick concentrated on the landscape. This part of the state was new to him. Yesterday he studied the topographic maps and online aerial photos of the upper Kuskokwim. He read summaries of its history and ethnography, learning that Sleetmute, his destination, lay at the boundaries of three Native groups, the Deg Hit'an, the Dena'ina, and the Upper Kuskokwim people. They were Athabaskans, Alaska Natives anthropologists lumped within a large language group that included the Gwich'in, the Koyukuk, and surprisingly, the Navajo and Apaches.

They were 'Indians.'

This made Nick slightly uneasy.

He was 'Eskimo.'

There weren't many, maybe less than a thousand people living in this remote area. There had never been many. The Kuskokwim headwater was a hungry place, not like the rich coastal areas where Nick's family lived.

Even today the inland settlements were small. Stony River and Lime Village were Dena'ina. Red Devil and Crooked Creek were Deg Hit'an. McGrath, Nikolai, and Telida were Upper Kuskokwim mixed with non-Native in-migrants, especially at McGrath.

But Sleetmute, Nick's destination, was a Yup'ik Eskimo village. Sleetmute lay at the edge of these three groups. Apparently some Yup'iks had pushed inland from the coast, moving up the rivers, crowding the Athabaskans and their traditional homelands. A puzzle. Nick was from the lower Yukon River. Why would Yup'iks move so far from the ocean? Why choose the greater hardships of the interior forests over the richer coastal areas?

Why stir up trouble with Indians?

In the steam baths, Yup'ik elders told old stories about Indians and Yup'iks. They were usually cautionary tales of mistrust and war. As a child Nick had feared Indians, though he had never seen one. When he finally met his first Indians at boarding school he was surprised to find them so friendly. He told them. They laughed with him about it. They had grown up afraid of Eskimos.

Nick wondered if the war stories were exaggerated. If they were, why tell them that way?

To keep us closer to home, he concluded.

The stories hadn't worked with him.

The Kuskokwim River flowed westward, a modest channel cutting through lowland hills. A hundred miles further, the Kuskokwim became a substantial river. At its mouth it formed a vast delta with the Yukon River, the homeland of the Yup'ik people, fifteen thousand strong, many times the upper Kuskokwim peoples. Maybe the Yup'iks had spread upriver because of that... too many fights within too large families. Success had costs.

A small village appeared, cabins on an island in the frozen river, Stony River, a Dena'ina settlement. They passed above it. The plane began its descent.

In short order they came over Sleetmute, the most inland of the Yup'ik villages, two hundred and fifty miles from the ocean. No seal hunting here. It stretched along the north bank of the Kuskokwim near its confluence with the Holitna River, a tributary.

Sportsmen floated the Holitna, the pilot said. What did Sleetmute think about that? Floaters waiting at the airstrip for rides back to civilization?

The plane touched down on the icy runway. The pilot braked, gunned the engines, spun the plane around, and cut power. Nick's ears rang with the silence.

"Sleetmute," he announced with satisfaction.

A sole figure approached from the edge of the strip bulked in cold weather gear. Nick finally recognized the face inside the parka hood. Camilla Mac Cleary, his boss. Somehow she looked different. Nick realized what it was. He'd never seen her dressed for winter.

He found his heart pounding. Why was he feeling nervous? He stepped from the plane to meet her. She smiled broadly, her deathly-pale face framed by a wolf ruff.

"Nick!"

Before he had prepared, Camilla wrapped her arms around him. She held on. When she finally released, Nick saw she was crying.

"I missed you," she said.

She wiped tears with a bulky glove.

"Yeah?" said Nick awkwardly, reading the wet eyes. "Not... a migraine?"

"That happens later," she laughed.

Nick finally smiled.

"It's good to see you," she declared.

She hugged him again. This time Nick hugged back.

Boxes came off the plane. The pilot cranked up the engine and took off, leaving Sleetmute to others.

"There's a sled to push your stuff."

Camilla produced a short dogsled at the runway's edge, its worn bent slats bleached with age.

"Where did you find that?"

"Frances Egnaty, the woman we're going to interview. She said to use it for hauling our stuff. We can walk to our place. You can walk to most of the village. Everything is on this side except for somebody's store. I haven't gone across yet because the ice. It's kind of intimidating, for me anyways."

"You been here long?" asked Nick, loading the sled.

"Since yesterday."

Camilla, the expert by her single day, showed the way. They left the runway in silence, Nick pushing the sled. Camilla was comfortable with silences, Nick had learned. In some ways, she acted more like a Yup'ik than a kass'aq. Kass'aqs didn't like silences.

Sleetmute stretched along a track between the airstrip and river. About one hundred people made it home. The houses looked compact and neat, some constructed of logs taken from the forest, others framed and finished with flat wood exteriors painted dark blues and whites. Stovepipes smoked above roofs in the subzero air. It felt about minus ten, perfect for outdoor travel.

Except for them the path lay empty. But Nick expected his arrival had been noted. A village had eyes and tongues. Already there would be talk about the kass'aq who met a charter. The news would spread. Camilla walked comfortably beside him in large pack boots. She should be unused to snow. She came in from San Francisco. Her most recent fieldwork had been in Mexico. She admitted she was unsure of the river ice. But she walked as if she knew about snow. Camilla noticed him watching.

"Like my parka?" asked Camilla, running a glove around the ruff. The goose-down parka was a type sold by outdoor suppliers in Anchorage. The wolf ruff had been added by somebody, silver hairs tipped in black. The ruff was trimmed with beaver.

"Stylish."

"Belongs to Mel Savidge. I'd be dead without it. It feels really cold to me."

Camilla seemed to take pleasure in ordinary moments, Nick knew. Like the simple walk from the airport to their quarters. But maybe to her, this was not ordinary. And maybe it just seemed that way. Nick wasn't sure with Camilla, what was real or not.

"All these are hers, over-pants, gloves, boots."

This surprised Nick. Mel Savidge was stocky and shorter than Camilla. His face must have shown it.

"What?"

"Well uh, I don't know. Do they fit? She's, uh, different, physically, from you."

Nick blushed.

"Not as tall," said Camilla, stopping to show how the snow pants rode up her boots. "I loosened the shoulder straps. A little short. She's saved me a bundle. We go that way."

They took a side trail through alders. The path passed a clearing with a dog yard. A dozen or so dogs watched from small houses.

"Hi good dogs!" called Camilla.

Several stood, nosing the air.

"They know me already, poor things," said Camilla.

"Why do you say that?"

"What?"

"Poor things."

"Well, look at them."

Nick stopped to look. The dogs watched with interest. He saw nothing amiss.

"They're chained to their houses," said Camilla.

"Uh, yeah?" nodded Nick.

Camilla frowned at him.

"They're chained, staked to their houses," she said for emphasis.

Nick rocked uncertainly. Camilla seemed upset about something.

"Yeah, staked... somebody's sled dogs," ventured Nick carefully.

"So that makes it okay? Staked to the ground because they're going to be hitched to a sled?"

The logic was right, the passion strange.

"Working dogs," agreed Nick.

"Working dogs? They can hardly move! They're like... prisoners. Chained up. In prison."

Nick assessed the yard with a more critical eye. The clearing was open, snowy, cleaned of debris, sheltered by the alder thicket. Each dog had a separate cubby. Short chains restricted movement to the house. None of the dogs was tangled. The team seemed alert, well fed. There was nothing unusual about it. It was like he had kept his own team, before his snowmachine. When he was young, his dogs had hauled firewood.

"Uh... they don't have leash laws in San Francisco?"

"Dogs get to be dogs."

"In apartments?"

"At parks, beaches."

Nick had seen his share of urban dogs on walks, pulling the pooper-scoopers.

"Loose dogs get shot where I'm from," said Nick.

"Shot?" she said, shocked.

"Yeah."

"What, like escaped prisoners? Escaped slaves?"

"No, dogs. That's what dogs are... you know, what dogs are for."

"Getting shot?"

"No, work, working, pulling."

Camilla looked more than peeved.

"They're just resting," said Nick quickly. "The stake... it keeps them out of trouble. You ever untangle a fight between teams?"

Camilla said nothing. She imagined a brawl between sled dogs hitched to sleds.

"You ever see loose dogs, hunting in a pack?" asked Nick.

Camilla seemed less sure.

Nick walked a few steps and reached beneath an alder. He pulled a thick branch from the snow, dusted it, cleaned it of twigs, and swung to test its heft. He passed it to Camilla.

"For when you walk around here."

Camilla stared at the club in her hand.

"For loose dogs," said Nick.

Camilla smiled.

"I throw and yell, fetch! Right?"

The joke caught him off guard.

"There's our place," said Camilla easily, pointing with the dog stick. An old log cabin lay tucked within a stand of black spruce.

"Bye guys!" yelled Camilla to the imprisoned.

She took the track to the cabin, climbed the short steps, stomped free of snow, and entered. Nick parked the sled and followed, worrying about stakes and chains. Had they been arguing? Was Camilla mad at him? Was she seriously upset or not about the chained dogs? He honestly couldn't tell.

The short entry opened into a hot compact living room. A cast iron stove cranked out heat from a wall. The kerosene had not yet burned away the musty smell. A multi-paned window above a worn and sagging couch offered a fine view into the snowy forest. The living space felt cozy.

"The kitchen's there," said Camilla happily. "It's got a good table where we can write and another large window. There's no running water. But Frances said to use the sled to haul it. This was her son's old place. Her daughters sometimes use it. Oh, bedroom's back there."

The single bedroom had no door. A queen bed on raised box springs filled the entire space.

"Where's the son?"

"He's in Oregon... Edward Egnaty."

"The daughters?"

"In Anchorage. One is married with kids. The other's a single mom."

"So Frances lives alone in Sleetmute?"

"Recovering from the second surgery. I spoke with her yesterday. But I don't know if she followed everything I said. You can translate for us."

"Okay."

"There's an outhouse behind there," Camilla waved out a bedroom window. "It's chilly, but it doesn't smell. This is an older place, so it's not hooked up to anything."

The bedroom looked snug enough. But Nick saw the snag with the setup, a single bedroom, one bed. This was a problem, wasn't it? He couldn't read Camilla.

"I brought my sleeping bag," offered Nick.

"So did I," said Camilla.

Nick assessed the ambiguity. On this project, like the last one, he worked for Camilla under a contract. They were partners, Camilla said. But he considered Camilla to be the boss. She *was* the boss. She was also a friend, though they scarcely knew one another. Previously, they had worked in Togiak about three weeks. Given all this, she should have the bed.

"I can sleep on the couch," said Nick.

Camilla gazed at it.

"Looks kind of saggy."

"I don't mind."

Camilla studied Nick.

"I don't feel right about that. We're partners on this project, right?"

"Well, yeah. But, you know, I'm working for you. I don't know what it's all about. You're the lead, like last time."

"But we're sharing the house."

"Well, yeah," said Nick, worried about what was coming next. She was going to say, 'let's just share the bed.' What would Nick say to that? How did he feel about sleeping on the same bed with Camilla? He wasn't sure how he felt about it. He stood unmoving, carefully disguising his discomfort.

"So," said the smiling Camilla, "let's flip for it."

Nick let out his air.

"Okay."

"You got a coin?"

With difficulty, Nick dug inside his snow pants and fished out a quarter. He flipped.

"Tails," called Camilla.

The quarter hit the plywood floor and rolled under the bed.

"Shit," said Nick, digging for another coin.

"No!" laughed Camilla. "The winner's been decided. The Chinaman will get us if we cheat."

"The Chinaman?"

"That's what my grandpa always said."

"Who's the Chinaman?"

"I don't know. But it's bad to cheat him."

Camilla plopped on the bed grinning and shook off her hot parka. Finally, here was the Camilla he remembered, tall and lean and smiling. She looked even thinner than the last time they had worked. Her cheekbones on her pale face were ruddy from cold. Her black hair, cropped shorter than Nick's, frizzed with dry static like a corona. Her large dark eyes were shadowed as if she needed to sleep a week. Fine lines creased the corners, the telltale sign of pain.

Camilla looked worn.

But she looked genuinely happy.

"I'm glad to be working with you again, Nick."

"Me too."

11

The beaver den felt wrong.

She rested on slick cold mud and worried. It was damp. Water had risen in the entryway. To enter and exit required wading through an icy sump along the tunnel's bottom. The floor was constantly wet. The dark had lost its dry warmth.

The refuge felt unsafe.

In the pitch black, the playful one ducked into the hole in the den's floor and waded the chilly tunnel. She squeezed through a jumble of debris into cold bright sunlight. Her body barely fit. Her midriff had expanded since she had first broken an entrance into the beaver house. She clambered out upon the frozen pond, wet and uncomfortable, and shook herself dry.

The dark wolf watched.

He rested at the pond's margin in his usual spot in the early morning sun, waiting for her appearance. She trotted over. The dark one came immediately. He kissed her face. She kissed back. He frisked around her like a puppy, flouncing to a place where they often ate. He had a hare.

He rested to the side while she ate, placidly watching the pond, occasionally sniffing the air. Crows gathered in the trees, attracted by the kill. The dark wolf ignored them, a proud hunter.

Food appeared at the edge of the beaver pond soon after her first arrival. The scents showed the dark wolf brought them. He had tracked her to the pond. He was the only visitor. He waited and watched, guarding the kills. When she emerged from the den, he disappeared. She saw him hiding in brush. The rogue watched from the margins.

After the fight with her sister, her wounds hurt. Her muscles were stiff. She moved with pain. She ate the offerings. She healed at the pond's edge, sensing changes. She was pregnant. The dark one who watched sensed it too. She rested alone in the pale winter light, staring across the frozen pond to the brush where the dark one hid. This became routine.

He showed himself openly one morning, approached tentatively, leaning to one side, ready to bolt. He was larger and stronger than her, but approached this way. He survived alone, had no pack, a solitary male at the fringe of community. What he wanted, he asked for with diffidence. She had grown to know him. She was ready. It took no time to make the friendship, to find affection. Ever since, he waited attentively for her emergence each morning. He brought food. Seeing him made her happy. His greeting lifted her mood. She no longer hurt. She became playful again.

She finished the hare, shook dry a second time, gauged the air, and moved into the wood to explore. Crows descended to the bloody snow. They scattered as the dark one passed. He trailed near her hip. Sometimes he led and she followed. They did it either way. They were partnered.

She took a path that led into the draws. The day was windless and mild, a good day for travel. At a frozen streambed they discovered tracks of a moose. The dark one sniffed with her. The scent was fresh enough. He took the lead. They tracked and followed the meandering spoor down the draw into brushy patches filled with snow. Here they foundered in chest-deep drifts, backtracked, came by a side slope to look further up. During the search they heard it.

A howl floated over the hills.

The playful one instantly stopped. The dark one came to her side. They listened.

The howl came again.

Her brother.

Something was wrong.

She abandoned the hunt, working off the ridge toward the call, running with some difficulty, her midriff heavy. The dark one loped behind. She traveled a rill, crossed a stream, went up a major ridge. At the top diverged paths made by many others. She took a trail along connected ridges, traveling a familiar course to a slope. She slid down without pausing. Her heart beat strongly.

The snag protruded near the standing rock. The dark one went to sniff it and found his mark. He replenished it. He moved to the nearby stone and read its messages. This was the boundary. It designated the new couple from the original pack. The boundary had come easily. The dark one had marked the snag beside the stone. She had marked it too. None had contested.

The playful one smelled the standing stone. It triggered conflicting urges… brothers, sisters, home. She stepped onto the river's ice, hesitated, whined, looked to her partner for help. The dark one turned aside and assumed the lead. He left the frozen river and took a faint steep path upwards, zigzagging among dense brush to the top of a ridge. She followed.

The slopes fell steeply here. He took a series of ridgelines, dipping down and rising up, edging toward the troubling howl. He knew these marginal paths. He had made some himself. The traces led to a ridge above the pack's canyon. She came beside him, her first return home since the fight with her sister. She had never viewed it from this vantage.

She stared into the narrow canyon, fearful, excited. She saw confusion. Young ones, bigger now, milled about the creek bed. What was happening? The dark one flopped on his belly to watch. His breaths came deep and regular.

This was not his pack, but he knew it well. He was used to watching.

The playful one moved back and forth along the ridge top, absorbing the agitation of the young ones. She felt distress. Her heart beat wildly. What was happening?

Abruptly, her brother appeared below.

Without hesitation, she barked.

He looked high, saw her, barked too, a greeting, a plea.

She immediately stepped from the ridge, sliding down the slope. She had to greet him! She skidded on paws dug into ice, working hard not to tumble. She leaped between outcroppings and slid more. Her brother bounded up to meet her. She ran as the slope lessened. They came together in a great collision of shoulders, kissing, and rubbing, her older brother, her hunter, her dearest companion!

A deep growl sounded.

The playful one spun.

The strong one! The leader!

He stood with legs spread, head low and menacing at the mouth of the den, shoulder hairs stiff, lips peeled back.

The playful one stumbled. Her belly pulled her over.

He launched upwards.

A shadow plummeted past her.

The dark one! He had slid as she had, coming behind her. The first time he had entered the canyon! He planted before her, snarling savagely, showing teeth without fear or submission, blocking the attack.

The strong one stopped short. He slipped back, ferocious, frantic.

Fear gripped her. Confusion.

Where was her sister?

She drew up, prepared to run, to escape to the tunneled debris along the creek bed. But where was she? Where was her sister?

The young ones milled and whined. They looked for direction. The strong one gave no clear signals. He threatened the intruders, glued to the den, unwilling to move. He seemed paralyzed.

Something was terribly wrong.

The playful one searched for her brother. She found him in the brush, stiff, poised for battle. He did not face her. He faced the leader!

Cautiously, the playful one moved from behind her partner, stepped with wary deliberateness on the icy slope. She quivered with tension, her condition displayed to all, close to delivery. The strong one hung by the den with desperation.

Where was her older sister?

The dark hole disappeared into the hillside.

The strong one shifted, keeping between her and the den. His face moved between the detestable rogue, the rebellious female, and her brother. His rear legs raked the ice, signaling the young ones.

He attacked.

He flew at the rogue. The challenger leaped to meet him. No help came. The strong one dodged and bolted, tearing along the slope. He disappeared into brush. The dark one chased a few steps. The young ones scattered.

The creek bed emptied.

The den was abandoned.

The playful one felt exhilaration... and dread.

She approached the den carefully. Lifted her nose. Disturbing scents flowed from it. She turned about several times, bewildered, anxious, reexamining the canyon, the frozen creek bed, the steep walls. This was the home. This was the center.

Two wolves reappeared below, a niece and nephew. They watched her apprehensively.

Memories flooded her. She went to the dark one. He stood resolutely, staring away. She turned to her brother, the one whose howl had brought her. He also stood, watching her, ignoring the dark one.

Everyone waited.

They waited for her.

She was horribly frightened.

Emboldened. Physically sick.
She turned back to the den.
The dark mouth beckoned.
The final passage home.
With a shudder, she entered.

12

Emergency meeting... wolves.

Mel Savidge learned just before its start. Typical.

The emergency didn't surprise her. Fish and Game had lots of emergency meetings. The state handbook said emergencies rarely happened, by definition. Fish and Game called nearly one a week.

Derby Peters, the assistant commissioner, wanted her at this one. She didn't know why.

Mel entered the second-floor conference room. A lazy gaggle of wildlife biologists and managers lounged around the long table waiting for things to start. Dan Crawford, the commissioner of Fish and Game, hulked at the table's head. He drank from a coffee mug shaped like a pig head, his name embossed beneath its snout. His prim secretary read from her day planner, outlining his schedule for the rest of the day.

Gary Gunterson and Hank Reisdahl, biologists with Wildlife Management, stood to the side with somebody Mel didn't know, a field biologist by his head bobbing. Gunterson, ugh! God's gift to manhood. She could smell his stink. He polluted everything he passed. A walking ashtray! To consolidate space, the department had moved the smoking room to first-floor storage, a windowless space where the department stored publications. It had become Gunterson's de facto office. Now even the technical reports stunk like Gunterson.

"Let's get this going," grumbled Crawford. "Okay Derby, who gets to start?"

Mel opened her notepad and jotted, 'Emergency Meeting, Wolves.'

"We'll start with Ben Langstrap," said Derby.

The mystery man between Gunterson and Reisdahl straightened a notch.

'Ben Langstrap' she noted.

"Dan, you may not know Ben. He conducts wolf research on the Kenai…"

"Yeah, that's fine," Crawford interrupted. "Pleased to meet you, Ben. Before we start all that, can somebody just please tell me, in simple sentences, what's the emergency here? Why do we now all of a sudden have an emergency with Kenai wolves?"

Derby's mouth still hung half open.

Gary Gunterson seized control.

"Because we've got a runner," declared Gunterson.

"A runner?" said Crawford.

"One of our transplanted wolves hasn't stayed put. It's running."

Mel scribbled. 'Kenai transplant. A runner.'

Crawford gave a bemused laugh.

"Yeah, I heard all that. So what? I mean, these are transplants, right? We pick up wolves from one place and dump them in another. A wolf doesn't stay put. What do you expect? What's the emergency here?"

Crawford was on a short fuse.

"Well that's right," agreed Gunterson, clearing his gravelly throat. "Everybody knows that. Dumping wolves is a crap shoot. A wolf doesn't like where we put it. I wouldn't either if you dumped me on the Kenai."

Gunterson laughed at his joke.

The commissioner chuckled. Nobody else did.

Gunterson doesn't consider this an emergency either, concluded Mel. Then who called an emergency meeting?

Apparently Derby Peters, Crawford's assistant, who tried again.

"Given the sensitivity of the wolf program, we thought it best to assess this development in-house and quickly," said Derby.

Crawford listened with a forced tolerance, an expression that said, 'I'm surrounded by idiots.'

So Derby had called the meeting, Mel decided. Crawford and Gunterson attended reluctantly. Why had Derby risked a meeting like this? Derby was the guy who had pretended indifference about wolf politics, waiting with Mel beside the State seal in the capitol building.

"I think it would be good for us to hear from Ben first," suggested Derby once again. "The issues should become clearer. Ben?"

Ben Langstrap.

Here was a wolf researcher Mel didn't know. Nor did the commissioner, apparently. This was not unusual in a sprawling outfit like Fish and Game. Field biologists rarely got to sit with the big cheese at headquarters. A considerable gulf separated line biologists from the top brass. Field workers were scientists. Top-level bureaucrats negotiated a world of money and political power. Each respected and needed the other in wildlife management. But the gulf was considerable.

"Thanks," Langstrap began. "I've been asked to describe the status of UK-7, the seventh transplant from the Upper Kuskokwim management area. This wolf was captured and moved five days ago from the Big River drainage."

Langstrap stole a glance at his division's head. Gunterson wasn't happy.

"UK-7 was released on the middle Kenai southwest of Ninilchik. Telemetry indicated that UK-7 immediately moved east from the release site. Since then, UK-7 has covered about fifty miles daily."

Mel wrote 'fifty miles a day' and underlined it. An audible intake of air around the table showed others thought this a fair clip too. Fifty miles a day! This wolf was in a hurry.

"Where's it on the Kenai now?" asked Crawford.

"It's not," said Langstrap. "UK-7 has left the Kenai."

Crawford lifted his eyebrows. He leaned forward, more interested. He gave a sardonic smile.

"I thought we said that wouldn't happen."

"No one said that," corrected Hank Reisdahl, the straight-shooter manager in Wildlife Conservation.

"Well, I remember saying that," said Crawford. "That's how we sold it. Like Siberia. Alcatraz for wolves, surrounded by water and ice."

"And it is, mostly," Reisdahl frowned. "But it's a peninsula, not an island. Wolves found a way onto the Kenai. They can find a way off. This one has."

"How?" asked Mel.

Langstrap looked at her blankly.

She had never been introduced.

"We're not sure of the exact route," said Langstrap, assuming Mel was somebody. "We think she's following established trails, the snowmachine tracks. She snuck past Kenai Lake. Then we think she scooted down the Johnson and Ingram creek trails, crossed the flats by Portage, and found the trails up Crow and Raven creeks out of Girdwood."

Crawford began laughing.

"Alcatraz!" he said to his secretary.

"What do you mean, 'she'?" asked Mel, lost by the geography but not gender.

"UK-7 is a female," said Langstrap.

Mel felt a new empathy. UK-7 was a feisty female, running from the big boys. Go girl!

"A lactating, alpha female," added Derby Peters.

"What?" said Mel.

"That's not right," growled Gunterson.

"It says so here," said Derby, waving papers.

"What are those?" asked Crawford, suddenly more relaxed, no signs of being in a hurry. Derby passed the papers into the commissioner's meaty hands.

"The field logs," said Derby. "She was lactating at capture, an alpha female."

"You helped capture this one?" Crawford asked Gunterson, surprised at finding his name on the log report.

"Yep," said Gunterson.

"She was lactating?"

"Yep."

The room fell silent.

Mel wrote 'lactating alpha female' followed by an exclamation point. She watched the commissioner peruse the log, stroking a cheek with a fingertip. Your little wheels are turning, aren't they, smirked Mel. You're thinking how this plays politically.

What a great meeting!

"Why isn't this an alpha?" asked Crawford, coming out from the log to Gunterson.

"Because we know squat about the Big River packs," said Gunterson.

"She was lactating," said Derby forcefully.

Derby seemed to care about this wolf.

"That doesn't mean anything," said Gunterson.

"It means she had pups," said Derby. "Only alpha females reproduce. That's why she's running."

"Okay, okay," said Crawford, intervening.

"She's trying to get back to her pups," said Derby.

"Okay, help me think this one through," said Crawford, pressing for calm, no longer smiling. He read the log again. He looked to Derby, Reisdahl, and finally to Langstrap, the field biologist momentarily forgotten in the exchange. "Where's this wolf now, Ben?"

Mel smirked. Oh, what a golden boy you are now. The commissioner used your first name.

"We're not certain," said Langstrap. "We think she's at the Matanuska River flats near Palmer and Wasilla."

"Really!" said Crawford, impressed.

Mel turned to the map of Alaska pinned to the wall. She got up and walked to it to visualize this astonishing report. This wolf had not just escaped the Kenai. It had found a way through the Chugach Mountains, avoiding the urban sprawl around Anchorage. She was at the mouth of the Matanuska River in the vicinity of Palmer and Wasilla, semi-rural suburbs northeast of Anchorage and south of the Alaska Range.

"Here?" asked Mel, pointing on the map.

"Yeah, somewhere around there."

"Going where?" asked Mel.

"Home," Derby answered. "She's going home."

"Really!" said Crawford again.

"We don't know that," said Langstrap.

"It's obvious," said Derby. "She's heading for home. She's trying to get back to her pups."

Several people began talking at once.

Mel examined the map in awe. How could she do that? How could this wolf find the way back home? It staggered the mind. She had been transported by plane from the upper Kuskokwim to the Kenai Peninsula over a major mountain range and saltwater inlet. Drugged. Blind. How could she know the way back?

"Wasn't she drugged?" blurted Mel, but no one heard her over the babble.

"Okay, okay, let's get focused," said Crawford, exerting order. "Let me see if I've got it. We've got a runner. She's left the Kenai Peninsula. Maybe she has pups. Maybe she's heading home."

"And maybe she's infected," said Derby baldly.

"What?"

"Maybe she's infected... with lice," said Derby. "That's the emergency."

He pointed again to Langstrap.

Mel scribbled 'lice,' underlined it.

"Well, again, we don't know," began Langstrap, spreading out his hands upon the tabletop, embarrassed to bear the bad news. "But it's possible."

"Lice?" said Mel. "Sorry, but I don't know what that means. What do you mean, infected by lice?"

"This is Mel Savidge," said Derby, introducing her finally. "She's with Subsistence."

"By 'lice' we mean 'dog lice,'" said Langstrap. "*Trichodectes canis*... the dog-biting louse, a common parasite of domestic dogs, a dog pest. But it can infect other animals. Outside Alaska, it infects coyotes and some gray wolves. Fortunately, our wolves are free of it. Alaskan wolves are clean. All except for the Kenai Peninsula. Its wolves got infected decades ago."

Mel was shocked. She knew a lot about wildlife issues in the state, but she knew nothing about this.

Dog lice had infected wolves on the Kenai.

"What's it do?" asked Mel.

"Nothing good," said Langstrap. "Dogs tolerate the louse. They evolved together, you know, dogs and lice. They're used to each other. But with wolves it's different. The infection has dramatic effects, especially with coats. Lice-infected wolf pelts are virtually worthless. Patchy. Broken guard hairs. Smelly matted underfur."

"They bite themselves to hell," said Reisdahl.

"The infestation itches intolerably," said Langstrap. "It makes them miserable. They rub and bite and scratch, shoulder blades, groin. That breaks the skin. It starts oozing, smells horrible, sort of like earwax and rotting flesh beneath the underfur."

"Ugh," said Mel, scrunching her nose with a hand.

"We've worked aggressively to prevent its spread off the Kenai, when we've had funding," said Reisdahl.

He looked darkly at Gunterson.

"We've found that ivermectin is effective," said Langstrap. "The drug kills the louse. We've treated the infected packs on the Kenai by live capture, inoculating wolves, and by scattering bait treated with ivermectin at sites of wolf-killed moose for other wolves to eat."

"Has it worked?" asked the commissioner's secretary.

Her small voice surprised Mel. She hardly spoke at meetings, sitting quietly beside her boss, taking notes, whispering by his ear. This problem had grabbed her.

"No," Langstrap shook his head. "All the packs on the Kenai have become infected. We can't catch and treat every wolf or clean up every den."

"Re-infections from dogs," said Reisdahl.

"And coyotes," said Langstrap. "The coyotes eat up the bait. They can catch it too. Maybe ten to twenty percent of the coyotes are infected."

Mel assessed Gunterson. He had said nothing during this exchange. He sat with a scowl. He doesn't like the intervention, decided Mel. He must think it's a waste of state money, treating lousy wolves.

"Does it kill them?" asked the secretary.

"Ivermectin?" asked Langstrap.

"The lice," she said. "Do the lice kill the wolves?"

"Not directly. It weakens them. The hair loss makes them more vulnerable to cold weather, especially young wolves. Adults can live with it for some time."

"If you call that living," said Derby darkly. "It makes their life hell."

"Probably," said Langstrap.

"It destroys their trapping value," added Derby, "it totally destroys their pelts."

"Wait, let me get this straight," said Mel hotly. "We're dumping wolves on the Kenai where the wolves are infected with dog lice?"

"Yes," said Reisdahl.

Mel's indignation brought things to an awkward halt.

Gary Gunterson looked at Mel directly.

"Yeah, it's stupid," he said to her without malice. "I always said this relocation program was stupid. If you're going to cull a wolf pack, just cull them. Why torture them to death?"

The first time ever, Gunterson said something right.

"Okay, okay, we've had this discussion before," said Crawford.

"Be ready for it again," said Derby. "It will get out with this runner. The press will be all over it."

"She's not infected," said Gunterson.

"How do we know that?" said Crawford.

"No time for it," said Gunterson. "She's moved too fast. No time for her to get infected."

"Is that right?" Crawford asked Langstrap.

"Well, I don't know," said Langstrap, cautiously. "Normally I'd agree. She's traveled fast. But on the second day... she killed a dog. I examined the yard. The dogs were full of lice."

"Killed a dog?" said the secretary.

"To eat," said Langstrap. "The dog probably had lice, but we don't know for sure. So there's the contact. The wolf may have caught it from that meal."

"She's not infected," said Gunterson.

"But we don't know for sure," said Crawford.

"That's right, we don't know," said Reisdahl.

"Any visual confirmation?" pressed Gunterson.

"No... just telemetry," said Langstrap.

"What's visual confirmation?" asked Mel.

"You can spot an infected wolf," said Gunterson, once again addressing Mel as if she were a legitimate person. "They do a jiggle and shake, something like shaking off water. You can spot it from the air."

"Sometimes," agreed Langstrap.

"So what are you telling me?" asked Crawford. "Can somebody sum up this last exchange?"

"What we're saying," said Derby, "is that the runner may have caught dog lice. If so, the runner could start it going elsewhere. If it spreads like it did on the Kenai, it could become a fast-moving epidemic that infects all the wolf packs in Alaska. Once started, we'll never get rid of it. Our wolves would be ruined."

Crawford sat silently, rubbing his forehead.

"Shit," whispered Mel in the hush.

"Yeah," muttered Crawford.

He tapped fingers on the table, turned to his troopers, Reisdahl and Gunterson.

"Well, let's do something. Catch her. How hard is it to catch her? She's radio collared, right?"

"Yes, but..." began Reisdahl.

"It's busted," said Gunterson.

"The collar transmits intermittently, erratically," said Reisdahl.

"She busted it," said Gunterson, smiling. "Smashed it the first night out. She's a tough little bitch."

"It goes on and off," said Langstrap. "We get short, periodic fixes. That's why we don't know exactly where she is. The signals come and go."

Crawford leaned his bulky body back in the armchair. It creaked dangerously from the weight. He put his hands behind his thick neck. He looked around the table and smiled at his people.

"Well, maybe we do have an emergency."

13

Frances Egnaty was expecting them. Leaving the log house for her place, Nick and Camilla discovered Sleetmute transformed by children. School was out. Four-wheelers roared. Students ran between houses, shouting and laughing in the low afternoon light. Kids made a place better, thought Nick, fresh, funny, and disorderly. He preferred it that way. He had heard of closed retirement communities outside of Alaska with covenants to exclude the young. He could hardly imagine it. Elders denied the joy of goofy grandchildren?

It seemed perverse.

"Who are you?" shouted a small girl bundled for the cold, lips chapped from a runny nose.

"Camilla. This is Nick!"

"Is that your boyfriend?" asked her friend.

"Not yet."

Camilla took Nick's arm affectionately.

"See, Nick, they always try to pair us up."

"Just pity," joked Nick.

"Hardly! Hey! Isn't Nick cute?"

The girls giggled into gloves and scampered off.

"They're so jealous!"

"Yeah," said Nick, enjoying Camilla's arm in his.

Nick was grateful for this unexpected reunion. He had imagined their last parting as final after the herring survey in Togiak. Yet here he was again, working with her on a project, a short mid-winter break from classes for him, earning some money. Maybe research with Camilla could become a regular thing.

"Frances Egnaty's house is over there," said Camilla. "She's nice, but her situation is sad."

The path wound among several caches on high posts. From the undisturbed snow, they looked unused. The Egnaty house was a log cabin, newer and larger than the place they used. Smoke rose from a stovepipe. An old dog barked from a chain staked by a woodpile. A four-wheeler sat at the front steps. Frances could mount it without stepping on snow. Like the storage caches, the lack of paths about the house spoke of abandonment. Her children had forsaken home.

Sort of like me, thought Nick.

Nick had shipped off to boarding school and never fully returned. As a university student, he reappeared on the lower Yukon River for short snatches to catch up and assist his grandmother with salmon fishing. He'd leave with boxes of provisions. He felt guilty each time he said goodbye. He never knew his mother. A low mound at a lonely fish camp marked her sad, short life. He had an aunt and cousins who preserved his grandmother's hope for the family's future.

She must have given up on me long ago.

He hardly fit at home. He never had. He was a social outcast because of his alcoholic mother and the rumors that surrounded her death. Yet he didn't fit in the city either. He felt adrift, an urban Native among many others searching for meaningful paths.

Why did Frances Egnaty live her final years alone? What drove her people away? He entered the house feeling morose.

Frances Egnaty was a substantial woman, plump and friendly in a colorful shift trimmed in gold braid. Nick saw why her knees gave out. Lots of weight to carry.

She laughed to see Camilla, this time with a young man. She ushered them to a table marked by long use.

Framed photos of children and grandchildren covered the log walls. She navigated the rooms on aluminum crutches with bulbous rubber ends. When she maneuvered to the table with a hot teapot, leaning on a single prop, Camilla hopped up to assist. Camilla laid out plates of dried fish and pilot bread as directed. Frances plopped down heavily, breathing hard, smiling because Camilla helped.

"Cama-i," she greeted Nick.

"Cama-i," Nick greeted back.

Sleetmute might be the most inland of Yup'ik villages, but it felt right to Nick. He had known many old women like Frances Egnaty. He instantly liked her. She seemed pleased with him too.

"You are from Bethel," said Frances in Yup'ik.

She was guessing. Lots of people came from Bethel, a regional center of transport and commerce near the mouth of the Kuskokwim River. Its deep channel allowed sea barges to unload supplies during summer.

"Kuigpagmiu," answered Nick, 'a person from the big river,' the Yukon River.

"Ahhh," said Frances, impressed by a visitor from so far off.

"Nicholas John," he offered his hand, gently pressing hers. "But I go to school in Fairbanks."

She smiled and nodded and turned her attention to Camilla, the skinny kass'aq.

"Have strips," she urged, pushing a plate of smoked king salmon. Camilla looked undernourished to her.

"Thanks, I will."

Camilla took a piece, gripped with her teeth, and ripped the oily red flesh from the skin. She had learned to eat salmon strips at Togiak when she worked with Nick. He took one too. The rich smoky salmon burned wonderfully going down. Oily strips from the Kuskokwim were famous. Frances seemed pleased to feed them.

"Did you put these up?" asked Camilla.

"Oh, no. My knees," said Frances.

Apologetically, she lifted her cotton skirt and patted them with a hand. She looked at Nick and laughed, exposing so much to a stranger. But that was why they visited… her knee replacements. An ace bandage completely wrapped one knee. The other displayed white scars.

Camilla had briefed Nick about the botched operations. Two years ago, Frances entered the Native hospital in Anchorage for a knee replacement. Somehow the doctors replaced the wrong one, removing her good knee by mistake, leaving her to painfully hobble on the bad leg as the replaced knee healed. That was the knee with the scars. She had lost a year from that. The surgeons eventually replaced the arthritic knee, the one wrapped in elastic bandages. She was part way through the convalescence for that second operation. She had lost two years of subsistence activities because of the ordeal. Their job was to calculate the monetary worth of those lost years.

A peculiarly kass'aq view of things, thought Nick.

"How did you get these?" Camilla waved the dark salmon skin.

"Oh, I bought them," said Frances, shaking her head sadly. "I never used to buy them. Twenty dollars a pound!"

Nick instantly felt guilty. Frances was reduced to buying salmon strips. This was an embarrassment for an elder. An elder like her could not afford to buy many strips. She had served her guests her best and most expensive food. He wiped his fingers on his pants and didn't take another.

"Terrible!" said Camilla.

"Have tea," Frances offered.

Camilla filled the cups, Canadian Red Rose extended with tundra plants. It tasted wonderful.

"They asked about you," said Frances.

"Who?" said Camilla.

"The mayor and… you know," she replied, suggesting others. "They wondered why you came and took my son's place. I think they worry."

"About what?"

"Those doctors are going to cheat me!" she laughed.

"They know why we're here?" said Nick.

"Because of the operations?" said Camilla.

Frances nodded.

"Well, even so, Nick and I will treat our interviews with the utmost confidence," said Camilla. "What you tell others is your choice. But we work for you. What you tell us will be kept in confidence. You get to okay the report I write for your lawyer. Nick and I will not be talking about the case to anybody unless you approve. Should Nick translate that? Go ahead Nick."

Nick translated.

He was partway through when Frances bent over double, like somebody tickled her.

"What?" smiled Camilla.

"His words," grinned Frances with glee.

Nick stopped, his face burning.

She was laughing at how he spoke Yup'ik!

"Oh, I'm sorry," said Frances, catching her breath. "I just… I just haven't heard some of those words for a long time."

"He shouldn't translate?" asked Camilla.

"No, no, he should! He should! I like it! I just haven't heard some of those words for a long time."

Nick sat mortified.

"Well, okay then," said Camilla cautiously. "We'll translate most everything I say between English and Yup'ik, just to make sure. Right, Nick?"

"I'm sorry," said Frances, trying not to smile. "You speak good, real good, real plain."

Her eyes nearly disappeared above her huge grin.

Frances Egnaty obviously had a quick humor. Nick generally liked that in people. It was the Yup'ik ideal. But he hated being the butt of jokes!

"Is that okay about privacy?" asked Camilla.

"Yes," said Frances smiling.

"If it's okay with you, I want to be clear about what we talked about yesterday," said Camilla, politely ignoring

Nick's discomfort. "Can I go over your family's situation again, this time in Yup'ik with Nick translating?"

"Yes," said Frances.

"Nick?"

Nick frowned and nodded.

Over the next half hour, Camilla asked questions. Frances gave detailed responses in Yup'ik. Nick translated, both directions. Except for an occasional smile, Frances said nothing more about Nick's 'words.'

Partway along, Nick decided it wasn't him. It was Frances who spoke funny. Her Yup'ik displayed odd lexical features. They understood one another fine, but at times they used different grammatical constructions, divergent cadence, and variant roots for words, like standard American differed from Queen's English or British cockney. To Nick, Frances cut verbal corners. His own speech was grammatically complete. Occasionally some of her word roots didn't quite sound Yup'ik, like loans from Athabaskan. A linguist would have fun analyzing it.

The interview confirmed Camilla's understanding of the situation. Frances was a widow. Her adult son lived in Portland. He had trained in small engine repair at Mount Edgecomb in Sitka, found employment outside Alaska, married a kass'aq, and never returned. He occasionally visited with his children. They viewed their father's birthplace like another planet. Currently, Frances' two daughters lived in Anchorage with three grandchildren. When at Sleetmute the daughters assisted Frances with fishing at the family's fish camp just upriver. They helped to operate gill nets and a fish wheel, depending upon the runs and water conditions and season. Frances oversaw the smoking and drying.

"Even the little ones help," said Frances.

Then came the operations.

Her arthritic knee bothered her more each year. Doctors recommended a knee replacement. When Frances went to Anchorage for the procedure, the daughters came along. They first stayed with relatives.

The grandchildren enrolled in school. Then the mistake happened. The doctors replaced the wrong knee. Frances found she couldn't do anything. Instead of walking on a mending knee compensated by a good one, she still had the painful bad knee and an artificial joint that had trouble healing. The new joint became infected. She developed viral pneumonia. The recovery took much longer than planned. Unexpectedly, the family was stuck in Anchorage.

"It got bad," said Frances sadly. "My youngest, she likes to party. She began to do that. My oldest got work in a hotel. I watched the little ones. I couldn't walk. I couldn't work. Lots of drinking. Lots of arguments."

Her eyes teared up telling the story.

"The entire family moved because of the operation," Camilla restated.

"Yes."

"They've been there two years."

"Almost two years."

"When did you come back to Sleetmute?"

"After the second one. I get around on those crutches and that four wheeler you saw out there."

"Your daughters didn't come back?"

"Yes," she sighed, meaning they didn't.

"Why not?"

Frances wiped her eyes.

"They want to stay. Better jobs. Schools. Stores. It's easier. They got lazy, I guess."

Nick translated, feeling depressed. Here was the reason for the abandoned caches in the yard. The family had lost its workers. Frances didn't mention another probable reason for the absent daughters... addictions.

Sleetmute was dry. Anchorage wasn't.

Nick had personally experienced the pull of town described by Frances. Abruptly, village life seemed boring and antiquated, even though it had never felt that way before. Rural communities died because of this pull, bleeding residents to the city, person by person.

"You came back," said Camilla.

125

"I got homesick."

Camilla sat quietly, giving Frances time.

"They say it's harder here. No money. Just subsistence. But it's home."

Frances pointed out the portraits on the wall, bright faces smiling at the camera.

"I wish they came home. It's lonely."

Nick felt terrible for her. The son was gone because of the boarding school system. The botched operation had taken the others. Frances suffered from the incompetence of surgeons who couldn't tell right from left on a medical chart.

"So you went after those doctors," said Nick.

"Oh no, no," said Frances, surprised.

"What do you mean?"

"Not me."

"You didn't go after the doctors?"

"My daughters did it."

Nick translated. Camilla registered no surprise.

"They hired the lawyer," said Camilla.

"Yes."

"Your daughters pushed to sue."

Frances nodded but said no more.

"Why?" asked Camilla finally. "Why did your daughters want you to sue the doctors?"

"For the money," Frances sighed.

She looked wistfully out a window at the spruce boughs, drooping with snow.

"It takes money to live in Anchorage."

14

Joel Haggarty, outdoor legend, gulped beer in the hotel bar. His snakeskin boots tapped out a dance on the parquet floor. Protestors chanted outside the double-paned windows like muted music, shouting to pedestrians negotiating the icy streets of downtown Anchorage.

"Boycott Alaska!"

"Save the wolves!"

"Ban the snares!"

He drank to kill time and dampen his pent-up energies, the internal forces barely held in check as he waited to testify. Even outdoor legends had to wait at board meetings. The only way he could sit still was with a beer. Even so, his boots hammered under the table.

He flew from Farewell into Anchorage that morning through the stiff crosswinds of Cook Inlet. His buddies dropped him off near the Hilton, the Board of Game venue this cycle. He filled out a card to testify, then announced to the trappers he'd be in the bar. Get him when they got to snares. The Board was deliberating bow hunting in the Anchorage basin. He cared squat about bow hunting.

Haggarty detested Anchorage, a little Los Angeles dusted by snow. It had rush hour traffic, suited businessmen, and teenage malls. Tourists from Japan. Art museums.

That wasn't Alaska.

Now Fairbanks, that was a frontier town. His base was home to free-spirited outdoorsmen with big trucks and homesteads carved from vast forested ridges. Plenty of room for privacy. From it he trapped, gunned, and guided. He was within striking distance of the Brooks Range for sheep, the Kobuk for caribou, the upper Kuskokwim for guiding. He had trapped the whole Interior, a hundred winding river valleys free of roads, dropping from the sky to work his magic. At Fairbanks he reigned as unofficial king, the paramount chief of trappers, outdoor ruler by hard example and proven success. He held forth at roadhouses from Ester to Tok. Momentarily he drank alone, the hour before noon, waiting for the board, but at home, the trappers bought him the beers.

More chants came from the street.

He hated regulatory meetings. Yet he attended them. It was part of his duties as king. The Alaska Outdoor Council kept track of agendas and informed him of times and places and issues. Sheep seasons. Moose rack limits. Closed areas. Trapping restrictions. The threats were endless. He attended to represent the common man, to protect real Alaskans against ever-increasing inroads on their liberty. Outdoorsmen were an endangered species in America, losing ground to preservationists, anti-hunting organizations, and gun-control lobbies.

Today it was snares. Tomorrow it would be something else. He swigged beer, boots clicking.

When he entered the Hilton that morning the protestors waved signs in his face. He had ducked easily and entered through the whoosh of revolving doors. He thought he was late for public testimony. By mistake the boys had dropped him off at the Captain Cook, the wrong hotel. He had walked six blocks to the Hilton, surrounded by wolf lovers. But the board had fallen behind schedule. A crowd of trappers milled in the mezzanine. So he submitted his card and headed for the bar. He was on his second beer.

"Joel!" rasped a voice.

Gary Gunterson, the old toad from Tok, entered the bar. He was now the big cheese at Fish and Game.

"Hey, Gary," Haggarty nodded.

He motioned for him to sit. Gunterson did and signaled the waitress for the same as Haggarty.

"They finally ready for snares?"

"Naw, still fighting about bow hunts. They've formed a committee that's called a long break."

The chants of protesters drifted from the street as the waitress brought the extra beer. Gunterson snickered.

"You run that gauntlet outside?"

"Almost got stopped by a sign."

"Me too," laughed Gunterson.

"Couple of police units. Channel Thirteen News."

"They interview you yet?"

"The cops or the news?"

"The evening news."

"No, why?"

"They were asking about you. Nina Blair, she wants your interview."

"What for?"

"Snares. Blair on snares. She needs some talk. Everybody tells her that you're her man, the original originator."

"Well, I didn't."

"I know. But she needs a trapper. She already did me. But I'm Fish and Game."

"Yeah, okay, iffen she can catch me."

"That girl will."

The two drank, feeling well matched. They watched the lobby fill during the break, a real mix, trappers, biologists, outfitters, greenies, animal rights, bureaucrats. It sounded like ducks.

"Thought I was late," said Haggarty.

"They're always behind," said Gunterson.

"I rushed over from Merrill Field. Flew in from Farewell. There's a bitch of a wind over the inlet."

"How's Farewell?"

"Cold."

"You trapping over there?"

"A bit. What are they going to do with that proposal? Limit the number of snares?"

"Naw, not this Board. They won't do that, not after their wolf control vote."

"So what will they do?"

"Best practices."

"What the hell is that?"

"Today's buzzword. They'll form up a committee to discuss 'best practices' for trapping. The committee will recommend next spring. You like committees?"

"Hell," growled Haggarty.

So the trip was a waste of his time. This was why he hated meetings. Mostly it was all smoke and no fire. Rush and wait. Damn politics.

"Anyway, there's a thing I wanted to talk to you about," said Gunterson, bending closer. "Got us a little problem."

"What's that?"

"We got a runner."

"What do you mean?"

"One of our wolf transplants. You know, the Kenai? One of our transplants didn't stay put. Hightailed it. She's running. She's run so far, she's run clean off the peninsula."

"Yeah?"

"All the way to Wasilla."

"No shit?" grinned Haggarty.

"No shit," smiled Gunterson, pleased with his story.

"That's something. I hadn't heard. 'Course, I've been out at Farewell."

"Nobody's heard yet. But it will hit the papers Friday. The Dispatch has found out."

"Runner. That's good."

"Female from your area… Big River."

"She's made Wasilla? How'd she do that?"

"Over the Chugach, maybe Bird Creek."

"That's a good one, the runner," joked Haggarty.

Wolves moved when they wanted to, he knew. This wolf confirmed it. It was three hundred miles from Kenai to Wasilla.

"Yeah, but that's the problem," said Gunterson. "It's not all a good show. That wolf may have caught something on the road... the lice."

Haggarty stopped grinning.

"She's likely clean," said Gunterson dismissively. "But you know, there's lice on the Kenai."

"You think she caught it?"

"She killed a dog," said Gunterson.

Haggarty sat back to consider this. Wolves and dog lice. He'd seen it once on the Kenai with a friend who trapped out there. The wolf was moth-eaten. The smell had turned his stomach. Could killing a dog transmit lice? Maybe. That's how wolves got it on the Kenai in the first place. Too many people, too few moose. The wolves fell to eating dogs. The lice jumped species. But would killing one dog be enough?

"The story on Friday will be that," said Gunterson. "You know Terry, right? Their outdoor writer? He interviewed Reisdahl and Langstrap. That's the headline... epidemic."

"Who's Langstrap?"

"He does wolves on the Kenai. Terry's okay. He's got no ax to grind. But it will go down bad. More for the greenies."

"Yeah," said Haggarty. The environmentalists would make a fuss about this. And, well, maybe they should.

"So here's the thing," said Gunterson. "You want some work?"

"What do you mean?"

"A contract."

"For what?"

"To catch her."

Haggarty examined Gunterson for the joke. But Gunterson was serious. He was offering Haggarty work, catching the runaway wolf.

"Can't you guys?" asked Haggarty.

"We'll try, but you know, the more the merrier."

"No, I guess I don't know. That seems like a waste of my taxes."

"Because there's a hitch. No transmitter. The runner's busted it. It's got the burps. Now you hear it, now you don't. Mostly we don't. She won't be easy to find. She don't stay put. And our boys are busy. But for someone like you…"

Gunterson was doing the flatter thing, giving him a chance to strut his stuff, improve on the legend.

"She's at Wasilla?" asked Haggarty.

"Last we heard."

"Going where?"

"Who knows?" shrugged Gunterson. "She's one of yours. You tell me."

"A female from Big River?"

"Yep. Oh, and she was nursing."

"Nursing?"

"Yep. Pups. She's one hell of a wolf," grinned Gunterson. "One for you gunners. But I tell you, with what she's done so far, and her pups out there, bet you dimes to dollars she's headed into the Alaska Range."

"Yeah?"

"A beeline for home."

Haggarty mulled it over. Here was a challenge, finding a specific wolf running through the Alaska Range to the upper Kuskokwim. He thought he knew how he might do it. It would be expensive.

"State covers costs?" asked Haggarty.

"Within reason," said Gunterson.

"I get the transmission frequency?"

"Yep."

"And a salary?"

"Naw, no salary! Expenses and ten thousand plus another five thousand if you bring her in."

"Fifteen thousand and another ten if I catch her."

"Shit, you think I'm made of money? Okay."

"What do mean 'bring her in'?"

"Yeah, well, we'd prefer you catch her alive, treat her, and return her to the Kenai."

"You're kidding."

"Listen, it's a joke in Juneau. We're not in the wolf killing business right now. They want a live capture. But, you know, if you can't, you can't. You do what you have to do to stop her."

"I still get paid?"

"Yep. But this isn't a bounty," added Gunterson. "Can't use that word either. This is a contract. And if you can, land the plane before shooting."

"Okay," said Haggarty thinking, then smiling. "Okay."

He and Gunterson shook hands.

A crowd had filled the bar for lunch. Haggarty saw a familiar face, Nina Blair from Channel Thirteen News. An accomplice with her carried a camera pack and sound equipment. She chatted up somebody else who looked vaguely familiar... tall, slender, bearded, curly haired, backpack.

"Son-of-a-bitch."

His snakeskin boots smacked the hardwood.

"Nina! Over here!" called Gunterson.

Nina Blair turned.

"Nina, this guy here is Joel Haggarty."

Nina Blair put out a hand to Haggarty, who quickly rose to his feet. She was shocked when Haggarty lunged past her and threw a fierce right-arm punch at the face of the curly-haired companion. The wild punch missed. Curly-hair saw it coming and sidestepped. The swing carried Haggarty into the cameraman. Equipment went flying. Everybody began grabbing and shouting at once.

"Whoa! Whoa!" yelled Gunterson, grabbing Haggarty's shoulder. The cameraman grabbed Curly-hair, who seemed more than willing to throw his own punches. The two were held apart in a quick scuffle that sent plates and flatware crashing to the floor.

"You son-of-a-bitch! Come on!" shouted Haggarty.

"Let's see it!" shouted his rival.

Hotel workers descended.

The antagonists allowed themselves to be pulled apart.

Smoothing his curly hair, Haggarty's foe smiled wickedly and strode from the bar. He disappeared into the crowded lobby. Gunterson sat Haggarty down. The buzz died down while hotel workers cleaned up.

Nina Blair sat beside Haggarty, wide-eyed and eager.

"What was that?" she gasped, checking her cameraman's status.

Haggarty reclaimed his beer. He took a furious gulp.

"Nothing," he said.

"Nothing?" she asked amazed.

"Thought I knew that guy."

Blair looked into the crowded lobby then back to Haggarty.

"Geoff Sturgis?" she asked.

"That his name?" said Haggarty flatly.

He took another gulp and angrily remembered that evening last summer drinking hard in North Pole, getting free drinks and a free ride, waking up chained to the ground with a million goddamn bites and a new nickname people used with peril. Mosquito Man. Haggarty never forgot a stranger's face. Now he wouldn't forget the name.

"Geoff Sturgis," Blair repeated.

Haggarty calmly nodded and turned his steely attention to the newswoman.

"You still want an interview?"

"God, yes," said Blair.

"I'm going," announced Gunterson.

"Send word if they ever get to snares."

"Yep," replied Gunterson, heading outside for a smoke. The noise from demonstrators rose and fell.

"What was that about?" asked Blair again.

"Nothing at all," said Haggarty. "A temporary misunderstanding. You want to talk about trapping?"

"Snares," said Blair, seeing her cameraman struggling with equipment. "I'd like to film. But let's talk first."

Haggarty answered the newswoman's questions, his origins in rural Minnesota, his stint in the military based at Fairbanks, his decade of trapping.

"They say you use snares to take wolves. Lots of snares?" asked Blair.

"It's pretty simple," explained Haggarty. "Anybody could do it. You set around a kill. A moose in a woodsy place works good. I didn't invent this. Trappers always did it. I just put out a few more than most. A dozen, two dozen, depending."

"That's why you call it saturation snaring?"

"I don't call it that."

"What do you call it?"

"Snaring. It's not that unusual."

"I heard you once caught eleven wolves in one set," said Blair.

"That may be a record," Haggarty chuckled. "That doesn't happen every day."

"That's not too many?"

"It's legal, if that's what you mean."

"So you don't think eleven is too many?"

"Look, a good trapper takes that many wolves over a winter, one trap at a time. It's no different from that. It's just the efficiency that catches attention."

"But it's not too many."

"There's still plenty of wolves," said Haggarty dismissively. "Hell, the biologists export them now, we're so rich with wolves. The Board wants us to take more. I figure out how to do that and somebody gets mad."

"Uh huh," said Blair, jotting notes. "You're a studied wolf expert, they tell me."

"Well, I've lived among them, if that's what you mean. I've studied them up close. They're smart. You wouldn't believe the things I've seen them do. They'll survive. Snaring isn't going to hurt wolves in Alaska. It'll help them in the long run."

"How?"

"Restore the balance."

The cameraman put his back to the bar, prepared to shoot. Blair moved into position. The camera rolled.

"What do you think of the 'save the wolves' demonstration going on outside?" said Blair to Haggarty, positioning a microphone.

"It's a free country," said Haggarty, looking into the camera. "But it's a tempest in a teapot."

"Why is that?"

"There's plenty of wolves in Alaska. More than enough. Ask the moose and the caribou. They've declared some emergency because there's so many wolves. I don't know about that. But I'll tell you this, the hunters, they're the real endangered species. Politics are destroying our children's heritage."

"Should the number of snares be limited for trapping wolves?"

"I support regulated trapping. If there are too many wolves, I can't see why the number of snares is a problem."

"Are snares humane?"

"Now that's a different issue. I favor humane ways of trapping. I support using the best practices for trapping in Alaska. I'll work with reasonable people to develop them. But I'll tell you this, watching wolves starve to death by driving moose to near extinction in an area, that's not humane either."

"Do you favor wolf control?"

"We ought to let trappers solve the problems first. That's better than government wolf control, if that's what you mean. But maybe as a last resort, I guess sometimes special things are needed."

"What do you say about those calling for tourists to boycott Alaska?"

"I say that's fine with me. It leaves more of Alaska for you and me. I say, go for it! More power to them!"

Nina Blair signaled a stop to filming.

"Thanks!"

"No problem," replied Haggarty, grabbing his near-empty beer mug.

"I was going to ask, but didn't, it seemed off topic," said Blair, "but I was going to ask how you felt being a trapper. You know, how you feel killing wolves. I mean, you've studied them. You said you've learned how smart they are. So how do you feel when you kill them?"

"Let me ask you this first," said Haggarty. "Wolves study moose. I've seen them do it. Wolves get to know moose really well. How do you think a pack of wolves feels when they pull down a moose?"

"I don't know," replied Blair, her blue eyes reflecting his. "I guess maybe they feel glad to get it?"

"Because they have something to eat?"

"Yeah."

"Because they're successful hunters in a food chain?"

"I guess."

"Well, maybe all those years trapping wolves has made me feel a bit like them."

"A hunter in the food chain?"

He wiped his mouth and smiled.

"The one at the top."

15

Camilla Mac Cleary felt the first twinge of pain.

Nick translated and she felt the subtle slip of gray matter, silent readjustments of ganglia around vessels, initial bursts of an electrical storm, hidden and baffling.

The doctors rarely blinked when she described her private torment. They stared intently as if trying to decipher a code. 'Migraine' they eventually pronounced, returning to that word like priests to doctrine, a reaffirmation of holy mysteries, a litany of faith, the intricacies of the marvel called the human brain and its neurological maladies, all revealed in time. Meanwhile, try this pill. If that doesn't work for you, if it produces insufferable side effects, try these off the list. Caffeinated analgesics. Beta blockers. Calcium channel blockers. Anticonvulsants. Selective serotonin reuptake inhibitors. A long list... all developed for other ailments and of dubious worth with migraines.

As an anthropologist Camilla had held the perforated skulls in museum collections, the prehistoric skulls with precisely drilled holes, trephined heads that once cradled human brains like hers, empty crania with square excised plugs. They filled museum cases, the works of shamans or witch women or Paleolithic surgeons who carved the exits with obsidian knives to release the pain locked inside the human heads. So many!

'Migraine' intoned the doctors.

One in five women suffered.

The twinge spilled its poison, drippings of black agony, desperation, and hopelessness. She scratched notes on paper as Nick John translated from Frances Egnaty's narrative, brassy words that beat on her brain. She squinted past a painful veil into knife-edged light. She nodded, forced her smile, found the proper questions with increased difficulty.

"They hired the lawyer?" she asked while her stomach roiled, the poison sinking deeper. When Frances said 'yes' she loathed the daughters as she loathed herself.

"Why did your daughters want you to sue the doctors?" she asked, fighting with nausea.

"For the money," sighed Frances, looking wistfully out the window, like Camilla, wishing only for normalcy.

Camilla could endure no more. She shut the notebook with a great effort, stood and smiled.

"Thanks. Let's end it for today," Camilla whispered. "Can we come tomorrow?"

"I just need a pill," she apologized, stumbling along the snowy trail, Nick beside her. He must detest me. They passed the chained dogs, watching from their own private holes. She entered hers, groped a duffle for bottles, swallowed the pill, and fell onto the musty bed.

A blanket covered her.

She took the hand before it withdrew.

"Thanks Nick," she whispered, holding tight. She didn't want to be hated.

"Sure," Nick answered, his voice distant, forlorn.

"Stay," she whispered. Her cold slender fingers held him. "You must hate this. But the pills will kick in. Wait a bit. The pills will kick in."

Nick didn't know what to say to that. He felt sad and useless. Camilla had no pills when they first worked. The headaches had been something new, unexpected, a curse from post-partum hormones.

"What are they?"

"A sumitriptan," she murmured, eyes shut. "A tricyclic antidepressant at night. The triptan sometimes works if I catch it quick, at the first twinge. I should have brought them to Egnaty's."

"It happens a lot?"

"Every day. Every afternoon. When my progesterone's up, I may get a free day." Camilla cracked her eyes, trying to see his face. "Do you think I'm addicted, Nick? Am I an addict? Is it rebound? The pain's unbearable. The doctors say, take them. Pain, every day."

"I don't know."

He knew about alcohol, nothing about this. He could drink and he could stop. Others couldn't and drank themselves dead.

Personal biochemistry. Fate.

"I don't know what to do," groaned Camilla.

The room fell silent.

Nick propped against the wall.

Camilla gripped his hand, an anchor, like Togiak again, unbearable pain except for Nick. A leech, she grimaced. He must hate me. But maybe he can rest too, sitting beside me on the bed. Her agony drifted into a haze. She almost slept. The pain gradually lessened. The neural fog began to slowly lift.

"It's going," she whispered, squeezing his hand.

They sat in silence again.

It was Nick who finally broke it.

"Did you grow up with snow?"

Camilla felt a slight shudder.

The first inquiry.

This was the first question Nick had ever asked about her personal past. She had never asked about his. Before, in Togiak, they had worked in blissful ignorance together, content not knowing.

"Sometimes," she whispered.

It would be up to her. Nick wouldn't probe. But he had opened the door.

"Lots of places," she said carefully, wondering what to disclose. "We moved... constantly."

"Constantly?"

"Thirty different schools by the time I was fifteen, when I was in school."

"Wow," said Nick.

The room was silent for a while. Nick's brain worked on the puzzle.

"How come?"

Camilla felt Nick had just crossed some line. He was probing deeper. Camilla felt a shiver of elation and fear.

"Construction," whispered Camilla. "My dad... he started jobs. That's what my dad was hired to do, start jobs that others finished. Big jobs. Bechtel, Brown and Root, you know them? Big companies with big projects. Once he got them going, they'd send him somewhere else to start the next one. Even when they didn't, he left. He couldn't stay put, a bad itch, he had to get out. My mother hated it, the packing and shipping and unpacking, he left all that to her, hauling me and my brother into every kind of place and situation. He never helped."

Nick looked out the bedroom's small window to the shadowed forest. He had never heard of these companies. But he could imagine it, a kind of nomadic wandering. Like the trans-Alaska oil pipeline. The massive project linking Prudhoe Bay with Valdez drew workers from everywhere, even his own village, transforming the state.

"You have a brother?"

"He left when I was small. My dad kicked him out. My father had to have his way. They actually had a fistfight over something stupid, like eating peas. So he threw him out."

"Where's he now?"

"Colorado, I think."

"Your parents?"

"They're gone," sighed Camilla. "Dead."

She hoped to say no more. Nick sat in silence, leaving it up to her. She liked this about Nick.

"So I've seen snow," said Camilla, recalling the cold places of her childhood. "Nova Scotia, Quebec, Peru..."

"You lived in Peru?"

"I remember Peru. Chile. Bolivia. The Andes."

"I'd like to see the Andes."

"I learned my Spanish there. But mostly it was hot places. Venezuela, Panama, Saudi Arabia, Syria, Texas… too much Texas."

"Jesus. What did your father build?"

"Pipelines, dams, electrical generating stations, petrochemical plants, mines. Anything oil and gas or electric or mineral, big things, you know, thousand-mile pipelines in the desert, mega-pit mines at fourteen thousand feet. He didn't build them. He'd get them started and pull out."

"I never saw a big town until I was twelve," said Nick.

Camilla began remembering the flow of places. They often blurred together. Some she had tried to forget.

"In my earliest memories, I'm always standing beside a trailer or some cinder-block house, my mom unpacking boxes. I'm looking at other children staring back at me. I was the skinny white kid with crossed-eyes and bottle glasses. Yeah, I had crossed-eyes. Everything looked double. I thought that's the way the world was, two of everything. And everybody spoke a different language. That's just how things worked. So I'd watch the jumble and listen, just listen, trying to figure things out, you know, easing in, getting to know the place. Then I'd be out there in the mud getting so dirty you couldn't tell me from them. But I always knew when it was time to move. When I finally made friends, that's when we moved."

Camilla opened her eyes.

The pain and nausea had left. Only echoes remained.

"That's when I was little. You know, later on, eventually you quit."

"Moving?"

"Making friends."

She found Nick leaning against the wall at the bed's head post staring into space, imagining her childhood. Nick grew up in a small intimate village, a completely different experience. But in some ways he acted like her. He couldn't quite fit anyplace. She liked that about Nick too. But for him the dislocation would be temporary, she knew this. He was a traditionalist at heart, though he would deny it. He had roots. He'd return to them some day. His sensitivity to the feelings of others came from a lifetime of closeness. Camilla was attuned to others too. But hers was the interloper's.

"Gone," said Camilla, weakly smiling.

"Yeah?" said Nick, sounding hopeful.

"You cured me."

Nick said nothing to this foolish statement.

He stood and stretched.

"Let's find something to eat."

* * *

In a Yup'ik village, Nick cooked only in emergencies. He had told Camilla this before. Why cook when others did? And why eat alone? Yup'iks liked company. Food tasted best when shared with others. Sharing increased your luck. These were basic principles for Nick. He was an unapologetic lazy bachelor. So in a strange village, a first order of business was finding dinner with somebody who would enjoy feeding you. Nick led Camilla down a track. He searched for a particular house.

"How do you know this guy?" asked Camilla, hugging the parka closer against the subzero cold.

"Family friend," said Nick, taking a side path. "My aunt said to find him."

"How do you know his house?"

"Frances Egnaty told me."

"When?"

"When you were getting crackers."

Dogs began yipping. They passed a dozen barking sled dogs standing atop their tiny houses or straining on their chains. A large black husky mix bounded toward them, unchained, tail wagging. Nick put out a hand. She sniffed.

Nick slipped her a piece of something to eat.

"What you feeding that dog!" a gruff voice demanded. An old man in stocking feet stood at the house beside a cracked door.

"Maklaaq," answered Nick cheerily.

Young bearded seal.

"Don't waste it on her!" yelled the old man, opening the door wider. He began laughing. "Come in! Come in! I was watching for you!"

Nick left the black dog chewing the dried seal meat. Camilla patted the dog's head, then entered the log house, amazed they were expected. The entryway smelled of beaver pelts and fish. Wooden butter barrels framed an unplugged freezer unit. A long wood-slat fish trap was wedged in a corner. The old man grinned at Nick, his moist eyes nearly lost above round weathered cheeks. Inside, an old woman stood shyly, grinning too.

"Here's that nephew we heard about," he explained to his wife. He sniffed like he had a cold and shook his head in happy disbelief. Such good fortune!

"Nicholas John, Nick John," said Nick, gently taking her hand in his. "Lizzie Kopuk is my auntie."

"Joseph Kopuk," exclaimed the old man, naming the deceased man who connected them. He wiped his eyes.

"Camilla, this is James Epchook, my great uncle's old partner. This is my friend, Camilla Mac Cleary from San Francisco, California."

"Ahhh!" they both exclaimed.

The old man and his wife took Camilla's hand warmly.

"Hello," said Camilla, smiling brightly. "What was your name?"

"Sophie. Sophie Epchook," smiled James' wife.

"I'm very happy to meet you," said Camilla.

Nick and Camilla were made to feel at home. They sat side-by-side on a comfortable sofa across from the Epchooks. A warm woodstove hissed and rattled like another occupant. Sophie brought out tea. And James Epchook began talking.

The old memories flowed. He spoke of Nick's uncle glowingly. Camilla saw Nick relax, sipping his tea and listening happily. Here is his place, Camilla saw. He thinks he doesn't fit, but he does. This is his world. Camilla felt happy too, relaxed beside him. She saw Sophie watch knowingly, misinterpreting the relationship. It didn't matter. She hadn't felt this good for a long while.

Nick listened with interest to James Epchook's history. He had known the barest outline of the connections between Joseph Kopuk, his dead great uncle, and the old partner from Sleetmute. Now he heard details. The two had met as young men in the salmon canneries of Bristol Bay. At that time, roustabouts recruited workers from the Kuskokwim and Yukon rivers. Unmarried men and women took the seasonal work. The canneries flew them to Bristol Bay to pack fish. Epchook came from the upper Kuskokwim, Kopuk from the lower Yukon. The grueling schedule on the canning lines had forged a friendship that lasted a lifetime.

They worked other jobs as partners thereafter. Woodcutting. Commercial fishing. Firefighting. The most memorable and profitable was trapping. Nick's uncle spent three winters with James Epchook working traplines along the Hoholitna River. They trapped marten, mink, beaver, wolverine, and wolf, living in trapline cabins. They tracked caribou with their dog teams just before snowmachines revolutionized winter hunting. The three winters were exceptionally lucrative, prime pelts and high fur prices. The money staked them successful futures. After that they went separate ways to start families. But they still kept in touch. He last saw his old partner at an elders' convention in Bethel, a year before his death. It seemed as if they had never been apart.

Nick found his own eyes tearing up. This was true friendship. Nick was only a nephew of Joseph Kopuk. Even that was by marriage, for Lizzie Kopuk was Nick's blood relative. But that didn't matter to James Epchook. Nick's presence woke the affection in his heart. Nick was happy to do it. He felt honored to hear the old man's stories. And besides, he'd eventually get fed.

"Are you hungry?" Sophie said the magic words.

"Yes," beamed Nick, and Camilla smiled.

She knows my tricks, he thought. But she never laughs at me. Nor judges. Too much anyway. He appreciated her for that. And she was looking better.

Sophie Kopuk served a savory stew of beaver meat and rice. A piquant red berry sauce covered a side of frozen whitefish, tumagliq, a bush that grew next to dwarf birch in open woodlands she told Camilla, confirming it as lowbush cranberry. A small bottle held seal oil beside the salt and pepper. James and Sophie poured it sparingly on their plates to dip slices of freshly-baked bread. They traded for it from the coast.

The food tasted wonderful. In gratitude, Nick presented his hosts with a sack of dried seal meat. Sophie gasped as if she'd been given a sack of gold.

Camilla asked about Sleetmute.

It began as an Indian fishing spot, explained James. The Deg Hit'an set traps for salmon at the tip of a nearby island. The seasonal settlement grew more permanent when families from the Holitna and Hoholitna rivers consolidated during winter, compelled by mandatory attendance at the public schools for the children. Even before then Yup'iks had been moving upriver. Some settled at Sleetmute. Families intermarried.

So we look Indian, laughed Sophie.

But the village considered itself Yup'ik, said James.

Cellitmiut, the Yup'ik name for Sleetmute, meant 'whetstone people.' Nearby slate outcroppings used to be mined for sharpening knives. The settlement's original name was Tovishq'ul Ghunh, 'whetstone place' in the Deg Hit'an tongue. So place names confirmed that the Yup'iks had settled an Indian place. But still, the Yup'iks and Indians got along well.

Nick explained why they were in town. They came to interview Frances Egnaty about the knee replacements.

"That poor old woman," said Sophie, shaking her head. "Her legs wobble. I saw her pick berries this year. She fell right over!"

"She picked berries?" asked Camilla.

"She tried," said Sophie, laughing. "She slid on her butt from bush to bush, pulling her bucket. That woman is always working. When her husband died, she'd ask around for extra fish to cut."

"I'd give her some," said James.

"She didn't fish?" asked Camilla.

"Oh, she did," said Sophie.

"But he ran the fishwheel," said James.

"Her daughters helped?"

"They did," said Sophie.

"But it got hard. So I gave her fish," said James.

"You know how a fishwheel works, right?" Nick asked Camilla. "It takes several strong arms to set a wheel, wrestling it into the water."

"The water goes up and down around here, depending on the rain," said James. "You got to move it. Lots of drift. It jams up the baskets. You got to watch it."

"She sets a net," said Sophie. "But not with those crutches. She's by herself in that house. Those girls ought to come home."

"The daughters?" asked Camilla.

"Those daughters."

Sophie began to clear plates. Nick leaned back, pleasantly full.

"Are those your dogs out front?"

"My grandson's," said James proudly. "He keeps them here. I'm too old for dogs. Except that black one you spoiled with maklaaq."

"Camilla feels sorry for them, tied to their houses," said Nick cheerfully.

"Nooo," said James, drawing out the word in surprise. "Those dogs are happy. You should see them run! They are so eager. He just hangs on tight."

Camilla smiled and nodded.

"She says they're like slaves, always tied to sleds, pulling things."

"That's what a dog likes, qimugta," declared James.

"What's that?" asked Camilla.

"Qimugta," repeated Nick, "what I said before. That's 'dog' in Yup'ik. It's from qimaug-, 'to pull,' uh... 'to pull hard.' Qimugta. Hard-puller. That's a dog."

Camilla looked amazed. That was the Yup'ik word for dog? They *were* poor slaves.

"They're tied down like felons," said Camilla.

"Yes, they are happiest to pull a sled," agreed James.

He left the table and lifted a fiddle hung from the wall. He strummed it with his thumb and tuned up a flat string. He passed the fiddle to Camilla.

"Yours?" asked Nick, knowing the answer by the easy way he handled it. Fiddling was common in some villages, a type of music picked up from miners during the gold rush. Fiddlers played at winter dances.

"A dog is like that fiddle string," said James to Camilla. "That string is not free to be a string until tied to the fiddle."

Camilla held the fiddle doubtfully. It felt light and warm, the strings stretched tightly. Dogs were like strings? She strummed. The strings sang, rich and resonant. She passed the fiddle to Nick, searching for a convincing argument.

"They're not hard pullers if they're tied to houses day after day," said Camilla. "I mean, what can their spirit masters think when they're staked like that?"

"Ah! Dogs have no spirit masters," exclaimed the old man.

This assertion intrigued Nick. He stopped strumming to listen.

"I thought animals had spirit masters," said Camilla, repeating what she had read about Yup'ik cosmology.

"They have names instead," said James.

Camilla frowned, working through this statement.

No spirit masters.

"Because dogs get names?"

"They are dogs, not wolves."

Camilla reflected on this contrast between wolves and dogs. Unnamed versus named. Wild versus domesticated.

Spirit masters versus human masters? Dogs worked for humans. Wolves lived for... what?

Spirit masters?

"Like that old dog you spoiled with maklaaq," said James. "My old leader. A hard puller, real strong, a good mountain dog, not like those skinny sprinters they run now. Tepsaq. That's her name."

"Stink?" Nick grinned.

"She rolls in smelly things," laughed James. "That's why she is Tepsaq. Strong and smart, she always gets loose. So I gave up."

Camilla saw the affection the old man had for his old lead dog. James Epchook felt bad about tying his best dog to a stake, despite what he claimed about dogs being born for servitude. He let her run free.

"And that other one, my mistake," said James laughing. "She won't stay tied up too. Always tries to mother things."

"What mistake?" said Nick.

"You didn't see her? Come," said James, standing from the table, stretching with audible cracks.

Bundled in parkas, they stepped under a black sky filled with stars. In the yard, several dogs left their houses, nosing the smells from the cabin. Suddenly, the black dog bounced happily from the shadows. The old man grabbed her neck and spoke to her in Yup'ik, laughing and patting her side.

"Tepsaq," chuckled James.

His big stinker.

The dog bounded to Nick. She shoved her nose into his parka pocket, knocking him backwards.

"She's looking for that maklaaq," said James. "You got a friend."

James searched around the yard.

"There she is! She's never far from that one."

They looked where James indicated. A gray shadow materialized from behind a snowmachine.

"A wolf!" Camilla gasped.

She took a step backwards.

James laughed.

The wolf stood with her head low to the ground, shoulder partly turned. She watched Nick petting Tepsaq.

"Let that one go," said James.

Nick released Tepsaq. She immediately bounced over to the wolf. They rubbed shoulders and nosed affectionately. The wolf began kissing Tepsaq's face.

"She thinks that's her mother," said James, shaking his head doubtfully.

Nick had never stood this close to an uncaged wolf. He remembered his last encounter with the wolf-dog at the party in Fairbanks. The animal had planted a flying back-kick near his head.

"How did it happen?"

"Somebody shooting around here," said James. "Like they used to do when wolves had bounties. Last spring this one comes, looking lost. Tepsaq found her. She kind of adopted her. Tepsaq likes to mother things. That wolf has learned it too. So there she is. My mistake."

The yearling wolf stood a half shoulder behind the sturdy black mountain dog, head now up, ears cocked forward. White patches accentuated each eye. She was lean, muscular, already taller than her adopted mother. No wolf-dog mix. A full-blooded wolf.

A wolf raised by a dog in a dog yard!

What must she think?

Did she think she's a dog too?

Nick remembered what George the dog trainer had said about wolves at the party. By their nature, wolves run from humans. But this wolf didn't run. She stood her ground beside Tepsaq. She stared directly at Nick, pale blue eyes clear and cold as ice.

Nick felt absolutely no urge to call her.

"What's her name?" asked Camilla.

"She has no name."

Camilla watched entranced. To the old man, this animal belonged in the wild, not a kennel. He kept her unleashed. He kept her unnamed. But she chose to stay around, close by Tepsaq, the adopted mother.

To Camilla, she was eerily beautiful.

"So you still have your spirit master," Camilla whispered to the orphaned wolf.

James heard and said nothing.

But his eyes said, 'yes.'

A spirit master still watched that one.

A wild wolf living in James Epchook's dog yard.

That was the mistake.

16

The rubble of muddy ice stretched to the horizon. Beyond it a snowy mountain range glowed, lit by a sickly moon. Everything felt dead. No water, no surf, no birds.

Salt. All she smelled was salt.

The wolf stared beyond the grounded ice at the lonely desolation.

She lifted her nose and howled to the sky.

The call rose, hung on a high note, and died.

No wolf answered.

The paths along the riverbank petered out on these empty mud flats, the black inlet, an impassible barrier.

She shivered, turned, and retraced her steps.

She could not reach the mountains this way.

Her stomach ached. She weaved among tuffs of salt grass beside the cut bank, watching for signs of prey. Ice groaned and clattered in the distance. The dog trail quit at the dangerous channels, a treacherous confusion of floating ice and roaring beasts.

She came to the oily path.

She had encountered many.

It blocked her passage again, hard beneath her feet. It repelled her. She crouched at the edge, nervously watching. The beasts roared upon them. Large. Fast. Horrific. She hid by day because of them. Traveled only at night, cautiously. Even so, they would find her, charge with sudden blasts of sound and light. They claimed the oily paths.

She kept away from them, took the smaller trails, and waited, concealed, listening. She did this now. Nothing moved. All dark. Silent. With a surge of will, she scurried across and ducked into brush.

She panted from the effort.

A hare!

She smelled it, hidden in the patch. Her insides cried.

It bolted!

She leaped and caught hind legs. A flick snapped its neck. She dropped beside it, licked warm blood from the punctures, momentarily placated.

Brush rustled.

A coyote!

They shadowed her. Wherever she went, coyotes trailed. The paths carried their reek, their signs scattered everywhere.

Specks of light shined from the brush.

She leaped at the eyes.

The coyote dodged and vanished.

Brush cracked behind her. She spun. A coyote snatched the dead hare and bolted up the bank.

She tore in pursuit.

Atop the bank, the coyote ran along the oily path, hare in its mouth, legs flopping. It turned its head, saw the danger, and galloped.

She bore down, hot with anger.

The coyote swerved, this way, that, skidding on ice, never dropped the hare.

The brushy edge vanished.

Winds buffeted.

Water rushed beneath.

She faltered, dangerously exposed.

The coyote sprinted, widening the gap between them.

She charged again. Slipped on ice. Found her feet. Ran savagely.

All at once, it roared.

Black shadows exploded with blinding light.

A beast!
She leaped.
Wind blew past.
With a rough splash, she rolled.
The roar faded into darkness.
She scrambled from the muddy fall to the foot of the dark bank, trembling. The beast was gone. The coyote too. The terror faded. Water sounded.
Behind her!
She carefully reconnoitered. A half-frozen marsh surrounded her. Icy water crackled at her rear. Somehow the water was behind.
Hateful coyotes!
Lights twinkled far ahead.
Places with people and dogs.
She searched the new spot carefully. The terrain fell into order. She understood. The oily path crossed the channel. It crossed the marsh toward the twinkling lights.
A snowy range gleamed beneath the moon.
She sniffed the air.
Nothing was right.
She longed for home. It ached within her.
She turned toward the white mountains, the one familiar thing, and cautiously took the oily path.
The twinkling lights grew near.

* * *

Fifteen below and a brisk wind off the Alaska Range.
Joel Haggarty figured he was earning his money today.
He explored the Susitna Flats plying his special trade, outsmarting wolves. Snow squealed under his heavy sled. He put the Renegade into an idling putter, got off, and surveyed the natural glade. This was the best spot yet. Thick brush surrounded a small clearing on three sides, just off the main dog trail to Rainy Pass west of Wasilla.
This was where he'd make it.
The trap.
For the runner.

He began by laying the bait, a substantially mangled moose, courtesy of the Alaska state troopers. Yesterday's train had killed the unfortunate beast as it walked the snow-free tracks of the Alaska Railroad toward Talkeetna. Dozens died this way each winter. The troopers distributed them to needy families and nonprofits. Alaskans hated to waste a good moose. This one got dragged beneath a coupler for the quarter mile it took the train to stop. The troopers were happy to give the bloody mess to Haggarty.

The runner seemed stuck in the Palmer-Wasilla area. Erratic radio transmissions and a smattering of sightings established her general location. Of course the Matanuska-Susitna drainages had wolves, but the local packs normally kept clear of the towns. Haggarty figured the runner was having trouble navigating the highway strip. This bush wolf had never seen paved roads or highway traffic. She must be frightened silly. A semi-truck might even finish her, a quick solution at sixty-five miles per hour. The wolf had been bogged down a week. It was long enough to draw Haggarty to the Mat-Su.

He tied a rope to the carcass and ran it out to a stout spruce. The Renegade eased forward. Held by the rope, the moose slipped off the sled near the clearing's center. He parked about one hundred feet off. No drips of fuel or oil should spoil the trap. He donned his special gloves, cotton boiled in river water and spruce tips to remove commercial odors. He walked back to the clearing with a bundle of snares, similarly boiled.

The wolf had finally found a way to cross the Knik and Matanuska rivers, Haggarty guessed. They had proved formidable barriers. The rivers were wide and braided where they entered the tidal flats of Cook Inlet. She'd been running on the south side of the Knik River, traveling from the mudflats to the glacier, based on the radio transmissions. Somehow she'd got across.

The brush around the clearing had narrow openings made by snowshoe hares. Small round pellets littered the narrow paths. He untangled a snare at an opening.

Carefully, he hammered a stake into the frozen ground, ran a cable along a branch of the bush, and secured it with plastic electrician ties. He carefully spread the loop around the opening so it hung partially hidden within the brush, one edge of the loop resting on the ground. With a spruce branch, he brushed snow over that part of the flexible cable. Backing out, he brushed away signs of his presence with the same branch. The first snare was set. A wolf pushing through that rabbit path would shove a head through the loop, catch the shoulders, and draw the snare tight. The woody brush would absorb energy from the wolf's thrashing while the stake kept the snare anchored. Haggarty moved to the next opening and began the process again.

Last night a woman in a panic called Fish and Game. A few crazies raised llamas in the Mat-Su Valley. Haggarty never understood the attraction. The animals were like persnickety children. The llama lady was frantic. A wolf had vaulted into the fenced yard. But a spitting llama and broom-swinging owner proved too much for the intruder. It escaped the same way.

The wolf had a radio collar.

That confirmed it. The runner had crossed the rivers.

Haggarty brushed snow around the second snare, moved a few paces, and began to set the third. Before selecting this site, Haggarty had studied the maps. He talked to local off-road enthusiasts. He phoned a dog driver he knew in Wasilla. Then he called the troopers for his mangled moose.

A buddy loaned him the Renegade and sled. He considered it an honor. Haggarty, the famous trapper, used his equipment for the mission.

Of course, his buddy knew about the runner. Everybody did. The wolf had become famous too. She was the talk of town, the buzz of texts and radio chat, the fugitive wolf that eluded Fish and Game.

As predicted, the wolf lovers adopted her, their newest poster child. They took her side. The Sierra Club, joined by the Alaska Outdoor Council, expressed concern about dog lice infecting Alaska's wolf populations. They called for the runner's recapture and cure. They differed about what should happen next. The Outdoor Council said to ship the rogue back to the Kenai. The Sierra Club disagreed. They opposed the relocation program.

Alaskans followed the story closely. They read updates on private posts and Dispatch News. Many rooted for the wolf, the 'underdog' so to speak, the rebel fugitive from government. Others oiled their guns. Fish and Game issued advisories about firearm safety and hunting restrictions near populated areas. Vigilantes had already shot several loose dogs in the Mat-Su area, thinking they had stopped the runaway wolf.

Haggarty moved to the next opening and unrolled a snare. The runner might get killed in the frenzy. But more likely not. The Mat-Su was big and empty, more country than people. And this wolf was smart. Based on her previous behavior, Haggarty guessed that the runner would keep close to established dog trails and avoid human settlements. He believed the wolf was working her way toward the Alaska Range given these constraints. She had successfully avoided Anchorage. She had bogged down a bit around Palmer and Wasilla, blocked by the rivers, roads, and subdivisions. But if she got through that madness, Haggarty figured she'd head across the Susitna Flats for the mountains. She'd find a doggy trail that went that direction.

That's where Haggarty worked today. He set his snares near a major dog trail heading northwest toward the Alaska Range. About fifteen miles from the last road, he placed it off the trail where dogs would not likely venture. He was almost to the Susitna River where it flowed south into Cook Inlet. That river would pose another barrier for the wolf. The wolf would likely turn along the riverbank as she had with the Knik River. She might travel until she found the dog trail with its crossing. That's what Haggarty would do if he were a wolf. So that's where he placed the baited trap.

She would be tired. She would be hungry.

But would she be careless?

Haggarty stood and stretched. He moved to the next opening in the brush and untangled another line. He whistled a tune and pounded the stake for snare number six.

Twelve more to go.

* * *

The wind brought her the smell.

A dead moose. Food.

She turned from the river's edge, drawn by the scent.

She was famished.

The she wolf saw the ravens next. They rose and fell into heavy brush. Overcast hid the moon and stars. Nothing showed clearly in the dim flat light.

She approached, flitting between concealments. Finally she had left the horrible lights and noxious paths of the roaring beasts. No coyotes trailed her. The silence had calmed and restored her senses. She followed paths that smelled of dogs and lead toward the mountains. She had crossed one river, come to another. Finally food.

She moved slowly, investigating.

Beneath the scent, something felt wrong.

Circling, she discovered an opening into a brush-lined clearing where the ravens gathered, the moose within it. The ravens hopped on the carcass unmolested, squabbling as they fed. Her stomach clenched. Her jaws dripped. She circled suspiciously.

Scents stopped her. The sweetness of broken spruce. And a rank burning in churned snow. She pushed her nose into both. Warnings. She walked cautiously, nose to the ground, following slight disturbances in the snow. She paused, scanned for signs of danger. Nothing moved or sounded except the feeding ravens. Several saw her. They launched to nearby trees, swayed on air, cawing protests.

She didn't trust ravens.

A trail smelled of hares. She took it. Littered with droppings. It pushed toward an opening in the brush.

Abruptly droppings vanished. The fragrance of broken spruce appeared. The changes stopped her. She searched the transition carefully. It was the same spruce smell beside the rank burning in the broken snow. She peered into the dark tunnel made by the hares and sensed the danger. She edged aside, circling again.

Her insides cramped. She had to eat.

Carefully placing each step, she arrived again at the main opening. Here the snow was packed and scoured like the dog trails she followed. Just beyond lay the moose. Ravens jumped skyward in angry squawks, relinquishing their find to the intruder.

Food, steps away!

Trembling with fear and hunger, the wolf stepped away from the scoured path, pulled by the food, inching into the clearing. No spruce smells. A remnant touch of burnt metal. She didn't like it. But she was famished.

She arrived. Her nose touched the belly, torn and bloody. Lingering odors no longer mattered. She ripped into the frozen flesh and gorged, filling her body's need.

She was nearly sated when she heard the ravens' raucous shouts.

Look out!

She jerked around.

Her bloody lips curled back in a snarl.

Outside the clearing a pair of wolves crept toward her, canines uncovered, shoulders bunched. Beyond them, other wolves circled and positioned. Strangers. She set her haunches against the stomach of the moose.

They attacked.

She lunged.

Her teeth found a muzzle and ferociously bit. The wolf yelped, jerked aside. A wolf hit her shoulder. She rolled, heaved herself free. The attacker flew into brush. In the recoil, she hit the moose heavily. Her attacker whirled. A snarl turned into a high-pitched scream. The wolf jerked completely around, tail whipping the air.

Another howl sounded. The other wolf squealed with panic. It thrashed with something in the brush.

More wolves charged the clearing. The she wolf saw them coming. She launched directly at one. They locked chests and rolled, tumbling free of the clearing. Shrieks sounded behind them. More screams.

The she wolf shook off, bolting toward the river.

No one chased.

Howls and shrieks rose behind her.

She stopped at the trees and risked a backward look.

Wolves thrashed and screamed around the moose. They howled in strangled, high-pitched squeals. Others rushed about in panic or escaped into the dark.

Ravens beat the air, screeching madness.

Hideous!

She fled the terror.

17

Nick replenished the hot kettle.

Camilla rinsed her soapy hair above the kitchen sink. She ladled the last of the hot water with an enameled measuring cup dented from years of use. She dripped everywhere. A wet tank top clung to her lean torso. After more noisy pours, she emerged from the kitchen, a towel wrapped around her head.

"That felt so good!" she proclaimed, dabbing at drips down her neck.

Short-cropped hair.

Practical, Nick supposed. She probably didn't need to wash it often. Some girls in the dorms shampooed daily. Their washing obsessions seemed silly. He did his about once a week, usually when he steamed. But oft-washed hair did smell good. Roses. Lilac. Coconut.

Camilla flopped on the saggy sofa, closed her eyes, and smiled contentedly.

"This feels so good," she repeated.

"Clean hair?" said Nick.

"No headache."

The pressure lamps pulsed slightly, breathing life in the cozy space. Nick watched Camilla relax, smile lines etched about her closed eyes. When he first met her, he mistook her for a boy. But the full lashes gave her away, and the lips. With her hair nearly hidden beneath a towel, she resembled an exotic manikin, long neck, angular jawline, sunken cheeks, a small scar on her chin. No wonder the Yup'ik ladies wanted to feed her.

"How are things in Togiak?" asked Camilla, eyes still closed. "How's Lydia?"

Nick balked. He hadn't prepared for this question. Of course, he should have. Camilla was catching up on news. Nick had met Lydia in Togiak the last time they worked together, a fish camp nymph who briefly captivated him. Then everything blew to hell. Nick thought of Lydia often, a disconcerting presence at night. He had made no effort to contact her. The memories were too disturbing. She hadn't contacted him either. Togiak and Fairbanks were worlds apart.

"I don't know."

"You haven't talked to her at all?" Camilla cracked her eyes to examine Nick's face.

"No."

"Did you tell your grandmother about her?"

Lydia and Nick's families might be connected, if rumors at Togiak proved true. But he hadn't told her. Nick was keeping his grandmother clear of the trouble with Lydia. He might regret this later, especially if his grandmother died before explaining family histories to him.

"That whole thing... it was a mistake," said Nick uncomfortably.

Camilla closed her eyes, laced her fingers across the wet top.

"I'm the expert of mistakes," she said.

Nick relaxed. She was sparing him, redirecting the conversation. She referred to her own big mistake... the surrogate pregnancy. In Togiak she revealed it. She carried and bore a baby for another couple. It completely messed her up. The migraines began soon after, probably a result of the pregnancy. He knew little else.

"How's that going?" inquired Nick carefully.

"Bad," said Camilla simply.

Nick waited. She said no more.

He stared out the window at large flakes falling over caches in the yard. Alaska Weather had forecast snow for the middle Kuskokwim. The caches lost their shapes. They became vague blobs at the forest edge. A winter separated Nick and Lydia from the mishaps in Togiak. A winter could erase a lot of mistakes.

He chuckled.

"What's funny?" asked Camilla, opening an eye and adjusting the towel. "My headdress?"

"No," said Nick, gesturing out the window. "The buried sheds."

"Why's that funny?"

"Bethel... a girl I once knew in Bethel. We worked on a project together, my first year at college."

"Tell me," smiled Camilla.

"A project about Eskimo kinship. I stayed with friends in Bethel. She rented this dinky house, the perfect place to work, she said, a big lot near the center of town, surrounded by piles of snow, just like that."

"Piles of snow."

"Yeah, and I wondered, why is that house empty, the place she rented? It was a nice little house on a big lot. She made paths over and around the snow humps to get in and out. I kept wondering, why's that place empty? Especially Bethel, houses get filled by somebody."

Nick chuckled again.

"Yeah?" said Camilla, smiling to hear Nick laugh.

"It got warm. The snow began to melt. We found out why. The lot was an old dog yard. The house was surrounded by dog shit! Hills of frozen shit! The guy had never cleaned up, years of shit, shoveled into mountains."

Camilla hid her mouth.

"It thawed into a swamp. She couldn't get out. I got pallets from the store and made a path over to the house so she could balance over the shit pools. God, did that place stink! You couldn't eat there without gagging."

"Did she move?"

"No! Her boyfriend showed up. He was like a greenie from Santa Barbara, wire-rims, ponytail, vegan. He loved it! Put on chest waders, jumped in with a shovel, making channels, directing runoff, happy for days! 'I'm restoring the wetlands!' he said shoveling shit.

"That's why the house was empty. It could only rent in winter. The owner never said what was underneath the snow. That's what I call a real snow job!"

Nick laughed at his cleverness.

Camilla groaned, joined him laughing, and removed the wet towel from her head, pinning it to a line above the hot stove. Then to Nick's astonishment, she pulled off the wet tank top and pinned it too, standing before him in a small black bra, her skin the color of milk.

"Just a second," she laughed.

She disappeared into the bedroom. Nick had just recovered his breath when she emerged, dressed in a baggy sweatshirt.

"I'm making tea. Want some?"

"Sure," said Nick, his face red.

He sat in silence while she worked in the kitchen.

What was Camilla thinking, or not thinking, pulling off her top in front of him? Was this how girls from Berkeley did things?

Camilla reappeared with hot mugs. She sat again on the broken sofa, he at the small table. The snow fell outside, much more than a dusting. The caches disappeared behind veils of white.

"So what should I do, Nick?" said Camilla.

"What?"

He was still imagining the black bra.

"They won't even let me see her."

"Who?"

"Kaylin."

"Who's Kaylin?"

"My baby. That's her name, her first name. On the second birth certificate she's named Cassandra. That's okay. I like Cassandra, even Cassie. Kaylin's better. Kaylin Cleary is her real name. That's how I think of her. Slender and fair... that's what Kaylin means."

Camilla's mood had shifted again. She spoke matter-of-fact, like a friend might talk. This felt odd to Nick. He'd little experience discussing personal things with Camilla, or with many women. In Yup'ik villages it seemed as if subcultures existed side-by-side, male and female. Girls talked with girls, guys talked with guys. Traditionally, single men even lived separately, sleeping together in the gasgiq, the men's house, set apart from women. Nick observed that university housing sort of worked that way too. But Camilla spoke like a friend. At Togiak, she said they were partners. Here, she just stood before him in a frilly black bra like nothing had happened. Now she asked him about her lost baby, something he knew nothing about.

She was a puzzle, unlike anybody he'd known.

"Who won't let you see her?" asked Nick, forcing his thoughts to the question.

"Everett and Brenda Schofield. I think Everett's doing it. I haven't seen Brenda since the delivery. He stole Kaylin from me at the hospital. I get nightmares about that. Footsteps… and I can't run. He got an injunction against me. I've never seen her since then. I don't even know where she is."

Camilla's face began to weaken.

"How can they do that?"

"The contract," said Camilla, brushing teary eyes. "I've got two lawyers. They say the courts treat surrogacies like business contracts. They're not like adoptions where the biological mother and the child's welfare get equal consideration. It doesn't matter if the mother changes her mind, just what's in the fucking contract."

Camilla couldn't see her own daughter? The Schofields claimed an exclusive relationship? Perverse, thought Nick. Yup'ik adoptions didn't work that way. Adoptions among Yup'iks were common and flexible. Adopted children gained dual sets of parents, the new ones who raised them and the old set who gave birth, both recognized in the community. A person couldn't have too many relatives. More help in times of need.

"Who wrote it?"

"The fertility clinic. I was dealing with Brenda. She begged me for help. She couldn't give Everett an heir, his own child. I felt sorry for her. Really, I did it for her. But she's dropped from the picture. The only one I deal with now is the asshole Everett."

"An heir? For property?"

"He's old and he's rich."

"Oh," said Nick. "She was too old to have a kid?"

"No, she's young. But she got irradiated to treat Hodgkin's. It ruined her ovaries. She was desperate. Really, I did it for her."

"Was he going to dump her?"

"Maybe. She was wife number four. You know, half his age. Arm candy. But I liked her. I was trying to help her. I was an idiot."

Camilla dug into her backpack for a folder, extracted a stapled sheath of papers, and passed it to Nick.

"The contract. I hate to touch it."

"You carry it around?"

"My lawyers meet with the judge next week in San Francisco. Judge Zimmerman. He's a family guy, they said. They hope he'll treat it like a contested adoption. I won't sign away the birth certificate."

She pulled out more.

Nick looked at two California birth certificates, 'Kaylin Cleary' on one, 'Cassandra Mills Schofield' the other. On the first, 'Camilla Mac Cleary' was named the mother, on the second, 'Brenda Schofield.' Nick shook his head. In some ways this resembled his own murky past. Who was Nick's mother? Was it the drowned teenager buried at the fish camp miles from his home, the grandmother who raised him, or somebody else?

"I won't sign off to make it legal," said Camilla. "But that's not enough. I saw it in my lawyers' faces. I don't know what to do."

Nick handed the papers back.

"You read them," said Camilla, pushing them to him. "Maybe you can think of something."

Nick looked at the thick papers in his hands, astonished. He knew nothing about surrogate contracts. What could he think of that two lawyers hadn't?

"I just don't know what to do," said Camilla again. "I wish I could see her, even just once."

A tear ran down her cheek.

She stared at the falling snow and whispered.

"Maybe that would be enough."

* * *

Interviews with Frances Egnaty took the morning. They worked hard, Camilla recording and questioning, Nick translating, and Frances providing answers. Through this collaboration, the economic circumstances of life on the middle Kuskokwim River emerged in greater detail.

The last decade had been filled with pain for Frances. A stroke claimed her husband, the family's main subsistence provider. With her son permanently removed in Oregon, Frances assumed the central economic role for her extended family of two daughters and grandchildren. She fished. She gathered. She processed foods. Frances couldn't hunt, but others in the village gave her moose, caribou, birds, and small game. Her arthritic knee progressively worsened. Walking and working became painful ordeals. Nevertheless, she worked. And she enjoyed the work. To Camilla, her attitude was remarkably positive right up to the operation.

"They say, why don't you just sit?" laughed Frances, speaking to Nick in Yup'ik, who translated to Camilla. "But when I sit, I think of all the things I could be doing. I'm not a good sitter."

"You sit still in winter, don't you?" suggested Camilla.

"Oh, yes," she laughed. "I sit when we manaq, go ice fishing. We jig for lush. Really fat livers! Whitefish. Those trouts. We sit on the ice, jigging, sometimes all day."

Frances sighed happily, thinking of the old pleasures, sitting on hard ice in subzero weather with friends, catching fish. Frances remembered something else. She pointed to a table in a corner of her living room, covered with scraps of cloth and fur. The workspace had pieces of beaver, marten, fox, wolf, and wolverine, even swatches of spotted seal traded from the coast. Camilla felt the tanned moose leather, soft and sweet with smoke.

"I sit when I sew," laughed Frances. "I make hats, mitts, little baby things. Boots. Eskimo yo-yos."

"You sell them?" asked Nick.

"Sometimes I just give."

"How do you get the furs?" asked Camilla.

"From people. The trappers. Or I trade for them."

Camilla lifted a pair of thick gray mitts joined by a colorful cotton cord.

"What kind is this?"

"Marmot," Frances smiled. "Parka squirrel inside."

"Those are worth a lot," said Nick. "A collector would pay a lot for marmot mitts. Nobody makes them anymore."

"Who are they for?" asked Camilla.

"I don't know," shrugged Frances. "Somebody will want them."

"Have you been able to sew since the operation?" asked Camilla.

"Not in Anchorage," said Frances in Yup'ik. "I didn't have anything in that place. My knee hurt so badly, the bad one I had to walk on. I couldn't concentrate."

"You lost two years of sewing?" asked Nick.

"Two years, maybe a little more."

Later that afternoon, Camilla sat quietly at the table of the small cabin, working over the morning's notes. Nick made strong coffee. He found no drip equipment or percolators in the house supplies, so he poured hot water directly over the grounds in an old enameled coffee pot. Nick liked it this way anyway. Camilla didn't complain.

She had not developed a headache. Miraculous, she said, rapping the table for good luck. It was the broken couch, Nick joked. He'd won the toss when they dragged the coin from beneath the bed to satisfy the Chinaman. Camilla slept beneath French windows. Nick fell asleep in the musty bedroom, thinking of Camilla in the next room. He woke with a stuffed nose, smelling pancakes. Camilla remembered he liked them.

"She's given things," muttered Camilla, half to herself, toting up the list of wild resources that Frances Egnaty used over the past several years.

"That happens a lot with elders," said Nick. "People just give to elders."

"I was originally going to document the foods she catches and calculate the loss for two years. But she's given as much as she harvests herself."

"Look at the storage space," Nick gestured to the caches outside the window. It turned out that this tiny cabin was a repository for food.

"She gets it raw, uncut, unfinished," said Camilla. "She does processing, drying, smoking, fermenting. Finished products get redistributed. She's a node in a village production network. Raw goods come in, finished products go out. She doesn't eat or use most of what she works on. Others do. Other people benefit from her activities beyond her immediate family. She processes thousands of pounds of wild foods each year. Look, three moose the year before the first operation. That's over fifteen hundred pounds of moose meat alone."

"Yeah," said Nick. He knew old people like Frances Egnaty. "That's not uncommon."

"Isn't that exploiting the elderly?" said Camilla, half in jest.

Nick shrugged. Some young people were lazy. So were some old people. In every village there were always hard workers like Frances Egnaty. Traditional foods got harvested and processed and distributed through them.

"She likes it. She gets bored doing nothing."

"Even with bad knees she's out on the ice, fishing. Or going to fish camp to set a net and cut salmon with her daughters. Or gathering plants, like these medicinal roots she talked about."

"Elders are tough," said Nick. "They've already survived hard times. My grandmother's like that. When I go back home, I know I'll be working. She lets me know what needs doing. Her stuff gets used by my aunt's family and lots of others."

"So we have to calculate this differently than I originally planned," said Camilla. "It's not just what she harvests herself. It's the value of all the food and products that she touches, the goods that pass through her. It wouldn't happen without her."

"Well," said Nick uncomfortably. "It might happen without her, but by other people. Somebody else might be doing it, you know, because she's not."

"Of course, that happens eventually," said Camilla. "But her absence was unexpected. It happened suddenly. So it's justified treating shortfalls as due to the operation. We can calculate what those are."

"Uh huh," agreed Nick.

"And what about the transmission of culture that has been interrupted?" said Camilla. "Her grandchildren can't learn how to catch and process fish in Anchorage. They're deprived of the opportunity to learn traditions because the fish camp is idled. How long does it take for a family to lose cultural traditions? In my experience, it can happen quickly. A single generation is all it takes. If the transmission is interrupted, traditions can be lost quickly, a language, the knowledge of where to put a net, the tastes for certain kinds of food. Those losses can extend beyond the years of interruption. The cultural losses can be permanent."

Nick knew this to be true. He had witnessed this in his own area. People stopped speaking Yup'ik to their kids. They used English only. Nick was bilingual because his grandmother spoke Yup'ik at home. But many families didn't. In some villages, the language had been lost. But it took two generations, not one. The oldest generation spoke Yup'ik with some English, the second generation was fairly bilingual, but the third generation spoke English only. He knew families where the grandchildren could not communicate with the grandparents. The oldest generation couldn't teach the youngest, at least with words.

"How do you put a dollar value on that?" asked Nick.

"I don't know. Those kind of losses are almost incalculable. It's like me asking you, 'how much money will you take to never smoke salmon again, plus, no one in the village would smoke salmon again?'"

"I would never make that deal. You couldn't pay me enough."

"Exactly. But the operation forced her family into this situation. It wasn't a voluntary choice for them to lose the fish camp. As voluntary compensation, it would have cost a lot to buy the cultural practice from them."

"Nobody would sell their culture like that," said Nick.

But as he considered it, he knew it wasn't true. People did it all the time. Buying frozen chicken instead of going moose hunting. Ordering a synthetic jacket from a catalog instead of making a sealskin parka. Leaving for college instead of staying at home.

And they sold out cheaply.

Him included.

"Of course, nobody does it that way," agreed Camilla. "But what would it take to pay you off? A million? Two million? I think the hypothetical exercise gets at a more accurate evaluation of the importance of smoked salmon to a Yup'ik than the price of a fast food hamburger in Anchorage, which is what those grandchildren are getting. And the food substitutes increase their health risks for heart disease and diabetes and other nasty things."

Nick watched Camilla working her notes, filled with ideas about calculating losses for the Egnaty family after the operation. She took the task seriously. He admired her for that. She caught him staring.

"What?" asked Camilla.

He lifted his cup.

"This coffee isn't traditional," joked Nick. "You know the Yup'ik word for it? Kuuvviaq."

"Really? Coffeeaq?"

"Yeah, spelled kuuvviaq. When we say, 'have some coffee!' we say, kuuvviaraa! And this old coffee pot is kuuvviarcuun. The word came along with the coffee, a loan that Yup'ik made into its own. Kuuvviialiuq... 'he's making coffee!'"

"I'm glad he did."

She flashed him a smile.

Nick decided there was a lot to like about Camilla.

18

The Piper Cub landed at the Farewell strip just before dusk. A tall figure in cold weather gear stepped out and strode toward a second plane waiting at the end of the runway. A fierce north wind swept the strip into a band of pure white. The Piper Cub immediately taxied and took off, shuddering in the broadside blast of wind.

"Evening, Chet," declared Joel Haggarty, the new arrival, throwing down heavy duffels and a daypack by the plane's ski.

"Howdy, Joel."

"Waiting long?"

"My first cigarette."

"Good," Haggarty nodded.

"My place tonight?" asked Chet Miller.

"Sounds good, if you'll have me."

"You're always welcome. Big duffels."

"Refreshments."

"I'll stuff them in back."

"Careful with the daypack. Put it on top. It's the receiver."

"Receiver? Another receiver?"

"Yeah, but this one's Fish and Game. They want it back in one piece."

"Okay," said Chet doubtfully. "What's it for?"

"To track that runner. You hear about her, the runner wolf?"

"Who hasn't?" said Chet, stuffing the heavy duffels and the receiver into the rear storage compartment, twisting tight the latch. "They talk about her at Stony."

"It's on loan to track her. Got me a real job."

"No shit?" laughed Chet. "They're finally going to pay you to kill wolves?"

"Nope," said Haggarty, lighting a cigarette in the growing dusk, shielding the flick of the butane lighter from the stiff breeze. "They're paying us to catch her."

"Us? Am I part of this?"

"If you want. I need a pilot."

Chet Miller frowned.

"Shit, Fish and Game..."

"Yeah, I know."

Chet lit one too.

They smoked in silence in the lee of the plane.

"Sounds a bit dangerous," grumbled Chet.

"We'll be discrete."

"State equipment in the plane."

"We can hide the other stuff."

"I don't know. Fish and Game." Chet shook his head skeptically.

"I can get Hal Martin. Don't worry about it."

They smoked some more, blowing into the whistling wind.

"Well, okay. I guess so. But what's the deal?"

"If we go after her, we wait 'til she comes through the pass. She'll head for her den."

"Which den?"

"Big River."

"We don't know where that is. Nobody knows where that is."

"I said 'if' we go after her. I don't know, I'm thinking to just let her run. She's something. She's got spunk."

"Shit, when have you cared about that?"

"Real spunk. I nearly had her. I got half the Lower Su pack and a pecker-full of trouble for it, but she escaped."

"How you know that?"

"Rigged me a flash. Got a series."

Haggarty reached into a pocket and pulled out his cell. He tilted to avoid the glare of the fading sun and called up the images.

"There she is, clear as day."

"Jesus, look at the teeth! And eyes!"

"That's from the flash."

"There's the collar," declared Chet, pointing at a dark hump on the wolf's neck.

"Yep, that's her. I got half the damn pack, but not her. She's something."

"They say she's full of lice."

"Naw... probably not."

"They say she could ruin everything, one lousy wolf."

"Now who cares?" joked Haggarty.

Chet said nothing, smoking sullenly.

"Less wolves around here if that happens, more moose," said Haggarty. "But I said 'if'... if we go after her and if we find that Big River den. I'd like to do that."

He admired his picture of the runner.

"How? Nobody knows where that den is."

"A Judas goat."

"What?"

"You don't know about Judas goats?"

"No goats around here."

"In a slaughterhouse, that's what they call the goat that brings the sheep to slaughter. You know about Judas... the betrayer."

"Judas goat?"

"To help us find that Big River den."

Chet smoked. Mulled it over. He didn't look happy.

"But, you know, there's our other things," said Haggarty.

"Yeah," said Chet, tossing his butt.

"First priorities come first. We'll work it in, and only if we want to."

"You had me worried there a bit," said Chet, laughing nervously.

"Well don't," said Haggarty, moving for the cockpit. "Business first. Fish and Game don't pay enough."

"Hey," said Chet lightly, "the other talk is the wolf howlers."

"Wolf howlers?"

"The greenies. They're sending somebody over to catch the runner. Somebody called the Stony River council to let them know he's coming over to catch the wolf."

"Who's calling?"

"Hell, I don't know. Somebody named, uh... Sturgis."

Haggarty pivoted like he misheard.

"You know him?" asked Chet.

"Geoff Sturgis," growled Haggarty.

Abruptly, he smiled.

"That's good," nodded Haggarty, hauling into the plane. "Me and him were just having our first real conversation at the Hilton and got interrupted. I'll be glad to see that guy again."

"Yeah?"

"Me and him have got some unfinished business."

* * *

With sputters and belches of black exhaust, Nick maneuvered the Skandic to the cabin's front door. Camilla came out without a jacket. She'd seen him through the French windows.

"Let's go!" laughed Nick.

He patted the leather seat behind him. It was a large, powerful snowmachine with plenty of room.

"Where'd you get that?" shouted Camilla above the loud idle. Nick flicked it off. The air reeked of fumes.

"Epchook," laughed Nick. "His son's. Two years old and hardly used. He's been gone."

"Why do you have it?"

"Because he likes me. Get on something warm. We have to break it in for him!"

Camilla threw on several layers beneath her borrowed parka. Still she felt the cold, clinging to Nick's middle as they flew along the river. Nick drove like a seasoned maniac, hitting speeds near seventy on the straights.

The Kuskokwim curved in great bows. He took the curves carefully. He was an excellent driver. To Camilla, the ride was exhilarating. Now miles from town, she found only parts of her cold. The chill wind whipped her pant legs and her neck behind her goggles. Otherwise, she felt toasty. Attached to Nick, she leaned with the curves and rose with the bumps, exercising like aerobics. She'd never ridden a snowmachine before. She immediately understood the allure. It felt wild and free.

The main channel spanned less than a quarter mile. Smaller channels twisted around islands. Black spruce and birch topped tall banks. They double-backed and rode down the middle in bright sun. Nick suddenly detoured up a side channel, turning a series of curves.

"The Holitna!" he shouted.

The Holitna River joined the Kuskokwim upriver from Sleetmute. Frances Egnaty spoke of it during interviews, a substantial drainage flowing off the Alaska Range. Many Sleetmute families traced their roots to it. There used to be inland Yup'iks who hunted the mountains. Some families still lived along it. Others traveled it seasonally to trap, fish, and hunt.

Nick twisted up the course. They passed a few cabins tucked in the forest along the river's edge. Nick brought the Skandic to a standstill. He cut the engine. Large bay windows glinted with sun on a substantial log cabin. No smoke came from the stack.

"Homesteaders," pronounced Nick. His breath billowed in the cold air.

"What do you mean?" asked Camilla.

"Epchook told me about them. I wanted to check it out, a state land sale along the Holitna, 1970s. Homesteaders built cabins and lived on their parcels long enough to prove up. That's one of them."

"Homesteaders."

Camilla said it like an anachronism.

"Most of them failed, Epchook said. It's a floodplain, got flooded out. Or they ran out of money. It's hard to live out here if you're not used to it. Most are seasonals. They visit during summer."

"I wouldn't mind having that one."

"Some work as river guides."

"Huh," said Camilla.

What must villagers think of outsiders who acquired free land and guided tourists? This large cabin looked like a vacationer's dream.

Nick flicked the engine to life and turned around.

"Let's find Egnaty's fish camp!" he shouted.

Nick drove back down the Holitna, turned up the Kuskokwim, and traveled for some time. He slowed, took detours, searching for landmarks. Frances Egnaty had described her family's camp. She located it on topographic maps with other places she fished. Nick looked for features matching verbal descriptions.

To Camilla, the land presented a confusion of frozen channels and forested uplands. She couldn't interpret half of what she saw. Islands looked like main riverbanks. Snowy sloughs looked like river channels. But she knew that Nick was an experienced winter traveler, an expert on frozen rivers.

Finally, he directed the snowmachine toward an island, found a side trail, and gunned up a short steep bank. They came to a halt in a snow-covered flat among birch trees that hugged a bend in the river. A bare fish rack sat along an edge. He cut the engine and stepped off.

"Found it," he grinned.

He pulled off his gloves, reached into a side compartment, and pulled out a topographic map. Atop the cowl, his finger began a meandering trace.

"See, we went this way, then went across here. That's the place the ice was thin and we turned around there."

"What?" said Camilla, surprised to hear about thin river ice. She hadn't noticed.

"So we came this way. This island was the one we passed back there. That brought us here, where Frances has the camp. Those are the racks. Yeah, and there are the smokehouses."

The smokehouses were tucked in the woods by the clearing. Camilla smiled at him, admiring his skills. She would not have found this place so quickly. On her own, she would have driven into the river.

"It's beautiful," she said.

"Her cabin must be back there too. Let's find it."

They strolled past the racks through the grove of birch. As expected, they found a small log house near the smokehouse. The door was latched but unlocked. They pushed inside and found a fair-sized one-window room. Rough furniture of birch wood lined the walls. There was a wide frame for sleeping bags. A stove made of a converted 55-gallon oil drum sat in a corner. A squirrel had made a nest on top.

"Cozy," said Nick.

"Brrrr," said Camilla, "cozy like a freezer."

Their breaths puffed in the cold air.

"There's firewood outside. We could start a fire in there if we needed. I'll bet there's even food."

Nick checked the cabinets and found meat and beans.

"Enough for a feast."

"We can't eat their food!"

"If we had to," laughed Nick, replacing the cans.

They stepped outside, closed the door, and reset the latch. Camilla saw movement on the river. Somebody worked on the ice.

"What's that?"

"A net!" said Nick enthusiastically. "Let's check it out."

Nick restarted the Skandic. Camilla climbed behind. She felt like a biker. It was fun. Nick engaged and slipped down the bank to the river.

A line of rough poles protruded from the ice. At each end, holes had been chipped to open water. A man in canvas overalls pulled a net from one of the holes, piling it on the river ice.

Nick cut power. Camilla got off with him.

They approached the net.

"Cama-i," said Nick, pulling up his goggles to reveal his face. "Nice day."

The man said nothing. He wasn't smiling.

Late thirties, Camilla guessed. They had interrupted him pulling fish from the net set under the ice. They looked like a type of whitefish with pointy noses and a small hump. An old Polaris with a plywood sledge was parked to the side.

"Hello," said Camilla, offering her glove hand. "I'm Camilla Mac Cleary. They call me Mac."

The man looked at the hand.

After a moment, Camilla withdrew it.

"Where are you from?" the fisherman barked. His breath reeked of half-digested alcohol.

"Sleetmute," said Camilla. "I'm from California. Nick's from Fairbanks."

Nick looked past him at a distant point, saying nothing, moving nothing.

"We're friends of Frances Egnaty," said Camilla. "We visited her camp."

The man turned on Camilla.

"That's not her camp!"

"It's not?" said Camilla with surprise, backing a step.

"This isn't her place!" he shouted. He waved angrily over the river.

Nick slowly adjusted his goggles over his face. He walked back to the Skandic, mounted, and started the engine.

"I think we're going," said Camilla. "Sorry to bother you."

Under the fisherman's glare, Camilla returned to the snowmachine. She climbed behind Nick.

"What's that about?" she whispered by his ear.

"Drunk," muttered Nick. "I don't talk to drunk Indians."

He gunned the engine and shot upriver.

The incident broke the afternoon's beautiful spell. Camilla clung behind Nick, examining the awkward encounter. The man was hostile. He grew angry when she mentioned Frances Egnaty. He claimed the camp wasn't hers, or the fishing area.

Was this some sort of territorial dispute? Trespass, encroachment, or maybe an unresolved fishing claim. The fisherman took fish from a net in front of the camp. Was Frances the encroacher? Or him?

He was clearly drunk. Maybe that was the primary explanation. Nick called him an Indian. He didn't look particularly Indian to Camilla. In fact, he didn't look too different from other men she'd seen at Sleetmute. Nick said he didn't talk to drunks. After the initial greeting, Nick had completely ignored him. The behavior was chilling.

Did the fisherman live at Stony River? That was the next community up. James Epchook said relations were good between Sleetmute and Stony River. Sophie Epchook said there was considerable intermarriage, that the Yup'iks of Sleetmute looked like Indians. But this encounter suggested tensions, at least between some families. Yup'iks had pushed upriver from the coast. Was this a problem caused by that expansion? Had the Egnatys taken over a fishing area once used by Athabaskans? Or was it the reverse? Was the fisherman encroaching on the Egnaty camp left empty for two years? She should consider that in the subsistence valuation... the potential loss of land through disuse.

Nick took a long bend.

Sunlight glinted off glass. A plane on skis parked on the river at the base of a bluff. Above it, houses smoked in the cold. They had arrived at Stony River, the Athabaskan community. It was as beautiful as Sleetmute.

Instead of excitement, Camilla felt a mild apprehension. She instantly identified this as silly. A single awkward encounter with a surly fisherman shouldn't color her feelings toward an entire community.

Nick slowed as he approached the bluff. Two bulked up men moved boxes by the plane. One of them, a tall man, walked toward the Skandic. Nick stopped and lifted his goggles. The man smiled and waved a gloved hand.

"Hey, little buddy! Welcome to Stony!"

"Shit," Nick growled to himself.

"What?" whispered Camilla.

"Cama-i!" greeted Nick half-heartedly.

He cut the engine and dismounted. The tall man shook Nick's glove. He came grinning at Camilla.

"Hello there!" he held out a hand. "Joel Haggarty."

"Camilla Mac Cleary," she smiled, brushing out eyelashes bent behind the goggles. "They call me Mac."

He took her hand in his.

"Mac," joked Haggarty. "You a friend of this guy?"

Nick stood aside, already fuming, trying not to listen to Haggarty's insults. What bad luck! First the ugly drunk. He was still pissed about that. Now the asshole Haggarty. He was already boasting and putting moves on Camilla.

Nick escaped toward the plane. Its cargo sat beside the skis. Haggarty's companion waited by a wing, watching sourly. Nick nodded.

"Nick John."

"Chet Miller," the man replied stiffly.

"Nice plane," said Nick.

"Suits me," said Chet flatly.

Something was amiss here. Chet didn't want to chat. They had interrupted something. Chet threw angry glances toward Haggarty, who stood by Camilla, blathering about nothing.

Sealed boxes sat on the ice.

Nick figured it out. Booze. They were unloading boxes of alcohol. He and Camilla had interrupted an illegal booze delivery.

Bad luck.

This was his punishment for showing off to Camilla with the Skandic.

Nick turned from the cargo to the plane. Under the wing nearest his eye was an odd bracket fixed to the strut.

Only the right wing. Chet followed Nick's eyes to the bracket. Haggarty arrived. He had finished sweet-talking Camilla. She remained by the Skandic, stretching cramped muscles.

"You guys get introduced?" grinned Haggarty.

"Yep," said Chet Miller.

"What's this?" asked Nick.

He touched the sturdy bracket under the wing strut.

Chet tensed. Haggarty smiled.

"What do you think, sharp-eyes?"

"A mount," said Nick.

"That's right, a mount," agreed Haggarty easily.

"For what?" asked Nick, just as easily.

"Camera gear," said Haggarty, brushing the bracket with a finger. "Slips in there and bolts. The cable runs along there so it's controlled from the cockpit."

Nick looked and saw the cable supports.

"Aerial photographs?" asked Nick.

"Yep," said Haggarty, "for when Chet gets jobs taking pictures for the mines, or geologic surveys, whatever. He flies the transect and clicks away. Right Chet?"

Chet gave a silent nod.

Nick nodded too.

"Better go. See you guys around."

"You betcha," smiled Haggarty.

Nick felt the eyes on his back. He slowly walked to the snowmachine, an unconscious sway from side to side, the careful cadence of a hunter on slippery ice.

A mount.

Perfectly clear to Nick.

Affirmed by Haggarty.

Certainly a mount under the right wing.

But all the rest was a bald-faced lie.

19

Sophie Epchook slathered ointment on Camilla's injury. It felt cool and deadening. Camilla watched the treatment with interest. She had never suffered frostbite before. The skin of her left leg had burned to a reddish bronze. That was a good sign, Nick said. It meant her skin was still alive.

"Will it blister?" asked Camilla.

"No," said Sophie. "It's just a nip."

"Next time I'll pin my pant legs."

"Or drive slower," said Sophie, eyeing Nick.

Camilla twisted her leg to inspect. The injury formed a red stripe across the back of her calf. As she sat behind Nick a gap in her pant leg had caught air. At the speed they traveled, the wind chill was eighty or ninety below zero. Her skin had partially frozen. She hadn't noticed. She had felt nothing as her flesh crystallized, nothing beyond cold wind and numbness. When her leg warmed, the near-frozen skin burned like a scorch from a hot iron.

Sophie applied an anesthetic for sunburns.

"It's in a good place," said Nick.

"My leg is good?" Camilla posed the white smear.

"Better than your face, or your nose."

"What's wrong with those?"

"Not a thing," he laughed.

Nick felt guilty his romp on the Skandic had frostbit Camilla. But it could have been worse. He needed to remember that Camilla knew little about real cold even though she had lived with snow as a child. He should have warned her. Then again, he shouldn't have been pushing seventy on the straights.

James Epchook teased her about skinny legs. He used to be afflicted with that, he told Camilla, but his wife had cured him. He patted his large middle. It was time for his medicine, Sophie announced. Supper was ready.

The four sat around a pot of moose stew with fresh-baked bread. The food tasted wonderful after the cold ride. Nick began to sweat in short order. He watched Camilla eat large portions of everything. Why was she so lean? He saw no evidence of her recent pregnancy.

As they ate, Nick described the drunk at the whitefish net near the Egnaty fish camp. James and Sophie listened carefully. It sounded like Hosea Jimmy, guessed Sophie. He was a moody boy. Recently he lived a semi-dissolute existence between Stony River and Red Devil. He drank too much and brooded. But fishing… that was a good sign. He might be growing up.

"He said it wasn't Egnaty's camp," said Camilla.

"Everybody knows that place is where she fishes," said James. "Lots of people fish there, three or four nets in that big eddy. She lets anybody put a net there. He must be sore about something."

James Epchook described the history of the fish camp. When James was younger, the Moores from Stony River used the place with the Egnatys. The Moores had been there first. The families fished together, each with a separate fish drying rack. Frances Egnaty was related somehow to the Moores.

"Her husband's sister was married to Sam Moore senior's son," said Sophie.

"That's right," remembered James.

When Sam Moore died, his children stopped using that camp. They fished at another place just inside the mouth of Stony River. That left the camp to the Egnatys, who built a cabin and larger racks just before Frances' husband died. Frances and her daughters still fished there.

"Is Hosea Jimmy related to the Moores?" asked Camilla.

James looked to his wife.

"He's the son of one of Sam Moore's daughters," said Sophie.

That might explain the outburst, thought Camilla. He was jealous the camp had passed to the Egnatys instead of the Moores.

"So maybe he thinks he should have that fish camp because he's the grandson of Sam Moore," said Camilla.

"He should just ask Frances," said Sophie. "She would let him fish there. He's a cousin to her nieces."

"People think they own things," said James with disapproval. "That boy is sore about something. I always hear him complain about downriver hunters."

"What downriver hunters?" asked Nick.

Nick always had an interest in these kinds of issues. He remembered elders who warned about trespassing in somebody's territory, using it without asking permission. Sleetmute and Stony River sat at boundaries between cultural groups. Such conflicts might play out here.

James Epchook took more hot tea. He described the history of moose hunting along the middle Kuskokwim. In the old days, he said, families lived up the Holitna and Hoholitna rivers to trap near the mountains. People made livings selling furs. The trading posts provided grubstakes. The furs paid them off. Families hunted moose, caribou, and brown bears in the mountains. They fashioned boats from bear hides to float down to the Kuskokwim after breakup. He could show them photos of the old bear boats. The whole family floated down, sometimes with the dogs aboard. When the schools opened, families couldn't move around like that anymore. The children had to stay in town. So the men went up alone to hunt.

Commercial fishing downriver changed things. It started with salted fish at Bethel. Barrels of salted salmon got traded when the missions operated. Commercial fishing took off after that. Suddenly the Yup'iks of the lower river had money. They bought bigger boat motors and started traveling farther upriver to hunt, three or four drums of fuel in a boat. They hunted the Holitna and Hoholitna. He knew these families. He traded with them for seal oil when they showed up looking for a moose.

"What do people say about that?" asked Camilla.

"I always tell them, no one owns the moose," said James. "They have families to feed like us. We always share. But you know, it got hard to find them. I used to get two moose in a week after salmon fishing. Then it took two weeks. Then three weeks. Then it was one moose in three weeks. I had to go way off the river. One year, I couldn't find any."

"Because of the sport hunters," said Sophie, recalling the moose-less years.

Sport hunters arrived too, said James. They hunted near Farewell until it got too crowded, then started flying to the headwaters of other rivers. They discovered the Holitna and Hoholitna. Outfitters dropped them off and the sport hunters floated down. It began with one or two Zodiacs, then became dozens. Charters picked them up at the village strip. That's when moose became hard to find.

"All that waste," said Sophie.

"What waste?" said Nick.

"They get a moose early on the float," said James. "They put the meat in plastic sacks, leave behind the head, the legs, all the bones, things we use. Never the antlers. They always keep the antlers. They float five or six more days. It gets hot in September. The meat cooks in the sacks. Turns green."

"What happens to it?" asked Nick.

"They try to give it away at the strip, but it's spoiled," said Sophie. "That's when the moose left."

Waste drove away animals.

Nick had always been taught that. He imagined how Sophie felt, opening sacks of putrid meat.

"Stony River too?" asked Camilla. "Have they had a hard time with outsiders?"

"Yes, Stony River too," said James.

"Maybe that explains why Hosea Jimmy yelled at us," said Camilla. "We're outsiders."

Nick understood her point, but said nothing. Hosea Jimmy was rude to treat them that way. A real person greeted strangers with hospitality. You shared, even meager stores. The more you shared the more everyone had. The fisherman was drunk. Booze had damaged his judgment, booze like that being delivered in unmarked boxes beside Chet Miller's plane. Hosea Jimmy was responsible for his bad choices. But bootleggers helped.

Crystalline snow crunched like brittle twigs as they walked the snowy path to their tiny cabin. Low overcast from the west hid the stars. Alaska Weather forecasted fog, James told them. Fog sometimes appeared this time of year. It made it difficult for bush pilots to land. Sometimes the fog cut them off for days.

A shadow flitted along the path, bouncing to their side.

"Tepsaq!" said Camilla.

Camilla petted and praised her.

Tepsaq looked pleased. But she was most interested in Nick's parka. Nick reached into a deep pocket and found a chunk of dried seal meat. He threw it to the snow. Tepsaq took it a few paces and began gnawing.

"Don't tell Epchook I'm spoiling his dog."

"Look," whispered Camilla.

Another shadow appeared.

The adopted wolf emerged from the brush behind Tepsaq. Epchook's mistake. Ears cupped forward, she listened to Tepsaq's sloppy chewing.

"She doesn't know whether to come," whispered Camilla.

"What's that in her mouth?" asked Nick.

"Oh, her sock baby!" laughed Camilla, delighted to see it. "Sophie told me about them. She wants to mother things, like Tepsaq. She once adopted a family of voles. Sophie stuffed her some sock toys. She carries and puts them places."

"She mothers voles?" exclaimed Nick.

Voles and sock babies.

This was a mixed-up wolf.

The wolf stared with blue eyes.

Nick found more seal meat. He tossed it to the snow.

The wolf put down the sock, looked at the meat, but didn't move. Nick stepped backwards. Camilla did likewise. After a fair distance, the wolf approached the meat. Without a look at Nick or Camilla, she took the meat and vanished into the dark. She immediately reappeared, grabbed the sock, and disappeared a second time. Tepsaq continued to gnaw hers in the track.

"Not entirely like her mom, I guess," said Camilla.

"Because that's not really mom," said Nick.

"She's beautiful."

Nick said nothing. Maybe the wolf was beautiful. But he could think of a dozen other adjectives before that one. Suspicious. Misplaced. Maladjusted. What was it about Camilla that made dogs poor things and wolves beautiful?

"Don't you think?" pressed Camilla.

"Yeah, a beautiful wolf," Nick concurred without enthusiasm.

As a reward, Camilla slipped her arm in his as they walked toward the cabin. Halfway there, a boy appeared along their path. Nick recognized him. This was a son of the village council president. Nick had met him at the tribal office.

"I looked for you back there," the boy gestured toward Epchooks' house.

"Yeah," answered Nick with a friendly smile.

"I'm supposed to tell you. She got a call today."

"Camilla got a call?"

"Yes," said the boy.

"Somebody called me?" asked Camilla.

"He's coming tomorrow," said the boy, relaying the message to Camilla. "He called my father. He said to tell you."

"Oh," said Camilla. "Who called?"

"Some kass'aq."

"Somebody I know is coming to Sleetmute tomorrow?" asked Camilla.

"Yes," said the boy. "He's coming to get that wolf."

The boy scampered off happily for home because he had successfully delivered the message, despite his nervousness.

"What wolf?" Camilla asked Nick. "The orphan?"

Nick didn't know.

* * *

The trail narrowed.

The she wolf followed it beneath a darkening sky. Heavy clouds covered the tops of the ridges. They hid the stars. She had entered the mountains. Steep slopes squeezed the river into sheer canyons. As she climbed, the silent, shrouded land lost its dangerous feel. No lights, no strange pathways, no terrified wolves. She felt right moving this way. The trail changed beneath her feet. It shrunk and lost the foreign smells, more like the tracks made by dogs and humans around home. Coyotes did not come this way. No wolf packs.

This was a track made by dogs and humans.

The slopes fell steeply. Deep snow lay on either side. She stopped often to check the air for others. She did not want to leave the trail here. She walked lightly and quickly. At several places, new snow from the steep slopes covered the track, sweeping it clean of footprints. She picked her way across those places cautiously. She moved like a shadow within shadows, a shape flitting between the dark press of canyon and clouds.

She climbed eagerly. Her muscles felt rested. Moose filled her stomach. Her body gained strength. With every stop, smells became more familiar, the landscape more recognizable, the temperature and humidity more correct. Her body responded with anticipation, feelings like the pack as it tracked caribou.

She was gaining, gaining, gaining.

She was closing in on home.

* * *

Frances Egnaty beamed.

She had family this morning!

Dora, her youngest daughter, nibbled toast at the breakfast table, coolly appraising Camilla and Nick. She flew in yesterday before the fog settled. Dora heard from the lawyer that anthropologists had begun to work with her mother at Sleetmute. She flew over to meet them.

Dora Egnaty scared Nick.

She had a hungry look, like a fledging waiting for dinner. She eyed them eagerly, especially Nick. He had seen this look before. It always made him nervous.

Dora was young, a year shy of Nick. He knew this from the interviews with Frances. But years of hard living showed. Purplish wells surrounded hard eyes. Her grin, yellowed and broken, was completely unlike her mother's open smile. A narrow scar cut across her chin. Another jagged through an eyebrow, emptied of hair. Abusive boyfriends, guessed Nick. She was wall solid, not plump like Frances. Her laugh was a tool ratcheting.

Frances beamed. A daughter had come home.

"Your kids?" asked Camilla, checking the room for small gloves or jackets.

"My sister's," said Dora flatly.

That was enough about that.

"They couldn't come," said Frances sadly.

Dora wanted to talk about the Native hospital in Anchorage. She wanted Camilla and Nick to know in detail the suffering of her mother at the hands of the incompetent caregivers, from the nurses to the surgeons. Camilla opened her book to take notes. Dora delivered a discourse that sounded both plausible and well-rehearsed.

Frances listened at the edge, looking embarrassed.

Nick said nothing, drinking coffee, hiding his disapproval. The complaint obviously drew on true events. But it was very un-Yup'ik. The Yup'ik ideal was to forgive human error. Errant Yup'iks freely admitted mistakes and typically achieved absolution. That approach led to healing in close communities. Lawyers hated this cultural penchant for confession by Yup'iks. It compromised them in the western legal system where 'truth' was established through adversarial contests. Dora had learned the rules of the western system. For Camilla, she laid a foundation of grievances for the malpractice suit. The hospital, it seemed, did nothing right.

With Frances' permission, Camilla presented to Dora the materials collected to date. Dora listened carefully and added details, filling out the picture of her mother's central role in village subsistence patterns. The additions were helpful. Nevertheless, Nick continued to feel dirty. Occasionally, he translated a point for Frances. Dora gave him sour looks, as if translating slowed things down.

Camilla worked effectively, Nick observed. As usual, she appeared completely non-judgmental. She trusted the speaker's expertise. Her manner proclaimed an interest to learn. Camilla drew people out. Respondents like Dora wanted to talk with her. She did anthropology well.

But what did Camilla really think of Dora? Didn't she see Dora's greed? Didn't she care?

Nick and Camilla walked home in chilly fog. Chimney smoke refused to rise, falling into the thick air. Lights in the village became bristling balls that shot out like searchlights, optical phenomena created by suspended ice crystals. Spruce branches sagged with hoarfrost, cracking in the cold silence.

Nick brooded.

Dora had asked it directly just as they closed.

'How much will it be?'

Camilla didn't know yet.

'When will you know?' Dora pressed.

How much? When?

Questions of greed.

Her eager eyes turned to Nick.

'Come back later,' she smiled.

Not Camilla. Only him. Come back later. He knew what she meant. Come late, after Mother is asleep, the later the better. We'll make some fun.

All he could see were razor teeth.

Nick knew he could over analyze. But he trusted his gut. He had rarely spoken to Camilla about personal feelings. But tonight he needed to talk about his growing distaste for the lawsuit. It wasn't Frances Egnaty's lawsuit. It was the daughters'. He wanted to know what Camilla felt beneath her neutral front, to find if her feelings matched his.

Was it really the case she didn't care?

As they approached the house, Nick saw it wasn't going to happen. Every light in the cabin was on, bathing the yard with light. Footprints crisscrossed the snow as if the headless had run around looking for brains.

The front door banged open.

"Mac!"

A bearded stranger leaped down the stairs.

He grabbed Camilla and kissed within her hood.

Camilla staggered back, her white cheeks ruddy in the cabin's foggy glow.

"Nick," she gasped. "This is Geoff Sturgis."

And Nick's gut suddenly felt worse.

* * *

Sturgis talked non-stop while Camilla fixed dinner.

Energetic, passionate, and committed, he covered globalization. Climate change. Wilderness. Wolves. Saving wolves especially. These were the issues. He trailed Camilla around the small cabin, helping at her direction, carrying plates, stirring tomato sauce, filling the kettle. The lecture never stopped.

Nick sat with Nils Eckholm, Sturgis' partner, watching him dismantle and oil an odd-looking rifle. Nils was a Swede, a pilot who flew Sturgis in, fairly young, maybe late twenties. His plane sat at the airstrip.

The odd rifle shot darts. Nick examined them, packed in rows within an aluminum carrying case. They were thin anesthetizing missiles. Explosive caps propelled them. Nils passed the rifle. Nick tested the balance. It had the feel for caribou. He sighted down its scoped barrel. Like any hunter, Nick wanted to try it.

"For the runner," said Sturgis.

"Are you hearing this, Nick?" asked Camilla.

"Yeah," said Nick.

He had been listening.

He was unsure about Sturgis, the political activist, Camilla's 'old friend' from Berkeley. In Sturgis he observed semi-mastered mania. Was he medicated?

Nils worked from another duffle. He pulled out a hand-held device with wing-like projections. A radio tracking antennae. Nick had never seen one of these either. Nils passed it over. He pointed out features.

"We haven't heard anything about this," said Camilla. "Kidnapped! Her poor pups!"

"She's famous!" Sturgis gushed. "Three million followers on her site! We head off tomorrow."

"The forecast is for low ceilings," cautioned Nick.

Fog sat thickly outside the window.

"When it lifts," said Sturgis confidently.

"You're going to look for her?" asked Camilla.

"She's coming through Rainy Pass. She's run hundreds of miles. She's amazing! We have her frequency. We'll fly that way and position for the next transmission."

"What for?" asked Nick.

Sturgis looked at him funny.

"To save her. Did you hear what's happening?"

Sturgis launched into a history of the treatment of wolves in North America. He marched waving a teacup. Wild wolves used to range the continent, he explained. When settlers arrived, the slaughter began. Government supported it. Wolves were demonized, nearly extirpated. Only remnants remain. Wild packs survive in the Far North and Yellowstone.

When left alone, wolf packs form territories and complex social orders. Only the alpha pair have pups. The whole pack rears them. Wolves aren't demons. They help to balance ecosystems. Wolves don't attack people. There was not a single authenticated case of healthy wolves attacking humans in North America. But the slaughter continues. They are still at it.

"Who's that?" asked Nick.

Sturgis paused. He studied him. Nick could see the calculations. Sturgis might be manic, but he was shrewd. A Yup'ik Eskimo asked the question. Eskimos killed wolves. They had killed wolves for thousands of years. How would Sturgis answer a Yup'ik?

"Look behind the curtain," said Sturgis. "You'll find who pulls the levers, the land dealers, the corporate magnates, the marketers. Wilderness destroyed for profit."

Tonight the evil was money. Sturgis the eco-freak would not directly challenge the Yup'ik hunter. Sheltered in a Yup'ik cabin, kissing into a wolf ruff, Sturgis fingered corporate greed. Who did Sturgis accuse other nights?

"She's infected with lice?" asked Camilla.

"Kenai packs have lice," said Sturgis.

In poor regions where Camilla had worked, kids routinely contracted lice. But lice were specialized, she knew, adapted to particular species. Humans didn't catch dog lice. How easy was it for wolves to catch dog lice?

"But she wasn't there long, right?"

"Langstrap said she killed a dog," said Sturgis. "The kennel had lice."

"Who's Langstrap?"

"A wolf biologist on the Kenai."

"It's bad," said Nils, repacking the antennae. It was his first contribution to the conversation.

"What's bad?" Nick asked.

"The lice. It's bad for wolves."

"How bad?" asked Nick, surprised the man who worked with his hands actually spoke.

"The hair comes out in great fistfuls."

"How awful!" said Camilla.

"It makes them suffer," said Nils. "Better off dead."

Nick considered the Swede's assessment. Better to be a dead wolf than contract this disease. Nick knew what had happened when outsiders brought foreign diseases to the Yup'iks. New maladies destroyed entire communities. What would happen if lice got started among wolves? Nick had believed the era of devastating epidemics was over. He had no idea domestic dogs posed such a threat to wild wolves.

"But we can save her," said Sturgis. "Show them, Nils."

Nils took a small case from another duffle. He popped it open. It contained a syringe and several small vials. He passed it to Nick, as he had done with everything else.

Nick read from a vial.

"Ivermectin."

"An injection cures it," said Sturgis.

"One injection?" asked Camilla.

"That's what they say," said Sturgis. "But we'll see. Maybe she'll need more."

"How will you do that?" asked Nick.

In answer, Nils touched a large flat pack that leaned against the wall. He peeled back a Velcro seal.

An aluminum cage, ready for assembly.

"You've got a cage?" said Camilla, shocked.

"Of course," said Sturgis.

"Why?"

"Because they'll kill her unless we find her first. Keith Nichols is looking. He's Fish and Game in McGrath. And they've hired that bastard, Joel Haggarty from Fairbanks. He'll be looking too."

Nick examined the cage, six walls designed to latch together. He hefted a corner. It was lightweight, just room enough for a wolf to turn around.

So Haggarty was hired to find the fugitive wolf. He remembered his encounters with Joel Haggarty. They had surprised him running booze into Stony River. He had sweet talked Camilla and lied about brackets under the right wing of Chet Miller's plane.

Camilla frowned at the cage. Nick saw the creases about the eyes. She needed her pills.

"Temporarily, right?" said Camilla.

"What?" asked Sturgis.

"The cage?"

"Of course, of course!" agreed Sturgis. He put an arm around her. "It's only for transporting. If Fish and Game finds her first, Keith Nichols will dump her back on the Kenai. That's a death sentence. That bastard Haggarty will just kill her. What's one more wolf to him? They can't see that she's special. She's the most famous wolf on the planet right now. Everybody knows about her. They've even named her… Penny. From the Odyssey, the journey, Penelope, true and constant, trying to get back home. It's vital we rescue her."

"Rescue her for what?" pressed Nick again.

"To stop the killing," said Sturgis. "I know, she never asked for any of this. She never chose to be kidnapped in the state's goddamn wolf program. But she's made it real for people like nothing else has done. She's incredibly important. The public understands her. She's become the ambassador for wolves everywhere. She'll stop the killing."

Nils sealed up the cage.

* * *

Nick couldn't sleep.

Camilla decided sleeping arrangements. Nils shared the bedroom with Nick. She and Sturgis slept in the living room. Sturgis had an air mattress and sleeping bag. Nils slept in his bag atop the double bed, lightly snoring. He fell to sleep immediately. Nick lay awake, playing through the day's events, imagining what might be happening in the living room. He knew the saggy couch was not big enough for two. He didn't know the width of Sturgis' air mattress. Sturgis was an old friend from graduate school in Berkeley, according to Camilla. He had yelled 'Hi Mac' and kissed her. He followed her around the cabin. She gave him domestic tasks.

This was how his mind played tonight.

Nick didn't have to be there. He had a standing invitation from Dora Egnaty. Nick checked the clock. The display glowed midnight. This was when she expected him. It would be a simple thing, pull on his boots and parka, tiptoe out the door, walk the foggy path to Egnaty's. Dora would be up. The house would be warm, the lights low. She'd have a bottle of something. There wouldn't be a need for much talk. He had a lot in common with Dora. Nick wouldn't be bothered where Camilla woke in the morning.

Nick knew this was stupid. Camilla showed no signs of intimacy with Sturgis. He was just a friend. Already she was asleep on the saggy couch, dreaming whatever Camilla dreamed, maybe her nightmare about Everett Schofield coming for her baby. Sturgis was awake on his air mattress, plotting how to save the world from humans.

Nick flicked on the nightstand light.

Nils didn't move.

He reached beside the bed and found the thick folder given to him by Camilla. Propped on pillows, Nick began to read through it. The file contained correspondence between Camilla and the lawyers, between the lawyers and the Schofields, between the lawyers and the lawyers.

Stupefying.

He set the folder down and found a pamphlet on the nightstand. Nils had given it to him. A 'wolf center' in California. The center bred wolves. Its mission was to save the endangered Mexican gray wolf. Once found in northern Mexico, Arizona, New Mexico, Colorado, and Texas, the wolves had been driven to within seven animals of extinction. The center had saved this population. Small photos showed wolf faces, a pair of wolves walking, a wolf howling. By sponsoring a wolf, a person got a photo, biography, certificate, and newsletter.

Nick rubbed his eyes.

His stomach felt sick. Spaghetti. It always went down good but made him sick. He thought of the moose stew at the Epchook's. Moose stew never made him sick.

Nick put down the pamphlet.

He picked up Camilla's thick folder again. He thumbed through it a second time, his mind a jumble of disparate thoughts. He discovered the hated contract. Camilla couldn't stand to touch it. Nick began reading. Mostly legalese. Legal boilerplate. But the contract was the key, Camilla said. He forced himself through it. Condensed, the contract stated the obvious. Camilla was to carry a baby for the Schofields. Upon payment, she'd give the baby up. The contract terms were voided if the baby had birth defects. Nick thought through the elements. Camilla had carried the baby. There were no birth defects. The payment sat in a Mexico City bank, untouched. The Schofields took the baby at the hospital. The courts slapped Camilla with an injunction. She couldn't see the baby. Camilla refused to sign the revised birth certificate. A judge was going to hear the case within a week.

Nick shook his head.

How could he help? He wasn't a lawyer.

He lay awake, listening to the soft snores from Nils. Swedes snored like Yup'iks, Nick decided. Snoring... a cultural universal. The digital clock glowed one fifteen. He was still annoyingly awake.

Nick picked up the contact. He read through it again. This time was quicker. The elements stood out clearly. Even the legal boilerplate made sense. When he finished the last page with four signatures, the two Schofields, Camilla, and a notary, nothing had changed.

Camilla was screwed.

Nick heard footsteps.

A form appeared in the half-light.

"Nick? You still awake?"

"Camilla?"

Nils stirred and sat up.

"Nils, do mind sleeping on the couch?" asked Camilla.

Nils mumbled something and immediately disappeared into the living room, dragging the sleeping bag. Camilla took the warm, vacated spot. Nick felt his heart beating. What was she wearing? Nick couldn't tell. She pulled beneath the sheets and blankets and grabbed for Nick's hand.

"I'm fucked," she moaned.

She began weeping, gripping his hand within hers.

Migraine.

Nick dropped the file folder and cut the light. He reached for Camilla's forehead. He began to stroke it.

"It's always the same, night after night," she wept. "When will it ever end?"

Nick knew this wasn't true. She hadn't had a migraine for several nights. Just yesterday, Camilla remarked on this. But tonight was tonight.

"Did you take a pill?" asked Nick.

"Yes," whimpered Camilla. "God, it's horrible." She continued weeping.

"What can I do?" asked Nick forlornly.

"Press here," said Camilla finally, bringing his hands to either side of her head above her ears. He pressed. "Harder," she whispered. He pressed harder. He pressed until his muscles shook from weakness. Then he released.

"Again," whispered Camilla.

Nick repeated, pressing long, hard, released.

"Again."

Nick continued until he lost count.

"Did that help?" asked Nick, worn out.

"Yes," whispered Camilla.

She pulled his hand over her eyes, holding it there. He felt the wet of her long lashes. He put the other hand into her hair. He pulled through the short snarls. She just lay, hiding her eyes in his palm while he stroked.

"That's good," she whispered.

He could hardly hear her.

They lay doing this a long while. Nick combed her scalp with his fingers, hiding her eyes within his palm. Comb, reposition. Comb, reposition. He thought of nothing. Just the motions. Over and again. He began to drift off. He looked at the clock. Two fifteen.

"Camilla?" whispered Nick.

"Yeah?" came a mumble.

"You're still awake?"

"Yeah. But it's better. Thanks."

Nick took away his hands. She didn't move.

"It still hurts?"

"Yeah, but it's better."

Nick lay beside her in the dark. He was cold.

"Get under the covers," whispered Camilla.

Nick got under. Camilla snuggled against him.

"Don't worry," she mumbled.

Then there was silence.

Nick didn't worry.

In the warmth, sleep took him.

20

There was sadness in his eyes.

So the playful wolf kissed him.

Her brother kissed her back. This was their morning ritual, a display of mutual love. But today he seemed especially sad. Her favorite brother turned and left for the hunt. He descended into the fog. This morning, thick chill air filled the cleft that hid the community. The playful one stared after him.

He disappeared into a swirl of mist.

The canyon lay in shadow for the winter. The low sun entered only for snatches. Spring warmed it. The high summer sun washed it brightly. Winter kept it dark. The clammy fog clung to the cleft like a wet web. It stuck to every hair and stone. It stole the joy of living.

Something vague ached within her. She whined, already missing him, her hunting partner. She couldn't follow him. Instead, she turned to reenter the den.

Movement at the edge of her vision stopped her.

The strong one stood there, watching. He had watched the kiss and the parting at the mouth of the den. He no longer entered it. That had passed to others.

The playful one returned the strong one's gaze. She respected him. He was a good hunter. He contributed to the community. He led the young ones who were his children.

She moved from the den to greet him on the hillside. The instant she shifted, the strong one turned and disappeared into the brush. At the same moment a shape appeared above her on the ledge. It was the dark wolf, her mate. His blackness loomed large in the mist. He wouldn't allow her to greet the strong one alone. The strong one always gave way to the dark wolf. That was the new order.

Outside, the dank of winter weighed.

The playful one turned from it wearily.

She disappeared into the den.

* * *

Joel Haggarty examined a well-used game trail through a brushy patch. It followed a snowmachine track that passed over a knoll between small drainages. The far stream ran narrow and deep. He saw signs of many kinds of animals descending to its broken ice to drink, hares, weasels, martens, and moose. This was a good watering spot. In the trail's center he saw them, the fat pads of wolves. He stepped off his Viper and studied the impressions. He observed three distinct prints. Wolves had recently used this path.

Haggarty walked off the trail through the brush several dozen steps to a standing granite stone partially covered in snow. The brush tore at his canvas overalls. No wonder the animals used the snowmachine track. Or maybe it was the other way around. The local snowmachines used the established game trail. He leaned against the stone and lit a cigarette. The animals came for water at night. Several footprints looked fresh this morning. A moose had recently browsed the willow bark along the trail. The moose sign might have attracted the three wolves.

As he smoked, Haggarty drew up a mental picture of the drainages around Big River. It was his recent pastime, searching in his mind for that elusive den.

Where was it?

The Big River pack roamed a large territory. They traveled from Sleetmute up to McGrath. Several packs overlapped in the hills of the middle and upper Kuskokwim. Big River lay at the center. Fish and Game had never found that pack's den. It must be well hidden, probably in one of the steep, narrow canyons draining west of that braided river. Under this granite stone, he probably stood only miles from it. The wolf prints showed that members of the pack used the small rivers. He would try a test set to see what came up. Given the foul weather, he could experiment.

Thick morning fog had grounded Chet Miller's plane at his homestead. This turned Chet into an unbearable grouch. Fog was bad, he worried. The moose would get ahead of them. He had stared beyond the cabin's picture windows nervously. Then he forced Haggarty out of the warm cabin on this wild goose chase. How was Haggarty supposed to deal with the moose alone on the ground with a snowmachine? But Miller insisted. So Haggarty went. It cost him nothing, it was Miller's fuel.

He smoked. Might as well experiment.

Haggarty put out his cigarette and walked back to the snowmachine track. He drew on his cotton gloves. From the sled he pulled out a shovel and a burlap sack of wood shavings. Walking carefully along the snowmachine track, he found a place showing all three sets of wolf prints. Whistling a tune, he sunk in the shovel and began digging a round hole, carefully placing the excavated snow onto the burlap. At about an eight-inch depth he stopped, smoothing flat the floor of the circular hole. From the sled he returned with a twenty-inch-diameter section of conduit, cut exactly eight-inches deep. He set the conduit into the hole, tapping it firm. From the sled he retrieved the trap, a large spring trap with toothless padded jaws, an experimental soft design from Canada. He placed the trap inside the hole, its perimeter reinforced by the conduit. He hammered it secure with a stake and set the spring.

He stuck in the shovel's handle.

The trap snapped shut.

Haggarty smiled, removed the shovel from the padded jaws and reset the spring. The trigger would sit just below the surface of the trail. He sprinkled the trap with wood shavings from the burlap sack to prevent the surrounding snow from freezing solid. Then he carefully shoveled broken snow over the top, bringing it level with the trail. He dispersed the remainder of the unused snow into the brush. On a nearby bush he tied a red plastic sash to mark the trap's location. Finally, he brushed the surface of the trail with a spruce bough, erasing the marks of his efforts.

Haggarty repacked his equipment and started the Viper. He eased it forward and ran over the top of the newly-set trap. Once over, he looked back. The trap remained set and hidden. The buried conduit had taken the weight of his machine. The snowmachine's track marks passed right over the trap, obscuring the spruce sweepings in the snow. The trap lay just underground, waiting for a wolf that walked down the center of the trail.

"Check you later," said Haggarty, smiling.

He gunned the Viper down the ridge toward the Kuskokwim. He'd find brunch somewhere, maybe Hosea Jimmy's house at Stony River. Hosea always had coffee and news.

* * *

The fog broke around noon.

Geoff Sturgis fretted. He'd been pacing about the cabin for the last three hours. Nils had packed the plane's equipment by nine. Camilla lay in the bedroom's dark, recovering from the night's migraine. The last traces of its pain lifted with the fog.

Sturgis explained the plan to her when she emerged from the back. They intended to fly between the Kuskokwim River and the mountains, listening for transmissions from the runner's radio collar. They'd refuel at McGrath and spend the night there. Camilla and Nick might see them tomorrow night. If it got too foggy for the search, they'd head for McGrath.

"Be careful," said Camilla. She wore dark glasses against the hazy sun.

"Always," grinned Sturgis, kissing again inside the parka hood. This time Nick saw Camilla was prepared. She offered a cheek.

The plane roared down the runway. It lifted over the far trees. The drone receded and disappeared.

"Patchy," said Nick.

Gauzy white obscured the distances.

It wouldn't be easy to tell ground from air.

"God, I hope they're careful," whispered Camilla.

"Yeah," said Nick. "Are we interviewing today?"

"Do you want to?" sighed Camilla. "I feel like crap."

"No."

"Let's just sit inside today," said Camilla. "You can make me tea and tell me stories."

"Okay," said Nick.

Camilla took his arm.

"I think we're almost done anyways," said Camilla.

The words sounded dispirited.

* * *

They lost the sun within the first ten minutes.

They flew blindly. Nils locked coordinates on McGrath and navigated with instruments. He radioed the airport in McGrath. Fog along the entire Kuskokwim, they reported into his headset. IFR conditions.

Cloudy air bumped and jostled the plane.

"I can't see a thing!" shouted Sturgis, staring from the window into the blank white.

"We can't go lower," said Nils. "There are hills."

"Shit," said Sturgis.

The receiver sat silently at Sturgis' feet. No transmission came from the runner.

"We need to get closer to the mountains!" shouted Sturgis. "That's where she'll be."

"Okay. Let's go up," said Nils, watching the instruments, keeping a line on McGrath, bringing the plane higher.

"Hey, it's light ahead."

The plane broke from a fogbank into bright sunlight. The broad Kuskokwim River glittered in crystalline whites beneath a deep blue sky. Fog billowed on either side. River channels meandered between scatterings of trees covered with hoarfrost. Snowmachine traces gracefully curved beneath them catching the sun like silver bows.

"Beautiful," said Nils.

Fog swallowed the view.

"That's how it's going to be," said Nils.

"It'll be the same for Haggarty," said Sturgis.

The receiver squawked suddenly. It emitted a flutter of piercing squeals. Sturgis jerked down the volume and grabbed the hand-held antenna. He donned earphones and scanned.

"It's her! It's Penny!"

"Which way?" yelled Nils, watching his instruments.

"Two o'clock!" shouted Sturgis.

Nils adjusted the aircraft, eased the plane higher.

"Good!" yelled Sturgis.

They flew in and out of breaks in the fog.

"It's stopped!" yelled Sturgis, flipping switches on the receiver.

The plane burst into bright sunlight. Crumpled hills flowed beneath them, scored by tiny rivers. The plane had left the main Kuskokwim.

"What's that?" shouted Sturgis.

"Where?" yelled Nils.

"There! Wolves! Turn back! Turn back!"

Sturgis saw a wolf on a narrow white trail. It seemed to be thrashing. A second wolf ran.

"Turn! Turn!" shouted Sturgis.

Nils brought the plane into a tight turn.

Straight below him, Sturgis saw a shape like a thick man.

"Turn!"

The shape swiveled in synchrony with the plane.

Sturgis looked into insect eyes bright with sun.

They exploded!

"Up! Up!" shouted Sturgis, slapping his hands against the dash, instinctively bracing.

Nils hauled on non-responsive controls. The plane tilted as it fell. Sturgis remembered a tree, pushing toward the window like a stiff thread into a needle.

The plastic stove in with a shattering blast.

Then black.

* * *

Camilla worried.

Nick was unfamiliar with this side of Camilla. As he told her stories, she fretted with the slow passing of the afternoon. He finished with his killing his first sandhill crane. It was almost as tall as him. Lugging it home made him walk crooked for a week.

"Let's go to the Epchooks," she said.

They owned a speakerphone for family calls.

James and Sophie Epchook were delighted to see them. Of course they could use their speakerphone.

Juggling the local phone directory, a very thin book, Camilla dialed the airport in McGrath. After transfers, they got airport dispatch. They learned that the McGrath airport had received a transmission from Nils Eckholm about thirteen hundred that afternoon. One o'clock. Nick looked at his watch. It was now four. Eckholm had not filed a flight plane. McGrath was now fogged in. Bush carriers had canceled all flights. Was there a problem?

Camilla said she didn't know. She described the pilot's plan for flying transects between the Kuskokwim and the Alaska Range. Could the plane have flown to Anchorage instead? Camilla didn't know. She'd call them back soon. She hung up and stared at Nick.

"Those boys who came in yesterday?" asked James.

"They went out at noon," said Nick.

"To McGrath? They should be there by now."

"They're looking for that wolf toward the mountains."

"It's worse that way."

"Can I make another?" Camilla asked.

She punched a series and hit speaker. A familiar voice spoke above a fizz of static.

"Fish and Game, Subsistence. Mel Savidge."

"Mel, it's Camilla! And Nick! We're in Sleetmute."

"Camilla! I was just thinking about you. Are you on a speaker? You sound like you're inside a barrel."

"Nick's here. So are James and Sophie Epchook, friends of Nick's family. It's their phone."

"Hi Nick. Hi to all," said Mel, sounding relaxed and pleased.

Nick was surprised. Mel wasn't rushing.

"What's the occasion?" asked Mel. "You want to talk about the medical malpractice suit? I can't talk long. I'm just leaving for a meeting on the hill."

So much for that, thought Nick.

"Do you know about that wolf, the one called the runner?" asked Camilla.

"Oh God, you bet I do," said Mel. "She's giving our big boys heartburn. That's why I thought of you. I hear she's headed your way."

"We just learned about it," said Camilla. "Where is she? Do you know? A couple of guys flew out of here to look for her today. I'm worried they're stuck in fog."

"Who? Nobody's flying today."

"Geoff Sturgis and Nils Eckholm. Nils is the pilot."

"They're Fish and Game?"

"No, they're with the boycott. Geoff Sturgis is from San Francisco. Nils Eckholm is Swedish, a student at Berkeley."

"Oh yeah, now I remember that name. Sturgis. He's with the howlers. That's working."

"What's working?"

"The boycott. I shouldn't be saying this, but what the hell. The governor is about to pull the plug on the wolf transplants. Tourism is scared shitless by the boycott. The publicity from that runner ratchets things way up. The boycott is gaining steam."

"That's why there's heartburn in Fish and Game?"

"No, not that. It's the lice. That's the heartburn. They're worried the runner's a plague ship."

"Plague ship?" asked Nick.

"It's that bad?" asked Camilla.

"That's what they say," said Mel. "Some of them, anyway. They've convinced me. A wolf pack with lice is screwed."

"How fast does it spread?" asked Camilla.

"Once it gets into the dens, it's done. Endemic. They really want that wolf. So now everybody follows the daily weather reports from McGrath. It's foggy, eh?"

"Yeah," said Camilla.

"How are you, Nick?"

"Okay," said Nick, his head full of plague. Suddenly he felt mad.

"Why are they doing that?" said Nick testily.

"Doing what?"

"Moving wolves around and spreading lice."

"You got me," said Mel. "It's stupid! Everybody says it's stupid. But the governor didn't want to be accused of killing wolves. It's supposed to be non-lethal wolf management."

"Because of moose?" asked Nick.

"Too many wolves for the moose. That's what the Board of Game says. They say it's an emergency on the upper Kuskokwim."

Nick looked at James Epchook. He was carefully listening to the conversation, a rare ear on the inner workings of Fish and Game.

"From what I'm hearing here, the problem is too many sport hunters," said Nick.

"How's that?"

"Too many floaters. Too much waste," said Nick angrily.

"You still there?" asked Camilla.

"Yeah, just a second, I'm getting a pen. Okay Nick, go ahead. What do you mean, floaters and waste?"

"They fly in through Farewell," said Nick. "There are trails all over that place. Outfitters put them down on the headwaters. They float and they hunt. The meat's spoiled by the time they're finished. Wasted. They can't even give it away. That's the problem."

"What headwaters?"

"Holitna, Hoholitna, Kwethluk,"

"Nick didn't mention it," said Camilla, "but there are hunters from downriver too. They come up from Bethel with big outboards. They come for moose too."

"We've all heard about that one," said Mel. "The upriver-downriver problem. But this sport hunting waste by floaters is news to me. You think that's a bigger problem than wolves?"

"I don't know," said Camilla, eying Nick.

"Why are they moving wolves all over the place when the problem is those sport hunters wasting moose?" said Nick angrily. "It's spreading lice!"

"Yeah, totally stupid," agreed Mel. "Hey, I'll look into this. I got it down. Farewell. Floaters. Headwaters. I got it. Look, I gotta run. But what about those two guys, Sturgis and... what was his name?"

"Nils Eckholm," said Camilla.

"They're grounded by the fog somewhere?"

"I don't know," said Camilla. "They took off about noon. They didn't get to McGrath."

"Nobody's flying today. That's what I heard," said Mel. "You want me to do something?"

"What could you do?"

"Call FAA or the troopers. But if it's bad fog, no one's going to be able to fly out to find them."

"Let me call McGrath again," said Camilla. "Maybe they've heard something more."

"Call the troopers too. I'll be on the hill for the next couple hours. Let me know if I can do anything. Leave a message."

"Okay."

And the phone call ended.

* * *

Nick loaded food from Sophie Epchook. Dried salmon and hot coffee. He secured it under the pack of emergency equipment that James Epchook always kept handy. Tent. Blankets. Small stove. Fuel. Flares, though he'd never used them, so maybe they were bum, James said. Ax. Shovel. Rope. All beneath a tight tarp on the sled behind the Skandic.

James described each item as Nick secured them.

Nick was going out to look.

Camilla fretted. Her migraine returned. She downed more pills. Second and third calls to McGrath turned up nothing new. The only contact with Nils Eckholm was precisely at ten past one. They notified the troopers about the missing plane. But with no flight plan and dense fog, no air search could be reasonably launched until sometime tomorrow. The plane might be anywhere.

In a call back to Mel in Juneau, Camilla and Nick learned of a short transmission from the runner at about one twenty. The transmission placed her just south of Farewell. The wolf had come completely through Rainy Pass. Against all expectations, the runner had found her way back into the Upper Kuskokwim drainage.

It was now eight o'clock at night. Dark and foggy. Temperatures rising. Nick would go out to take a look.

"How will you know where to go?" said Camilla. "The troopers said they could be anywhere."

"Not anywhere," said Nick.

He pored over topographic maps pieced together on the kitchen table. James leaned at his shoulder, pushing his finger around drainages, remembering places and events and conditions connected to the lines on the maps.

"They left here at about twelve forty-five going toward McGrath," Nick said to James. "Where would they be when they radioed McGrath at one ten? That's a half hour out of Sleetmute."

James pushed his finger in a space above the Kuskokwim River beyond Stony River.

"About here," James said.

"Okay," said Nick, marking the map. "Now, the transmission from the runner came about one twenty. It originated just south of Farewell, here." Nick put a finger on a point two quadrangles over. He made a mark. "Do you have a straightedge?"

Sophie brought a yardstick from her sewing.

Nick laid an edge on the spot south of Farewell. Holding it there, he rotated the yardstick until its edge touched the mark on the Kuskokwim upriver from Stony River indicated by James.

"Maybe farther up if it was one twenty," said James.

Nick adjusted the ruler up and made another mark.

Camilla now understood.

"They had a receiver in the plane," said Nick. "They were listening for transmissions. Before that they followed the river toward McGrath, I'll bet, because the fog was worse toward the mountains. Then they heard the transmission, maybe around here. They'd have turned toward it, following a direct line."

Nick took a pencil and traced the line along the yardstick.

"It was a short transmission," said Camilla.

"But it gave a bearing," said Nick. "That's where I'm going tonight. Along that line."

All four heads converged over the line on the map.

James Epchook put on his reading glasses. Nick watched him. Epchook knew this land. His finger moved this way and that along the line. He shook his head.

"You can't follow that line, unless you're a bird."

"No, but they could."

"How far would they go after losing the transmission?" asked Camilla. "There was no visibility. They would have given up and turned toward McGrath. They could be anywhere off that line."

"Yeah," said Nick, his mind made up.

"See this?" said James Epchook.

He indicated a mouth of a river.

"Swift River. It's the first mouth up from Stony River. Take that one. Then take the river to the left. The first left. That's Jonetno', the Cheeneetnuk. That one leads close along the line."

His finger traced the Cheeneetnuk to the Big River. The route was fairly near the line Nick had drawn. His finger waved above the drainages on the map between it and the Kuskokwim.

"It's hilly in there. Steep."

"Okay," said Nick, memorizing the terrain.

"The Cheeneetnuk goes up almost to Big River. Maybe they followed Big River toward McGrath after the transmission."

"Yeah," said Nick.

Big River bent northwest, connecting to the Kuskokwim just upstream from McGrath. James indicated the hilly region near the Cheeneetnuk.

"This place here, in Deg Hit'an it's called Digidithqaggidi. That means 'we can't get down that way.'"

"Can't get down," repeated Nick.

"Too steep," said James. "All along here, too steep. Watch for the avalanches."

"Okay," said Nick.

"Don't go up this one, the Talgurrsaq, the Tatlawiksuk. It's one mouth past the Swift. If you miscount, you'll be in that one."

"What's wrong with it?" asked Nick.

He stared at the river on the map. It almost paralleled the Cheeneetnuk. The two flowed south from uplands.

"It's okay, all right," said James, "if you know what you're doing. That's Passiksuar, the mountain this side. And Passilugpak that side. Steep. You can fall through the ice around here. It's okay. Cheeneetnuk is better."

This was in Yup'ik. Nick realized James had automatically switched to Yup'ik to describe the terrain of the Tatlawiksuk. In typical Yup'ik fashion, he spoke optimistically about that drainage. But Nick understood him. He should avoid it. Camilla suddenly looked scared. She didn't understand what James Epchook was instructing. The last she heard was 'avalanches' and 'don't go up this one.'

"Nick, this sounds dangerous."

"It's okay," James assured her in English. "He's going to look for those boys. That area back there is good."

And Nick saw the finger avoid the Tatlawiksuk.

Camilla said her goodbyes standing inside the doorway. Her dark brows were furrowed. She hugged him and held tightly. She seemed reluctant to let go.

"How will I hear from you?" she asked.

"I don't know. I'll call from Stony. Or McGrath."

"You're going all the way to McGrath?" she whispered.

"I don't know."

"Call me."

James Epchook was waiting at the Skandic, a black shape in the fog. He held a hunting rifle and a box of cartridges.

"Take this," he said simply.

Nick strapped the weapon on the seat just behind him within easy reach. He tucked the cartridges into a pocket and pulled on his thick driving gloves. Epchook was still thinking about drainages.

"You'll find those Bobbys up the Cheeneetnuk," he said.

"The Bobbys?"

"Isaac and Michael Bobby. Big Ike and Little Mike. They'll help you."

"They live up there?"

"You'll see the cabin partway up."

"Okay," said Nick. Why was this the first mention of people living up the drainage? Who were the Bobbys? Trappers?

"And that other place, it's okay. Just watch out."

"Yeah."

"Some strange things happen in there."

"Okay."

Nick flicked the powerful engine to life. Following the headlamp's ghostly beam, he roared into the night.

His last thought was of Camilla.

'Call me.'

21

The world compressed.

Light foreshortened by fog.

The headlamp illuminated a compact moving space.

Nick was used to night driving. In the Far North, winter nights were long and people had to travel. He wasn't afraid of dark journeys. But dense fogs added peril to night trips. They blurred and blocked, absorbed and tricked.

Tonight Nick drove inside a lighted box. He could see nothing but glare a short reach ahead. The effect was movement without progress. The engine whined, the tracks revolved, the wind blew past, but the light box stayed fixed. Obstacles appeared suddenly. A log. A bump. Ruptured ice. Adjustments had to be instantaneous. The box was small. No room for error.

Nick concentrated on snow tracks.

The best solution to the blindness were other trails. Leaving Sleetmute, he found the snowy tracks on the Kuskokwim River, the thickest set heading upriver toward Stony River. He stuck to their center, driving unerringly upon them, ignoring traces breaking left or right. Regular traffic connected the two villages. As long as the river ice hadn't suddenly fractured that night, the main trail was trustworthy. He knew the ice hadn't fractured. So he opened the throttle. He leaned into curves that appeared immediately before him, took bumps with flexed legs, felt the air flow by his goggles, warmed by the fog. He drove fast and alone on the trails of others in a short box of light.

The real challenge lay ahead.

Finding a lost plane.

Nick's mind went over James Epchook's instructions. Take the first mouth past Stony River, a right-hand turn. That was Swift River. After that take the first left mouth, the Cheeneetnuk, a left-hand turn. That would put him along the plane's bearing if Nils and Sturgis had locked on the wolf runner's transmission from Farewell.

It presumed much. It was all he had.

Tonight Nick followed a long tradition of search and rescue. When someone disappeared in bush Alaska, people regularly did what they did tonight, make educated guesses and dispatch parties to look. He knew by tomorrow, if Nils and Sturgis had not materialized, other parties would head out from Sleetmute, Stony River, McGrath, and Nikolai, searching until the lost were found. That's what neighbors did.

What had happened to them?

Nick considered possibilities. Nils put down somewhere because conditions became too dangerous. They landed to wait out the fog. That was a good scenario. But there were others. The plane flew too low. The engine quit. The wings iced up. If they had crashed and were injured, tonight might be critical. But temperatures had risen. They had blankets. They wouldn't freeze if they used the blankets. That was all good. But how would Nick find a crash in dense fog?

The mouth past Swift River was the Tatlawiksuk. It curved and paralleled the flight line toward the runner's last transmission, like the Cheeneetnuk. James Epchook advised Nick to avoid it. The hills were too steep, the snows unstable, the ice too thin.

'Strange things happen in there.'

Nick did not consider himself superstitious. Most Yup'iks weren't. They were a practical people firmly grounded in the empirical world. They had to be. The Far North of the Bering Sea was far too unforgiving. The Yup'iks survived by being observant and smart.

But Sleetmute hugged the margins of the Yup'ik world. Somehow Indians seemed more superstitious to Nick. They had more worries. More taboos. Beyond Sleetmute, Nick had crossed into Indian territory. The Talgurrsaq... that was a Yup'ik name, anglicized to Tatlawiksuk on the map. Its mountains, Passiksuar and Passilugpak... they too were Yup'ik words. Big Pestle and Little Pestle. But the area Epchook called 'we can't get down,' that was a Deg Hit'an name. So was Jonetno', anglicized to Cheeneetnuk. Despite the shifting of names, Nick knew... this was an Indian place.

Epchook handed him a rifle.

Strange things happen.

Nick nearly missed Stony River village in the fog. The trail he followed split. More than half the tracks veered left. Nick stopped to reconnoiter. The lights of Stony River village glowed faintly in the fog above the island embankment. Nick checked the time. Ten o'clock.

Should he call Camilla from the village? Would she have more information? Nick considered the hard task ahead. He was just getting started. Nick gunned the engine and took the right split.

The village disappeared in fog.

Navigating would now prove trickier. The first river mouth past Stony River... that's what he wanted.

Snowmachine tracks peeled off the main track to the right. Nick took them. In short order they led into the mouth of a river. This was Stony River. Even with the dense fog, Nick was certain. The outfall of the substantial tributary lay across from the village. Snowmachine tracks showed it had a heavy use from Stony River village residents. Farther up these tracks a traveler would reach Lime Village, a remote Dena'ina settlement.

Would there be a similar set of tracks to guide him into the Swift River mouth? He couldn't count on it.

Nick turned back toward the main Kuskokwim, holding close to the east bank of Stony River. The fog lay thick. He drove near the edge, making his own trail. At some undetermined point he reentered the Kuskokwim, holding tight to the bank. Progress turned slow and bumpy with drift logs, ice fractures, and irregular terrain. An overflow welled from a fissure. He backtracked, circled, and returned to the bank. Traces of other travelers crossed here and there. He ignored them, hugging the edge in the fog.

After an hour of rough travel, the cut bank abruptly disappeared. Nick turned right a short distance. Circled. Tested another direction. Looped back to his tracks. He had found a river mouth.

He sat on the idling Skandic, assessing his position. Unless this was a slough of the Kuskokwim, he had found Swift River, the first mouth past the Stony. He turned into it. Snowmachine tracks appeared in his headlamp beam. Traffic going upriver. Compared with Stony River, far fewer tracks. Travel up Swift River was not as regular, if indeed this was the Swift. If he had miscounted and gone too far, this might be the Tatlawiksuk. But Nick thought not. He had carefully hugged the bank. This was the first mouth.

Nick checked the time. Near midnight.

He cut the rumbling engine. Cupping his mouth with his gloves, he shouted.

"Nils! Sturgis! Nils! Sturgis!"

There was silence.

Nick found the thermos. He sipped coffee from its lid, listening to the silence. No one was traveling tonight. Too foggy. He felt goose bumps. His body shivered slightly. Air temperatures had warmed, but the fog had crept into his clothes. The moisture chilled him. The coffee that Sophie had brewed was hot and bitter. No sugar. James Epchook style, Nick concluded. He stowed the thermos and wiped frost from his goggles. From here on, he looked for a grounded plane.

Nick flicked on the headlamp.

The fog absorbed and reflected.

Back in the fuzzy box.

He urged the Skandic forward and entered Swift River. Nick edged across the mouth, finding its west bank. He turned right, keeping the bank at his left elbow. In this manner, he traveled upriver. At twelve fifteen he stopped and cut the engine.

"Nils! Sturgis! Nils!" he shouted.

There was silence.

This would be the strategy. Travel fifteen-minute stretches. Stop and shout. He knew nothing better in fog. He restarted and pushed ahead. The snow on the Swift River ice was soft and smooth. Dry grass poked through along the edge. There were no tracks where he traveled.

Before the third interval, the bank failed.

Another river entered.

Take the first left, James Epchook had said. That was the Cheeneetnuk. Nick cut the engine.

"Nils! Sturgis! Nils!"

A breath of wind responded. It came from the mouth at his left. Nick shivered, his body chilled from inactivity. It was bedtime. He was tired.

"Nils! Sturgis!"

A sigh came from the river.

Nick restarted. He turned left into the new tributary. His mental map had been right so far.

The river ascended. The fog lessened.

Trees appeared along the bank, shapes in the heavy mist. It was a substantial woodlands. The trees moved with the breath of wind that ran down the drainage. Nick smelled pine. Uplands lay ahead, why there was wind. For the first time, he saw shreds in the fog. The moving air stirred and lifted. He discerned far-off shapes like banks and hills.

Nick cut the motor and light.

"Nils! Sturgis! Nils!"

Nothing. His skin prickled.

He switched on and pushed ahead. The banks rose further. The woods thickened. The fog began dispersing. The fuzzy box opened around him. The sky appeared.

Moonlight shined on an enchanted scene. Trees covered in hoarfrost breathed in the crystalline air. They glowed silver beneath the pale light. Bits of ice and snow dropped with the sway of branches. A raven croaked. Nick motored slowly, absorbing the beauty of the place. It was nearing one o'clock. Ahead the river constricted. At the narrows dense fog billowed.

He stopped to consider it.

Like a narrow gate, blocked.

Frowning, he restarted and entered the thick fog. The light box closed around him.

Just inside, he saw them.

Lights.

White and red.

"Nils! Sturgis!" he called.

He juiced the Skandic forward.

The lights immediately shifted. They moved away.

Another snowmachine.

Nick plunged behind it.

The fog clamped tight.

Just ahead of him a white headlamp glowed. It reflected off the fog. Red break lights also winked like fuzzy blood spots. A low motor rumbled like an echo.

He must see me. Why doesn't he stop?

Nick pushed his throttle. He moved to catch up.

The other did likewise. It kept just ahead in the narrow channel.

He knows I'm behind him. He's running.

Nick opened more throttle. Wind began to whip him. Ice crystals stung his cheeks. He hunkered behind the windshield. The other snowmachine opened up too. It turned this way and that, Nick on his tail.

Nick fumed. Why won't he stop!

Abruptly, it left the river.

It leaped a slope as the channel turned.

Nick leaned and followed. He nearly missed the entrance to a narrow trail. He gunned up the incline and kept behind. Brush whipped his legs.

It was an old trapline.

The trail bent and twisted up a steep ridge. Trees sprang up in the fog and disappeared like leaping beasts. The trail climbed higher and higher, dense brush pocked with clearings.

Why won't he stop!

Suddenly it straightened.

Nick opened up full. He roared toward his quarry.

The other did too. Kept just ahead.

Thick air whipped. Fog thinned.

Nick burst free.

A black vault opened above him, ablaze with stars.

Wind blasted.

Great shadows flew like black wings of night.

They flapped! Beat at him, straight at his face!

Nick ducked and jerked hard.

Tracks lifted, freewheeled, screamed.

The Skandic flipped.

Nick flew into dark.

The machine sputtered and quit.

Nick lay on his back in thick berry bushes. Bright constellations winked above him with a quarter moon.

Far off, a wak-wak-wakking receded into remoteness.

He struggled upright, found his feet and his goggles. The Skandic lay on its side in a snow berm just beyond him. The sled was attached and upright.

Nothing broken. Nothing hurt.

He grabbed its edge and hauled the machine upright. The flashlight was in the rear storage. He flipped on the beam and stepped into the trail, scanning left and right.

He stood on a high ridge free of fog.

Wind sighed in the tree tops.

The other snowmachine was gone.

Nick walked up the trail, swinging the beam. Two-dozen steps. The trail abruptly failed. Stunned, he stood at a brink. Nick flashed the light over the edge of a precipice.

A black void.

"Hey!" yelled Nick into the chasm. "Hey! Hey!"

The dark swallowed his voice.

"Hey! You down there!" he shouted again.

It had to have gone off the cliff!

Nick swung his light left and right, searching for the tracks going over. Undisturbed snow flashed. Nick swept the light behind him and found his footsteps. He backtracked, looking for the passage of the other snowmachine. Two-dozen steps brought him to the Skandic.

He walked past it, examining the downhill trail. He found tracks, clearly marked in snow.

One set.

Nick shivered.

No other tracks.

With some difficulty, the Skandic came out from the brush. Pointed down the trail, sled hitched, Nick followed his beam, slowly retracing the twists of the narrow trapline. One set of tracks. The ridge winds fell. Fog swallowed him again. It thickened.

Nick shook as if from fatigue.

The downward journey seemed to take a long time. Finally, a cleft appeared, the place where he had left the river. His headlamp lights flashed off ice.

Something moved.

Nick's heart jumped. He cut the engine.

A beam hit his face.

"Hello!" yelled Nick.

"Hello!" a muffled voice yelled back.

A dog began barking.

Nick stumbled from his seat, grabbed the flashlight, and slid down the bank. A man stood on the river beside a snowmachine. A black dog barked at his knees. A beaver hat and muffler wrapped his head and face. His eyes looked like they watched a ghost.

"Nick John," Nick said, trying to sound alive.

The stranger looked at the Skandic in the gap on the high bank. Air flowed down the cleft, shredding the mist.

"From Sleetmute," added Nick.

The dog bounded forward. Its tail wagged. It stuffed its nose into Nick's glove, moving to his legs and boots, smelling Tepsaq and seal meat.

The stranger fidgeted. His eyes shifted nervously from the Skandic to Nick to the river behind him. He pulled the muffler off his nose.

"I heard shouts."

"That was me," said Nick.

The stranger pointed.

"There's a plane."

"What?"

"Down there," said the man, motioning. "My brother can call McGrath."

Without further explanation, he mounted his snowmachine. The dog scampered away. Nick scrambled up the bank and started his. The stranger passed beneath the cleft, the dog running at one side. Nick slipped down the slope and locked in behind.

This time the foggy lights didn't run.

Nothing was said, but Nick knew who he trailed. James Epchook had told him.

He had found the Bobbys.

Nick guessed Isaac, called Big Ike. His brother was Michael, called Little Mike. They would have a CB at their trapping cabin.

Isaac Bobby turned off the river. Nick came too. He drove a narrow trail brushed in places, just wide enough for a snowmachine. Fog closed thickly. But Isaac didn't slow or hesitate. He knew these trails.

Isaac turned several times, Nick right behind. His brake lights fluttered. Nick slowed. A detached sled sat to the side of the trail. They cut engines. Nick followed Isaac through knee-deep snow, flashlights out.

It was thick forest, large spruce and pine.

The plane dangled just above them.

No wings.

That was the first thing Nick noticed. They had snapped off during the plunge through the trees. The fuselage listed to one side, nose down, the cockpit not quite touching ground. A spindly spruce shoved through the front and out the top. One door dangled.

"I couldn't get them out," said Isaac.

He pushed his head through the door.

Nick squeezed beside him.

Nils Eckholm, splattered with blood, was wrapped in a blanket. Isaac had covered him.

Nick flashed his light upwards. The light caught Geoff Sturgis, also wrapped in a blanket, hanging in his belt. The spruce had penetrated the window between them.

"Are they dead?"

"I don't know," said Isaac.

Nick pulled off a glove and felt inside Nils' jacket. Warm. Still alive. Nick grabbed a broken branch and pulled beside Sturgis. His chest felt warm too.

How were they going to get Sturgis out? The tree through the windshield blocked him.

"You have a chainsaw?" yelled Nick.

"It might fall," said Isaac.

Nick saw this was true. The tree held the plane off the ground. Cutting might release it. Nick found a tree branch above him with the flashlight beam.

"We could hoist him out," suggested Nick.

"Okay," said Isaac.

With few other words, Nick and Isaac worked. They set up lanterns to free their hands. They severed the belt around Nils. Nick guided him into Isaac's arms. Together they carried him to the sled and slid him into a sleeping bag, tucked tight beneath a wool blanket, and tied him down. He showed no external injuries. The blood had dripped from Sturgis' dangling arm.

Nick climbed above the other door. He wrestled it open and fixed it with rope. He threw a line around a branch of a neighboring spruce and secured it around Sturgis' chest. He groaned and woke.

"Sturgis, you okay?" asked Nick.

"Wha…" mouthed Sturgis.

"You crashed. We're getting you out."

Isaac tied the rope the snowmachine.

"Go slow," said Nick.

"Yes," said Isaac.

Isaac slowly eased forward. The rope hauled like a pulley. Nick guided Sturgis out of the door.

"Okay!" yelled Nick.

Nick shinnied down. They lowered Sturgis to the ground and moved him to the other sled. He was heavy. Like Nils, they drew a sleeping bag around him and covered him with a blanket, secured with line.

Sturgis opened his eyes.

"We fell," mumbled Sturgis.

"Yeah, I know," said Nick.

"Nils?"

"He's okay."

Isaac reattached the sled.

"They should be medevaced!" yelled Nick above the idling engine.

"McGrath," agreed Isaac.

"How far to McGrath?"

"Three hours. You got gas?"

"Yeah. I don't know the trail."

"Follow me."

Isaac Bobby headed off, pulling Nils in his trapper's sled. Nick drew behind, pulling Sturgis in his. Isaac's dog ran a few steps and jumped next to Nils for the ride.

Smart dog, thought Nick.

They left the crash site by the narrow trail. Nick wondered how Isaac discovered it. Checking his traps at midnight in the fog? That made no sense. How badly injured were they? Nick found no bleeding wounds except the scrapes on Sturgis' arm. Maybe internal injuries. McGrath had a big runway. Planes could land there in fog. They could get to Anchorage.

Isaac took a series of trails over low ridges. Nick tried to keep them straight, but knew he would fail. Too much fog. They descended into flats. Cottonwood. The trail widened. He smelled wood smoke. Isaac's dog barked and jumped from the sled. Lights glowed. A log cabin emerged from the fog.

Nick followed Isaac inside. The room was small and hot with cluttered worktables and corner bunk. Furs on stretcher boards covered walls like head markers for a cemetery.

Little Mike stood at its center, blinking.

"Cama-i," Nick greeted.

Michael nodded warily.

"Call McGrath," said Isaac.

He waved at the CB and instantly left.

"We've got two injured men," said Nick. "They need a medevac to Anchorage. Tell them it's for two. Internal injuries. A plane crash."

Little Mike nodded. He'd seen the loaded sleds out the window. Nick looked at his watch. It was three thirty.

"Three hours to McGrath?"

Little Mike nodded.

"We'll need it by six thirty."

"Okay," said Little Mike.

Nick followed Isaac out, wondering if the tongue-tied trapper would make the call. Isaac was already on his snowmachine.

"I don't know the trail," said Nick again.

"Big River," said Isaac. "Follow me."

"Okay."

They roared off together.

The ride to McGrath was foggy and fast and exacting. Isaac Bobby knew the trails and flew. Nick hugged his rear, imitating his moves. Parts of the trail rode smoothly along rivers and small lakes. Other segments were rough and hilly. Isaac took them all fast. He drove like every minute mattered. Nick pressed hard behind him.

Nick remembered the maps at Epchook's. They first ascended the Cheeneetnuk, it seemed. It grew steep and narrow. Toward its end, they meandered through a spruce forest. Then they plunged down a steep ridge. After that, they traveled a wide, braided river. Big River flowed northwest, Nick recalled, joining the Kuskokwim near McGrath. Dense fog covered it. Isaac Bobby never faltered. He knew the way blind.

McGrath appeared with a suddenness that woke Nick from a daze. Lights blazed in the fog. Isaac brought them right to the airstrip. Broad and lighted, the strip held a plane. Paramedics waited. Little Mike had successfully radioed ahead.

It took only minutes to get Nils and Sturgis on stretchers and into the plane. The paramedics took vital signs and hooked up IV drips. Nick was relieved to see Nils awake. He spoke into the ear of an FAA official. Nick waved but didn't interrupt.

"How are they?" Nick finally asked.

"Blood pressures okay," the medic answered.

"Nick," said a weak voice from a stretcher.

"Hi Geoff," said Nick.

"Nils?" asked Sturgis.

"Okay. Awake. How are you?"

"Hurts like hell."

Engines revved for takeoff.

"You gonna scoot?" asked a paramedic.

"I'm scooting," said Nick.

"Nick," mumbled Sturgis.

"Yeah?"

"Tell her... tell her she was right."

"Yeah, the fog," agreed Nick at the exit.

"No... the bug."

"Huh?"

"The bug... bug shot us down."

"What?"

"Tell her."

* * *

Nick was famished.

Coffee had corrected his bleary vision. But his stomach needed attention.

They completed paperwork at the FAA office. He and Isaac Bobby answered questions about the crash. Isaac located the site on a map. They described the condition of the wreck. Nick did much of the talking. Isaac gave simple sentence answers. He acted like a nervous fugitive, though several at the airport had greeted him by name.

Nobody knew Nick.

McGrath was cosmopolitan. The village of five hundred people included Upper Kuskokwim Alaska Natives, government workers with FAA, and Fish and Game biologists. Compared with the trapper's cabin, it was a foreign country. The office was hot. Isaac never removed his jacket. He was ready to leave.

A stocky kass'aq with a blue cap entered. Nick had seen him assisting on the airfield.

"Morning, Ike."

Isaac nodded.

"Keith Nichols, Search and Rescue," he held out a hand to Nick.

"Nick John, University of Alaska, Fairbanks."

They shook and Nick stared at the familiar logo, a flying goose and caribou.

"Oh," Keith Nichols smiled, touching the bill. "And Fish and Game."

"I've worked for them too," admitted Nick.

"Ike, why don't you and Nick come over to the house for breakfast? Midge has bacon and eggs."

This sounded perfect to Nick. McGrath was nice, he decided. Even Fish and Game. They drove to Nichols' place, a substantial house beside a lake on the edge of town. Small faces peered from the straw of doghouses. Noses sniffed as they passed, trying to identify the visitors.

"My boy's team," said Nichols proudly when they entered. His house smelled of bacon, eggs, and toast. Nichols' wife, Midge, a compact woman with toothy smile, welcomed them. Isaac finally removed his jacket. Midge was interested in Nick and what brought him to Sleetmute. Over a full plate, Nick was happy to talk.

Isaac ate quietly.

The twelve-year-old boy watched wide-eyed.

"Terrible crash," said Midge. "How did it happen?"

"Don't know yet," said Nichols. "The pilot said they went down during a slow turn. He likely stalled."

"Stalled?" said Nick.

"If you turn too slow and tight," said Nichols. "You can fall like a rock. Steal your own air. One of our pilots did that doing stream counts. Killed him."

"Why were they out in this fog!" said Midge.

"The wolf, I guess," said Nick, spearing more bacon.

"The wolf?"

"That runner."

"I thought this might happen," said Nichols glumly.

"Your wolf?" Midge asked her husband.

Nick looked at her surprised.

"He caught that wolf," she said.

"Wish I hadn't," said Nichols.

Nick wanted more. But he wasn't going to embarrass his host by asking. The biologist obliged anyway.

"I knew they came over to look," said Nichols. "They called ahead to tell us. Somebody's going to get killed, I said. They were damn lucky. Lucky to be found. How is it you found them so fast?"

Isaac stared beyond the picture window and said nothing.

"Oh, school!" declared Midge.

She grabbed jackets and rushed her son out the door. The truck rumbled away.

"How'd you find them so fast?" Nichols asked again, this time to Nick.

"When they didn't reach McGrath, I went out looking," said Nick simply.

"They friends of yours?"

"No."

"You search and rescue?"

"No."

"But you went out? Why?"

Why *had* he gone out? Nick thought about it. It wasn't friendship. He had liked Nils. Not Geoff Sturgis particularly. It was Camilla. He went for her.

"They're friends of my partner in Sleetmute. She got worried. So I went out to look. I was calling for them in the fog. That's how Isaac found me."

Nick chewed his bacon. He couldn't say more.

Nichols looked puzzled.

Finally Isaac spoke.

"They crashed on my trapline."

Nichols was dissatisfied. He turned back to Nick.

"How'd you know where to look?"

"The last transmission from the radio collar. We got that from Fish and Game in Juneau. I took a bearing."

Nichols frowned at this. He retrieved a large map from a corner and unrolled it on the living room table. It was a well-used topographic map filled with colorful pencil marks and hand-written notes.

"That's the crash site?"

Nichols pointed to a small ridge between the Tatlawiksuk and Cheeneetnuk drainages.

Isaac nodded.

"You followed a bearing?"

Nick studied the map. He traced the presumed bearing from south of Farewell to a point on the Kuskokwim upriver from Stony River. It crossed the Cheeneetnuk.

The topographic sheet showed more detail than the chart he used. Nick saw he had strayed off the Cheeneetnuk when he chased the mysterious lights in the fog. The map showed an unnamed highland near the mouth of the Tatlawiksuk. It rose seven hundred feet above that river. The trail he followed had led him there.

"Your trapline's in here?"

Nichols' finger indicated the crash site.

Isaac said nothing.

Suddenly, Nick understood what was happening. Isaac wasn't cooperating with Nichols. He was offering nothing but the barest outline. He hardly looked at the topographic map. He wouldn't touch it.

Keith Nichols sat back and studied the guests.

"You know, that runner, that wolf everybody is after, she may be infected with dog lice. I captured that wolf. I wish I hadn't. She got put on a plane to the Kenai. She may have caught lice there."

"Does she have it?" asked Nick.

"I got to imagine the worst possibility, because if that lice gets into the wolf packs here, it's all over. You know about canine lice?" Nichols directed this to Isaac. "It would ruin our wolves. Ruin them. Our wolves would be finished."

It became clearer to Nick. It was Isaac he wanted to talk to. Nichols invited both to breakfast. But he was after something from Isaac.

The biologist tapped the map.

"When this fog lifts, I'm going out myself."

"To find her?" asked Nick.

"If I can."

"Then what?"

Nichols looked at him darkly.

"You going to shoot her?" pushed Nick.

"I'm going to catch her and treat her."

Nick waited for more. But Nichols was finished.

Sturgis had a cage for the wolf he named Penny, his internet darling, a good-will ambassador for wild wolves everywhere. Sturgis said Fish and Game would put her back on the Kenai. That was a certain death sentence.

Nichols was Fish and Game.

The biologist's finger moved above Big River.

"We found her here," he spoke again to Isaac. "Hal Martin put down on this little pond. A black male shadowed her. Across this other ridge."

Isaac's eyes followed the finger.

Nick knew that for Isaac, a Native trapper born in the area, every pond and valley and ridge beneath Nichol's finger meant something.

"Gunterson said they were a solitary pair, kicked out from the main pack. But she wasn't an outcast," said

Nichols, trying to catch Isaac's eye. "She was Big River. She was the leader, the top female, nursing pups.

"Now she's back, through Rainy Pass."

Nichols said it with awe.

"She's going to make it, by God, all the way back to the Big River den. And if she makes it, if she's infected, that pack is ruined. All the wolves of the upper Kuskokwim, the middle Kuskokwim, the whole damn system, if they get infected, they're ruined."

The finger spiraled aimlessly above the drainage.

Nick now understood what Nichols wanted. The biologist sought the answer to an unspoken question.

Where was the den?

Where was the den of the Big River pack?

He believed Isaac Bobby must know.

Isaac stared beyond the picture window toward the town of McGrath, its pole lamps winking off with the growing light above the fog. His face remained expressionless.

He wouldn't divulge it.

He wouldn't give a pack of wolves to Fish and Game.

Nick examined the map again. He saw the colorful marks were data points, references to research by this game biologist who had lived and worked in McGrath for years but was still mistrusted. A bold red line cut across the map near the foothills of the Alaska Range.

"What's this?"

Nick moved his finger down the line.

"Unit boundary," said Nichols, sounding defeated.

"A Game Management Unit boundary?"

"That's right... 19D on this side of the line, 19C on the other side."

McGrath and Nikolai were in 19D. Farewell and its lodge were in 19C. Elsewhere on the map were other red unit boundaries, all meandering.

"It's straight," said Nick. "Don't Unit boundaries usually follow ridges between watersheds or something like that?"

"Yeah," said Nichols. "That one's straight."

"Why?"

Keith Nichols ran his own finger down the straight boundary line. It cut across several drainages.

"Predates me. Could be the only straight unit boundary in the state."

"That's Farewell up there near the mountains?" pressed Nick.

"Yeah, Farewell. 19C is Farewell's subunit."

"They get their own moose hunt in 19C?"

"Yep," said Nichols.

"Separate from 19D?" said Nick.

He pointed near McGrath and Nikolai in 19D.

"Yep, separate hunt."

Nick frowned. He thought about the reason for the wolf relocation program... poor moose-wolf ratios. Too few moose. He recalled James Epchook's complaint about sport hunters wasting moose while floating the rivers. Here might be another piece of the problem... the ground hunters at Farewell. The sport hunters traveled the network of trails on four-wheelers, ferried to and from Anchorage by the bush pilots. Moose meat left the region out of Farewell.

When Nick had landed there, the airstrip at Farewell was the only straight line he saw while crossing the Alaska Range into the upper Kuskokwim. Straight lines didn't exist in nature, like this boundary on the map.

"Does that mean the moose population around Farewell are not the same moose as around the villages?" asked Nick.

Isaac Bobby reengaged. His eyes returned to the topographic map.

"That's how the Board regulates it, how we manage it," said Nichols. "That's what that line means. Separate moose populations."

"Why would that happen?" said Nick, perplexed. "I mean, what's to keep moose here from moving there? I don't see anything that blocks this subunit from this subunit. Wouldn't this be one group of moose that moves along the rivers?"

"That's what you might think," said Nichols, touching the Farewell area delicately. "That's what I once thought too. But that's not what they do."

"How's that?"

"We've been tracking them, investigating that question. Right now I've got radio collars on twenty moose. For the first time we're checking the validity of that line."

"You're tracking moose?"

"Twenty moose. And the preliminary findings are surprising, at least to me. Turns out there are upland moose and there are lowland moose."

The biologist pointed to the marks on the map. Nick saw blue marks on one side of the straight line, red marks on the other.

"There are two different moose populations, just like they've been managed," said Nichols. "Whoever drew that original line knew what they were doing. There's an upland group and a lowland group. They don't mix."

As Keith Nichols said it, he shook his head as if he still didn't believe it.

He disbelieved his own tracking data.

Nick saw that Isaac stared out the window once again.

He had disengaged. He was ready to go.

He had already left.

22

Sun thinned the fog. The tops of the Alaska Range appeared, floating above layers of gray. Nick trailed Isaac Bobby again. They ascended the Big River drainage toward the far mountains, climbing above the hazy light to vantages with long views, then plunging into lingering pockets of fog. The brisk ride cured his fatigue. Day revealed where he had blindly raced the previous night.

Nick called Camilla in Sleetmute before their departure. He found her with the Epchooks. They had just heard the news about the rescue from the FAA in McGrath.

"How were they?" asked Camilla, tired and worried.

"Banged up, but okay, I guess. Their blood pressures were normal," said Nick, passing along the only diagnosis he had heard.

"They weren't bleeding?"

"A little."

"I'll call Anchorage. Providence Hospital?"

"I don't know," said Nick, realizing he hadn't learned any details, rushing them on the plane. Camilla must think him an idiot.

"Nick, you're wonderful!"

That's what floated through his head as he drove. A bright sun and Camilla's praise... a beautiful day.

James Epchook asked for Isaac Bobby.

Nick had passed the phone.

Isaac mainly listened. He grinned several times and said a few things in Deg Hit'an. Nick didn't know that Epchook spoke that language. Refueling at a McGrath station soon after, Nick asked Isaac what Epchook had said that was so funny.

"He said, take care of my son's new Skandic," Isaac grinned. Now that Isaac had Nick firmly connected with Epchook in Sleetmute, the trapper relaxed. He suggested Nick follow him home.

They left Big River to climb a wooded upland. Nick remembered descending this steep slope in the fog. The Cheeneetnuk and Tatlawiksuk flowed off these highlands toward Swift River. The rim commanded astonishing vistas of the Alaska Range. They towered behind Big River, glistening white.

Nick lingered to take it in.

Isaac pulled beside him, studying his homeland. He pointed to the middle distance. Nick shielded his eyes. A moose browsed along a far bank of Big River. Isaac found field glasses to watch. He passed them to Nick.

The moose browsed complacently.

"They move along that way," said Isaac, waving his gloves from the Alaska Range toward the Kuskokwim lowlands.

It made sense to Nick. If he were a moose, he'd prefer the sheltered lowlands to the harsh winds he'd encountered at Farewell near the mountains.

Nick smelled pines. They soon meandered through forested uplands of spruce, birch, and lodge poles. Multiple small rivers creased it, a complex topography of ponds, clearings, and dense copses, prime for marten, beaver, and fox. Their trail picked up a stream that widened as they descended... the Cheeneetnuk.

They broke into a clearing bright with snow. A barking dog bounded out to greet them, the same black dog in the fog last night. The cabin smoked just within the eves of cottonwoods. A beautiful spot.

The trapline shelter was a year-round home. Drying racks and log caches lined the clearing. A wall of firewood stretched behind it. A small pile of junk sat nearby, the spare parts department. The Bobbys stayed even after trapping season ended. Not many people lived in cabins like this, separate from a village.

An old Polaris was parked by the house. It sat in a state of disrepair. Its track lay detached and in pieces. A cracked windshield leaned on a wall.

They found Michael Bobby asleep on the bunk inside the cabin. The younger brother woke and came to the table in unbuttoned overalls, rubbing his eyes. Isaac filled the kettle, put on stew to heat, and spoke softly in Deg Hit'an. Nick presumed he told about the rescue and medevac. Some of what he said had to do with Nick. Michael examined the stranger with wonder.

Isaac switched to Yup'ik to ask if Nick wanted coffee or tea with his stew. Nick said tea. Stretching boards covered the walls. Nick asked about the furs. Beaver was good this winter, Isaac said. But fur prices were bum.

Nick placed the Bobbys between himself and James Epchook, late forties or early fifties. The brothers lived alone. They had relatives in Sleetmute, Stony River, and Lime Village. Lots of Bobbys in Lime Village, Isaac said. His father originally came from there, a village where they spoke Dena'ina. His mother was a Yup'ik from Sleetmute, related to the Epchooks. Michael's mother was Deg Hit'an from Stony River. Isaac said his grandfather also spoke Russian, the language of the church. Nick was astounded. The two brothers were polyglots, proficient in at least four different tongues, yet they lived without people to talk to. Michael hardly spoke at all. He mainly listened and smiled. As the food warmed up, so did Isaac. He talked freely in Yup'ik and English. Michael grunted in assent to whatever his older brother said.

The stew was excellent, beaver flavored with fish oil. Nick praised it and the Bobbys seemed pleased. Isaac used the wild onions that grew in large patches along a nearby pond. The oil came from burbot livers, with frozen greens, cooked down. Nick's tea was laced with bitter tundra plants, sweetened with sugar and condensed milk from a tin.

The cabin was neat and sparely furnished. Furs lined the walls in various stages of preparation. Traps of all sizes hung along the beams. There were no pictures, no frills, no signs of feminine influence. The Bobbys had never been married.

"It's beautiful, really quiet," Nick motioned to the perfect view out the window. "The women don't know what they're missing."

"Who?" said Isaac.

"The women," Nick repeated the joke.

"They all left," said Isaac simply.

"They did? To where?"

Isaac shrugged his broad shoulders.

Michael also shook his head.

He fed a log into the clattering stove.

Then Nick understood. The Bobbys trapped as they did because there was no one to marry. The Bobbys grew up before local schools. Teens got shipped off to boarding schools in other places. Many women never returned. They found spouses and jobs outside.

Nick thought of Frances Egnaty and Dora, the daughter. Would Dora ever choose sewing skins on the Cheeneetnuk over cleaning hotel rooms in Anchorage? He doubted it. Nick considered the furs lining the cabin, the products of thousands of years of knowledge and practice. Was this the last generation of fur trappers on the Upper Kuskokwim? Without women, it would be. Was this how an ancient culture died?

"Your Polaris outside?" said Nick to Michael, feeling slightly depressed.

Michael clanged the stove door. He nodded toward his older brother. The broken Polaris belonged to Isaac.

"What happened to it?"

Isaac hunched slightly.

Michael suddenly found his tongue.

"We dug it out."

"From snow?" said Nick.

"Two days to find it."

"Avalanche?"

Michael nodded.

"James Epchook warned me about that," said Nick, spooning more stew. "Unstable slopes. You on it?"

Isaac nodded and motioned to Michael.

It was his story to tell.

"My back hurt," said Michael.

He indicated the oval pelts tacked on plywood sheets lining the walls, no doubt by him, the youngest brother.

"So I went out. I drove up Second River. Large prints over there, maybe like an animal waking up. I saw his Polaris tracks. I thought, what's he doing up here? I followed them to the rim. I looked over. Lots of snow went down right there. His tracks went down too.

"I got scared. I looked this way. I looked that way. Nothing. Just snow. Then I saw it. Sticking up."

"What?"

"A glove, sticking up."

"Huh!" said Nick.

"I dug around that glove."

Michael started laughing.

"He was still stuck to it."

Isaac grinned mischievously.

"There was an arm. A shoulder. He was all there."

They laughed together, like this was a fine joke.

"You were okay?" asked Nick.

"I had an air pocket, like this," said Isaac, demonstrating with an arm around his nose. "One arm like this, the other stretched up. That's the glove he saw. I knew it was outside. I could wiggle my fingers."

"How long were you buried?"

"Long enough to think of lots of cuss words."

"We couldn't find that Polaris for two days," said Michael. "It's all messed up."

"So I use his," teased Isaac.

The reward for saving his older brother's life.

Isaac handed a weathered marmot mitt to Nick… the glove that saved him. He stood at the window to look at the dismantled Polaris.

"It can be fixed. I got to get some parts."

"With all this beaver, you could buy that one I'm riding," joked Nick.

Isaac shook his head. He liked the old Polaris.

Nick turned to Michael.

"Good thing you found him, so he could find that plane."

That recalled the puzzle Nick wondered about.

"You were checking traps… after midnight? That's how you found that plane?"

"No, he heard that dog, Ciuk," said Michael, answering for his brother.

The black dog slept outside in the pale sun beside a cache. Hair flopped over his eyes.

Ciuk meant 'bangs.'

Isaac leaned against the sill to tell that story. It was the one he wouldn't tell to Nichols in McGrath. But Nick was okay. He was James Epchook's partner's nephew, a Yup'ik who liked his stew and tried to sell them a borrowed Skandic. Isaac put a finger on the pane, pointing into the yard.

"He barked at that sled. A wolf climbed in it."

"A wolf?" said Nick, surprised.

"That wolf climbed in to die. Ciuk didn't like it. He woke me up. I thought, why is he barking at midnight? Weasels after the meat? I got up and looked."

"A wolf?"

"I knew him, all right," said Isaac. "I used to watch that one. A good hunter."

Isaac watched wolves.

No wolf pelts hung on the walls of the cabin.

"You trap wolves?"

"Sometimes," said Isaac.

Michael worked his fingers.

"Six years," said Michael.

The last time the Bobbys had trapped for wolves.

Nick had never heard of a wolf in a sled.

"Was he sick?"

"He climbed in to die. He had no blood left," said Isaac grimly. "Cuts… here and here and here behind the knee. He lost his blood."

Michael listened, mesmerized.

This had happened just last night.

Nick remembered the brother's face. Michael looked frightened when Nick came through the door.

"Who did that?" said Isaac angrily. "Not a fight between wolves. He was so weak, I picked him up, he didn't even mind. I put him there beneath that cache.

"Then I got my gun. I told him, 'I'm going hunting.'"

Michael nodded, remembering.

"Hunting?" asked Nick.

"For that one who did it," said Isaac. "This was not the first wolf. It killed another at Big River. Ripped up its back. I saw it from the bluff with my scope. Then it chased me into that avalanche. Big green eyes. That's how it happened."

Into the avalanche?

"I got mad. I took that dog, Ciuk. A hunting dog. I put his nose on that blood. He would follow it, even it's foggy.

"That's how I found it in the trees. He took me to that plane. By myself, I couldn't get them out. I wrapped them in blankets. Then I heard shouts like search and rescue. I found your tracks."

Isaac looked at Nick strangely.

"They went up a mountain."

Nick nodded.

"Then you came out. I thought you were a ghost or something. But that dog decided you smelled okay."

So Ciuk had found the plane.

None of it made sense to Nick.

"What killed that wolf?"

"I don't know. I saw him once. Big green eyes."

"A carayak," whispered Michael.

Isaac said nothing to that.

A carayak?

In Lower Yukon villages, 'carayak' meant a monster, something ferocious like a bear. This carayak killed wolves. Through the window, Nick saw Ciuk beside the sled, nothing beneath the cache.

"Where's the wolf?"

"He walked away," said Michael.

"Walked away?"

"When I looked, he was gone."

"Why were you up there?" said Isaac. "Up on that mountain? I thought you were a ghost."

Nick poured more tea. It was his turn.

He told his part of last night's strange events, how he found the Swift River, the first mouth past the Stony. Then he found the Cheeneetnuk, the first left up the Swift. He shouted at intervals in the fog, trying to find the plane if it had gone down. Then he saw lights. As he neared them, the snowmachine took off.

"I chased it," said Nick. "It went up that mountain to a cliff. A duck stopped me. It flapped into my face. I thought it went off the cliff. I searched with a flashlight."

"No tracks."

Neither Bobby spoke.

They waited, just listening.

"That's why I was up there. I chased that snowmachine. I looked with the flashlight because it must have gone over the edge. Then I saw you and the dog. You said a plane was down."

Still, neither spoke.

"What was that?" said Nick finally.

"It left no tracks?" said Michael.

"No tracks."

"A phantom," Isaac nodded grimly.

"Never chase it," said Michael, unsurprised.

Nick sat dumbfounded.

"A phantom? What's that?"

"You saw, it left no tracks," said Isaac.

"Just let it alone," said Michael again.

Isaac stood for his parka.

"Let's go," he declared.
"Where?" asked Nick.
"That trail of blood."

* * *

Isaac drove with Michael seated behind.
Ciuk rode in the sled.
Nick followed on the Skandic, reworking the strange conversation. Phantoms left no tracks, Isaac had said. Never chase it, Michael declared. Neither seemed surprised by Nick's story.
Were they saying?
A phantom snowmachine wasn't real?
A phantom was something like an optical illusion?
Was it something caused by freezing fog?
Suddenly, this made sense.
Ice crystals could do strange things with light.
Nick knew this to be true. At times they created circular bows around the sun or moon or streetlamps. Nick had flown above circles of light that appeared to travel in the clouds below the plane, created by sun and ice crystals. At times, fog projected light like lasers. Nick saw that at Sleetmute just yesterday, light shooting skyward from the pole lamps. Fog and ice could shrink and expand objects. When traveling on ice, large distant mountains turned out to be bumps just feet away. Imposing walls turned into small cracks in the river surface. These were all illusions.
Was the phantom he chased an optical effect?
Had he chased his own lights in the fog?
If so, it was a remarkable illusion. He had seen both white headlamp and red taillights. That meant his red taillights had been reflected forward and reproduced directly before him. It was possible, he decided. The fog surrounding him may have formed a reflective chamber that reproduced images. He thought could replicate it with three mirrors, one in front, one behind, and one to the top or side.

Nick recalled how the lights behaved. They sped up and slowed down when he did. Of course they did, because the lights were the Skandic's lights. They turned corners. But so did he. He imagined he followed them, but as likely they turned as he reacted to the curves of the narrow river. They ascended a slope and he followed. This happened at a tight bend in the river. It went straight because he hadn't yet turned. The old trapline at the top was happenstance.

It all made sense.

But what about the bird, the duck that saved his life, flying into his headlamp?

There were no ducks, Isaac said as they prepped for travel. All the ducks flew south by October. Ducks did not overwinter.

A raven or crow, Isaac suggested.

A snowy owl, said Michael.

But it was a duck. Nick heard its wak-wak-wak fade into the distance.

On the other hand, Nick also had been certain he chased a snowmachine.

He nearly drove off a cliff.

Strange things happen in there, James Epchook said.

The crash site looked even more impressive in full daylight. How had anyone survived it?

The wings of the plane were in pieces. One still stuck to a high branch. The fuselage hung nearly vertically, impaled on a spruce. Debris lay scattered everywhere. Nick wandered beneath it, imagining how the plane fell. It looked as if it had come straight down. FAA investigators might get out here at some point. They would analyze the wreckage for causes. Keith Nichols said the plane stalled turning too tightly and too slowly, losing lift, slipping and falling sideways. The tilted fuselage fit the stall theory.

Sturgis said they were shot down.

He was in pain, barely coherent.

Something about a bug. Tell Camilla, a bug shot them down. That didn't make sense. How did one find answers to being shot down? He supposed a careful investigator could do it. To bring a plane down, a bullet would have had to hit something vital, maybe a wing or tail flap.

The Bobbys disappeared down a nearby trail. They followed Ciuk, who tracked the wolf's bloody spoor. Game trails crisscrossed the woods on the broad ridge. Isaac occasionally trapped it for marten and tree squirrels. Moose browsed between drainages and created the paths.

Nick came upon an aluminum satchel in a berry bush. He opened the latches. The rifle for shooting tranquilizer darts. Styrofoam forms protected it. It waited to be pieced together and used.

Nick scanned the debris. By a wing section, he came upon the cage, boxed and intact. He began a pile. Someone would want the equipment back.

He found the tent and sleeping bags and a digital video camera, completely sound. Sturgis was prepared to film the captured wolf. Under a wheel he discovered the case with vaccine and hypodermic needles, still unharmed. Nick now understood that the plane had not fallen hard. The spread of branches had absorbed the energy and slowed the plane's descent. It shook things out. Snow and brush had cushioned the final impacts. The slow fall had saved Nils and Sturgis.

Nick brought his snowmachine around. He packed the salvaged items into the sled. He still missed the darts for the rifle. He hadn't found them in the snow. Nick walked to the fuselage and stuck his head inside its hanging door. A sturdy spruce rammed through the front window. Miraculously, the tree had passed between Nils and Sturgis. The plane hung on it precariously. Driven by the emergency, Nick had climbed around inside.

In the light, he felt less certain about it. But as the plane hadn't fallen then, it probably wouldn't now. Nick grabbed the pilot's seat and hauled himself inside. In the co-pilot's well Nick found the dart case, an oblong aluminum box caught beneath a foot pedal. He retrieved it. As he did, he saw another thing.

A small round hole punched through the floor. Bright snow showed through like a shiny quarter. Nick touched it. The metal edges punched inwards. He put his eye carefully to it. He looked through a mangle of severed cables into the woods beyond.

A bullet hole.

It ripped upwards through the plane.

Or was it?

Nick examined the inside of the cockpit. Sheered tree branches had shattered the plexiglass windows. Any of these limbs could punch a hole in the skin of a falling plane. He saw dents, rips, and tears everywhere. Imagination made this round puncture into a bullet hole. Like turning reflected light into a phantom snowmachine.

Nick slipped from the cockpit to the snow. The case wasn't heavy. He opened it. The thin darts and their tranquilizing cartridges lay intact, precision tools for bringing down a wolf. The plane crash was all because of that. In an unusual causal chain, a transplanted wolf had led to this near-fatal crash. Another wolf brought Isaac to it along a trail of blood.

He closed the case, shoved it beneath the sled's tarp, and cinched the bundle down.

Nick found Isaac and Michael less than a quarter mile away. They had parked the snowmachine, blocking a narrow trail through heavy brush. Michael wandered the brush with Ciuk, who explored game tracks as if on a romp. Isaac knelt in the trail. Blood splattered it.

"This is where it happened," said Isaac grimly, pointing along a path of red rosettes on the snow. "He went that way. He couldn't run. See how he limped."

Isaac walked a few steps and knelt again at a place of disturbed snow. He took a knife from his belt and pushed the blade into the ground. It disappeared easily into granulated ice. He did this in several spots.

"Something was buried here," said Isaac.

The blade brought up curled wood shavings.

"Spring trap," declared Isaac.

"Whose?"

"I don't know."

"The trap cut him up?"

"No, that's where he got cut up," said Isaac, pointing at the bloody snow close by. "Then he limped that way."

The trail of blood ended at the cabin.

Nick tried to imagine what had happened. The wolf was trapped, then cut a few feet away. It limped off, dripping blood. Had the wolf escaped somehow? Where was the trap now?

Michael approached with Ciuk at his ankles. His gloved fingers held something. He placed it in his brother's palm, a brown paper cigarette butt, barely weathered. It still smelled of tobacco.

The green-eyed monster smoked.

23

Camilla's pain grew.

The dull pounding of a persistent hammer, prisoners beating iron bars, harder, harder.

She tried to defeat it, adding columns of numbers, aggregated, analyzed, one brain lobe opposing another. Thoughts moved slowly against the pounding, a struggle along pain-filled paths. Neural channels flooded. Cold panic rose. She felt it as a smothering in her chest.

She closed her eyes, took large breaths.

Willed herself calm.

Nick, she silently called.

That first night, Geoff missing, she waited in dread for news with the pain, restless, a growing apprehension. She hadn't really slept. The footsteps came. The echoes and calls. 'It's time.' She needed to run but her body failed her. 'No, please,' she pleaded. 'Don't take her!'

She jolted awake.

Nothing but emptiness, unending despair.

The lawyers had phoned that evening, subdued. Two more days, they reminded her, then the preliminary hearing. 'But don't come,' they had decided. Shouldn't she meet the judge? 'Not yet, not without risk,' they advised. 'He's traditional, a family judge, he might misunderstand your hair, your profession, anything. It's a preliminary hearing. Let us handle it. But was there anything else?'

They asked at the end, as if they'd already found the rope short. She'd wept and the night of pain began after the useless pills.

Nick, she called through the agony.

She cracked her wet eyes to the cabin's yellow light, squinted at the dim numbers, felt the fear settle. The prisoners hammered. She added. Numbers. Dollars. Subsistence losses and recovery. Damages and compensation, injuries and remediation.

To make it whole.

After the rescue, she had phoned the right hospital. Geoff was stable, post-op, repaired and sedated, three broken ribs and a bruised spleen, said Nils. Thank God. They saved us, he said, dragged us, roped like logs on the sleds. He hadn't said a proper thanks. The door closed and the plane took off. Tell Nick that Nils said thanks.

Camilla closed her eyes, imagined the falling plane, a plummet of metal and flesh in slow motion. Panic rose to meet it. She fought for deeper breaths.

God, I'm fucked.

Her fear ran like the wolf.

Where was Kaylin now?

She'd never find her, never see her child again, never again. She was so tired of the endless running... the constant pain. So hopelessly tired.

She woke to a sputtering into silence. Boots knocked hollow in the entryway. Cold flowed through the door.

"Nick!"

She came up from the table and collapsed into him.

"You okay?" she heard him say.

She nodded and clung.

"Nils says thanks," she whispered into his neck.

"Yeah," whispered Nick.

"He didn't have a chance to say thanks."

"Okay," whispered Nick.

"Thanks for saving them. For saving Geoff."

She found herself crying.

"Migraine?" whispered Nick.

Camilla nodded.

"Let's get sleep," whispered Nick.

He gently pulled her off.

"Yeah," muttered Camilla.

She stumbled down the hall and fell onto the bed. She felt blankets cover her, fingers through her hair, a descent into blackness. The fear rose up.

It began running.

Running. Running.

* * *

"She's still asleep," Nick said wearily as James Epchook poured him coffee from the breakfast pot.

"Is she sick?" said Sophie. "What's wrong with her?" She brought smoked fish, bread, and canned peaches.

"Migraines."

"Oh?" said Sophie unsurely.

"Headaches so bad they make her cry," said Nick sadly.

"Poor…" said Sophie, drawing out the word in sympathy.

Nick ripped into breakfast. Hunger had waked him at six. The fog had lifted. So he walked beneath the morning stars to the Epchooks, finding them awake. Elders never slept late. James Epchook sat with him at the table, glad for company. He ate in a comfortable silence for some while. Then he quietly described the rescues. He told of the search for the plane in the fog, his meeting the Bobbys, the race to McGrath with the injured, and the airlift to Anchorage.

James listened proudly. It was a fine story.

"Did they talk to you?" asked Sophie finally.

"Who? The Bobbys?" said Nick.

Sophie began laughing.

"They don't always talk," said James.

"Remember we went over there with Sarah?" said Sophie to James, her eyes twinkling. "Little Mike peered around the corner of the house. He looked scared."

James laughed, remembering Michael's face.

"They must not see too many people," said Nick.

"Not too many girls," said Sophie.

"They talked to me. We talked about trapping."

"They know how to trap," agreed James. "They know that place better than anybody. He found that plane fast."

They had followed the trail of blood from the butchered wolf. Nick left them near the crash site, still trying to decipher it.

"Better than that biologist at McGrath, Keith Nichols. You know him?"

"He comes around, the big one."

"Oh, that one," said Sophie.

"Isaac wouldn't answer him," said Nick.

"About what?" asked James.

"Big River wolf dens."

"Why did he ask about that?"

"Because of the wolf called the runner. He wants to catch her at the den. He's afraid she has lice."

"We heard about that wolf."

"What do you think about it?" asked Nick.

"I don't know," said James, thinking.

He turned to his wife, started laughing again.

"When we were kids, we would have been in trouble, huh? Everybody had lice back then. If they shot you for lice, there'd be no more Eskimos."

"Dog lice ruins a wolf," said Nick. "Better to be dead, they say."

"Shoot us too," said Sophie testily.

"What?" Nick said, surprised.

"Then shoot us too. Look at that old woman you've been pestering. Bum legs, scarred up knees, swollen red, but where does she go? Everywhere. She does more than anybody, fishing and cutting and sewing. I saw her going for berries on her butt!"

James laughed. He too had seen Frances Egnaty during fall berry picking, scooting on her butt.

"Or that boy, Joseph Icaran," said Sophie to her husband. "Burned up in that fire. No fingers left, just stubs. Scarred-over eye. They said he would die like his sister. But he was strong. He lived! Got married. Five kids."

"He's a good shot, one eye, no fingers," said James.

Here was Sophie's point. Who lived without troubles? Despite them, Yup'iks succeeded.

"I hear it's like booze," said Nick. "The lice kills them slowly, spreads, one after another, until it ruins the whole pack. It's hard to stop."

"Why did they catch that wolf?" said James. "I heard she had pups."

"A relocation program. Too many wolves. That's what Fish and Game says. Is that right?"

"Yes, there are too many wolves," James agreed.

"Why?" said Nick, glad to be consulting an expert. "I don't know about wolves. There aren't any wolves around my home."

"No wolves?" asked Sophie surprised.

"There used to be wolves when there were caribou. The elders say the caribou left. The missions brought in reindeer. One hard winter the wolves crossed the Yukon and killed them. They only ate tongues. Then they disappeared."

"I've heard that story," said James. "Something bad happened there. I don't know what it was that happened."

"Caribou are coming back now," said Nick. "The Western Arctic herd is moving south. St. Michaels saw them. It's been a hundred years."

"Then you'll see wolves too. The caribou and wolves come together."

"There are too many here?" Nick asked again.

"It happens," said James simply. "The moose go down, the wolves don't."

"What's 'relocation'?" said Sophie.

"They catch a wolf and fly it someplace else," said Nick. "To reduce wolf populations."

Sophie looked skeptical.

"It happens sometimes," repeated James. "In the old days, there got to be too many wolves."

"What happened back then?" said Nick.

"They would do something about it. Only when things got real bad, when there was not enough food."

"What did they do?"

"Find the dens and kill the pups."

"Kill the pups?" said Nick, surprised.

"That was the quickest way," said James. "You killed the pups. You let the older ones alone. You don't mess with them. Wolves have their own ways. They are like us. They have their ways of doing things. The hunters did that only when things got real bad, like not enough food."

Killing pups.

Nick had never heard of this approach for reducing wolf populations.

"You can't do that today," said James. "If Fish and Game heard you killed pups at a den, you'd have big trouble."

"Is it real bad now?"

"What?"

"Not enough food."

"Oh, it's bad, all right," said James. "In those places upriver from us, Nikolai, Medfra, Telida, there's not enough moose. People have moved out. They say those places are just one or two families now. It's okay here. But you have to work to find a moose."

Nick remembered the earlier conversation about outside floaters and waste. More hunters. More competition. More waste. Fights over fewer moose. When you fight over animals, they disappeared. That's what the elders had taught Nick.

"But they'll do these other things," said James about Fish and Game. "Relocations, shooting from planes. Now we hear about lice."

"I hope they don't shoot us," huffed Sophie.

"Isaac Bobby knows that den?" asked Nick.

"I don't know. He knows that area better than anybody," said James. "If anybody knows where it is, he does."

"Do you know where it is?"

"No," said James, shaking his head.

He sipped coffee, thinking.

Sophie left for the kitchen.

Nick felt worn out. He should check on Camilla.

He rose to leave.

James Epchook smiled at him.

"But somebody could find it."

* * *

School was starting.

Kids ran along the paths of town, laughing, fooling around. Four-wheelers zoomed with students. A boy with a familiar face ran up. The mayor's son.

"Cama-i," smiled Nick.

"Cama-i," he replied. "They said to tell you to come to my house."

"Where's your house?"

"Over there," the boy waved. "The big antenna."

"Who said to come over there?"

"Your girlfriend. Bye."

He ran off for school.

Nick walked the direction indicated.

Passing the airstrip, he spied a familiar plane... Chet Miller's. The bootlegger was in town. Nick diverted toward it. He touched its engine. Cold. It had sat for a while, maybe the night. He could guess why. A delivery. By ordinance, Sleetmute was dry. Alcohol possession was illegal. But booze deliveries were hard to stop on the Kuskokwim.

Nick saw the mysterious bracket under the wing strut. He touched it again. A camera mounting? Who could tell? Beneath the wing was something crunched in the snow.

A cigarette butt.

Brown paper.

As he walked, Nick mulled over the green-eyed monster that mutilated wolves. Somebody had smoked a brown-paper cigarette by the granite rock near the crash site, probably off trail to keep it clean. That smoker had set a trap and caught a wolf that Isaac knew, a good hunter. The wolf had escaped, mutilated, and limped as far as the cabin.

It curled in a sled to die.

Enraged, Isaac Bobby had tracked the blood trail with Ciuk, looking for a monster with green eyes. Michael said a carayak. Isaac had not challenged that suggestion. They found the trap site near the crashed plane, and the brown-paper cigarette.

Was Chet Miller the monster?

Nick recalled the topography, a game trail crossing a brushy ridge between streams. There was no place for a plane to land. Also, it was too foggy to fly that day. If he was the monster, Miller didn't use his airplane.

Nick saw no wolf carcass at the Bobbys' cabin.

Michael said the wolf walked away. It found the strength to die elsewhere. Nick had seen the blood trail. Ciuk followed it easily. The brothers' story was too strange to be made up. Nick believed it.

The tall antenna stood above a newly refurbished house painted blue. A plump middle-aged woman with a friendly smile greeted him at the door, Mary Showalter, the mayor's wife. To Nick's surprise, Camilla and Frances Egnaty sat in her living room. A familiar voice spoke from the speakerphone. It was Mel Savidge in Juneau.

"Nick, come in!" gestured Camilla.

Her long lashes squinted like she stared at the sun. She looked worn, abused, a fairy waif in the grip of some terrible enchantment.

"Mel, Nick is here."

"Hi Nick!" said a voice cracking with static.

"She found us," explained Camilla.

"They said to call the mayor's house. How are you, Nick? You're the talk of the town!"

"Which town?" said Nick warily.

All his life he had worked to avoid being the talk of any town.

"Juneau. It's gotten crazy here, so I thought I'd call. Actually, I was sort of ordered to call you. You and

Camilla are now on the governor's radar screen. Congratulations!"

Nick sat beside Camilla, puzzled. Her eyes were nearly closed. She fought the headache.

"I'm at the capitol," said Mel. "You probably can't hear it, but just outside there's a huge rally going on. It's wild. Speeches. Bullhorns. There are dueling groups with police in between. The anti-control group is shouting, 'Save Penny! Save Penny!' They've just heard a speech from Geoff Sturgis, patched in from the hospital in Anchorage. Listen, now they're shouting 'boycott, boycott!' The other group is for wolf control. They've got bullhorns too. They're shouting 'save the moose' and 'save our food,' things like that. Geoff told the crowd that he was rescued by an Eskimo named Nick John, so congratulations, you're on national public radio somewhere."

Frances Egnaty and Mary Showalter shook their heads. Nick looked forlornly at Camilla.

"Nick? You still there?"

"He's here," mumbled Camilla. "But I think he needs some sleep."

"I'll bet," agreed Mel. "You too?"

"You want to talk to us?" asked Camilla, shielding her eyes from pain.

"I was told to call you. The governor's office is frantic. His political coalition is getting hammered. The runner has given the boycott national attention. It's taking off and doing weird things, like the Korean trade delegation. Trade talks are suddenly on hold. The governor is beating on Fish and Game to do something. So we're suspending wolf relocation for a while. What a hoot, eh? They ordered me to call you, to find out what's happening out there. So, here I am. What's happening in Sleetmute?"

Nick frowned at Camilla.

"Fog," said Camilla gamely. "Really, nothing much here. Uh… Nick is back from the rescue. And we have Mary Showalter and Frances Egnaty with us. This is the mayor's home phone."

"Nick?" said Mel.

"Nobody is talking boycotts here," said Nick.

"What are they talking about?"

"Not enough moose."

"People want fewer wolves?"

"Nobody has told me they like wolf relocations," said Nick. "Maybe the governor should just let the local hunters solve the wolf problems, you know, out of the limelight. People want to be left alone."

There was a long pause.

Nick didn't know what else to say.

"What about the runner?" pushed Mel. "What are they saying about that?"

"Uh… Keith Nichols said he's going to look for her," said Nick.

"Yeah, the field biologist in McGrath. I heard that too. Nichols will look for her. Nothing else?"

"Not that I've heard."

"Well, I don't think he'll find her," said Mel.

"Why not?"

"She hasn't transmitted since Farewell. That radio collar is finally dead. How big is the Upper Kuskokwim? Tennessee? He'll never find her."

"What's he going to do?" asked Camilla.

"What's that?"

"If he finds her, what's he going to do?"

"Put her back on the Kenai, if he follows orders."

"I thought they suspended the program."

"Yeah, but she's a fugitive from the old program, so they'll want to put her back. There's pressure on Fish and Game to kill her, to free her, to put her on display, all sorts of things. The state won't give her to Sturgis and the boycott, that's for sure. And they can't let her stay on the Kuskokwim or the governor loses votes, or so his handlers think. Fish and Game is so desperate, they're calling zoos."

"Zoos? But what about her babies?" asked Camilla.

"Her babies? Oh, nobody thinks her pups are still alive."

"They're not?"

"They probably died weeks ago."

Camilla's eyes teared up.

"How else are you guys doing?" asked Mel. "How's the project?"

"Okay, it's okay," said Nick quickly. "Interviews. It's okay."

"Yeah," whispered Camilla.

A tear ran down her cheek.

"Well, I've done my duty," said Mel. "I'll pass along the news from the front. Let me know if I can do anything for you. Hey, good job finding that plane, Nick! That was great! Bye!"

And Mel was gone.

Frances hobbled to Camilla.

"You don't look too good," she said sympathetically.

Camilla closed her eyes and shook her head.

"Do you need aspirin?" asked Mary Showalter.

"Yeah, I could use some," whispered Camilla.

Mary disappeared to get it.

"I thought they'd be alive," whispered Camilla.

She looked to Nick, searched his face for hope.

"Yeah," said Nick sadly.

"Couldn't they still be alive?"

"I don't know," said Nick softly. "What would they eat?"

"Another wolf could feed them?"

"I don't know. I think there's one nursing wolf."

Other tears came down her cheeks.

"I thought she'd find them. I thought they'd see her again."

Camilla began weeping. Mary Showalter arrived with the aspirin. The two old women gathered around her.

Nick sat off to the side, feeling terrible. He saw what had happened. Camilla had identified with the runner, like herself, separated from children. Regardless what happened next, the runner had failed.

She would never see her pups.

"They don't know everything," said Frances kindly, patting Camilla's arm. "Wolves are like people, smart. They do what they have to do."

Camilla nodded silently.

"Maybe a sister took those babies and cared for them," said Mary. "That's what we used to do. Chew up a little food and put it into their mouths. That's how we always fed babies without milk."

"They don't know everything," said Frances.

Camilla wiped her eyes with her wrists.

"Thanks," she whispered.

They laid her on the couch with a blanket.

Nick got up to go. He was feeling useless.

"Nick," whispered Camilla, sensing him leaving, her eyes closed. "Can you do a favor? The blue notebook is at Frances' house. It's got the old numbers. Can you get it? I have the new one here. We need the blue book to show how they've changed."

"On the table," said Frances, looking anxious.

"We're supposed to call Feinberg," muttered Camilla wearily. "Talk to him about the numbers. You can help to translate."

Nick walked the glassy paths, slick after the fog.

He felt as weary as Camilla looked. What was happening to her? She looked beaten. He needed to steam, a real bath. He needed to purge his body of the stress. He'd join Epchook tonight. That's what he needed, a real steam. Maybe Camilla needed that too.

He came to Egnaty's place. Why did Frances look so anxious? On the table, she said.

He knocked once and let himself in.

The house was a gloom, every curtain shut. It smelled of liquor and stale cigarettes. He saw why Frances was at the Showalter's. She had escaped her own home. The living room table presented a clutter of dishes and old food around a square, well-used bottle of scotch.

He saw no blue notebook.

The kitchen was a mess of unwashed pans and cutlery. No notebook here. He heard low chuckling. He backtracked to the main room.

Dora Egnaty leaned in the hallway, grinning.

She wore a long unbelted shift that fell to her ankles.

"Want a smoke?" she asked.

She moved to the table in a post-party stagger. She found a rumpled box and flipped a cigarette into her wide lower lip, just above the scar. It slipped in neatly.

"Sure," said Nick, bending close.

She pushed one into his mouth, giggling, found a tiny lighter and lit them both. She lowered herself into a chair, her legs wide and relaxed, and puffed toward the ceiling. Nick sat too. He was worn out. He needed a smoke.

"The big hero," teased Dora, in the gloom her smile a blurry white without the jaggedness.

"Yeah," Nick laughed lightly.

"They're talking about you," said Dora, this time without the sneer, almost admiration.

Nick shrugged as if he didn't care.

Gossip traveled.

"They wonder how you found it so fast," said Dora, pushing a bit closer, looking into Nick's broad young face, a Bering Sea face, the face of a successful hunter.

"I got lost in the fog... chasing phantom snowmachines," joked Nick. "Then I stumbled into a Bobby. He found it tracking a dead wolf."

Dora checked his eyes for deception. Saw none.

"Chasing phantoms?" she asked, impressed.

"Nearly off a cliff," he pushed his hand over an edge.

Dora picked a glass at random and poured scotch. She took a sip and handed it to Nick. He sipped too.

"Scared me shitless," Nick laughed.

Dora took it back, listening carefully.

"A duck saved me," said Nick.

"What?" she smiled in wonderment, forgetting her pretensions.

"A duck saved me from the phantom. It flew at my face like a bat. Whoosh! Flapped at my headlamp! I panicked and turned like this and flipped over. Right at the edge of the cliff."

His hand pushed over again.

"No," breathed Dora.

She passed back the glass. Nick drained it.

"Then I stumbled into Bobby, that trapper and his dog. They tracked a dead wolf in the fog to the plane. It hung nose down from a tree. No wings. Ripped to shreds."

Nick shook his head. He remembered the scattered debris, thinking nobody had survived. He drew on his cigarette.

"Which Bobby?" asked Dora.

"Isaac," said Nick. "You know him?"

She laughed scornfully.

"I've seen them," she said, pouring more scotch. "They live up there?"

"It's really beautiful," declared Nick.

Dora looked at him, disbelieving.

"Cottonwoods, open white meadow, streams and ponds. It must be amazing in summer."

"Amazingly buggy," sneered Dora

"Beautiful and buggy," agreed Nick.

He took Dora's glass and finished it.

"You partied?" he surveyed the room.

"Come on, I'll show you something," grinned Dora.

She grabbed his hand and pulled him down the hall. The bedroom smelled sweet and grassy. His eyes adjusted to its darker gloom. Dora quickly worked in a corner. A flick of a lighter was followed by puffing. She jumped on the bed and passed the sweet-smelling pipe to Nick. He took it, drew a long hit. He felt the smoke mingle with the scotch, a fuzzy lightness that filled his brain.

He coughed.

Dora laughed, taking the pipe back.

"Good," said Nick, sitting on the bed.

"Yeah," said Dora, teasingly. "So is this."

She did something with her hands behind her, hidden by the gloom.

"What?"

"What you're here for," she laughed.

She showed the blue notebook.

"I've been studying it," she teased, accenting the 'study' because he was university. She opened the pages.

"It's been revised," said Nick, taking more hits from the pipe.

"Yeah?" said Dora, waiting while Nick held the smoke.

"Yeah," exhaled Nick.

"Revised... even better," smiled Dora, tucking the notebook beneath her.

Nick shrugged and passed the pipe.

Dora tucked it somewhere behind her too.

"Especially for you and that girl," she purred.

"Camilla?" said Nick. He shrugged again, feeling the buzz in his brain. He teetered uncertainly, coming to his elbow on the bed.

Dora laughed.

"Twenty percent," she purred. "Ten for you, ten for her, sixty for us. Not too bad."

She leaned back, finding the pillow for her neck.

"Sixty of two million. One million two hundred thousand... not too bad. And revised, getting even better."

She ran her hands to her ankles, grabbed, and slipped her dress along her thighs, spreading her legs. In the gloom, Nick saw the smooth firmness and the darker triangle below the gathered cotton. She laughed again.

Nick bent his frame down. He carefully placed a hand beside her neck. He leaned, guiding his face toward hers, finding her lips with the tiny scars. His other hand felt along the smooth leg. He kissed as his hand moved up the thigh. Their tongues touched lightly. He gently plunged his hand beneath her and found the prize.

He rose, the blue notebook in his hand.

"Thanks," he said.

Nick deftly kicked off the bed.

He strode down the hall, tucking the notebook into his belt. He found his parka at the table, grabbed the bottle of scotch, and stuffed it inside a large pocket. A cigarette butt smoldered precariously on the edge of a plate. He squashed it dead.

"Fucker!" she called from the bedroom.

Not today, he thought.

Outside the midday light dazzled.

He strode toward his cabin in a growing fury, his mind full of booze and hash. Drunken all-night parties... an elder has to flee her own home! Twenty percent, he heard her say. Ten for you. And in the ashtray he saw them among the dirty whites, crushed and reeking.

Brown-paper butts.

Inside the cabin, Nick collapsed on the broken couch.

He swigged scotch from the bottle, opened the notebook. His tired brain worked down the columns of numbers. 'Two million plus' the final total read, the plus for other kinds of damages like pain and suffering. Two million alone for the subsistence losses, the lost harvests, the lost sharing, the interrupted transmission of cultural knowledge between generations, the compromised rights to traditional areas, the lost role as an elder, the lost processing of foods for others, the lost sewed furs and crafted products, a comprehensive, detailed list, pounds and dollars attached, three years aggregated. Annotations referenced interviews with Frances. Careful. Meticulous. The wonders of anthropology.

Camilla had converted Yup'ik traditions into hard cash.

One more revision, a call to the lawyers, the claim, the settlement, and the children cashed out.

Another family displaced.

An envelope fell from the notebook, wedged like a bookmark, addressed to Frances Egnaty from Feinberg's legal firm. Nick read it, a short statement of final payment should the suit prevail. Sixty percent went to Frances. Twenty percent to the legal firm. And twenty percent to the anthropological consultants.

He stuffed the letter back, closed his eyes.

He saw Dora's rapacious grin.

'Not too bad.'

He heard nothing.

But he felt it. Something moved. Outside.

Dora? Back for the book?

Nick cracked his eyes to the windowpanes above the couch. Beyond the sagging glass he saw movement beneath the abandoned cache. A furtive shadow. Nick squinted again. It vanished.

In the entryway he found Epchook's rifle. Checked the load. Drew on his parka.

The outside cold cleared the fog from his brain.

He cautiously moved to the weathered cache.

Knelt beneath it.

Red rosettes splattered the hard snow. Bright. Barely frozen. Drips trailed away.

Blood trail.

An eerie feeling gripped him. He took a deep breath to calm his insides and rose to his feet. The splattered trail led into the wood. He followed.

The trail left the village. It weaved among snowy humps and hollows, crossed a frozen slough, and entered a thicker wood. Nick climbed a low ridge to its top and descended. The blood trail entered a crisscrossing of game trails. He quickly lost it in brush.

Ahead, the wood ended. He stalked carefully to a glade, bright with sunlight.

It stopped him cold.

Caribou dangled at the far edge. Gaunt antlers tangled in trees, stretching necks, heavy heads high off the snowy ground. Noosed. The caribou strangled from rawhide snares.

Shadows flitted beneath them.

Wolves!

They fed on the carcasses.

Noses came up, dripping.

Caribou blood. That's what he followed. It came off a wolf prowling the cache.

The pack broke and dispersed like smoke.

A solitary wolf remained. A female. She stood at the glade's edge, a gray coat, bright face, young and lean and alert, studying Nick with an unthreatened gaze.

The wolf lowered her face, dipped playfully to the frozen meadow, and sprang back a few steps. She paused to look over a shoulder and turned to face Nick. She dipped playfully and sprang off again.

Nick entered the clearing, rifle before him. He strode to a caribou and knelt beside it. His glove stroked the coarse coat. Wolves had gnawed a side, exposing raw meat and ribs. He fingered the rawhide noose entangling the antlers, anchoring the beast to poplars.

He touched history.

No one set snares for caribou.

A shadow flickered.

The playful wolf watched him again.

Startled, she turned and bounded a few steps.

She stopped and waited.

Nick left the caribou. He passed among bleached poplars eyed with the scars of old limbs. The wolf danced ahead. The wood quickly ended at the edge of a white meandering glade opened to the midday sky.

The she wolf waited on its far side.

He stepped into the clearing.

With gunshot cracks, ice broke beneath him.

Nick grabbed as he fell.

He caught an edge by his armpits, arms stretched out on a shelf. His legs hung in empty air. Water rushed below him, a torrent in a cleft capped by snow.

He dangled.

The wolf approached warily, head to the ground, eyes level with his.

Nick felt his arms slipping. With a desperate kick, he lunged and reached, scrabbling for a handhold. The shelf cracked loudly. The wolf sprang. Nick grabbed, found her neck. His gloved fingers gripped hair. He felt neck muscles tighten and strain. They held in a tense lock.

The ice shelf shattered.

They fell together, hitting black water.

Nick went under. Frigid currents sucked him deep, tumbling him through a dark tunnel. The wolf tumbled with him. He grabbed and held, felt himself pulled, lifted.

He lay gasping.

A dim chamber... the wolf was locked within his arms. Her lean body felt hot and alive against him. He released from the strangling embrace. The wolf rose and stepped away. She turned toward him, her eyes fixed on his.

He knew her... the misplaced orphan in Epchook's yard, the nameless wolf who mothered voles and carried stuffed socks... Tepsaq's shadow.

No... the wolf clouded and morphed in the dark... it wasn't her.

A slender limb pushed the gray muzzle back. A face shined pale as death within the ruff. Wet hair gleamed black as night. Beautiful eyes pierced his. She cradled an arm. Eagerly she bent to pass it to him, dark eyes shining.

"Nick," she said.

He stared into her arms.

"Nick."

He jolted.

Camilla touched him.

"Nick, wake up!"

"Wha..."

"You're having a dream."

Nick struggled, eyes wide, barely seeing. He lay upon the couch inside the dim cabin. Camilla sat beside him. Cradled in her arm, she passed it to him...

"Nick, wake up, you're having a dream."

Nick lurched upright.

What was happening? His wild eyes swept the room.

"It's freezing," said Camilla.

She moved to the stove and adjusted the flow. Its pungent odor bit the air. She kicked the notebook.

"You found it," said Camilla.

She placed the book on the arm of the couch, carried the empty scotch bottle to the kitchen.

"You didn't come back. I got worried."

Camilla filled the kettle for the stovetop.

She came back to the couch, sat beside him, and searched his face. She reached a hand for his shoulder.

"You're so tired," she said sadly.

Nick jerked back. The recoil shocked her.

"I got worried," she said.

She began to cry. She moved to bury her head by his neck. Nick started to receive her, shoved her back.

He leaped up, heart racing.

"Sorry," groaned Camilla. "I'm sorry, sorry. I'm so fucked up."

"Why didn't you tell me?" cried Nick sharply.

"What?" she croaked.

"The deal! The shares! What do they call it? The cut!"

He was shouting.

"What are you talking about?"

Nick grabbed the notebook, shook out the letter, threw it at her. She read it painfully.

Nick's eyes searched the room.

"I've never seen this," whispered Camilla

Nick didn't respond. He frantically searched the shadows.

"I've never seen this before."

"You didn't know what you'd get?" yelped Nick.

"No. Salaries."

"You didn't know the cut? Twenty percent!"

"No," whimpered Camilla.

Nick shook the notebook in her face, furious.

"Millions for them! And an elder can't even stay in her own fucking house! Chased out of her own house! But that doesn't count, does it! And you pump it up even more. Millions!"

"Scott must have done it," said Camilla, pleading.

Her ex-boyfriend did the contract?

"He said he'd handle it. It didn't matter to me."

Nick slapped the notebook down.

"Of course it doesn't matter! Nothing important matters!"

He was done with it.

Done with the fucking project.

He grabbed his parka.

Camilla stumbled off the couch and grabbed him.

"Don't leave, Nick. Please, not tonight."

"Like your last one?" growled Nick. "That last contract? Anything's for sale! Everything's for sale! Families... babies!"

"Nick!" cried Camilla.

"You going to break this deal too?"

Camilla clung desperately as he moved to the door.

"You sleep with devils! I won't!"

He threw her off.

"They take her tomorrow!" moaned Camilla.

Nick jerked open the door.

"Don't leave! Please, not tonight!"

He stomped out.

24

Fog shrouded the yard.

He stood as if rooted. Where he had stood before, below the abandoned cache.

It rose above him like a threat.

Panic gripped him. And shame.

He sucked in deep breaths. His heart hammered.

He had abused her. Like a common drunk.

But they were real!

The blood, the caribou, the wolves!

The wolf pushed back her muzzle, cradled her arms.

Real!

He fell to his knees and retched.

The door cracked behind him.

"Nick?"

He heard worry in her voice. No deceit, no greed.

"Nick, are you okay?"

"Yeah," Nick swallowed, on his knees, mortified, his face in his own vomit. He stood unsteadily, unable to look at her.

"Come inside," said Camilla.

"I can't."

"Why?"

"There's something... I have to figure out."

There was silence.

"Are you drunk?" asked Camilla.

"I don't know."

There was more silence. Nick turned halfway.

"I'm sorry," he said. "I was mad. The project's fucked and I got mad."

"Yeah," said Camilla, her voice steady, her brow pained.

"Something just happened. Something strange has happened. I have to do something."

"Okay."

"There's something I have to do. But... I'll come back."

"Okay."

"Will you be okay... until I get back?"

There was silence.

Nick turned to leave, feeling even smaller.

"Nick," said Camilla gravely.

"Yeah?"

"I didn't sell or fuck anyone."

The door slammed.

The yard smoked with fog.

He felt like a fool.

His heart stopped racing. The terror left. Still, it took effort. He approached the cache warily, allowing his eyes to adjust.

No wolf crouched beneath it.

Nick knelt. Fumbled a pocket. Withdrew a lighter and flicked on the tiny flame. It shuddered in the cold. He brought it along the surface of the snow. The hard surface glistened.

No blood trail.

He stood unconvinced, faced the woods where the trail had led, and walked into them, feeling his way among the naked boughs. He walked a long while. No glades. No dead caribou entangled in rawhide nooses. No poplar groves. No treacherous torrents.

Nick collapsed with his back to a spruce.

"What's happening?" he groaned.

A raven croaked.

It was real!

Not like a dream!

Nick worked his way back. He came out of the woods by the runway. The plane was gone, Chet Miller, done with his business. Bastard. His cigarettes in Dora's stinking ashtray. His cheap scotch on Frances' table.

Nick's throat burned.

He wandered, out-of-phase, adrift and disconnected, stumbling down unfamiliar paths. Stovepipes breathed sparks into the night. A dog howled mournfully. A chorus followed.

The wolf had lured him. He held her.

She felt like fire. She was beautiful.

Epchook's path.

Small heads pushed from straw-filled houses to track his progress. A black shape bounded to him, Tepsaq, the lucky leader left unchained. She buried her wet nose beneath his arm. Her insistent shove brought Nick completely back.

He patted her shoulder.

"Where's your shadow?"

He couldn't see the orphan. But he felt her watching.

He smelled the steam bath working, finding it behind the house, half buried in snow. Nick dragged open the wooden door. Boots were tucked beneath a bench. Nick slipped inside and peeled off his clothes. A wooden barrel held chilled water. He took a long drink with an enameled cup and doused his face and hair. Dripping, he shouldered through the inner door.

Heat gripped with a hot fist.

The black firebox pulsed in the pit.

A half-melted form hunched beside it... a white lump like wax. James Epchook, his uncle's partner.

Nick positioned close beside him.

The pit breathed fire.

Pores opened. Released.

A hot pool spread on the plywood beneath him. His breathing slowed, each breath a searing of fiery air. He felt his insides cooking.

Through lashes, he saw the ladle lift.

The water poured.

SSSSSShhhhhhhhh…

Steam erupted.

Pain beat him down.

He shrank, sunk in penitence.

SSSSSShhhhhhhhh…

Another wave.

He shuddered, counted out the suffering, eleven, twelve, thirteen, fourteen…

SSSSSShhhhhhhhh…

He sank lower on the wood, twenty-one, twenty-two, twenty-three…

Nick hit the door. He shoved through and collapsed on the cooling room floor. The door shut hard behind him. He lay nearly senseless.

"Ho, ho, ho!"

Muted, it came through the door.

The half-melted lump had beaten him.

Nick believed it only right.

He gulped from the chilled barrel, doused his slimy body, and plunged inside.

Heat gripped again. His pores reopened, an outpouring of hot oil. It streamed off his back, thick and scalding. He shrank with pain and prepared.

The ladle came up.

SSSSSShhhhhhhhh…

The steam erupted.

Nick shuddered, bent low, and took the blows.

Again. And again.

Three more rounds, the old man poured. Twice he chased Nick out. The last Nick endured to the end.

The fire died low. James Epchook threw open the grate and poked the embers into a welcome flame.

"Soap," he pointed to basins.

They lathered and rinsed with water from the pit's reserve. Nick shampooed until his hair squeaked. He leaned his limp body against a hot wall to dry, licked clean by the heat. James did too. They rested in silence.

"That was good," whispered Nick finally.

"Ii'i," agreed James.

"I needed it."

James threw logs into the firebox and shut the grate. He wasn't ready for the cold night. Neither was Nick. The heat returned. They basked in it.

"I worried you had company," said Nick, thinking of James' wife but seeing only the men's boots tucked beneath the cooling room bench.

"Not tonight," chuckled James. "She thought you might come over to wash out lice."

Nick laughed, accepting the gentle teasing.

"Where's your friend?" asked James.

"The cabin."

"Is she better?"

"No," said Nick sadly.

James grunted.

"We'll miss her when she leaves," said James.

The ultimate compliment. They liked Camilla. There was much to like about her. He had abused her badly tonight. His exhausted mind replayed it, the freakish vision, his harsh words.

The unresolved mysteries.

"Uncle, can you tell me something?" ventured Nick cautiously. "What do they say... about phantoms?"

"Phantoms?" said James, surprised by the topic.

"Phantoms... like snowmachines."

"Ah! The phantom snowmachine," nodded James.

Nick looked at him, shocked.

"*The* phantom snowmachine?"

"You don't know about it?"

"No."

The old man leaned back.

He closed his eyes, gathering thoughts. He sipped his cup of cold water from the outside barrel. He cleared his throat. Then he began with the unhurried cadence of a practiced narrator.

"Some say it was a kass'aq."

He slowly shook his head.

275

"Some say he was a miner killed in an avalanche, trying to reach his claim. But that is wrong. It was not a kass'aq, not a miner, but a dina, one of the Digenegh, an Indian."

"Digenegh," said Nick.

"He stayed at Stony River, him and his wife. Oh, how they partied! How they drank to forget! Him and his wife. It was lucky people had dogs back then. The dogs always brought them home. The dogs knew the way, Red Devil to Stony… pulled them home in the sled.

"I don't know how, but he got some money. Maybe trapping. Firefighting. He got some money and bought a snowmachine. Lots of people did. After that started happening, who needed dogs?"

Nick nodded. Working dog teams disappeared.

"It was at a winter fiddle dance, they got real drunk like they always did. This time, no dogs to bring them home. So he drove the new snowmachine, drove it to Stony River, his wife in the sled behind him, real drunk. He made it all right. He got back home, fell into bed. But he forgot… what about his wife? What about her? He had no dogs to unhitch, no dogs to tell him.

"He found her the next day when he woke up. She sat in the sled, frozen dead. That's how he killed his wife.

"Later on, not so long, next winter, they saw him at the fiddle dance. Again, real drunk. So drunk, he forgot where he was. He stumbled around. Finally he just lay down to sleep, right there on the dance floor while the fiddlers played.

"Who began it? I don't know. A dancer kicked at him, lying on the dance floor. 'Get up!' Who did it? I don't know. Maybe that's why he kicked him. 'Get up!' Then another dancer came by, kicked at him too. The fiddlers played. Then another. Kicked him while they danced. And then another.

"They kicked him to death."

Nick shuddered.

"Nobody wanted his snowmachine. That's how she died, behind that snowmachine. So somebody drove it away, took it into the mountains, pushed it off a cliff.

"Ever since, you see it. It comes at night. The phantom... because it leaves no tracks. It wants you to follow. They say, let it alone. Just let it alone. It takes you to that cliff. That's where it goes. That's where it only goes. Just let it alone."

James chuckled.

"Kind of a ghost story," he laughed, slapping Nick's knee.

"Yeah," Nick whispered weakly.

They sat in silence, their bodies licked dry.

"Uncle," ventured Nick again. "You know that plane parked on the strip today? It had a bracket under the right strut. A welded bracket about this big. I hadn't seen that kind before. Somebody told me, that's a mount for taking aerial photographs."

James frowned with doubt.

"I think that bracket is how I got that wolf outside," said James, "that orphan, Tepsaq's shadow. Somebody has been shooting from planes."

It was a gun mount.

Joel Haggarty had lied to Nick at Stony River.

"What kind of gun?"

"I've never seen it. But I've seen what it does. It tears up a wolf like it's been through a war."

A large caliber machine gun.

That's what Chet Miller mounted on his plane.

Nick leaned back, tired and drained, and closed his mind to bootleggers and illegal aerial gunners and chronic drunks who killed through neglect. He was hardly better. He had failed Camilla tonight. She had begged him for help and he hadn't given it. He abandoned her.

'They take her tomorrow,' she groaned.

He had forgotten about it, the legal hearing for her baby, Kaylin, or Cassie, a child she had never seen after losing her at the hospital. She was worried sick. She had asked him for help to keep her, to read through the contract, to find some way.

Instead, he attacked her.

'Anything's for sale.'

'You sleep with devils, I won't.'

'I didn't,' she said.

Slammed the door.

In the dark she had cradled it, handed it to him expectantly. She pushed back the wolf ruff from her pale face, beautiful dark eyes.

Didn't sleep with anyone.

I don't remember that either, the dark cave, clinging to her wet neck, her cradled arms. He could almost see it, he wanted to see, within her arms... a child...

Like her? Or a child like a...

"I was thinking about that thing."

"Huh?" Nick roused.

"Somebody could find it," said James.

Find it? A thread from the old conversation.

Wolf dens.

"Those Bobbys wouldn't do it. But a real person could try it. There's a way to try to find it."

"Yeah?" said Nick, groggily.

Why was he saying this?

"Tepsaq."

Nick said nothing.

James started laughing, patted Nick's knee.

"She'd do it for you. You spoiled her good."

Nick nodded... dried seal meat.

"You know, I'm glad you came, you and that girl. You remind me of him, my old partner."

He shook his head and wiped his eyes.

Nick closed his... tried to see within her cradled arms... to see the child.

"Even you don't look a thing like him."

And Nick woke up.

That was it!

* * *

Headlamps flashed through the cabin.

A motor sputtered dead, waking her.

She heard the hollow steps on the stairs, coming slowly through the entry, cautious, side-to-side, a hunter on dangerous ice, uncertain of what comes next.

She rose from the couch to meet him, prepared for sleep. But she had waited up. She had waited for him.

"Are you okay?"

Camilla asked it first.

"Yeah," said Nick, relieved by its sound.

"I was worried about you," she said.

She put her hands in his.

He felt her cold fingers, drawing him closer. There was no pain on her brow. Just concern. He pulled her to him and held her tight.

"I was worried," she said into his neck.

"Thanks," whispered Nick huskily.

"You looked scared."

"I was."

He finally let her free.

"You had a dream?" offered Camilla.

"Yeah," said Nick, a nightmare. He drew her close again. "I'm sorry," he whispered, thinking of the things he had said to her.

"Me too."

The lights from the cabin's pressure lamps hissed softly. Camilla spoke with regret.

"I'm sorry about the project, Nick. It hasn't been what I thought it would be. I'm sorry I brought you in."

"Let's quit."

"It's way too late," she said sadly.

She pushed back and looked at him squarely.

"That would be unfair to Frances, you know that, Nick, a gross unfairness for her. She's already suffered so much to suffer that too."

Nick said nothing.

"Frances was wrongly injured," said Camilla. "This is her compensation for that injury."

"Her daughters are using her," said Nick sourly.

"She knows that. She's let them. She could stop it," said Camilla sighing. "She can still stop it. It's her money.

She can keep it. She can give it away. We can't run her life, Nick. That's patronizing. We can't run her children's lives. I can't even run my own life. And it's not the money. Not really. You know that. It's how they use it. Only they can decide that."

"That much money will destroy them."

"Will it?" asked Camilla sadly. "Would it destroy you?"

Nick could say nothing to that.

She put out her hand.

"Let's sleep."

Nick didn't take it.

"I have to go," said Nick, troubled.

Camilla dropped her arm. She gathered her nightshirt around her legs and sat at the table. She felt exhausted, fearful, nearly defeated. Tomorrow, a judge would hear arguments that might irrevocably take away her child. There was nothing more she could do. She couldn't even be there. Her own lawyers wouldn't let her. Now, even Nick was going.

"Something is happening," said Nick carefully. "Something strange."

"What?" asked Camilla, nearly at the end of hope.

Nick looked out the small panes, reluctant to speak.

"The nightmare?" whispered Camilla.

"You'll think I'm crazy."

"You're one of the sanest men I know."

"I saw blood in the yard, beneath that cache."

Blood beneath the cache. Camilla listened.

"A trail of blood," said Nick, "like the blood at Isaac's camp. I followed it. It took me through the woods to a pack of wolves. They were eating caribou caught by their antlers in rawhide snares. I touched the caribou, I felt the snares, I stared into their guts. I felt it all. It was real. The wolves ran, but one stayed. I followed her and fell through ice and almost drowned. I woke up with her in a cave or a den."

Nick paused, struggling how to say it.

"I think it was you."

No emotion crossed Camilla's face.

"The wolf was you."

Still, Camilla's face showed nothing. Nick knew what she was doing. She had detached, hid everything, listened, a receptive shell, a performance. She did this better than anyone he had ever met. He knew nothing of what she was thinking or feeling. He just had to trust her.

"She had something in her arms. She gave it for me to hold. I tried to see it, but I couldn't. I couldn't see. But I know what it was. A baby."

Nick sat on the couch. He felt helpless trying to convey what he'd experienced, helpless to know how Camilla felt about it and him.

"It was real."

He said it aloud as if to persuade even himself, not a nightmare, not ordinary, real, knowing how this sounded.

"What does it mean?" asked Camilla, a tinge of worry in her voice.

"I don't know. But I think it means I have to go back. It's about the wolves up there. There's something I have to do. I don't know what it is. But I have to go back upriver."

Camilla reached for Nick's hands. She took them in hers. Hers trembled.

"You have to go tonight?"

Nick nodded. She searched his face.

"Then I'm coming too," she said.

Her loyalty caught him unprepared. Relief flooded him. He wanted to crush her with gratitude.

"But you can't," he said reluctantly.

"I can't?"

"Because there's something you have to do too."

"What..."

"For your baby."

Color flushed her pale face. Her brow furrowed.

"I don't know if it matters," cautioned Nick, "but it's something. It came out of what happened tonight when I steamed with James Epchook, from the wolf in that den, showing me her child, so I don't even know if it's even right."

"What?" whispered Camilla anxiously.

"You said it yourself. You didn't sleep with anybody."

Nick squeezed her hands.

"...with the devil... I was wrong to say it."

Camilla closed her eyes and nodded.

"I don't know why I didn't see it before," said Nick, "but now it makes sense, about Kaylin, your baby..."

The lamps hissed quietly.

"Schofield's not the father," said Nick

"What?"

A dog howled in the distance.

"My God," whispered Camilla.

25

The dark wolf shook himself.

He fluffed his coat against the dank fog that filled the canyon. Nearby two young wolves paced nervously, watching him, the pirate, the outcast, now the alpha of their pack. He prepared for the hunt. The young wolves saw it, waited for his sign. They would go too, the last out. This morning the canyon had emptied. All had gone for food. There had been none for days.

A wolf appeared at the entrance of the den, the playful one, the dark wolf's mate. He sprang up to greet her. They rubbed faces affectionately. He almost frisked around her. She took it happily. She peered about the canyon for anything to eat, searching from the den to the steep ridges above to the frozen stream below. There was nothing. She was thin and hungry. But she couldn't leave.

She barked.

The dark one understood.

He sprang down the hill. The young wolves fell in behind. They disappeared into the brush passage that protected the community.

The playful one looked for others. All was empty and quiet. It felt terrible. She smelled the den's opening, catching scents, remembering companions.

Where were they?

Here was her brother, the great hunter.

Where was he now?

Oh, how she missed him!

She pushed her nose skyward and called. The sound rose and fell in a long, expectant note.

She listened.

A howl came back from down the trail. The dark one returned her call. Otherwise, silence.

Where was her brother?

The playful wolf turned several times, anxiously watching the brush, expecting to see his lovely face. But the canyon remained empty. Nothing stirred or sounded in the clammy white. Her body gave a helpless shiver. She felt stretched. Cold. Anxious. A sharp urge prodded her to follow the others. She yipped with hunger.

But the dark hole held her.

She plunged into the den.

* * *

The dark wolf finished his reply.

The young wolves waited on the hard river ice that left no tracks. It protected the trail to the den, perennially blocked by snags from the upper slopes. Only the passage of wolves kept the tunnels free.

The dark wolf loped off and the yearlings followed. Fog came and went along the narrow streambed. A wan sun briefly shone and disappeared. Hunting would be difficult. There were pockets of fog for hiding. Mists to dampen smells.

The stream met a larger way. The canyon broadened. The wolves jumped to snowy ground and investigated. Scents were old. The dark wolf trotted downstream. Prey would be further along. This was too near the den.

The dark wolf heard buzzing. He ducked under cover. The young wolves did likewise. The buzz moved off like a distant insect. The dark wolf pushed his nose into the air. He smelled nothing unusual. But he recalled the sound from other occasions. It was dangerous. The dark wolf resumed the downstream trot. The others followed.

The stream joined yet a larger bed. The sun came out. The steep hills lessened into long forested ridges. The dark wolf knew this juncture well, once a boundary between old territories. Trails radiated from the spot. At the convergence was the pissing stone and a snag bearing the marks of the community.

He moved directly toward it.

The ground erupted!

With a loud snap, his hindquarters jolted.

He set his legs and vaulted. Jaws jerked him short, flinging him into the snow. He flew around savagely. He attacked, biting furiously. It was hard and cold and fastened to his leg. He vaulted again. It dragged him back.

The yearlings ran about frantically. One jumped at the dark wolf's haunches, attacking the jaws. The second joined. They tore at the ground with fury. Soon, exhausted, they fell back.

The dark wolf lay panting on his belly in the snow.

Something moved. The wolves positioned to face it.

From up the slope a familiar wolf appeared, coming down a game trail. The old pack leader, the strong one, returned from a solo hunt. He stopped a short distance off, sniffed the air, a trio of wolves, two his own children. He approached cautiously.

The dark wolf spread his four legs, flattened his head, and snarled, showing teeth. Come no closer.

The strong one stopped, perplexed.

The yearlings split to either side.

The strong one circled. The dark wolf rotated, confronting his opponent, unable to move from the place. After a full circle, the strong one understood. He barked at the dark one, turned his back, and vanished up the foggy streambed.

The dark one returned to his leg, biting and scratching. He frantically gnawed the cold jaws. The yearlings stood by confused and fearful.

The fog cover broke.

* * *

Nick secured supplies on the sled.

He had food and a hot thermos as well as rope, blankets, and a kerosene lantern. These he stowed beside the gear still unloaded from the last trip. He filled auxiliary fuel cans, pumping from the Epchook's large tank. His breath billowed. He finished just after midnight. An east wind had scattered the night fog. Stars winked above him.

James Epchook stood with him, bundled in a bulky jacket, stomping well-worn pack boots, puffing in the air. Camilla stood too, hugging her parka.

James called for Tepsaq. He patted the sled. She jumped aboard. He snapped a line on her collar.

"She won't fall off," assured James.

Nick turned to Camilla.

"Be careful," she whispered.

"Okay," said Nick.

"I'm going to worry."

"Yeah."

"Kiss him and let him go," laughed James. "I'm cold."

She did.

Nick started the Skandic, suddenly not wanting to go. He drove off with a wave. They disappeared behind him. Nick rumbled a short distance through town and descended to the Kuskokwim. Tonight he could see the trail to Stony. He found its center and roared upriver.

Tepsaq held her nose into the streaming air.

The town of Sleetmute quickly hid behind a bend. As it left, a shadow tumbled from the bank. Nick slowed the snowmachine and looked back. A small shape appeared, running up the trail.

"Your shadow," said Nick to Tepsaq.

He wondered what to do. It took only a moment's thought. He gunned the engine and took off upriver. Keep up if you can, thought Nick to the orphan wolf. I won't help you. I won't hinder you. It's past time you saw the real world.

Nick's thoughts wandered with the wending trail… the elusive runner, the distasteful project, the Bobbys, James Epchook's instructions, the unsettling vision, tomorrow's court hearing, river obstacles, supplies he carried, Tepsaq in the sled. But mostly his thoughts returned to the kiss.

'Kiss him and let him go,' James Epchook said.

And she did.

His first real kiss with Camilla.

'I'm going to worry,' she had said.

'Kiss him,' James laughed.

And she kissed him, just like that.

The snowmachine skimmed the trail with a sudden lightness. It hummed a sweet tune. His body felt clean and wholly alive, his mind alert. The ground fog was breaking. A slivered moon set.

The wind kissed his lips.

So had Camilla.

He felt wonderful.

* * *

Camilla phoned from the Epchooks' house at breakfast. She placed the speaker on audio so James and Sophie could listen from the table. She welcomed their company. She felt extremely nervous. She dialed Hugh Glassner first, her lawyer-for-hire referred by her former lawyer-boyfriend, Scott Findley.

"Let me add on Scott," Glassner said anxiously.

She knew he would. She wanted them both quickly and without an argument from Scott.

"Camilla, hello, I wasn't expecting the early call," gushed Scott, added on and sounding rushed. "I'm pulling together last-minute details for the hearing with Judge Zimmerman. I'll bet you are too, Hugh, right? So how are you, Camilla?"

"Okay," said Camilla flatly. "I just saw a letter on the payment schedule for the Egnaty malpractice suit from Feinberg's legal firm."

"Uh… yeah," stumbled Scott, startled by the topic.

"Sixty-twenty-twenty, that's what I saw," said Camilla. "Twenty percent for the anthropologists."

"Uh, that's right, it…"

"The letter was addressed to Frances Egnaty. I've never gotten one. Did you negotiate this?"

"The letter was to who?"

"Frances Egnaty. Did you negotiate this?"

"Yeah," said Scott. "I thought after we talked that…"

"When we're you going to tell me about it?"

"Uh, gee, Camilla, I guess it…"

"I don't like to hear about agreements I've made that I've never seen," said Camilla, angrily. She looked over to the Epchooks.

Sophie looked embarrassed.

James sipped his coffee and nodded.

"My partner, Nick, has just quit on me because of this. He thinks I've been lying to him."

Sophie looked shocked. Camilla put her hand over the receiver and shook her head 'no' in reassurance.

"Camilla, I'm… I'm sorry," stammered Scott. "I didn't mean to cause problems. I thought you'd be pleased with the split. Your partner should be pleased."

"I can't imagine how that got approved without my knowledge or concurrence," said Camilla. "It shows one important thing, Hugh."

She waited. She was good at waiting.

"Uh, what's that?" asked Hugh Glassner, surprised to be brought into this dispute between Scott and Camilla.

"It shows that I'm the trusting type," said Camilla. "When someone assures me something, even a verbal contract like this malpractice project with Feinberg, I trust them. I don't double-check everything. And Hugh, it's the same with the surrogacy contract. When someone tells me something, I tend to trust that it's true. I don't always double-check, right?"

"Uh, right," said Glassner.

"Which is why, when they told me I'm carrying someone's baby, I believed it, even when it might not be true."

There was silence on the other side.

Camilla waited for the lawyers to catch up.

"What are you saying, Camilla?" asked Scott, no longer rushed or solicitous.

"Someone lied," said Camilla. "Everett Schofield is not the father."

"Wait, wait a second," said Scott.

"He lied," said Camilla.

"No, no," Glassner jumped in, putting some order to a mixed-up dispute. "Of course he is. The issue is whether Brenda Schofield is the mother on the revised birth certificate, or whether you are. That's the legal issue. Not whether Everett Schofield is the father."

"That was the custody issue," said Camilla. "But we got it wrong. The contractual issue is that Everett Schofield lied in saying he's the father."

Again there was silence on the other side.

"No, no," Glassner started in again, as if reading something. "I've got the contract here. It clearly establishes Everett Schofield as father."

"But is he?" challenged Camilla.

"It says he is, right here," said Glassner.

"No, but is he? Was it his sperm?" asked Camilla.

There was silence.

"It wasn't," said Camilla flatly.

She heard papers fumbling in the background.

"Don't bother looking, you won't find anything," said Camilla. "This was part of the trust, at least on my part. They shoot you up with sperm in the clinic and say it's Schofield's and you believe it."

"I'm looking too," said Scott, clearly to Glassner.

"Look all you want, but I'm telling you, I've never seen any certification from the clinic that it's his," said Camilla.

"We've never challenged this before," said Glassner. "It's just been a mutual stipulation that he's the biological father."

"Yeah," said Camilla, "because nobody raised it."

"Then why isn't it true?" asked Scott. "If there's nothing here, how do you know?"

"I don't," said Camilla. "But Nick, my work partner, he's the one who smelled the rat, the bait-and-switch.

Everett Schofield is how old? He's sixty-one. That's in the clinic records. Brenda Schofield, how old is she? She's thirty-three, also in the records. She's wife number four for Schofield. That's not in the record, but I learned that from her. She was terrified that he'd divorce her unless he got an heir. He'd done that to the other three. She begged me for help."

"Because she was infertile," said Glassner.

"Right," said Camilla, "she is. Bad eggs. It's my egg. But here's the deal, Everett's infertile too! Nick spotted it. It makes no sense that a rich egotist obsessed with producing an heir and married to four different women would be childless at sixty-one unless he's infertile too! I agree with Nick, guys like that leave babies somewhere along the line. He hasn't. He's shooting blanks."

Camilla looked over to the kitchen table. Sophie and James Epchook were listening intently. This time, it was Sophie who nodded.

"But wait," said Scott, "the clinic records are full of tests on Brenda Schofield's infertility. There's nothing about Everett being infertile."

"Exactly," said Camilla. "Why isn't there something on him? You'd think there'd be something, one way or the other. Either they've excluded the records from the files, or they never tested him. I don't know which. But with a powerful client like Everett Schofield, I can imagine it going either way. He doesn't want anyone to know he's infertile. It's his machismo, or something to do with legal inheritance, something like that. He wants people to believe my baby is biologically his."

"So we've got to challenge and ask for a paternity test," said Scott.

"Jesus…" whispered Glassner.

"But wait a minute, what difference does it make?" asked Scott. "This is a surrogacy contract. Of course the genes won't match the Schofields and the baby. You're the legal surrogate for them. That's the whole point. Biology doesn't count in who's the legal parent."

"That's precisely the legal point," pressed Camilla. "Look at my contract. It says I agree to be a surrogate mother using my egg for Everett Schofield as the father. You'll probably wind up arguing this ambiguity in the contract. But my understanding of those words was that the sperm came from Everett. That was the whole point of it for me, to help Brenda Schofield have *his* baby, not some other man's baby. If I had known it wasn't his sperm, I wouldn't have agreed to it."

"And if it wasn't his sperm..." said Glassner.

"He's broken the intent of the contract," said Camilla. "He's lied. Or the clinic has lied. Or at least misrepresented it. That's fraud. The contract's busted. I don't want my baby raised by a lying bastard like Everett Schofield."

Camilla listened as the two lawyers began a heated argument about legal theories, details of fact, the afternoon's hearing, and so on. She set the receiver down and hit mute. She found she was trembling and crying.

Sophie was immediately beside her, an arm around her shoulder.

"Poor..." she drew out the word in sympathy.

James lifted his coffee mug and toasted.

* * *

The breaking fog created more work for Joel Haggarty.

He eased his Viper around a difficult twist in the game trail he followed.

It meant that Chet Miller would be flying his plane, insisting on ground support. That was fine. Haggarty liked the work. He hated being cooped up. Yet he hadn't had a block of time to carry along his side project, catching the runner. He'd started trials here and there but with no real results. He'd been stymied by circumstances.

A voice crackled on the receiver at his elbow. He slowed and stopped the snowmachine, tuning the dial slightly.

"Joel, you there?" said Chet Miller.

"I'm here."

"Where's here?"

"Near the Swift."

"What's it like?"

"Patchy."

"How's it look toward Big River?"

"Better that way, but you know."

"That's where we got to be. I'm taking off in thirty."

"Okay. Thirty."

"Big River."

"Okay. Big River."

"Out."

Shit, thought Haggarty.

He shouldn't have taken on the runner deal with Fish and Game. Really, he didn't care one way or another about the state's troubles. Let them be boycotted. The governor deserved it. But Gary Gunterson was an old buddy. Haggarty promised to help him out. And it was a challenge. Haggarty liked good challenges. He liked to beat them. He had beaten Nichols to the punch and all the other boys in Fish and Game by finding the runner first before she crossed over Rainy Pass. Almost caught her. Then the radio collar went dead. Where was she now? Where was that den? How could he get her?

He had runner on the brain. That bugged him.

Haggarty restarted the Viper and set out northeast, the general direction of Big River.

Her radio transmitter went completely dead. She hadn't signaled since the night of the crash. Shit. What a mess that was. That plane coming down, right on his set. When he got back to business, Big Ike and that Eskimo were right there, hauling those greenies to McGrath, packing Geoff Sturgis, beat up to hell, off to Anchorage.

He never finished the private conversation.

Oh well, he would finish it with the wolf.

He'd steal Sturgis' thunder. He'd catch the runner, treat the lice, and fly her back to the Kenai.

Oh, that would aggravate Sturgis!

Haggarty thought about the other guy with Big Ike, that pesky Eskimo, what was his name?

Nick. Nick John.

He looked like one of those goddamn commercial fishermen out of Kodiak, built for dragging crab pots or skinning polar bears or something. What was he doing around here? Why was he helping Big Ike save Sturgis? He even cleaned up the crash site, hauling off the best stuff. Was he in league with the greenies?

Haggarty didn't think so. He was in it with that girl, Mac Cleary. Pretty. Tall and slim. Haggarty liked that type. He liked them with boobs too. They had caught him and Miller unloading a shipment of booze when he spotted the gun bracket. What were they doing, nosing around? Were they some kind of undercover narcs? Miller was nervous about it. He didn't like them. But Miller was always nervous.

Don't worry, Haggarty told him.

He could take Nick, whenever he had to.

Haggarty stopped near the crest of a ridge and killed the engine. This was one of his places. He had time. He wanted to check it out carefully on foot. The snow had crusted several days ago. No need for snowshoes.

He grabbed the rifle from its mount beside him. It was locked in place, carefully pointed forward, easily accessed while hunting in winter. If one inspected, it also was placed to allow for firing straight ahead while driving, the bullet passing between the windshield and cowl. He could slip an arm around the stock and pull the trigger, fingered through a slit in his right driving mitt. Illegal as shit. Inaccurate as hell. But he used it occasionally, just for fun, chasing foxes or caribou. This stop he unhooked the rifle from the mount. He needed stealth and accuracy.

Haggarty quietly ascended the ridge.

The fog had settled in the low areas.

Bingo! Three wolves flitted in the foggy bottom of the next swale. His padded trap held one, struggling to escape. The others paced nervously. Haggarty removed his mitts, adjusted the sights for the downhill shot, and aimed, placing a wolf in the crosshairs. The discharge was deafening. A wolf dropped. He swung expertly and squeezed off two more at the other wolf, frantically running up the creek bed. The second wolf dropped. The third wolf stayed put in the trap.

Haggarty grinned. Good shots!

The morning had begun just fine. He could work the side project while spotting for Miller.

Haggarty slid to the Viper, racked his rifle, and gunned a path over the ridge. He remembered this set, near a prominent stone in the riverbank. The stone obviously marked territory. Lots of wolf sign. He buried the trap on one of the trails to the stone, not the main one, but an uphill side trail. Lucky guess. The wolf had walked that path, stepped into it, probably within the last hour. Wolves out hunting, he guessed.

Haggarty approached slowly, watching for others. He didn't know this area well. It lay at the outwash of numerous small drainages coming out of the highlands. The hillsides turned dangerously steep here. The snow was unstable. Might be a good place for hiding a den. But which little creek? Which steep drainage? A person could spend winters looking and find nothing.

But he was trying something. Totally illegal. It hadn't worked yet. But maybe it would this time.

Haggarty retrieved the dead wolves, year-old males with beautiful pelts. Too valuable to leave. The ravens would ruin them. Not much time. About now Miller would be taking off. He dragged the wolves atop the seat behind him and tied them down. Buried in a deep drift somewhere, he'd retrieve them tonight.

The trapped wolf watched. He crouched, ready.

Large and black, in his prime, Haggarty saw.

Same age as that other wolf caught near here.

Haggarty cut a sapling. He rigged a noose, dangling from its end. He gingerly approached. The wolf lunged. Haggarty deftly noosed, slipping it over the neck. The rope jerked tight. Haggarty yanked the rope over and hauled it taut around a nearby tree, stretching the wolf between it and the trap. He tightened. The wolf's tongue protruded. He simply waited, smoking a cigarette, occasionally adjusting tension.

The struggle for air ended.

Haggarty went to work. He pulled his knife.

"Okay, old boy, better you than all the packs of the Kuskokwim, wrecked by goddamn lice, eh?"

Haggarty cut expertly. The haunch. The stomach. The neck. He sliced deep and wide until the blood ran. The wolf flinched with every cut. Finally, he sliced a tendon behind the main joint of a rear leg.

"Can't have you running too fast."

He wiped the knife on snow.

Deftly, he released the trap and the neck noose, jumping back with his rifle ready. The dark wolf exploded up. He yelped and fell. Struggling up, he hobbled another dozen feet before falling. He did this again and again, wobbling an escape up the creek bed.

Haggarty watched impassively. Then he followed a short distance and inspected, touching the snow. Dribbles of red blood marked the wolf's passage. They pointed up the drainage.

"Okay Judas, find me that den."

When his radio squawked to life, Haggarty had finished digging out his trap.

"Joel, you there?"

"I'm here."

"I'm not seeing anybody out today. Some traffic on the Kuskokwim. That's it."

"Good."

"But I can't see everywhere. And I can't see you."

"I'm in fog. It's patchy."

"I'm heading to Big River now. You somewhere ready?"

"You bet. Perfect timing."

"Let's go to work."

* * *

Gloom and fatigue stole the pleasure of the kiss.

The patches of fog grew as he neared the hill country. The eeriness grew too as Nick entered the Swift River mouth. Strange things happened there, James Epchook said of the nearby Tatlawiksuk, an unsettling place, a foreign land exceeding the boundaries of comfort.

They stopped to eat.

Nick munched dried fish from his stores. Tepsaq lay on her belly beside him eating the same, happy and alert. James Epchook was right there too. She had not fallen off the sled. She jumped off when he slowed and commanded. She really didn't need the safety leash. Nick unhooked it after the first hour, giving her the freedom to come and go, which she did. She occasionally explored, ran alongside, and jumped on again.

What must Tepsaq think they were doing?

Hunting, Nick decided. She must know they were hunting and accepted him as the hunt leader. Nick had never hunted with dogs. The Yup'iks had dogs for eons. But since snowmachines, hunting with dogs was becoming lost knowledge. But Tepsaq remembered how. She took interest in game trails, moose browse, caribou pellets, grouse scratchings. She ran off on short excursions, lost from sight, reappearing beside him. She peed often, leaving her sign everywhere. She seemed genuinely satisfied. The gloom hadn't affected her.

Nick considered what course to take next. Before the food break, they had traveled up the Swift River a short distance. Tepsaq hadn't found anything like wolf signs. Now they worked closer to the hills. It grew foggier and steeper. Look there, James Epchook had advised him. Let Tepsaq find it. Wolves liked a steep slope free of snow for a den, a secluded place with sun. Let her find it.

Nick patted Tepsaq's shoulder.

How would she know they looked for a den?

Tepsaq stood up and sniffed. Her nose caught a shift of air. She abandoned a piece of fish and took off. Nick straddled the Skandic, flicked it to life, and followed. She stopped about a half-mile's distance, nose to the ground.

Nick stared at it incredulously.

A trail of blood.

He cut the engine and stepped from the snowmachine. He knelt by droplets in the snow, frozen red caps, shining bright and fresh. He removed a glove and touched them. They warmed and ran along his fingertip.

Nick shivered.

He had touched a trail of blood like this at the Bobbys' cabin. It led to the crash site. He believed he had touched a blood track under the abandoned cache in Sleetmute. That led to snared caribou. These drops formed a trail through the brush at the base of the hills.

Tepsaq watched him expectantly.

"Okay," said Nick, nodding.

Tepsaq took off up the trail.

Nick mounted the Skandic to follow.

What was happening here? He felt for the rifle. A monster, said Michael Bobby. Isaac hadn't disagreed. By the crash site they found signs of a leg-hold trap, a gruesome butchering, and a brown cigarette. Like the one beneath Chet Miller's plane. Miller was a bootlegger, a drug dealer. Nick didn't want to stumble on monsters unprepared. He moved the rifle closer.

Tepsaq tracked the blood trail. It went upstream, turned, left the streambed, and climbed a short ridge. Tepsaq bounded up and waited. Nick had trouble getting the Skandic up. After several failed approaches, he gunned up an erosion scar, spinning the track at full throttle. At the top he got off. The blood trail fell into a vale filled with fog. He didn't want to force the Skandic down and get needlessly stuck. He'd go first on foot to check the terrain, then decide.

Nick shouldered the rifle.

He stepped off the ridge.

WHOOSH!

A wolf leaped past!

He fell, tumbled, and jammed to a stop. Painfully, he rolled from thick bush and brought the rifle around.

He spied the wolf nosing Tepsaq.

Tails wagged wildly.

The orphan! Nick groaned.

Tepsaq's shadow had found them.

The happy greeting was brief. Tepsaq took off in one direction, the wolf in another. Nick brushed himself free of snow. With large steps, he covered the remainder of the embankment, finding firm footing.

Fog filled the swale. Nick searched close to its edge. Ahead he saw Tepsaq's shadow, nosing the ground. Seeing Nick, she bounded ahead.

He knelt where she had nosed.

Drops of blood.

Here again was the trail. It lead into the gloom.

The orphan wolf trotted ahead. Her nose skimmed the icy ground. Nick came too. She bounded a few steps, stopped, and watched him. Nick followed, muscling through snowy brush. She scampered ahead, stopped, and waited. He followed, oddly discomforted.

Where was Tepsaq?

Why did the orphan track?

The ice broke with his next long step.

It shattered like glass.

With sickening suddenness, he fell.

Nick launched the rifle and frantically reached. His armpits hit a thick edge, knocking air from his lungs. He dangled on a shelf of ice, gasping for breath. Water rushed beneath him. He'd broken through ice above a narrow stream.

Jesus! It was happening!

He kicked and reached, scrabbling for handholds.

Tepsaq's adopted child stood steps away.

She watched, head to the ground, her face at his level, legs spread wide. Her ghost eyes locked on his.

His arms began slipping. More ice cracked.

He desperately lunged at the wolf.

The eyes were the last things he saw.

With a splintering sound, Nick fell.

He landed with a soft thud, a pile of snow a dozen feet down that preceded him through the hole. He lay sprawled on more ice. He heard water running near at hand.

And faint quacking.

Nick leaned on an elbow. He peered down a dim tunnel. A stream coursed beneath the level of the ground. He lay on a former surface, a frozen bank cut into the swale's floor when the river ran higher. The channel seemed roofed. Icy brush and snow overhung and covered it. Dim light shined ahead in places where the ceiling had broken.

Nick carefully crawled. The bank tilted to a sluice of swift water, a deep-cut, free-flowing stream. A warm spring, guessed Nick, coming from a heated aquifer that welled from the hills, warm enough to run during winter, sheltered by the icy roof.

Nick scooted toward the dim light and found the next surprise. The water flowed into a substantial pool. On its surface swam ducks! One dove. They all dove. Up they popped. They were feeding!

Black ducks.

Underground. In winter!

Suddenly, the chamber reverberated with sound.

The ducks exploded off the pool. Out of the icy ceiling they flew like bats from a cave.

Tepsaq's nose poked above him. She barked again.

"Shush! I'm coming," scolded Nick, ears ringing.

Nick pulled up through an icy crack into the foggy swale. Vapors rose around him like billowing steam. Tepsaq bounced to him and kissed his face. Nick grabbed her. He looked for the orphan.

Of course, she was hiding.

Nick spoke to his shaggy companion.

"Well, Tepsaq, we found the ducks."

* * *

The runner stood on a high vantage.

A vast sloping valley fell before her. Behind her white mountains reared, peaks growing from gray lowlands, tops blazing with new snow. The wind brought smells of black spruce and pine. It blew from up the valley.

It smelled right. Looked right. Felt right.

She knew this place!

A great river flowed off the mountains. Braided channels glimmered with morning light. White flats stretched in great curves that disappeared into a distant basin. Along its edge, dark specks moved. They formed a line over a far crossing.

Caribou!

She knew this river!

The she wolf circled with unrestrained excitement.

She checked the terrain. She smelled.

She knew that crossing!

She quivered as another sight unfolded below her. Other dark specks appeared behind the thin line of caribou. They followed, positioning. Her heart raced. She knew them too. Her pack! Her children!

She leaped down the ridge.

She ran boldly, no longer afraid.

She had found it! The hunt!

She was home!

* * *

The day lengthened, Nick wearied.

The trail of blood drew them higher into the hills. The fog shredded, grew patchy, gave way to dark blue sky. Pockets of dense fog thickened in the deep canyons. Tepsaq led and Nick followed with the Skandic. It was slow going. The line of blood traveled little-used game trails that traveled ridges, taking them upward. It became clear, they pursued a wolf. Large bloody paw prints occasionally appeared in the spoor. So much blood had been spilled, Nick wondered how the animal continued.

Who was this wolf?

Why was it gravely wounded?

The trail might end at the den of the Big River pack. Would he find the runner there? Would he know her? Did she still wear the radio collar?

What would he do if he found her?

Cure her, Camilla said.

He carried ivermectin with the dart gun. It could cure a wolf of canine lice, said the biologists.

But why?

There were too many wolves on the Upper Kuskokwim, James Epchook said.

It sometimes happened. Competition increased. Food became scarce. The runner was a breeding alpha female. Her release would compound that problem.

Fish and Game wanted her gone from the Upper Kuskokwim, relocated to the Kenai.

Nick didn't much like Fish and Game.

Appoint her goodwill ambassador said Geoff Sturgis. Let her represent the plight of wild wolves everywhere, the struggling groups like the Mexican wolves in the brochure Nils had given him. Sturgis and Nils almost died for this idea.

A caged celebrity.

Pacing for the smiling crowds.

'I'd shoot her and tell nobody.'

So said a stranger at the store in Sleetmute.

'That wolf is trouble.'

Nick wished he knew wolves.

Joel Haggarty knew them. No one knew wolves better than Haggarty. That's what the bush pilot had told him, bringing Nick to Sleetmute. What would Haggarty do with the runner?

Haggarty was an arrogant asshole.

Suddenly the afternoon sun burst full upon the trail. Tepsaq broke into a run. They traveled a high ridge. A panorama spread beyond them.

Big River.

Wide braids swept across the vista. Nick recognized it. He and Isaac Bobby had followed the drainage to

McGrath, saving the crash victims. After the gloom of the lower rills, its brilliance dazzled his eyes.

Tepsaq began barking. Nick closed in behind her.

High on the overlook, a form lay inert.

Nick cut the engine. He didn't bother to take up the rifle. He wouldn't need it.

"Shush," he whispered. "Show some respect."

Tepsaq quieted immediately.

It was the wolf. Large. Dark. A male in his prime.

He lay on his side in the sun.

He had run out of blood.

Run out of life.

The dark wolf had made the high place, one he knew well, a view he loved. He had succeeded. Here he collapsed, the wounded pirate, the outcast, his spirit to release and linger for the start of the next journey.

If the world deserved it.

Nick saw the deep wounds.

This one had suffered badly. It might never return.

From afar Nick heard buzzing.

He imagined it somehow connected with the wolf's death. But it drifted faintly from somewhere beneath the overlook. Nick shaded his eyes and searched. The sound grew louder. Suddenly a small plane appeared from a far bend in the river, flying low. It flew upriver toward the mountains.

Chet Miller's plane.

With it came an amazing sight.

That bastard!

Nick ran to the sled. He frantically unhitched and searched. He found the recorder beneath canvas at the front... Sturgis' video recorder from the wrecked plane.

Nick raced to the overlook. Hit buttons. The camcorder flickered to life. Nick found the plane on the display and punched record. The plane passed beneath him. He filled the screen, followed closely, zoomed, captured the action in detail.

"Bastard!" he growled aloud.

Chet Miller's plane dipped and soared. It swept the riverbed like a bird of prey, rose, circled, and dove, sweeping again. Over and over, it harried the ground. Before its shadow and noise ran an animal, a large ungainly animal, terrified!

A moose.

Its thick neck carried a radio transmitter.

The plane soared, swung around in a tight circle, and swept low again. Nick recorded.

The moose frantically ran upriver, away from the lowlands toward the mountains.

Miller was driving it.

Nick instantly saw why. This was a special animal. It was one of the twenty animals fitted with a transmitter by Fish and Game in McGrath. Keith Nichols tracked their daily movements. Nichols had said it was an important biological study to finally settle the merits of a debated question... the validity of a straight line on his map.

Were there two moose populations or just one within the Upper Kuskokwim region?

Nick remembered the map on the living room table, filled with color-coded marks. Nichols hardly believed his own data. The marks from the radio-transmissions showed there were upland moose and there were lowland moose. The two populations didn't mix.

The new data validated the straight boundary line that defined hunting units. Moose didn't cross it.

Nick remembered how Isaac Bobby disagreed. Isaac and Nick had stood on an overlook not far from where he was right now, coming back from the rescue. 'The moose move this way,' the trapper had explained, motioning from the mountains to the lowlands, contradicting Nichols' data. The moose moved seasonally to avoid harsh upland winds during winter. Based on years of personal observation, he knew there was a single moose population, not two. Upland and lowland moose regularly mixed.

Fish and Game's research had important implications for hunting. It potentially affected a lucrative sport hunting industry on one side of the line, and a struggling subsistence moose hunt on the other. It determined how each was managed.

Here was Chet Miller... messing with the research!

Miller worked as an outfitter and transporter. He wanted the straight line to stay. He made big dollars flying and guiding and provisioning sport hunters. He needed liberal moose seasons on his side of the line. That happened only if the Board managed the upland moose separately from the lowland moose. This winter, he was making sure the twenty radio-collared moose stayed away from the lowlands.

Miller had a receiver in the plane, reasoned Nick. He knew the transmission frequencies. He tracked the radio-collared moose, just as Nichols did from McGrath. When a moose got too close to the unit boundary, he flew out and drove it back. The Upper Kuskokwim region was so remote and so vast, no one had caught him at it.

The outcome of this research was linked with wolf control, realized Nick. If the upland sport hunt were managed more conservatively, more moose would move downriver for subsistence hunting near the villages. There might be more moose per wolf, better moose-wolf ratios. The wolf emergency might disappear on the Upper Kuskokwim. The issues intertwined.

Miller's plane soared in a higher arc. It banked and swung around. This time, it came straight at the rim above the river.

"Shit!" yelped Nick.

He had seen it in the view finder.

This plane had a mounted machine gun!

He ran from the edge and dove behind the Skandic.

The plane roared over him. The noise was deafening. His Skandic rocked with wind.

Time to go.

Nick shoved the camera in a rear hatch and jumped on the Skandic to leave.

The wood exploded!

Nick jerked back, astonished.

An insect blew from the trees!

Large eyes flashed green with the sun.

A great bug!

The insect stopped. The goggles came up.

Joel Haggarty smiled, his machine rumbling. He sat astride a powerful Viper. He'd come up a slope from Big River amid Miller's roaring pass.

He spotted the bloody wolf and grinned evilly.

"Hunting?"

An antenna stuck off the Viper, a receiver like the one Sturgis used. Nick understood… Haggarty helped Miller find radio-collared moose. He was the ground support, helping to drive moose with Miller.

"Tracking," said Nick, "same as you."

Haggarty brought up his rifle, still smiling. He rested the barrel atop his windshield, pointed off to Nick's side. He nodded at the bloody dark wolf.

"Got to be careful with those things. They can play dead. Never turn your back."

"You would know," said Nick, eyes still fixed on Haggarty.

Haggarty grinned, satisfied. He continued easily, like the give-and-take at Stony River, caught off-loading alcohol.

"Guess I told you, Chet Miller does aerial photography? That's what's happening today. He's out taking pictures for prospectors. I didn't mention, the way he does it. It's kind of proprietary. Industry secrets. So that camera, the one you tucked up in there, can't let those trade secrets out, you know what I mean."

He waved the rifle at the Skandic.

"Secrets?" said Nick dumbly.

"On that camcorder there. You know, how he takes aerial photos of geology from the plane. You snuck up here to learn how he does it, for some other outfit I guess. So, you just get off easy there. Find that camera, toss it here, and we'll call it good."

Nick assessed the rifle. Gauged distances.

Haggarty drove a powerful machine. So did Nick. He wanted the camcorder. Nick could give it up and still report what he saw to Nichols. These two would deny it. His word against theirs. Would Haggarty kill him over it? Nick doubted it. Haggarty could have killed him already. He wouldn't shoot because of this alternative.

Nick slowly got off.

"Let's be careful," suggested Haggarty. "Why don't you push that gun of yours slowly, back handed, 'til it drops off the other side, away from you."

Nick pushed on Epchook's Winchester.

It slipped from the seat to the ground.

"You know, Miller thought you and that girl might be spies," snickered Haggarty, "but I know you're not. You're out hunting wolves for her greenies, yeah?"

Nick frowned.

Haggarty now fished in darker waters.

Camilla.

Miller worried about Nick's partner and what she might know. How much did Camilla know about Chet Miller's moose drives? The bootleg trade of booze and drugs? Of course, she knew next to nothing.

Is that why Haggarty hadn't shot him? He wants more information on Camilla first. On how much was Camilla involved.

Nick felt the new fear.

If Haggarty killed him now, she'd have absolutely no warning about these maniacs. They'd have her completely off guard.

"You getting that camera?" pushed Haggarty.

Nick reached for the storage.

He had to warn her.

Nick saw it coming. Haggarty didn't.

Miller's plane dove.

The wind blast hit.

Haggarty rolled.

Nick leaped to the Skandic and roared off.

CRACK!

A shot whistled past his head.

"Shit!" yelped Nick.

He plunged into spruce.

A headlamp flickered behind. Haggarty pursued.

Where he was headed? Nick didn't know. He barreled down a game trail, narrow and steep by a knife-edged ridge. Nick remembered the topographic map, James Epchook's finger pushing around it, talking of avalanches, steep slopes, and drop-offs. Names like 'you can't get down there.' Haggarty seemed to be gaining. The ridge ended. The hillside broadened.

CRACK!

A shot from the moving Viper!

Nick swerved left and right, saw a trail, ducked into it. It was no wider than the Skandic. He prayed it stayed wide. If it closed, he was dead.

Haggarty moved behind him.

CRACK!

Another shot.

Nick burst from brush into meadow. A pond spread out at its center. Open water shimmered, overflow on ruptured ice. How deep? No chance to gauge it.

Nick gunned the Skandic, leaned back, and shot across. He felt the ice quit beneath him. The Skandic skimmed atop open water on momentum.

Haggarty followed.

A wall of wood loomed. An entry. Nick took it, plummeting down another steep slope. In moments fog swallowed him. Visibility disappeared. He drove almost blind. Just as suddenly the fog patch ended. He again rode in light.

He swerved to a different trail.

Haggarty burst from the fog, right behind.

CRACK!

Nick saw how that worked. Haggarty drove one-handed. Somehow he shot with the other. A maniac!

The trail had once been groomed. An old trapline. It ran wide and straight. Nick opened the throttle.

CRACK!

The shot whizzed above him.

Nick hunched low between pommels.

The Skandic soared off a low bank. Nick hit a streambed and skidded sideways. He chose a direction, straightened, and gunned full bore. Ice showered behind him. Haggarty did the same. They sped on a twisting river. Haggarty's Viper slowly gained. Nick turned a corner to find a split in the river, the convergence of two streams. The right fork looked straight and clear. The mouth of the left fork, partially blocked by a boulder, billowed with fog. Nick turned left.

Fog stole the view. Temperatures plummeted. Nick's visor fogged and froze. He ripped it up to see. Ice crystals stung his face. He drove like a madman, zigzagging up the narrow stream that fell from the highland.

The fog thickened. The world shortened to a fuzzy nimbus. Haggarty moved close behind.

CRACK!

The bullet ricocheted off rock. It splattered him with fragments.

The world blurred.

Nick squinted through narrowed lashes.

A third bubble glowed.

A headlamp and red brake lights winked in the fog directly ahead. A snowmachine drove before him!

The streambed took a series of quick bends. The mystery lights swerved left, right, and left, just like Nick. Haggarty's Viper slipped in a turn, slowed, adjusted, and followed.

The streambed opened. Dim passages appeared alongside. The stream made a sharp right turn. But the fuzzy lights went straight up the bank. Nick did too, grinding up the steep incline.

The lights traveled upwards. An ancient trapline zigzagged up a steep slope, shrouded in dense fog. The lights tracked it. Nick did too.

Haggarty fell back. At curves, Nick lost sight of him.

Right, left, right… Nick chased the lights.

He sensed it coming, a slight clearing of air.

Nick leaned hard over. He killed the engine. Released the brake.

The Skandic shot off trail and crashed into dark brush.

Haggarty's headlamp appeared. The Viper roared past and slowed. Haggarty searched. He almost stopped. Nick held his breath.

The fog deepened.

Just beyond Haggarty, lights floated in fog, waiting.

CRACK!

Haggarty gunned ahead! The lights did too!

Haggarty resumed the mad chase.

They vanished, ball lightening in clouds.

Nick heard powerful engines like echoes reverberating from the upland, moving farther and higher. The roar grew fainter.

With a high-pitched scream, something freewheeled on air.

Then silence.

Nick rubbed his stinging face. His hands shook. With some difficulty, he started his engine, rocked the Skandic free, and turned downhill.

He didn't go up.

The track fell and joined the streambed. Fog boiled thick upon it. He sat for a moment to reconnoiter. What direction had he come? He turned right and slowly motored, his thoughts blurred like his eyes. The ground fog lessened. He came out of the fogbank surprised by low-angled sunlight. Barking brought him back.

Tepsaq.

She bounced down the streambed and turned onto a game trail. Nick didn't think twice. He steered the Skandic to follow.

She took him up, a branching network of game trails. Once again he came out of the woods upon the overlook, now partially shrouded in clouds. There was his sled as he left it. Beyond was the body of the dark wolf. Chet Miller's plane was nowhere in sight.

Tepsaq nosed him affectionately. Nick patted her shoulder. From a deep pocket, he dug out a piece of seal meat. She took it sloppily, flopped on her chest, and contentedly gnawed. At the edge of sight, something else moved. The orphan, Tepsaq's child, watched from the brush. Nick threw a piece in her direction.

She cautiously retrieved it and vanished.

The howls began soon after.

Wolves!

Tepsaq took to her feet and barked. She immediately disappeared into the wood.

More howls.

Tepsaq reappeared at a trail hardly wide enough for a dog. She looked intently at Nick. Disappeared again.

Nick snatched the daypack. He slung rifles across his shoulder.

A third set of howls.

And Nick ran.

* * *

Daylight faded.

The fog briefly cleared before its end. The canyon lay shadowed. The playful wolf sat in a last patch of light. The pale sun slipped behind the canyon rim. She shivered and surveyed the frozen creek below the den. The world remained empty. She felt drained, dispirited. Hunger gnawed her insides. A great urge gripped her, leave to find food. But she held at the mouth of the den.

She rose to her slender legs and paced.

She placed her nose on the ground. The community lived in it. She could smell it. The earth recalled them like a fading tale. So faint. Her brother. Her sister. The young ones. She found them as she searched, memories in the ground, the people of the canyon, the rivers, the mountains. Some were old, almost undetectable. Some newer. She recognized them all. None yet perished.

Great loneliness filled her.

She lifted her face to the sky and howled.

Sound echoed within the canyon.

Then silence.

A thought worried her. What about the den?

She scurried to the mouth and ducked inside. In a heartbeat she came out again, reassured. Hunger gnawed her. She needed food. The paths to food went through the tunnels of debris, out onto the river, up into the hills. That's where she would find food.

Instead, the playful one scrambled to the ledge above the den. It smelled strongly of the dark one. This was his perch. He sat here and waited in the morning for her. When she came from the den, he jumped down and they kissed. He romped. Then he left to hunt. He always brought food. He left it at the den for her.

She looked upwards, the rim of the canyon. Where was his silhouette, scratched on the edge? Where was he? His memory filled her with longing.

She lifted her face and howled, long and anxious.

She waited. His call didn't come.

Again, she felt a vague nervousness. She slipped from the ledge to the den's mouth and disappeared inside. In moments she reemerged, satisfied.

How hungry she was!

She stared at the canyon. She eyed the clogged exit. That was the way. They went that way, everybody but her. A great yearning pulled her. Go too. Follow them. But she stood fixed at the den. They would come from that way. She knew they would come from there. Each of them, one by one, all the community united in the warmth of the sun at home.

She lifted her face and howled.

Here! Come here!

What was that?

She turned in an anxious circle.

Faint responses. They came from down the canyon. A faint howl. A bark. A yip. She listened, fidgeting. She disappeared into the den and emerged to listen more. She whined softly.

Sounds like wind rustling.

She knew it. She knew who made it… the young ones rushing through the brittle corridors.

Suddenly, out came the first! Out came another! And another! They ran along the creek bed. It was wonderful! And amazing! Out came somebody so faint she had almost become lost to the hills.

Her sister! Her older sister!

With a gasp of joy, the playful one leaped from the den and rushed to meet her!

The she wolf burst into the canyon with mad elation.

She was home! Home! The familiar walls reached down for her. The yearlings circled joyously. They had done the same when she first appeared. At the hunt with the caribou, they welcomed her home. Round and round they frisked about the canyon floor, yipping, bumping shoulders. And suddenly from above, the playful one! Her younger sister! She appeared, tail high with joy. In the madness, the she wolf turned up the slope to greet her!

A great shape exploded from the side.

The strong one, her old mate, burst from the brush in an eruption of fury! He attacked!

He hit the playful one. Bowled her over.

The playful one, weak from hunger, rolled as she fell beneath his chest. His jaws snapped, closed upon her throat. He reared, ripped, flailed side to side.

The she wolf attacked.

She plowed into him. Bit his skull.

He turned a shoulder into her, not releasing.

She grabbed his back, bit hard.

He yipped in pain and released. The strong one turned with a snarl and skipped into a run.

The she wolf chased.

The yearlings, caught up in the frenzy, converged on the playful one. She hunched in shock on the ground. One bit a haunch. Another snapped at her jaw. Another bit her back.

The she wolf launched upon them, ferociously snarling. She knocked one over. Bit another.

The yearlings split and scattered.

The she wolf found her feet and spun wildly. The joyous homecoming had turned into chaos. She saw it above her, too late to react… the rim of the canyon, an outcrop moved.

An odious shape.

She stared into it, ready to leap.

A flash and crack.

She toppled.

* * *

Nick ran along the game trail.

Tepsaq went before him. The howling of wolves… Tepsaq knew. Something momentous was happening. Nick sensed it too. Time to run.

The trail skirted the edges of steep fall-offs. It skittered along the tops of a system of ridges, the backs of the crumpled hills around the prominent peaks, Big Pestle and Little Pestle. Nick remembered them from the maps. The slopes plummeted sharply to either side. The ridge tops offered wending ways for the surefooted. Animals made these paths. They rose and fell along the spines of the hills.

Tepsaq chose among the branching options. She and Nick ran atop the starts of drainages, one step falling into the headwaters of one, another step falling into another. In the gray of evening, Nick felt like he ran atop the roof of the world.

Tepsaq nosed the ground at a junction, made a choice. She bounded off. Nick followed again past a rocky rim like jagged teeth. Suddenly, Tepsaq halted beside a snow-free knoll. She stared down a steep slope.

Nick slid alongside, panting for air.

He stared into a narrow canyon, the headwaters of a frozen creek that snaked directly below. The light was fading to dim shadow. At one end, the creek was clogged with woody debris, obscured by winter's snow. As he stared, the canyon seemed to be filling with wolves!

Nick threw off the rifles and ripped open his pack. With field glasses, he scanned the canyon floor. A wolf stood directly below on the slope. Beside it was an opening. The den! Tepsaq had found it, the den of the Big River pack! One, two, now three wolves ran along the frozen creek. They had emerged through debris at the creek's end. As he watched a fourth wolf emerged.

Nick sucked a quick breath, steadied the glasses.

A radio collar.

It was the runner! The wolf wore a radio collar. He had found her. She had found the den!

Tepsaq barked. She looked poised to fly down the slope into the canyon. Nick grabbed a handful of neck hair and yanked her back.

At that moment, the mêlée began. Wolves attacked wolves. A large wolf charged laterally, across the slope to the den. Nick heard the collision. Combatants locked in battle, snarling and snapping.

The runner joined the fight.

This was it.

Nick frantically reached for the rifles, both on the knoll beside him, loaded and ready.

He hadn't expected it to be like this.

Sturgis' dart gun, or Epchook's Winchester.

Tepsaq went over the side.

She slid into the canyon filled with wolves.

Stupid dog!

Nick grabbed and whipped the barrel down. He cleared the lens with his thumb and found wolves in the scope. Magnified before his eye, they fought. They broke apart.

There was the runner! She wore the collar.

She chased a challenger.

Nick followed her in the sights.

She reversed and launched into another. Where was that Tepsaq? Nick couldn't pause to look.

The fight broke. Wolves scattered.

Where was the collar? There!

Nick found it in the scope again.

The runner stood alone, spinning at the den.

She had won. Every wolf ran from her.

She looked up the slope to the canyon rim.

Why is she looking up here?

She stared straight into the crosshairs.

'I'm shooting downhill,' Nick remembered, thinking of adjustments. Don't shoot high.

He was the last thing she saw.

He squeezed the trigger.

* * *

Nick was not a mountain goat.

From the daypack, he secured a rope to a large rock to assist him in the early stage of the descent. The slope lessened toward the bottom. Off rope, he slid taking large steps, his pack on his back, balancing with Epchook's rifle before him. When he arrived he found two wolves, both lying on the snow near the mouth of the den. And there was Tepsaq. She waited, panting, not touching the spoils. All the other wolves had fled. He checked the sky. He had about an hour of twilight before losing the gray shadows. He didn't want to be down here in the pitch black beside a wolf den.

Both wolves were females. The one looked young and lean, almost starving. Her ribs showed prominently along her gray sides. Her throat was ripped open. She'd been unlucky in battle. Or perhaps it was just her time… too weak to defend herself in a fight. He placed a hand on her soft belly. She still breathed.

His hand came up wet.

Milk, dripping from teats.

Nick felt sick.

He pushed that from his mind. He walked to the other female. She looked larger, stronger, well nourished. Had she really run four hundred miles? An area by her neck was bleeding. The collar had chafed it raw.

Nick took his knife and angrily cut through the collar. He almost heaved it down the slope. Instead, he slipped it into his pack. He searched her body carefully. He found the needle on the left haunch. He had aimed for the shoulder. He carefully removed it.

In the daypack he found the syringe. He loaded it with ivermectin, swabbed the wolf's haunch, and injected. He saw no signs of lice. But, it was dark.

He stood to stretch.

Somehow without his knowing, a wolf had quietly appeared at the den. Nick didn't even flinch. Tepsaq's shadow had arrived.

The orphan wolf cautiously approached the dying female. She sniffed the teats. Tepsaq rested some distance away, watching, doing nothing. The orphan wolf looked at Nick. Then she vanished.

"Jesus!" exclaimed Nick, blinking.

She'd gone inside the den.

Nick stowed gear, saw movement at its mouth.

The orphan wolf reappeared. She dropped a puppy at her feet! She disappeared again, quickly reappeared with another. In short order, there were seven pups outside, winking in the dim light. Most were tiny. Nick counted. Five tiny ones. There were two larger pups. They looked too large to be from the same litter.

The puppies cowered together, afraid to be outside among strangers. They gathered around their mother's belly, huddling close to her teats, finding comfort there. And sometime while they gathered close, she died.

A small shudder.

Nick could almost see her leave.

The orphan wolf nosed closer.

She put her head near the mother's wet belly. She began coughing, as if choking.

She vomited.

The seal meat.

The two largest pups struggled over to her and whined. They began to lick around her face.

She let them, feeding the regurgitated food.

And Nick saw she let each one eat in turn.

Even the littlest.

26

A light glimmered at the edge of the world. In Camilla's dream a wolf was running. She ran and ran toward the dawn. An unending fear moved with her. It blew across the surface of a lake, lines of never-ending riffles. The night's pounding came and went. But the prisoners waited, restive, prowling the cells, listening for footfalls. When they came, the entry echoed. The door cracked. She roused, rose from the couch in the dark, still clothed, gripped by dreams.

"Nick?" she asked groggily.

They embraced before the door closed.

"Thank God."

He held her a long while without speaking.

"What happened?" whispered Nick finally.

"What?" said Camilla, still lost in a dream.

"The hearing?"

Camilla pushed apart. Her voice quavered and broke.

"You did it... the judge, he ordered a test."

"A test?"

"A paternity test!"

"That's all?"

"He said he couldn't proceed. So he ordered it. They said he seemed irked."

"Huh! That's good?"

"Oh Nick, it's great!"

She hugged him again.

It wasn't over. But her desperate hope lived.

"I passed out," she murmured. "What time is it?"

"Six thirty."

"You've been up all night?"

"No, I got in about two."

Camilla pushed back, surprised.

"Two?"

"I've been at the Epchooks."

"The Epchooks? Since two? Why?"

"Because… I've got to go," said Nick.

He gestured feebly out the door.

"Go? Again?" said Camilla dismayed. "Because you couldn't find her?"

"No, I mean, yes. We did…"

"You did? You found the runner?"

"Yes," said Nick, embarrassed.

"Oh God, Nick! You really found her? What happened?"

Nick rocked on his heels, looking out the door as if waiting for some unwanted event.

"I… uh… darted her."

"You did?"

"Gave her a shot of ivermectin. Oh, yeah…"

He dropped to a knee and rummaged a daypack. He pulled out the remnants of a collar.

He pushed it to Camilla.

"Dump that somewhere."

Camilla stared amazed. The radio collar!

"Here it is. This is important," said Nick.

He pulled out a camcorder.

"This is important. It's the one Sturgis had. It's got evidence. Make copies. Give one to Fish and Wildlife Protection. Give one to Mel Savidge. She'll know what to do with it. It's evidence… against Chet Miller."

"Chet Miller?"

"The pilot at Stony River, remember him? The guy running booze? He's been driving moose with his plane to mess up the moose study, the one by Nichols on unit boundaries up in McGrath. It's all tied up with moose management and wolf control. Mel can call me later. But you need to get it out of here fast, before Chet Miller finds out."

"A video clip?" asked Camilla, hefting the camera.

"Of Miller driving moose with his plane. That's illegal. It's evidence. Stay away from Miller and Haggarty. Especially Haggarty. They're maniacs!"

Nick looked over his shoulder. A second snowmachine rumbled into the yard. Nick went out to meet it. Camilla threw on her parka and followed.

"Cama-i," greeted James Epchook.

He sat on his own snowmachine, dragging a substantial sled. It carried an aluminum cage, Sturgis' cage from the crash. It was stuffed with blankets.

"Nick, what's going on?" shouted Camilla above the racket.

"We've got to get away before it gets light."

"Why?"

"Remember I told you about that wolf... the one I slept with?"

"The wolf you slept with?"

"The one who handed me something to hold?"

Camilla tried to read Nick's eyes in the dark.

The wolf Nick slept with.

"I remember. A baby?"

Nick pointed to the cage behind Epchook.

Camilla peered inside. She gasped.

It was filled with puppies! And Tepsaq's shadow, the orphan wolf, she was inside too! Tepsaq rested contentedly on the sled, chained beside it.

"Nick! Where did these come from?"

"I told you..." said Nick awkwardly.

"They're wolves?" gasped Camilla.

"Yeah."

"The runner's puppies?"

"No, not the runner, the other wolf, the one I told you about, why I had to go up there."

Camilla stared in the cage, dumbfounded.

"A wolf killed her," said Nick.

He saw she didn't understand.

"They're orphans," he whispered.

"Nick... where are you taking them?"

"Home."

"I'm going too," said Epchook with a smile. "I haven't seen his auntie for a long time."

"Your home?" gasped Camilla. "Right now?"

"It's time," said Nick. "Over a hundred years... time for wolves again. We've got to get going, before anybody sees them."

"They're pups! Who's going to raise them?"

"She will," said Nick, nodding at the orphan wolf. "She wants them. They've got a better chance with her than up there with maniacs like Haggarty and Miller. Better than some zoo."

"But what about the runner? You said you shot her... with ivermectin?"

"I left her at the den."

"You found the den?"

"Don't tell anybody."

"Oh God! Nick, her puppies? Did she find her puppies?"

"Yeah. Two puppies. They found her first."

"Oh God!"

"They seemed pretty happy. That's the last thing I saw. She woke up with those two puppies."

Camilla grabbed Nick and hugged hard

"Let's go!" shouted Epchook. "I'm getting hot!"

He eased his snowmachine away.

"Kiss him and let him go!" Epchook shouted.

But this time, Nick did it.

27

The night squalls ended. The morning fog thinned above the bay. Once again, the bridge lifted its gleaming crown into the sun, its belly still sunk in gray. A turquoise sky pushed down upon the hills surrounding the great city. Light shimmered upon the surface of the steely sea.

Camilla watched from her desk.

Its top lay empty, cleared of the dog-eared dissertation.

Cars appeared through the mist, whisking across in an unending hypnotic rush. The beacons blinked dimly above them.

The phone rang.

"Camilla?"

"Yeah."

"It's Mel, Mel Savidge, calling from Juneau."

"Hi Mel. How are you?"

"Good, and you?"

"Watching the bay with my morning coffee," said Camilla.

"Sounds nice. You get that dissertation in?"

"It's in, just yesterday."

"Congratulations! That must feel good."

"Well, my desk is empty."

"Hey, I just heard from Feinberg that they settled the malpractice suit with Frances Egnaty. He sent me an email."

"Yeah, they did."

"Congratulations on that one too! The old lady got a good settlement for her subsistence losses, is that right?"

"I'm not supposed to say, you know, but yeah, she did pretty good."

"That's great! She's still in Sleetmute?"

"Moved back for good. She's getting ready to fish with her daughters."

"They moved back too?"

"Them too. They're using the money to fix up their places, upgrade to satellite, things like that. They didn't like Anchorage. Bad for the kids, they said. So they've all come home."

"That turned out okay for everybody, eh?"

"I guess so," whispered Camilla.

"Listen, I can't talk long. There's an emergency meeting I've got to run to. Wolves and moose, of course. I can't get hold of Nick, so I thought I'd try you."

"He's hard to reach."

"He's got no phone?"

"Try his grandmother."

"She isn't picking up."

"You can leave messages at the city office."

"Yeah, well, I thought I'd try you for an update on things."

"What do you need to know?"

"People are crazed here," Mel laughed. "That video clip you delivered from Nick really stirred the anthill."

"What's happening with that?"

"Chet Miller's out on bail. But he's out of business. They've seized his plane. He won't be guiding anytime soon."

"You can't harass moose like that?"

"Nope, or mess up a study. The Board of Game is questioning the validity of all the department's moose data on the Kuskokwim, how many, the real populations, the impacts of outfitters, that kind of thing. I guess you heard the wolf relocation program is history."

"I heard."

"The boycott's still on. The governor's kaput. He's a lame duck because of this mess with wolves. Government has come to a grinding halt in Juneau."

"That's too bad."

"Naw, that's good! Alaskans don't *want* to be governed. That's why we elect idiots."

"I see."

"But I was wondering, what's happening with Nick's little relocation program?"

"I thought nobody's supposed to know about that," said Camilla.

"They don't, officially," said Mel. "He's told me about it in confidence. But he should know that the department is getting some funny reports from the lower Yukon, weird wolf sightings and things like that. I wanted to tip off Nick. You know anything new?"

"Well, it's not supposed to get around."

"Yeah, I know."

"Last time I talked with Nick, the puppies weren't puppies anymore. They're good-sized kids, or whatever."

"Where are they?"

"Those hills above his village, between the Yukon and Norton Sound. He said he fenced off a yard for the first month to help keep them safe. He brought meat off and on. He worried about the early weaning but that hasn't been a problem. That orphan wolf turned out to be a good mother."

"He's feeding them? That's illegal, you know."

"No, he's not. The mom turned out to be a good hunter. She brings them beaver and rabbits and caribou. They're going after the caribou."

"Reindeer… that's what we're hearing," said Mel. "There's a wild reindeer herd over there south of Stebbins. People have called to complain about wolves eating their reindeer."

"I don't know about that," said Camilla. "Nick says caribou are coming down from the north. He's surprised they've learned to hunt so well. Their mother never hunted before."

"Instinct, pretty amazing, eh?"

"Nick's finished feeding them. They're on their own."

"We're getting reports about wolves close to the villages."

"Nick thinks that's going to stop after breakup. It'll be harder to travel and people will start shooting at them. They'll move up into the hills."

"What does he think about that, people shooting at his wolves?"

"He doesn't think they're his wolves. He never did."

"Well, it's all a bit wacky. If the department ever found out about it, he'd be in big trouble."

"Why? Fish and Game moves wolves."

"But we're the government," laughed Mel. "We never follow the rules."

"Yeah."

"Thanks for the update. There are six, right? The five pups and the mom?"

"Maybe seven or eight. They've picked up a couple of other wolves somewhere. Maybe that's why they've had no trouble learning to hunt. The new wolves are showing them how."

"Now that's interesting."

"What's instinct? What's learned? We won't know from this experiment."

"Look at the time! I've got to go! The other thing I wanted to ask Nick about was the runner. They're still bugging me about her. Every meeting, they ask me about the runner."

"What have you told them?"

"I told them that Nick found her and treated her with ivermectin. If I didn't have that damn radio collar, I don't think they'd believe me."

"Yeah, that's what happened."

"They keep bugging me about the den. They want to know where it is."

"Well, Nick says he doesn't know."

"That's not what Gary Gunterson says, our stud in Wildlife Division."

"How does he know anything?"

"He heard gossip from the boys in North Pole who drink with Joel Haggarty. He heard that Nick found it."

"Is Haggarty up there now?"

"He's back home in Fairbanks."

"He never got charged with Chet Miller?"

"He's not on the video clip. Nick never fingered him. I can't figure out why he won't."

"Nick avoids conflict, you know," said Camilla.

"Well, since he was picked up wandering the Swift River without his snowmachine, Haggarty hasn't said much of anything about what happened out there. I think he's afraid of another Mosquito Man name. But when he's drinking, they say he tells ghost stories. You know anything about that?"

"Nick needs to tell it, not me."

"Gunterson heard secondhand that Nick found the Big River den. He's pushing hard for Nichols to find it because the runner never got sterilized. Nichols says he's got more pressing priorities like fucked-up moose studies. Haggarty's not talking to Gunterson right now."

"Nick told me to say he doesn't know anything."

"Does he?"

"That's what he says."

"Yeah, okay," laughed Mel, enjoying the conspiracy. "Well, I got to run. Oh, one more thing! I was wondering, what's happened with your case? You know, the custody hearing. Last I heard it was scheduled. What happened?"

There was a long silence.

Finally, Camilla answered.

"They've run," said Camilla softly.

"What? Who's run?"

"The Schofields," said Camilla. "The judge ordered the paternity test. We were waiting for the results. Then we hear they've disappeared. Everett Schofield didn't show for his appointment. Nobody at the clinic knows where they went."

"Wow! So Nick was right?"

"Looks like it."

"The guy's not the father! Wow!"
"Yeah."
"Both of them gone? The mother too?"
"Brenda too."
"And the baby?"
"Yeah… the baby too."
"God, I'm sorry Camilla."
Mel waited for Camilla to say more, but she didn't.
"What are you going to do?" asked Mel.
"They've issued a warrant," murmured Camilla.
"God, that's terrible!"
"They're looking… maybe."
"You'll find her," assured Mel.
"Yeah?" said Camilla.
"You'll find her."
Camilla said nothing.
"Oh, the time! I'm sorry, I've got to go!"
"I know."
"I'll call you back."
"Okay."
"I'll be thinking of you, Camilla."
"Yeah."
With a click, Mel was gone.
Suddenly the full sun broke upon the bay.
Day conquered the fog of night.
Glittering light exploded like brilliant diamonds.
Camilla cradled the phone.
She watched it through her tears.

ABOUT THE AUTHOR

Robert J. Wolfe is a cultural anthropologist who conducts research on traditional hunting and fishing practices in the Far North. He is the author of *Playing with Fish and Other Lessons from the North*, the *Falling Walrus* mystery series, and other works.

CPSIA information can be obtained
at www.ICGtesting.com
Printed in the USA
LVOW13s1711160217

524503LV00012B/1318/P